# BEFORE THE STORM...

"They have lock again," Jamie called out. "Do it before they get a weapon on us!"

Hannah gritted her teeth and pulled back on the joystick, shifting their angle of attack. Suddenly the *Lotus* was pulling twice as many gees, eyeballs down, pressing them down hard into their seats with crushing force. More alarms instantly began hooting—and then cut out, as the overloads went away, at least for the moment, and the gee forces slacked off. The *Lotus* had literally bounced off the top of Reqwar's atmosphere, and was heading back out into space. The temperature alerts shut down and the strain gauges slid back into the normal range.

Suddenly the cabin of the lander was strangely quiet. But it was nothing but a lull before the storm. Things were going to get a lot worse before they got better—if they ever got better.

NOVELS BY
Roger MacBride Allen

The Torch of Honor
Rogue Powers
Orphan of Creation
The Modular Man*
The War Machine (with David Drake)
Supernova (with Eric Kotani)
Farside Cannon
The Ring of Charon
The Shattered Sphere
Caliban
Inferno
Utopia
Ambush at Corellia*
Assault at Selonia*
Showdown at Centerpoint*
The Game of Worlds
The Depths of Time*
The Ocean of Years*
The Shores of Tomorrow*

NONFICTION

A Quick Guide to
Book-on-Demand Printing

A Quick Guide to the
Hazel Internet Merchandizing System

*Published by Bantam Books

# **BSI** STARSIDE

# The Cause of Death

A NOVEL BY

Roger MacBride Allen

BANTAM ▪ SPECTRA

TM
SPECTRA

BSI: STARSIDE: THE CAUSE OF DEATH
A Bantam Spectra Book / March 2006

Published by
Bantam Dell
A Division of Random House, Inc.
New York, New York

ISBN-13: 978-0-553-58726-5
ISBN-10: 0-553-58726-9

Printed in the United States of America
Published simultaneously in Canada

www.bantamdell.com

OPM 10 9 8 7 6 5 4 3 2 1

To the memory of
James Maury (1719–1769)
James Maxwell (1790–1867)
James Rose (1810–1882)
James Franklin Rose (1874–1966)
James Stoughton MacBride (1893-1981)

and to
James Roderick MacBride
James Austin MacBride
James Scott Riling
James Campbell Witte
James Keeton Edwards
James Lawrence Maury
James Herbert Barnes
Benton James Allen
Roderick James MacBride
Christopher James Parrish
Nicolas James Arida
Evan James Blacker
Duncan James Collins
Calvin James Dean

and
especially
to
JAMES MAURY ALLEN

# ONE · FLIGHT

The shot struck the ground about twenty meters downhill from Georg, throwing up a flash of lurid yellow light against the night sky. Georg Hertzmann threw himself to the ground. Rock shrapnel and clumps of dust and dirt dropped out of the sky all around him for an unreasonably long time after the explosion. Georg remained motionless where he was until the last of the debris had fallen back.

"You can get up and start moving now, if you wish," said a small voice in his headphones. "Their shots are becoming increasingly inaccurate. I believe they have lost their lock on your position and are firing blind, by guesswork."

Georg replied in a low whisper, trusting his throat mike to feed an audible signal to his breast pocket, where the voice was coming from. "Then they're awfully good guessers. Those shots are close."

"But they didn't hit you with any of them—even when they had a tracking lock on you. I believe they are not trying to kill you—merely frighten you."

"And they're doing a good job of it." After a moment's silence, he spoke again. "Just how confident are you about all this?"

After a pause for consideration, the voice spoke again. "About seventy-five percent that they have lost lock, eighty percent that they are just trying to scare you."

"Which gives me twenty percent odds that they are *really* trying to kill me. If I show myself and they get a new lock, I could find out the hard way."

"Granted," said the little voice. "But you cannot stay where you are indefinitely. If you do so, and they are not merely trying for capture, you will likely be killed, to the great inconvenience of our mutual endeavor."

Georg sighed. "I know things are different for Stannlar, but do bear in mind: if I get killed, it will be more than inconvenient. It will be permanent failure—not just for our work, but for me." Killing Cinnabex, or any Stannlar Consortium, and doing the job thoroughly, permanently, destroying all the backups, beyond hope of reassembly or revival, would represent something like a major industrial research effort.

"Your point is taken. My apologies. But the point remains that you cannot stay here."

"I know, I know. Let me think." He decided to risk rolling over on his side, in hopes of seeing more than the clump of dirt into which his nose was wedged. He moved as slowly as he could, cursing silently with every little spill of dirt and gravel that tumbled off him. The object in his breast pocket had been cutting into his chest a bit, and it felt good to get up off it. Besides, quite irrationally, he felt guilty about dropping his full weight on it, as if so doing might inconvenience the passenger inside.

The object was a silvery alloy disc with rounded edges, widening toward the center, looking for all the worlds like a miniature flying saucer out of the old-time pre-space paranoid urban folklore stories. In a sense, that was exactly what it was—except there was no little green man inside. Just a purple starfish.

Georg patted the disc affectionately. That purple starfish—and all the rest of Cinnabex—had been a good and loyal friend. Georg considered himself massively lucky that Cinnabex and her split-clone Allabex believed it a worthy use of their time to deal with anything as insignificant as human beings. Though, of course, right at the moment, "lucky" didn't seem a good description of his situation.

What *were* the Pavlat security officers trying to do, exactly? Kill him? Catch him? Chase him off? Whichever it was, how good were they at this sort of work? This was, in a sense, their home ground, and that might count for a lot—or not. They were city folk, and likely to be even more reliant on technology to help track him than he was in attempting to escape.

"Cinn," he whispered, "have you gotten anything yet on who these guys are?"

"I have managed a certain amount of signal intelligence. No decrypts, but I can see who is suddenly generating message traffic: the Thelm's Guard, and no one else."

"So it's all of Daddy's good little boys," Georg growled.

"More to the point, they are *not* the Thelek's good little boys, to use your informal and sarcastic mode of reference," Cinnabex replied. "The High Thelek's operatives would be far more likely to approach you with maximum aggression."

"These guys are plenty aggressive." George tried to think. If it was the Thelm's forces, coming from Thelm's Keep, they were probably no more familiar with the surrounding country than he was. He might actually have a slight advantage. They'd be relying on their fair-to-middling tech gear to track him. If he was careful, his camo suit was probably good enough to counter most of what their detection hardware could do.

Just then, another shot went off, and struck a good two hundred meters away.

Without a moment's thought, he rolled in the opposite direction, got up on his feet, crouched as low as he could, and started moving away from the blast, hoping that it would blind their instruments and distract their attention for a few vital seconds. He resisted the temptation to run, concentrating instead on slow and steady movement, both to avoid setting off motion detectors—and to avoid the dangers of tripping over something in the darkness.

Georg was using night-vision goggles—but night-vision gear was an unsteady crutch, good enough to make you trust the ghostly, blurry imagery too far. The Pax Humana trainers had beaten that much into his head. You could walk at a steady pace using night-gogs—but don't try to run. Besides, his gear was meant for observing nocturnal animal life—not evading a military force.

Georg spotted a sparse little clump of scrubby vegetation ten or twenty meters ahead. He moved in among the plants and knelt, still trying to stay low. It was a nice bit of natural cover—enough to screen him from all but the very best detection gear, but with enough bare spots and openings for him to get a good look around.

He had been moving north, and steadily uphill, toward a high pass between the peaks of two tired old mountains. If he could reach the pass, he would be over the northern border, and out of the Thelm's personal domain, out into the wider world where the Thelm's direct Will was not the final word and Thelm's Law did not apply. Georg did not know if merely crossing the border would be enough to save him, but there had been precious few other options open to him.

But was the pass itself still open? The approaches to the pass were wide at the valley floor, but contracted rapidly as it rose toward the pass itself. He was moving toward the narrow end of a funnel. He cranked his goggles up to max power and highest magnification and strained his eyes as he studied the top of the pass. There seemed to be some sorts of moving heat sources there, and the glints of what might be polished surfaces reflecting in starlight.

"Cinn—does your component have better night-sensing gear than I do? I think there's some action at the top of the pass, but I can't tell for sure."

"It likely does," Cinnabex replied. "Please remove the container from your pocket and hold it in your hand."

Georg opened his pocket, pulled the heavy disc out, and placed it flat in the palm of his hand. "All right," he said.

The container popped open, and the top half swung open, hinging on the side away from Georg. There lay the purple starfish—or, more accurately, the Stannlar component that, to human eyes, resembled a six-legged purple starfish. Georg had known it was in there, of course, but this was the first time he had actually laid eyes on it since Cinnabex had handed him the component transport container.

This small part of Cinnabex was most decidedly an *it*, the way a bit of trimmed-off fingernail or an extracted tooth would be an *it*. But this purple starfish was still part of the whole, connected remotely to Cinnabex's main body. Slender wires, attached to tiny electrodes on the creature, were connected to the transport container and its built-in transmitter and receiver. The main portion of Cinnabex was linked to this small part in such a way that the starfish sent and received the same pseudosynaptic signals that it would have experienced when snuggled up with the thousands of other components that made up Cinnabex's main body.

"Aim the inside of the container's upper half at the area you wish to have scanned," said Cinnabex through the headphones. "Remain concealed as much as possible while you are doing so."

Georg did as he was told. The inside of the container's lid must have served as a sort of parabolic antenna, with Pax alone knew what sort of detectors tucked away inside it. "Getting anything?" he asked.

"Far too much," Cinnabex replied. "There are all manner of Pavlat up there. They have more weapons and detectors than I could list in any reasonable amount of time."

"Right," said Georg, hunkering down a bit lower. The container closed itself, and he absently stuffed it back in his breast pocket. So. He wasn't being chased, or hunted, or tracked. He was being herded, being *driven* toward the Thelm's servants, waiting to gather him in. The Pavlat behind and below him were like the beaters at a shooting party, flushing out the prey, urging it toward where the men with the guns waited.

"Change of plans," he announced. "We move sideways, then look for a chance to double back into the valley. We lie low in daylight and make another try by some other route tomorrow night." He knew how long the odds were against his plan—but what choice did he have? Moving forward, up toward the pass, could at best be no better than surrender—and might be no better than suicide.

But suicide—no, *not* suicide, the acceptance of inevitable death at the hands of another—would be better than some other possibilities. Suppose—suppose they *did* catch him, and, somehow, forced him to do their will?

Later. Worry about it later. If he *had* a later.

Georg studied the terrain immediately around him.

The patch of scrubby growth that hid him was in a slightly bowl-shaped depression, not more than twenty centimeters deep. When the rains came, it would serve as a catchment that held water in place long enough for the plants to make use of it and grow.

But if water flowed into this catchment, where did it flow out? There! It was nothing more than a notch in the eastern side of the depression, leading to a shallow sort of trench. But it led east, and down, and it would provide some small measure of cover. Keeping himself hunched over and his profile low, Georg got moving. To his delight, he discovered that the trench rapidly deepened and widened as he moved along, with other dry runoffs joining it.

Soon it was nearly waist high, and the scrubby brush on either side of the wash grew thicker and lusher, providing almost solid cover on both banks. Georg recognized two or three species he had been studying. It was good to see them growing and healthy, out in the wild, even if he knew it couldn't last.

The genetic time bomb that would kill all the living things around him was not merely ticking—in fact, it had already gone off. The whole reason that he and Cinnabex and Allabex were on-planet was to undo the damage that had already been done, or, failing that, at least to try to keep things from getting worse.

He risked straightening up a bit as he moved along what had grown into a full-blown dry creekbed. Plainly, there was running water there in the rainy season. Even now the dirt and gravel underfoot was damp, or even puddled-over in places. He couldn't have asked for a better piece of cover, or a better avenue to lead him right where he wanted to go.

He was starting to think there might even be some hope in his future. Get out of the Thelm's Valley, find some way off this planet and back to Pax Humana HQ, then wangle a way off-planet for Marta and Moira—though Marta would probably have managed that by herself by then.

"We might actually get out of this, Cinnabex," he said.

"The odds are strongly against that, friend Georg," Cinnabex replied. "The odds of your escaping are growing worse by the minute. Your odds of surviving—and of our venture succeeding—will be far greater if you turn yourself in and agree to abide by local law and custom."

" 'Local law and custom,' " Georg echoed. "That's an amazingly prettied-up way to describe it."

"Very well. Call it a duty incumbent on you as a result of the honor bestowed upon you. Call it what is expected of you. Call it what law and tradition demand."

"Tradition. That's always the reason people use when they want to act without thinking."

"Tradition is the voice of experience," Cinnabex said, rather stiffly. Georg felt vaguely and unfairly disappointed to hear Cinn make such a typical Elder Race remark.

There was an outcrop of rock that half blocked the

wash. Georg had to pick his way over it slowly and cautiously, and did not reply at first. His back was tired from running half–hunched over, and the last thing he needed was to cramp up. He decided to take a short break. He found a place to sit down and lean against a rock for a moment, and said, "Just because something is a long-standing tradition does not make it right. And traditions can change, even if it sometimes takes very heavy pressure to make them change."

"I grant those points," said Cinnabex. "But they will not have much bearing if you are dead. You must be alive in order to change things."

"Not necessarily. Dying in a good cause can often do a cause good."

"A clever phrase, and it might even be true. However, the death can only do good if others hear about it," Cinnabex replied.

"That will be your job if I don't make it," Georg responded. "Get word back to Pax Humana, to Center, to Earth, of what happens to me."

Cinnabex was silent for a moment. "Forgive me, friend Georg, but one would almost think that you *want* to die."

Georg laughed bitterly. "No," he said. "Far from it. But if I *do* die, I see no reason for my death to be wasted."

"But even if I do send word to Earth, what good would that do? How could it change things?"

"I know, I know," George said, nodding absently. "Humanity is very weak, and very unimportant, and has little influence. *But things change.* Humanity will grow stronger in the councils of the sentient races. The other races will find themselves obliged to care about what we care about."

"That is extremely long-range planning for a short-lived race," Cinnabex said drily. "And it is optimistic almost to the point of being delusional. Such great shifts in power simply do not happen quickly—and almost never happen at all."

Georg grunted, but didn't reply. Better to focus on the matter at hand. He stood up and started making his way through the shallowing ravine. Soon, he could hear running water up ahead.

He paused as he came to where the ravine petered out, ending in a still pool of water that was a sort of inlet to a small stream flowing along at right angles to the ravine they had been following. Even in the height of the dry season, it was about five meters wide and a half meter or more deep.

"Is your component's transport case waterproof?" Georg asked, patting the container in his breast pocket.

"It can be fully sealed for short periods. But, of course, my component needs breathing air and ventilation for cooling. It cannot stay closed down for long."

"Five or ten minutes all right?"

"That is acceptable. Might I ask what you are intending to do?"

"Lie down in that creek," Georg replied. "I want to give my camo suit a chance to dump some heat."

Among its many other functions, the camouflage suit absorbed and stored the wearer's body heat. It did so to keep the wearer from being spotted by animals that could see in infrared—but it also hid the wearer from technological infrared sensors.

However, the suit's heat absorbers could only hold so much converted heat energy before they were forced to shed it, one way or another. If the absorbers ran too long, they would overload and explode. The best way to dump the excess heat was in cold running water. It would also chill down the whole heat-masking system, so it would run better and for hours longer before it would need another heat dump.

"I doubt that water will be very comfortable for you," Cinnabex replied. "But better cold and discomfort than detection. Please proceed."

"Right." Georg decided to move before he had a chance to think better of the idea.

The ravine shallowed to almost nothing as it merged with the creek. Georg moved forward to the last little bit of cover the banks afforded, cranked his night vision up to max power again, and popped his head over the top. Scrubby growth, weeds, brush, and small trees crowded up against both banks as close as they could, shouldering each other aside to get at the water source. That meant good cover for Georg—but also for his pursuers. There could be fifty Reqwar Pavlat lining the banks of the creek, and he wouldn't be able to see them.

He considered asking Cinnabex to use her detection gear again, but rejected the idea. Better to rely on his own less powerful but more discreet equipment. Georg lowered himself into the ravine and crept forward as quietly as he could toward its mouth until the water was over his boot tops. The stinging cold flooded down around his feet. He waded out into the center of the fast-moving stream and found a spot with a good-sized boulder standing up out of waist-high water.

"As I understand it, your camouflage suit's heat-dump process is far more effective if the entire garment—and its wearer—are completely immersed," said Cinnabex.

"That's what we're going to do. Full immersion. Give the whole suit a chance to dump through its whole surface area for a full five minutes."

"Might I ask how *you* are going to breathe in those minutes?"

Georg laughed silently. "I have a real high-tech device that ought to do the trick," he said, and pulled a long, flexible tube out of a pocket on the left shoulder of the suit. He placed himself upstream of the boulder, turned himself to face downstream, and sat down in the water, cursing the cold under his breath. He braced his feet against the big rock, shoved the tube into a valve in his suit's mask, and lay down in the cold, cold water.

The fast-moving current made it almost impossible to hold his body underwater, and at first he took in nearly as much water as air through the breathing tube. After a certain amount of floundering around, he managed to find a rock he could wedge his left arm under to hold him beneath the surface and got the end of the breathing tube far enough above the water's surface for him to take in air more or less reliably.

Only once he had those details organized did he get around to activating the heat-dump system—and only when the heat dump started releasing its stored energy through the suit, warming it dramatically, did he realize how *cold* he had gotten in just a few moments under the chill water.

The heat dump seemed to take much longer than five minutes—and the last minute or two seemed longer still, as the last of the excess heat energy drained away from the suit and the surrounding cold soaked back in around Georg's skin. At last the heat-dump system signaled completion.

He resisted the urge to spit the tube out and pop his head back up above water the moment the process was done. Instead, he moved slowly, quietly, looping the tube around to one side of his head so he could keep breathing through it while he lifted only the top of his head above water. The moment his eyes cleared the surface, he froze.

"What is it?" the tiny voice whispered in his ear. Somehow, even tucked away in its container, the Cinnabex component sensed that something was wrong.

The sound of rushing water was all around him, and loud enough to mask the sound of his subvocalizing underwater. He pushed the breathing tube far enough out of his voice to mutter a reply. "Many

Pavlat," he whispered, using as few words as he could. "Crossing creek, hundred meters south. Taking up posts both sides." Then he used his teeth and lips to pull the tube back into position. He was going to need it for a while longer—but he couldn't stay in the water too long. Cinnabex's component didn't have much breathing air left.

In any cold-blooded, rational analysis the component as a living being was expendable—but the component was also his link back to Cinnabex, and any hope of outside help.

And he was going to *need* outside help. That much was clear. He watched as the last of the Pavlat vanished from sight into the brush on both banks of the creek. "Cinn—any new useful info?" he murmured into the throat mike.

"Stand by," Cinnabex answered. "I have managed to generate at least partial decrypts and localizations for some transmissions. Mainly by a process of elimination, they have decided you must have headed east and are concentrating search strength in that direction. The commander ordered that guards be posted on the creek, on the assumption that you'd have to cross it, but the guards protested that the vegetation on the banks was too thick, making it impossible to keep watch. Therefore, the guards are being placed on both sides of the creek, about every one hundred thirty meters apart, sixty-five meters back from the vegetation belt that follows the creek downhill and south."

George swore to himself. He shouldn't have done

the cool-down. If he had just crossed the creek immediately, he might have kept a good quarter kilometer ahead of the search parties. Of course, that wouldn't have done him much good if his camo suit had overloaded and initiated an uncontrolled heat dump. There hadn't been any good choices—and hadn't been for a long time.

Georg watched silently as the last of the Pavs crossed over. He waited until he couldn't see them, until the undergrowth had completely muffled the sound of their passing. If he couldn't hear them, then maybe they couldn't hear him.

"All right," he said after a moment, "I can risk talking a little here, with the water noise, but I won't want to chance even subvocalizing once we're out of the water. We have to move, and soon. They're expecting me to try to cross the creek and head east, and they're watching from outside the vegetation belt. I'm going to head back to the *west* bank of the creek, hug the inside of the belt, and move south, back toward the way we came."

"The odds against success are extremely high," Cinnabex replied.

"Yes," Georg agreed. "Can you suggest an alternate option with better odds?"

"No," said Cinnabex. "But I regret that I must insist on our previously agreed dispersal plan."

In other words, Cinn was assuming Georg would be captured or killed. And it might well do great political and legal harm if the Pavlat learned that Cinnabex had been trying to help Georg escape. "All right," Georg said once again, though precious little at all was all right about anything. "Let's do it fast before your component runs out of air or I freeze to death."

Georg levered himself up out of the water to a sitting position—and almost fainted dead away. It was shocking to realize how much of his strength and endurance the cold water had taken out of him—and, perhaps, how little he had left even before he had gone in the water. He shook his head to clear it, then, moving slowly and cautiously, got to his feet while staying as hunched over as possible, doing all he could to keep a low profile. His arms and legs were stiff and cold, and he found himself shivering uncontrollably, his teeth chattering so loudly it seemed impossible that the Pavlat could not hear the sound. He longed for some of the waste heat he had just gone to such trouble to lose.

He moved downstream in the water past the entrance to his ravine, then scrambled up on the western bank of the creek. Once hidden by the foliage, he allowed himself a few brief seconds to recover, then set to work.

He knelt and pulled out the container holding Cinnabex's component. He set it down on the ground and watched as the lid opened itself one last time.

The component lost no time in climbing out of the container, the thin wires that connected it to the hardware inside trailing after it. It stood up on two of its six legs, and faced Georg, looking up at him through the leg-eyes of its two uppermost legs. "I must speak now, before I detach myself from the comm gear," it said, Cinnabex's voice coming to him through his earphones. "I must speak, and you must listen."

Georg knew what was coming, and knew there was no chance of agreement—but also knew how much he owed Cinnabex, and how very much Cinnabex had earned the right to be heard.

"Go on," he whispered.

The starfish drew itself up to its full twenty centimeters of height and faced Georg as Cinnabex's voice chimed in his ear. "The only way—the *only* way—for you to survive this crisis, and achieve your goals, and, perhaps, save this world from collapse, will be if you do what the Reqwar Pavlat require. You must weigh your honor, and your beliefs, and your oaths, against all that will be lost if you persist in your present course. Go on as you have, and our project will be canceled, all our work wasted—and the very survival of Reqwar's terrestrial ecology will be set at risk." The starfish paused for a moment, then gestured with two of its arms, a remarkably good imitation of a human shrug. Cinnabex had always been good at that sort of thing. "That is all. Now I must detach myself, and go. You know what to do with the container. You have about six minutes."

"I know," said Georg. "Thank you, Cinnabex, for everything. Thank you, and good-bye."

"May it instead be but farewell. Let us think on the time when the rest of me greets all of you once again."

"Farewell then," Georg said, resisting the absurd

urge to reach down and shake the component by its nonexistent hand.

The component folded its four uppermost legs back, and deftly detached the wires connecting it to the compartment. Then it swung its legs forward again and dropped down to stand on all sixes for a moment. It raised its two side legs and extended them to give those leg-eyes maximum binocular vision.

One of the eyes glanced up at George, and the little creature started back a handbreadth, as if surprised to see him there. Detached from the rest of Cinnabex, the component had already forgotten everything, lost everything. It turned its back on Georg and headed out into the brush. The creature's survival instincts would drive it to find some place safe to hide—but there was no place it would be safe from the enzymes set loose in its body when it detached itself from the comm system. The enzymes would start to dissolve the little creature's organs within a few minutes, killing it. Those enzymes would continue their work past death, dissolving the creature's body entirely, leaving nothing but a puddle of unidentifiable organic goo that would quickly seep into the soil.

It was a standard security precaution, and quite sensible when dealing with an expendable component organism, but it still didn't sit right with Georg. A wave of guilt and shame washed over him. Cinnabex had been right to ask the price of his honor. Was the death of this little bit of Cinnabex merely the first small down payment?

Georg pulled his hunting knife from its sheath and stabbed at the soft ground, then clawed the dirt out with both hands. He quickly had a thirty-centimeter-deep hole big enough around to hold the container. He shoved it in, filled in the hole, and flattened the loose dirt with his hands, then spread leaf litter and other debris around the disturbed area. He knew the odds were extremely high that the Pavlat would find it, but it didn't hurt to make an effort. The real point of burying the thing was to dampen the series of small self-destruct explosions that were due in about three minutes' time. If the Pavlat did open the hole, they would find nothing readily identifiable as Stannlar technology.

*I'll have to think up what to tell them it was, once they catch me and start asking questions,* Georg told himself. He realized the implications of that thought, then shrugged, stood up, and started to move south. *I'm going to get caught,* he told himself. *No sense pretending otherwise. No sense at all.*

But there was no need to make it easy on them, either. He moved as quietly, as stealthily, as he could, back down into the Thelm's Valley, toward the fate he had tried so hard to escape.

"*...do what the Regwar Pavlat require.*"

The words echoed in his skull, and he battled against them. No. Not when he wore the insignia of Pax Humana hanging on a chain around his neck, the pendant bouncing gently against the skin on his chest with every step he took. Better, far better, to die, no matter what the cost.

Georg Hertzmann headed south, through the thinning darkness, toward the last morning of his freedom.

# TWO ∙ LOSS

BSI Special Agent Jamie Mendez sat at the worktable in his cubicle. He listened to the deathly silence that had engulfed the big central operations room of BSI Orbital HQ—the Bullpen. There were at least a dozen other agents on duty in the Bullpen, but the room was utterly quiet. All eyes were on the maintenance robot as it went about its task, removing the last of the dead man's personal effects from the desk he had barely had time to occupy.

Jamie had to work for a moment to remember the dead man's name. Cho, that was it. Charles Cho. He had only lasted a month, and now he was dead.

Jamie tried not to remember that he himself had been assigned to the Bullpen a mere eight weeks before, or that Cho had been exactly the same age he was. But Jamie never had been much good at kidding himself.

"At least he finished his assignment," said a voice from behind him. It was his partner, Senior Special Agent Hannah Wolfson, standing by the entrance to his cubicle.

"Just before it finished him," Jamie replied. It was the first time Jamie had seen the maint robots clearing out a dead agent's effects. It was, he had no doubt, far from the first for Hannah. "Makes you start to wonder who'll be next, doesn't it?" he asked.

"Don't start thinking that way," Hannah said sharply.

*Because the next stop from there is wondering if* I'll *be next*, Jamie thought. And the odds weren't all that long, either. He knew what the casualty rate was among new agents.

The robot finished its doleful task, and wheeled toward the main exit. The silence lifted from the Bullpen. Papers rustled. Chairs squeaked, and voices started up again. A commlink chirped.

Hannah pulled out her link and glanced at it. "That's me," she said. "Kelly wants to chat. Gotta go."

"That's always good news," Jamie muttered, still staring at the newly blank worktable in the empty cubicle. How long until another new recruit landed there? It looked exactly the same way Jamie's own cubicle had looked the day he arrived. He suddenly had a very clear insight into why most agents did everything they could to personalize their work areas with pictures and mementos. No one wanted their space to look that *blank*.

Jamie shook his head, blinked, and realized that his own commlink *hadn't* chirped. He pulled it from his breast pocket and confirmed there was no summons on it.

What could Commandant Kelly have to say to his partner that she couldn't say to him?

* * *

"We need to talk, Hannah," said Commandant Kelly, glancing up at her as she came in. Kelly closed the file she had been studying and gestured Hannah toward a chair. "Close the door."

*That means bad news*, Hannah told herself. Kelly made a point of keeping her door open to all her agents, of sitting where she could be seen through the doorway, of keeping no secrets that didn't need to be kept. But Hannah did as she was told and pulled the door shut, blocking out the sound of a Bullpen that was struggling to get back to work, to pretend that the day an agent died was just a normal day.

Well, given the run of bad luck they'd been having the last few months, it *was* a normal day. That was the grim reality of the situation. Hannah sat down in the visitor's chair.

Wilhelmina Kelly pushed back from her desk and leaned back in her chair with a weary sigh. She was a small, slightly heavyset woman, a purebred Australian aborigine, with lively, compelling eyes that framed a strong-featured face. Her outsized chair and desk, left over from her ego-obsessed predecessor, made her look even smaller. Hannah knew better. There wasn't anything Kelly wasn't big enough to handle. At least, nothing so far.

"Tell me about your new partner," Kelly said abruptly. "Evaluate him as an agent."

Sometimes Kelly was like that, just jumping right in without any preliminaries. No words of mourning for

Cho, no expressions of sorrow. Duty and the job came first.

Hannah cleared her throat and spoke in as professional and dispassionate a tone as she could. "Special Agent Mendez is very new, very determined, potentially very good. His research has been first-rate, and on anything to do with weapons and tactics he's way ahead of me. In another areas, he shows lots of potential, but he's still making lots of mistakes."

"What kind of mistakes?"

"Jumping in too fast, acting on the basis of assumptions he hasn't confirmed, allowing enthusiasm to outstrip caution."

"In other words, acting just like a promising young agent who doesn't have much experience yet."

"That's about right."

"How has it been working with him the last couple of months?"

"I'm not used to working with a partner," said Hannah, "but I know that's the point of your pairing me with him—to see if partnering makes sense for BSI agents."

"And does it?"

"Yes," Hannah said, almost surprised by her own certainty. "We work well together. I'd be happy to continue working in a partner system—if *he* was my partner."

Kelly swiveled about in her chair, and glared out the two-meter-wide viewport that was one of the very few privileges that the commandant's rank conferred. The planet Center was a gleaming ball of green, blue, and white far below, and the jet-black of space was spangled with a glory of stars. Earth's own sun was one of those tiny dots of light, all but lost among all the others. An almost perfect metaphor for the situation in which humanity found itself—insignificant and all but unnoticed in a galaxy that held all the myriad Elder Races.

"Look at that," Kelly said. "Just look at all that— and tell me how the devil we're supposed to police it."

"How do you patrol infinity?" Hannah asked.

"That about sums it up," Kelly said, and they both stared out the viewport for a moment.

*All criminal cases with human involvement outside Earth's home system, and/or all criminal cases with nonhuman sentient being involvement.* So read the charter of the Bureau of Special Investigations. No doubt the people who had written it, ninety-odd years ago, had known then that the assignment was impossible. Every day that passed proved that—and showed how necessary it was to try to do it anyway.

"We can't police it without police," Hannah said after a moment or two of contemplating the sky. "Cho's just the latest. We're losing too many agents. Way too many. It's not just bad for morale—it's cutting deeply into efficiency. We're using up a lot of time just investigating the deaths of our own people."

"I know," said Commandant Kelly, her voice weary. "We're losing them faster than we can recruit—and *that* little fact does its own bit to discourage recruitment." She swung around to face Hannah. "So what do we do?"

"That's your job to decide, not mine."

"You're a *Senior* Special Agent. It's part of *your* job to advise me," Kelly replied. "Besides," she went on, patting the arms of her chair, "it wouldn't surprise me one little bit if *you* sat here someday. You could use some practice on the policy side."

Hannah gestured with one hand toward the Bullpen, and the newly emptied cubicle. "Obviously, we fill that desk. Close ranks and move on."

"Move on how? To where?"

Hannah Wolfson frowned and shook her head. "How, I can tell you—by facing facts. Every time we—humanity, I mean—every time we move outward, make new contacts with other races, or just expand our contacts with a race we've been dealing with for years, we find new problems. And there are now humans on four times as many worlds as there were just twenty years ago—but BSI hasn't even *doubled* in size in that same time. We're stretched too thin, trying to do too many things at once with not enough people."

Kelly gestured at a stack of papers on her desk. "What you just said in a hundred words, that nice thick report in the middle of the stack tells me in five hundred pages. But go on."

"Those are the facts. We have to face them *and* we have to respond to them. We have to stop doing things the way we did them ninety years ago."

"For example?"

Hannah stood up, and moved around to stand behind her chair, as if to get a bit farther away from the truth she was trying to face. "I wasn't sure of it at first, but you've convinced me. We need to do more partnering," she said. " 'One case, one agent' simply doesn't work anymore."

" 'One case, one agent,' " Kelly said, a sour note in her voice as she echoed the quotation. "That bit of folklore has probably put half the names on the memorial in Central Hall. We're going to run out of room on that thing pretty soon. I've been fighting like crazy to get the higher-ups to understand that one-agent-one-case worked when we were only dealing with three or four alien species in five or six star systems. Agents had a chance to study up on the cultures, the languages, to specialize. That's much harder now."

"Actually, it's impossible," Hannah replied. "I looked it up. The British Museum's Nonhuman Cultures Index lists more sentient alien species than we have agents."

"Which ought to prove my point," said Kelly. "So we try something else. It's time to go past the pilot program on partnering up agents and do it large scale."

" 'Pilot program'? I don't think we can get away with calling it that. It's just one pair—Mendez and me—and you've only sent us out on a few cases. We'd have to expand the test to I don't know how many agents, and run them as partners for months to call it a *real* pilot program."

"By which time we'll have lost how many more new agents?" Kelly demanded. "I'd be willing to bet Cho would have made it back to his desk—*if* he had had someone there to watch his back. But if we wait until we've done enough tests and studies and surveys to make the planetside crowd happy, we're not going to have enough agents left to keep this place open."

"You're preaching to the converted," Hannah said. "Being out with Mendez convinced me. Agents need backup, support, another pair of eyes. Mendez and I have proved it by *doing* it and coming back alive."

"But you haven't proved it with paperwork and pie charts. Even so, if we don't start partnering on at least *some* calls until we get studies done, we're only going to have two or three agents *left*," said Kelly. "That's why we're going to pretend you two were a full pilot program." She rubbed her eyes. "And we're going with a full-blown partnering system, or at least we will—but not just yet."

"Why not? You just said yourself we need to do it now."

"We *need* to do it now—but we *can't*. I've got a lot of people to keep happy. I need more time." She gestured out the viewport at Center. "Our masters down there, planetside. *Their* bosses, back on Earth. Our budget for the next two years is just about to be approved—maybe. It's a couple of months late already. I *can't* make any policy changes right now that might make some smart bean counter reopen the whole budgeting process. One agent-pair I can get away with *if* I call it a test—as long as it's still working, still successful. But I *can't* risk expanding out to a full program until the new budget is approved and the funds are actually disbursed to our accounts. If I make changes now, it will make us look very bad. It might give someone an excuse to shut us down."

"Come on. You're saying you can't risk taking a step that might save your agents' lives because it might delay our *budget* allocation?"

"Not just delay it," Kelly said sharply. "Cancel it. Meaning the BSI itself might not survive." She gestured out the viewport at the planet Center. "The Director and the rest of the bigwigs at On-Planet HQ have asked for contingency plans for pullbacks. For being more selective about what cases we handle. So selective that we might as well not even *be* here.

"If we just take on 'near-zero-risk-to-agent cases,' to use the happy phrase of the Director's memo, some *other* smart little bean counter is going to notice that we're not doing anything the local cops couldn't do, and they'll shut us down. It will be the end of whatever good the BSI has done for human civilization outside the Solar System. And I happen to think we do a lot of good. We save lives. We uphold the law. We show the Elder Races that humans are willing to clean up their own messes. Maybe we've even prevented a war or two. So yes, reluctantly, I am risking my agents' lives to prevent budget cuts that might end up crippling our relations with the Elder Races for the next thousand years."

Kelly hesitated a moment, then turned to stare at a blank spot at the wall to Hannah's left. At last she spoke. "Off the record, Cho bought into the 'one-agent-one-case' idea. He declined when I asked if he wanted to partner up. With you."

Kelly let out a long and weary sigh, then went on. "I didn't make it a direct order. I should have. So Cho is on my conscience." She turned and looked sharply at Hannah. "I *don't* want you two on my conscience. Effective immediately, you have standing orders to keep Jamie Mendez alive. Just forgetting for one moment that he's a nice kid and we don't want to see him die, politically speaking, it would be a disaster for the BSI to lose any more new agents just now—much worse than suddenly making big changes to how we manage agents. I'll have a bad enough time with the higher-ups over Cho's death. And I can't just keep the baby agents in-house. I *have* to send them out. But if we lose any more agents—especially new ones—that could be the last nails in BSI's coffin."

Hannah nodded. "Orders received and understood," she said. There didn't seem to be anything else she could say.

"Good," said Kelly. "Then just let me page Mendez in here for the case briefing."

"Excuse me?" Hannah asked.

"You didn't think this conversation was just *academic*, did you?" Kelly asked with a grim smile. "I'm assigning you two to a fresh mission—right now."

# THREE · **BRIEFING**

Jamie wasn't all that surprised to get called into Kelly's office five minutes after Hannah. One quick look at each of their faces told him what—or rather whom—they had been talking about.

Kelly gestured Jamie into a seat, then launched in. "I've got a job for the two of you," she said. She shoved a message sheet across the table so that it rested exactly between Hannah and Jamie. "That just came in from Reqwar. And before you can say you've never heard of Reqwar, neither had I until I looked it up. It's one of the minor Pavlat worlds."

Jamie picked up the message sheet. There were various dating and chrono and coordinate codes, but the message itself was printed in larger type, in the center of the page.

> HUMAN GEORG HERTZMANN FREE
> NOT GUILTY NOT PAVLAT DEATH
> NEGOTIATOR HERE SEND CASE HEAR
> HOME TAKE.

"It's not very clear what that means," Jamie ventured. "At least, not to me."

"We've seen worse," Kelly said placidly, and pointed to a framed document, hung on the wall. It was a message form, identical in format to one he held in his hand. The date on the message was five years old. The message itself read:

BSI KNOW OUI NEAT HILFE HIER
KALM NAO

"We never quite worked out how many languages that's supposed to be in," Kelly said. "We gave up trying to dope out what it *means* a long time ago. Now it's just a framed reminder that we don't know what the hell's going on, and the xenos aren't always that much help."

"We need reminding?" Hannah asked, plainly amused.

"What happened?" Jamie asked, allowing his curiosity to distract him. "I mean, with that message. Did you send an agent?"

"Sure we sent an agent—to the coordinates attached to the message. They put the agent's ship at a point in deep space, well away from any star system, or anything else, for that matter. We tried maybe half a dozen variants on the coordinates—figuring anyone who sent a message that scrambled might have written the coords wrong, too. Put them in the wrong order, or written them in another number base. I don't know how many variations we tried. Finally, we had to give up. Never did figure out what it was supposed to be about. Maybe it was a prank, or a test message, or a trap that didn't get sprung. I doubt we'll ever know." Kelly nodded toward the message in Jamie's hand. "The current message is a model of clarity in comparison."

Jamie shifted uncomfortably. "It's not all that clear to *me*."

Hannah reached for the message sheet. She read it over quickly and looked up. "What *do* you read it as meaning?" she asked.

"It's a bit ambiguous, I admit," said Kelly, "but I read it as saying this guy Hertzmann has been convicted of murder, and they don't want all the headaches of keeping a xeno-prisoner, so they want us to pick him up."

"Why does a xeno-prisoner make for headaches?" Jamie asked.

"A xeno-prisoner?" Kelly asked. "From a species you don't know much about? What *isn't* a headache? What's the right diet? What's a legit medical complaint, or legal complaint, and what's bogus? Is there something that's standard operating procedure in our prisons that would offend the xeno's culture, or be harmful to the prisoner without our knowing it? Do you want a pack of *other* xenos—relatives, lawyers, reporters, diplomats, scam artists, Space knows what, showing up to try and get him out or score points off his being locked up? The list goes on. It's a *lot* easier to get the home culture to agree to make the prisoner take his or her or its punishment back home. I figure they want this Hertzmann character to serve out his term in a human prison."

"Do we have a prisoner-transfer and sentence-equivalence agreement with the locals—or with *any* group of Pavlats?" Hannah asked.

"No, we don't—yet. But you're going to get us one—a standard working-level law-enforcement basic agreement. Something the diplomats can pump up into a treaty when they get around to it."

"*If* the diplos get around to it," said Hannah. "There's a pretty good backlog going."

"About twenty years' worth," Kelly agreed. "But that's not our problem, except it means getting a good solid interim agreement is even more important. It's going to be in force for a while." Kelly turned and looked at Jamie. "I figure you ought to have a leg up on this one, Mendez."

"How so, ma'am?"

"Your personnel file. You listed 'extensive experience in the Los Angeles Pavlavian expatriate community.'"

"Oh, well, yes." Jamie reddened. "That."

"Well, *have* you had extensive experience with them?"

"Well, yes, I have. But I don't know how much use it's going to be."

"Why not?"

How could he tell the commandant of the BSI Bullpen that he spent a summer working a Pavlat-owned store, in a neighborhood called Little Pavlavia, surrounded by Pavlats, and yet knew almost nothing about them? "Pavlats work very hard at not letting you learn about them, or get to know them."

"Didn't you make any friends, establish any contacts?"

Jamie shook his head apologetically. "Ma'am, it was a grunt job. I was the stock boy in a corner store. Pick up a box and put it over there. Mop the floor. Yes, I was there, in the community. Yes, I had extensive contacts, I guess. But hardly any of the customers were even willing to speak while I was in the room, let alone speak to *me*. Everything in that personnel file is true—but I was writing to make myself look good on a job application. It doesn't make me an expert on the Pavlats."

"Frankly, that's about what I figured," Kelly said. "But you're as close to an expert on the Pavlats as we have in the Bullpen at the moment." She nodded, making it clear the subject was closed. "So: a nice, simple job. Collect the prisoner, get the locals to sign on the dotted line, bring the prisoner back here, and hand him over to the Star Marshals—sometime when the StarMars aren't on a doughnut break. A milk run. Any questions?"

Jamie had something like an infinite supply, but he focused on what struck him as the central problem. "Ah, ma'am—as you say, the message is ambiguous. Suppose it means something else, and it's not just a prisoner pickup?"

"Then we find that out when we get there and deal with the situation as we find it," said Hannah.

Kelly gestured toward Hannah. "What she said." She glanced up at the wall clock, then stood up—

plainly a cue for the others to do so as well, and they did. "Consider yourselves briefed. You have one hour before you boost," she said. She looked at Jamie, then at Hannah. "So what are you waiting around here for?"

# FOUR · DEPARTURE

Fifty-nine minutes after the clock started, Hannah Wolfson was strapping herself into the left-hand pilot's seat on the bubble-domed command deck of the *Captain Arthur Hastings* while Jamie Mendez strapped himself into the right-hand seat.

The *Hastings* was a short, fat cylinder with three decks. The lower deck held the propulsion, the environmental control, cargo, and aux gear. The main deck had living quarters and work areas. The command deck was a smaller cylinder, barely large enough to hold the pilot's and copilot's stations, centered on the topside hull of the ship and capped by a transparent hemispherical forward view dome.

The ship carried two small ballistic landers, the *Lotus* and the *Orient Express*. BSI tradition had it that certain classes of ships in the BSI were named for famous characters, events, places, and vehicles in detective fiction. Captain Hastings had assisted Hercule Poirot on several cases. The steamship *Lotus* figured in *Death on the Nile*, and the train of the same name in *Murder on the Orient Express*. There was a complete set of the works of Agatha Christie aboard the *Hastings*—another part of the tradition—but there wouldn't be much time for pleasure reading.

The two landers were strapped down on the topside hull, one on either side of the command deck bubble. A portable habitat module was also strapped down topside, collapsed and stowed, to serve as accommodation for the prisoner they were expecting to transport home.

The ship's designers had played a few games with gravitic orientation. On the main and lower decks, and on the topside hull of the ship, *down* was toward the lower base of the cylindrical ship, toward the engines, opposite the direction of normal travel. However, the command deck's gravity field was rotated ninety degrees, so that *down* was *out*, toward one section of the cylinder rim, so the two landers were to the "left" and "right," and the portable habitat module was "overhead." That put "down" below the feet of the pilot and copilot in their command chairs. The arrangement led to a disconcerting transition as one moved from deck to deck, but allowed the craft to be flown from a normal seated position rather than with the pilot flat on his or her back.

But more things than not knowing which way was up or down could disorient a person. Hannah glanced over at her partner as the ship left the docking pad. He was looking a bit worried—and Hannah was pretty sure she knew why. Lots of people still found the idea of a completely automated starship disconcerting. Enter the destination planet's coordinates, hit the START button, and the ship would take it from there. It just didn't seem right. Star travel was too complex, too challenging, too full of surprises to have faith in such arrangements.

It tended to be nonpilots who were most worried by automated starships—and Jamie had no flight training at all. Hannah, on the other hand, had managed to earn a basic pilot's certificate some years back—and she trusted robotic piloting. She could fly the *Hastings* and the landers if need be, but she viewed herself as a backup to the automatics—not the other way around.

The BSI was practically the only outfit that had fully automated starships—and practically the only outfit that *needed* them. The official reasoning was that it would take far too long to train someone as a BSI agent *and* as a fully qualified starship pilot. But there was another reason that no one liked to talk about. A BSI ship had to be able to carry a badly injured agent back home without pilot intervention.

Soon the *Hastings* was well clear of Central Transit Station. The ship pointed herself toward deep space, and all there was in the viewport was the quiet, placid stars in all their glory, calm and everlasting.

Hannah's control board indicators showed they were boosting out toward their transition point, accelerating at a high rate. But however fast the ship was moving, it was not so fast as to make the stars appear to move. The acceleration compensation was smooth and perfect enough to damp over every vibration. The illusion of being motionless, at rest, quiet and safe, was all but complete. They might be boosting at twenty gees, but outside of the control panel indicators, there was no way to tell.

Hannah unbelted herself from the command chair and turned to Jamie, speaking in a voice calculated to be as calming as the unchanging glory outside the viewport. "So," she began, "were you able to find enough to do in the copious amounts of time you had for your research?"

She was relieved to see that Jamie responded with a grin. "Actually, I have to admit I did a lot better than I thought I would. I just asked questions, questions, questions, and didn't wait to read the answers."

Hannah reached for a display pad, flipped it to show research status, and was duly impressed to see that questions posed by one Jamie Mendez had generated 23.34 gigabytes of answer-data—more than what she had drawn herself by a good four gigs. Of course, 99.999 percent of the data that both of them had turned up would end up being utterly useless. The challenge over the next few days would be in filtering it down, finding the remaining .001 percent that could help them deal with the situation on the ground—whatever it was, exactly—and keep them both alive.

"It looks like you did good work," she said. "But now it's time to do more." She glanced at the nav displays. "We've got maybe nine or ten hours of cheap and easy radio contact with Center before we're out of reliable range of everything but the really big dish antennae—which they aren't going to bother to use to talk with us. Then we can switch to lasergram contact, which isn't *quite* so cheap or easy. A while after *that* we'll be so far off, and moving so fast, that the laser transmitters in Center orbit will have trouble tracking us, and the signal delay times will get impractical. We'll be out of effective range of anything but QuickBeam messages, and we don't want to have to rely on QB more than we have to."

"We don't have a QuickBeam *sender* on this ship, do we?" Mendez asked, plainly alarmed. Human-built QB senders had a bad reputation for detonating now and again.

"Stars no!" Hannah replied. "A QB sender would be *bigger* than this ship. But we can receive QB, and we can relay via radio or laser, and ask for Center to send a query via QB to whatever other star system you like—within reason. They don't like us using QB any more than we have to. The BSI budget isn't everything that it could be."

"Hmmm. Okay. There was one query I was thinking of sending, or at least wishing I could send."

"What, and who to?"

Jamie looked a little embarrassed. "To my old boss," he said. "Bindulan Halztec. The Pavlat I worked for. Kelly didn't give me a chance to say so, but I *had* heard of Reqwar—it's where Bindulan Halztec was from. He had to leave in a hurry years and years ago. I never did get the whole story. Some sort of political trouble."

"I thought from what you said he was just a shopkeeper."

"Just a shopkeeper on *Earth*," Jamie said. "It was pretty clear from the way he acted, and the way the other Pavlats acted, that he was something more—a lot more—than that before he came to Earth. And, if it came to that, his shop was something more than a shop. Any Pavlat with a problem wound up there, sooner or later—and usually the problem got solved. He had connections. I never was all that clear what they were, but he had them. Still does, I'm sure."

"So you think he might be able to give you a little background help." BSI agents often used precisely this sort of back-channel friend-of-a-friend contact. The problem in the present case was that they knew so little about what the case was about that it would be hard to come up with a useful set of questions to ask, and even harder to come up with a set of useful questions that would be short enough to send via QB. "All right," she said. "Draft something short—very short—and show it to me. Do that first, while we're still in easy range of Center. Any other thoughts?"

"Well, maybe just the start of one. I ran the name of the man we're supposed to escort back—if that's what we're supposed to do. Georg Hertzmann. Ran searches and metasearches and did some datamine work."

"Yeah, so?"

"So what I came up with is that if you run a query on Georg Hertzmann, and on Pavlat or Reqwar or both—practically everything that references those items has one other common referent."

"Okay, I'll bite. What's the punch line?"

"Pax Humana."

Hannah made no attempt to conceal her surprise.

"*That* muddies the waters. If Hertzmann belongs to PH, how is it a guy who belongs to a nonviolent action movement was convicted of murder?"

"That's what I was wondering. I didn't have any chance at all to track it further than that—it might not even be that he *is* a PH member. But there's *definitely* some sort of connection. PH has a big office on Center. They might know something that could help us."

"If they're in the mood to share," Hannah said thoughtfully. "I guess we need to make that query too, before we're out of range. I'll work that side of it while you're writing your letter to Shopkeeper Halztec." It took no particular detective skill to spot the disappointment in Jamie's face. He had wanted to work the Pax Humana lead himself. Hannah was pretty sure she knew why, based on what she had seen in his personnel file. "Look, Jamie—I know you're a big admirer of Pax Humana. It's in your file that you applied for PH membership."

"And got turned down," he muttered.

"That might be more of a compliment than you think," said Hannah. "But it's off point right now. I can easily understand your wanting to be the one to deal with them. But you obviously *have* to be the one to write to Halztec, and we're pressed for time for both queries. That means I have to be the one to contact Pax Humana." *And I don't think it's any bad thing that they don't see a request for information signed by a failed applicant who's still a big fan.* Pax Humana was in no need of more uncritical adoration than it was getting already.

PH would be more likely to respond with useful information if the query came from a more senior person with a more detached attitude. But the odds were against their responding at all. Pax Humana didn't hold the BSI in the highest regard—and Hannah, like most BSI agents, returned the favor. In her experience, they were awfully big on demanding respectful treatment but not so great on extending it. "Let's go," she said. "We're on the clock."

* * *

Hannah tried to be a bit cagey in her signal to Pax Humana's offices on Center. She was asking for information, not help, after all. She felt obliged to include the text of the message received from Reqwar, on the off chance that it contained some coded reference that would make sense to someone there, but she did her best to downplay the seriousness of the situation—easy to do when she knew next to nothing about it.

Jamie, meantime, worked up a tight, well-drafted query for his Pavlat friend, in a format suitable for QB transmission, in less than twenty minutes. In less time, in fact, than it took her to draft her query. She could have told him that, just to give his ego a bit of a boost. But she allowed herself the luxury of keeping quiet—and of not knocking a corner off her own ego. She got busy, and got the signals sent.

* * *

REQWAR . . . Habitable planet currently occupied by the Pavlat (see cross-ref). Mass .703 Earth, diameter .91 Earth, surface gravity .85 Earth, atmosphere at sea level .940 bar (approx 92.5% Earth sea level normal.) Period of rotation 31 hours, 15 minutes, 4 seconds.

Jamie rubbed his eyes, blinked, and tried to focus again. His cabin aboard the *Hastings* was, all things considered, a reasonably comfortable place, if you didn't mind having to fold just about everything in and out of the floors, walls, and even the ceiling, but it was, nonetheless, a small, windowless box. He could handle that. What was really throwing him off was time. Fatigue and time.

He checked his wristaid, and tried to figure out what time it was, really. His wristaid had picked up the shipwide links and automatically defaulted to the standard shipboard timekeeper, which had already converted to the Reqwar's day/night cycle and time-keeping, localized on the capital region of Thelmhome and Thelm's Keep. But his body was still on Center City Standard, the time kept in the Bullpen. He was not entirely sure if, right at the moment, it was day or night, or yesterday, or today, or even tomorrow back home—wherever home was, for him, at this point. California? Center City? BSI Orbital HQ?

But whatever time of day it was, whatever *day* it was, time was the one thing he didn't have to waste. He soldiered on with his reading.

Atmosphere: Oxygen 17%, Nitrogen 81%, $CO_2$, water vapor, and trace inert gases 2%.

...Landforms: Five small-to-medium island continents, ranging from Greenland-sized to Australia-sized, all associated with coastal islands...

...Native life on the planet has evolved to a state roughly comparable to the very early Cambrian fauna era of Earth, more or less on a par with the Burgess Shale fauna: relatively sophisticated macroscopic multicelled life-forms have evolved in a large number of genuses, each with relatively few species...Plants and animals have colonized most regions of the world ocean, but native life has yet to establish any sort of foothold on land. However, imported life-forms, especially plant life, are well established on all the main continents and many of the smaller islands. These are, for the most part, lightly modified and bioengineered variants of species found on the Pavlat home world...

Well, that at least jibed with what he had read from other sources. He had found that some sources repeated sections almost word for word from other references, while other sections were wildly different or contradictory. Never mind. He'd find out soon enough which bits were correct.

There was something comfortable about the grind of studying. It was all very much like crunch time back at Stanford. *Except a failing grade here doesn't just ding my grade point average*, he reminded himself. *It might get me killed.*

That thought provided all the incentive he needed to keep going. For one thing, he definitely needed more information on the particular breed of xenos they would be dealing with. Unfortunately, the sources on the Pavlat weren't much help in a lot of ways.

Pavlat: A species of deceptively humanoid appearance, sporting much the same body plan as humans: bipedal and upright, with their arms and hands all but completely evolved away from their previous locomotive functions and available for lifting, carrying, manipulation, etc. The Pavlat are generally taller and thinner than humans, and with a thicker, more leathery skin. They have six fingers on each hand, arranged more or less human-style, but with an additional opposable outer thumb. However, they have only four toes on each foot. It is unclear whether the "missing" toes are fused with other toes or simply fail to develop.

There is some variation in coloration, but the Pavlat are mainly bluish-grey in color, with the face, the ventral area of the torso, the palms of the hands, and the bottoms of their feet tan or light brown. Their faces are longer and more angular than humans', but the mouth and eyes are arranged as per the human model. There is no nose; instead, there are breathing holes just behind the large and fanlike ears. The ears themselves generally lie flat, but are even more maneuverable than a cat's. Ear position is an important signal of a Pavlat's mood.

As with their general bodily appearance, Pavlat biology is deceptively similar to human biology. The similarities mask vast and subtle differences that have shaped traditional Pavlat culture in many ways, some obvious, and some quite surprising. . . .

Jamie scored *that* section at about 85 percent right, based on his own quite limited experiences with the denizens of Little Pavlavia in Los Angeles. At least the article warned that first impressions could be deceptive—but it would have been nice if it had gone a bit further and tried to explain exactly *how* the similarities were deceptive. Interestingly enough, nearly all of the information seemed to be from human sources, with no data provided by third races. Maybe the other Elder Races didn't know much about the Pavlat either.

Communities on Earth like Little Pavlavia in Los Angeles merely provided the *illusion* that humans understood the Pavlat. The Pavlat on Earth had done a fairish job of assimilating themselves—and of keeping their reasons for leaving the Pavlat world very murky indeed.

He remembered from his days in Bindulan's store how complex codes and oaths of secrecy seem to cover everything. The humans that lived in and around Little Pavlavia had a few standard jokes about them, told with more affection than otherwise.

"How can you tell if a Pavlat is keeping a secret?"
"It's breathing."

"How can you tell when a Pavlat has told a secret?"

"It's stopped breathing."

If there was a hint of menace in that punch line, it wasn't out of place. The Pavlat did not deal gently with those who betrayed a trust, or a secret. It had taken a good long time for the Los Angeles cops to work out a way to deal with the Pavs, and the situation still wasn't altogether satisfactory.

Jamie rubbed his eyes and got back to work, slogging through the endless data files.

As with any widely dispersed intelligent species, the Pavlat have developed any number of cultures, each more or less adapted to the local climate and other conditions. However, it is safe to say that nearly all Pavlat cultures are strongly hierarchical, and are based in large extent on a complex and dense web of family connections, and a tightly interlocking system of obligations and privileges...

Jamie read on, until long after the words didn't make any sense anymore.

* * *

It was morning in Los Angeles. Bindulan Halztec got Jamie's message over breakfast—or what a *human* would call breakfast, merely because it was the first meal of the day. In most Pavlat cultures, Firstmeal was something much more—it was the main social and ceremonial meal of the day, when visitors came to call, and supplicants came asking boons, and family business was resolved.

Except, of course, that Bindulan was eating alone, in his very human-style kitchen, dressed in his ill-fitting but quite comfortable human-style coveralls, and puttering about the place very much in the style of an elderly but spry human widower.

Every once in a while, Bindulan realized just how un-Pavlat his behavior had become. A human, a youthful human, seeking him out, no doubt for guidance on some matter. It had come to that: He had immersed himself so deeply in human ways that the *humans* came to him for advice.

That realization brought him up short. He had, after all, come to Earth, come to Los Angeles, to *escape* the Reqwar Pavlat way of doing things, to turn his back on their medieval habits, the way they clung to traditions that might have made sense long ago but were now little more than formalized brutality, savagery made respectable.

But even so, those ways were *his* ways, his people. And even if he had put distance between himself and those traditions, he had not abandoned his people.

And yet, there, on Earth, without even being fully aware that they were doing it, the expatriated Pavlat community had set itself up as a distorted mirror image of the very society it was rejecting.

Bindulan had been the patrician's scion of a very

important family, and so, as a matter of course, he had become patrician to Little Pavlavia, even as he established himself as a mere grocer of no pretensions at all, a lowly shopkeeper with a well-earned reputation for being very close with a dollar or a UniStar—or any other unit of currency. Somehow, he had played both roles, side by side, both to the same audience, and none had ever questioned it.

He poured himself another glass of whrenseed juice, carefully mixed in the proper amounts of salt and sugar, and stirred it thoughtfully for a moment. Then he sat down in front of his comm screen and opened Jamie's message.

It took a remarkably long time to decrpyt, several seconds at least, long enough that Bindulan had time to decide it must be a long and involved video message, full sound and vision. He was startled indeed to discover it was a remarkably short text message, but with very heavy, slow-to-parse encryption—and then was startled anew, more than startled, *shocked*, as he read its contents.

Jamie Mendez, a BSI agent, bound for Reqwar! And assigned to the Hertzmann case, of all things. Not a word concerning that incident—no, not incident, *scandal*, had made its way into the normal local news reports, of course—but the Pavlat community knew all about it and was absolutely abuzz. No two Earthside Pavlat could meet without sitting down to discuss the matter in detail over a glass or two of whrenseed. Bindulan remembered his own freshly made whren, reached for it, and took a large sip, hoping it would calm him down, serve to settle his thoughts.

Every word of the too-brief message shouted out to Bindulan that Jamie Mendez had not the slightest idea that he was headed straight for the center of the quagmire, toward the twin black hearts of intrigue and murderous tradition that had driven Bindulan—and nearly every other Pavlat on Earth—out of Pavlat society in the first place.

The boy was writing to ask for advice, for guidance. The message had come reply-paid. Good. Very good. For Bindulan had extended a loan to Qal Frenzic's new endeavor. No doubt Bindulan would see his money again in due time, but it did mean that his finances of the moment simply would not allow him to send any QuickBeam messages on his own credit.

He paused for a moment to realize how highly he must think of Jamie, human or no, even to have considered the thought of paying himself. Even the shortest of QB messages would likely amount to more than all the wages Bindulan had paid Jamie for a full summer of hard work. Never mind that Jamie was human. Little Pavlavia was full of *Pavlat* to whom he would never *consider* extending so large an assistance.

But what to say? Well, the proper guidance in this circumstance was crystal clear—even if there was not the slightest chance of Jamie *taking* the advice Bindulan was bound to offer. James Mendez would go to Reqwar and do his duty, as honor required.

But honor also required that Bindulan warn and advise Jamie when asked, just the same.

He glanced down at the reply-paid section of the screen, noted the amount authorized—and saw that, fortunately enough, there were no restrictions whatsoever on how he *spent* the amount. If he wished to send further messages elsewhere, there were sufficient funds to do so. He should take advantage of that.

Very well, he would send the advice that honor required to Jamie. But that message would be brief, very brief. That would allow him to send a longer and more detailed message—in fact, a command—to where it would do Jamie—and Reqwar, perhaps—the most good.

He sat, sipping his whrenseed, and thinking, slowly, carefully, methodically, how best to spend the BSI's money to accomplish his own goals.

# FIVE ∙ **PAXERS**

Hannah set down her fork for a second, shut her eyes, and leaned back in her chair, the image of contentment. "Good food," she said, opening her eyes to look over at Jamie. "Say what else you may about the BSI, but you'll have to admit they stock the galleys on their ships pretty well."

"Granted," said Jamie, as he tore another piece of garlic bread off the loaf. "I didn't know anyone made ready-to-eat meals this good."

Hannah shut her eyes and smiled again, just for a second. One day had passed aboard the *Hastings*, and another; long enough for a sense of a routine to form. Part of that routine was dinner. The other meals she had to insist on, and almost literally drag Jamie away from his work—but, at least for both nights so far, for dinner he came willingly.

After only a handful of missions together, she had yet to puzzle out everything about her extremely junior partner, but she was starting to get a handle on him. One thing she knew for sure already was that he was a hard worker, and a quick study who took things seriously.

And the issue she was about to bring up just might

get unpleasant very fast. She would have just as soon avoided the topic, but the job required that they both face it. She judged it was the time to do it. But there wouldn't be any harm in approaching the matter indirectly.

"We still haven't gotten any reply from Pax Humana back on Center," Hannah said, as casually as she could, serving herself another healthy slice of lasagna. "But I have managed to pull together some pretty intriguing information about the job that Hertzmann is on Reqwar to do. What I haven't come up with is anything that links it directly to Pax Humana. Do you have anything on that?"

"In a way," Jamie said. "It's really a pretty weak connection. Hertzmann is there with his wife and daughter. They're not there rescuing anybody, or arbitrating a war, or that sort of thing. Georg Hertzmann and his wife belong to Pax Humana, but they're on a business deal, with some Pax Humana money behind them."

Hannah nodded. "I'm not all that surprised. The Paxers do more of that than rescuing or war-stopping. Those sorts of jobs are *expensive*, and PH has to do a lot of fund-raising, lots of business deals to support their work."

Jamie looked at Hannah thoughtfully, almost accusingly. "You don't like them much, do you?"

Hannah set down her fork and shifted in her seat a bit. "I don't have anything *against* them," she said, "but no, I'm not as *for* them as much as I gather you are. They are brave people, and they do good work. A lot of them are genuine heroes. But not *all* of them are heroes, and not everything they do is heroic—no matter how hard they work to make the outside world and themselves believe it. Besides, the only reason Pax Humana can live up to all those proud mottoes about being willing to die, but not to kill is because there are outfits like BSI that *will* use force when necessary."

"What are you talking about?"

"Well, there are two angles to it. First off, there were a lot of times when some bunch of xenos were up against PH, one way or the other, and heard about their being willing to die but not kill—and decided to take the Paxers up on it, figuring there wasn't any risk in killing Paxers. PH people got themselves killed—then BSI agents went in after the killers, and caught them—or died trying. After a while, most of the xeno bad guys realized there *were* consequences to killing Paxers—and so fewer Paxers got killed. Some BSI agents grumble that what really happened was the Paxers traded their casualties for BSI ones."

"What's the other angle?" Jamie asked.

"Nearly every decent government prevents violence against its citizens by declaring itself the only entity allowed to *use* violence. If, say, there's a kidnapping, it's legal for the BSI agents to shoot the bad guys, though it's *illegal* for the bad guys to shoot back. But if a bunch of virtuous citizens shot the bad guys, *they'd* be breaking the law just as much as the bad guys. That's why vigilante justice is a contradiction in terms."

"But the Paxers don't do that sort of thing. They do just the opposite."

"Right. They walk right into the middle of our hypothetical kidnapping standoff, wearing big signs that say SHOOT ME pinned to their backs. But the bad guys know that the cops will come after them if they do shoot the Paxers—so they don't. The Paxers can afford to risk a nonviolent approach *because* the bad guys know there are risks involved in killing or harming Paxers."

Hannah took a sip of wine and went on. "It takes real courage to do what the Paxers do. But they can only afford to take the moral high ground of nonviolence *because* BSI and the other law-enforcement and military organizations *don't* take a vow of nonviolence. The point is you can be a very good and brave person and do good and brave things—and still cause a lot of needless trouble. There's the old saying—the path to Hell is paved with good intentions."

"I think that saying is supposed to mean you can cause harm by accident while you're trying to do good," said Jamie stiffly.

"Maybe," Hannah replied. "*I've* always thought it was another way to say the ends justify the means—or rather, showing that they *don't* justify the means. I want to buy food to give to starving orphans, so it's all right for me to rob a bank to get the money—and if three guards get killed in the shoot-out, well, it was their own fault for getting between me and my trying to do a good deed. The Paxers tend to assume that they are so good that whatever they do must be right.

If you disagree, then you must not only be wrong, but opposed to doing good—maybe you're even evil."

"That's laying in on awfully thick," said Jamie.

"I'm just exaggerating to make a point: A lot of times the ethics and morals of a situation are a lot more ambiguous than Pax Humana wants them to be. The best—or least bad—summing-up you could make of their involvement in the various human-Kendari disputes would be to say that the Paxers have made the problems more complicated. Some would just say they've made things worse. I've heard the Paxers being accused of betraying the human race."

Jamie toyed with his food for a moment, took a bite, and spoke. "You said something a while back about it *almost* being a compliment that they turned me down. Should I be glad that a no-good organization didn't want me?"

It was hard to miss the belligerence in his remark, but Hannah gave it her best shot. "No, that wasn't it at all—and I didn't mean to suggest that Pax Humana were bad people. What I thought was a compliment was that they *didn't* turn you down completely. According to what you said in the self-disclosure section of your file, they told you to come back in a few years and try them again because you weren't ready to join Pax Humana—yet. They were telling you to come back when you had a little experience under your belt."

"Experience provided by the Bureau of Special Investigations," Jamie said.

Hannah looked him straight in the eye. "Exactly,"

she said. She wasn't going to tiptoe around a discussion of her partner's limits and abilities—not when both their lives might depend on understanding them. "You're too smart not to know that you were sending a very mixed set of signals, applying to both organizations at once. But you should take it as a very strong compliment that *both* organizations considered your application very carefully. Neither rejected you. One just told you to try again later, and the other, the BSI, said yes—in *spite* of those mixed signals."

Hannah leaned in closer to the table. "Let me be very clear about what worries me. You might, someday, sign up with Pax Humana. If so, fine—but that will be the day you resign from the Bureau of Special Investigations, because the PH membership oath includes a renunciation of all forms of violence, and a BSI agent can't swear to any such thing. *Until* then— you are BSI all the way. You're ready to defend yourself, and defend me, and use all appropriate means to fulfill your assignment—even if that means shoot to kill. Are we clear on that?"

Jamie went pale, then flushed, but his face took on an annoyed, stubborn look that Hannah found very reassuring under the circumstances. "We're clear," he said. "That's the way I've played it so far, and I'll keep at it."

"Good." *Very good. And I'll make sure you* stay *clear on that point.* After all, her orders were to bring him back alive. Kelly hadn't said she had to be *polite* about it. She finished her lasagna and let her silence close that particular topic of conversation.

What she was hoping for was that *Jamie* wouldn't let the silence linger. If he wanted to brood and sulk, that would spell trouble. She wanted him to speak next, make it his decision to move past the argument.

But the silence sat there for a time, unchallenged by either of them, neither of them so much as looking at the other. It reminded Hannah all too painfully of the strained and angry quiet around her family's dinner table. Just the fleeting memory of it was enough to tie her stomach in knots.

"Did, did, ah, you get anywhere on what sort of business deal Hertzmann was working on?" Jamie asked at last. He stood up, cleared the dishes from the table, and loaded them into the cleaner. Plainly he was trying as hard as he could to pretend things were okay.

Hannah nodded, stood up herself, and reached around Jamie for the coffeepot and a couple of cups—and tried to hide her own sense of relief. If he had started to brood and sulk, it could have soured things for a long time.

She sat down and poured a cup for each of them. "I'm still working the details up," she said, "and believe me, there's a lot of holes in the sources, and I'm making some guesses that could be wrong. But, if I have this straight, Herztmann's company is working with a Stannlar organization, if you can believe that."

Jamie looked at her in surprise as he sat back down. "I'm not sure I do. I didn't know the Stannlar did business with humans at all." The Stannlar were friendly enough, but if humans were the younger of the two Younger Races, then the Stannlar were among the oldest of the Elder. Supposedly there were a good number of living Stannlar Consortia that were themselves older than the human race. What sort of common ground could a human have with a being hundreds of thousands of years old?

"Most Stannlar don't—but, and don't ask me how—Hertzmann managed to team up with a pair of *young* Consortia. I barely knew there were such beings. Anyway, Hertzmann got some of that Pax Humana money together and formed a corporation, more or less, with these two Stannlar Consortia. That corporation has been hired to do an out-of-warranty repair on Reqwar's terrestrial ecology."

"*What?* How could there be a *warranty* on the terrestrial ecology?"

"Well, not a warranty, really. It's more an option to renew with a new service provider."

"You're going to have to back up here a little bit," Jamie said. "Renew what? How?"

"*How* is the key to it all," said Hannah. "How is the problem. But let me go back a bit—like five hundred million years or so. That's what I've been digging into today, mostly. Comparative early biology." She grinned. "You have to study a little of everything in the BSI."

Jamie smiled back. "I've been finding that out."

"Anyway, the point is that all the life on Earth was in the water, the oceans, until about four hundred and seventy million years ago. The continents were lifeless barren rock. It took a long time for plant life to establish itself on land, and land animals couldn't really get started until there were enough terrestrial plants for them to eat. The oceans were full of complex life-forms—trilobites and early fish and so on—for close on a hundred and eighty million years before there was any significant colonization of the land.

"Reqwar is following about the same pattern—but it's a about five hundred million years behind. What this ties into is that the Elder Races have hugely complicated rules about settling on planets. You're not allowed to wipe out the local terrestrial ecosystem. But you *can* establish your colony on a world that doesn't yet have land-based life, but *does* have reasonably advanced sea life—the equivalent of those trilobites and primitive fish. Seaborne plant life will give you oxygen in the air, among other things. You can harvest sea life as food and feedstock until your own farms and so on are established. You'll have to process the seafood to make it edible for your species, but the Elder Races all know how to do that already.

"The catch is that while there aren't exactly rules or laws saying your species *can't* colonize a planet forever, the universal experience and received wisdom is that even the longest-lived intelligent species isn't likely to remain on a colonized world for more than a few million years at most.

"Sooner or later something will happen—politics, trade, a plague, a war, a change in fashion, even evolution of the intelligent species in question. *Something* is going to cause species X to abandon its colony on planet Y. And when that happens, the species is expected to clean up after itself, at least biologically.

"No one much worries if they leave cities or roads or whatever behind. Erosion and geology will take care of things like that, sooner or later. But they aren't supposed to leave any imported life-forms behind. The worry is that without intelligent species X around to supervise, you'll get overbreeding, or nasty mutations, or maybe critters that excrete something toxic, or that remove some vital nutrient from the environment.

"That's why it's handy to set up shop on a world without life on land. You can set up your own complete ecosystem, with all the plants and animals from home. You won't ruin the local terrestrial ecology, because it isn't there yet. And when your people leave, they can wipe out *everything* on land, again without worrying too much about interfering with the planet's development. The imported life-forms will have processed some nutrients that will get washed into the sea and get eaten, and maybe put more oxygen in the air. But stuff like that either won't harm the oceanic ecosystem, or the ocean life can actually make use of it."

Jamie frowned. "But even if intelligent species X evacuated a particular planet in the most orderly way possible, it could never be certain it had killed all the microbes and insects and so on it had brought along. If something like a rat or a cockroach managed to establish itself—"

"Exactly."

"And things would be even worse if species X went extinct, or their colony just collapsed. There wouldn't be any hope at all of a cleanup. Even if species X survived when the colony gave out, the rest of the population of species X might not have the time or the wealth or the inclination for the cleanup."

"Right again. So how do you solve that?"

"That's obvious. You genetically engineer every species you introduce. You insert a kill-gene, maybe multiple kill-genes, just in case one k-gene fails or mutates. Insert some bit of genetic code that wouldn't do anything until it was activated, but that would kill or sterilize the life-form when it *was* activated. Probably the tidiest thing would be to make every living thing susceptible to one of a series of viruses that caused sterility."

"You're almost there," said Hannah, "but suppose species X dies out before it can release the sterilizing viruses?"

Jamie thought. "I don't know exactly what sort of mechanism you'd use to make it work, but you'd have to rig things so that, instead of taking action to wipe out imported life-forms, you'd have to take action to *prevent* them from being wiped out. If the intelligent xeno species is still around and still running the planet, it can push the 'reset' button every hundred years or so. But if species X collapses or leaves the planet, it won't be there to push the button—and good-bye to the species with the kill switch—and every species that relied on it as a food source. I guess you wouldn't have to kill off *all* the species directly— just the core species that supplied the main structure of the ecology. Probably mostly plants or their local equivalent."

"Full marks—except for one assumption you made, on account of your not thinking like a member of one of the Elder Races, and a fiddly cultural detail you don't know about the Reqwar Pavlat."

"Okay. I'll bite. What did I miss?"

"Elder Races species take the long view. They rig that 'reset' button to be pushed every ten thousand or hundred thousand years, not just every century. And the Reqwar Pavlat won't or can't do genetic engineering themselves."

"So they hired someone else to do it? Another species?"

"Right. Some species called the Kreflar, if I have that right."

"Never heard of them."

Hannah grinned evilly. "No reason why you should have. They managed to go extinct themselves, about the same time the Neanderthals checked out. But the punch line is that they didn't just do the genetic mods for Reqwar before they died out. They encrypted their work."

Jamie sat bolt upright. "*What?* Encrypted DNA? Is that even possible?"

"I have no idea. But this isn't DNA—it's whatever genetic code life from the Pavlat home world uses. And encryption must be possible with that genetic material because the Kreflar did it. In effect, you have to know the password before you can reset the clocks on all the kill-genes."

"And the people who know the passwords are all dead."

"And the kill-genes are starting to activate," Hannah said. "Unless or until Georg and his friends manage to decrypt the code and reset the timers, Reqwar's entire terrestrial ecology is going to collapse and die out within one or two human lifetimes.

"In other words," Hannah went on, "the stakes on this case are a lot higher than where one man serves out a prison sentence. The question is whether much of anyone on Reqwar will be alive by the time he *finishes* serving it."

# SIX ∎ MIRACLES

Marta Hertzmann stared at the display screen as she slowly and carefully shifted the scan-scope's field of view to the next encoding site. She spotted the telltale encrypt-start sequence and used the marker controls to lock in on it. She glanced down at her status boards. The learning sequencer was following right along with her, recording all her actions. She highlighted the encrypt-start sequence and flagged it, then moved down the gene to the encyprt-stop marker, and repeated the process. That was the last one on that gene—and, praise be, the last encrypt site for that species.

She let out a sigh of relief, saved her work, and lifted her hands away from the controls, being careful not to joggle anything. Delicate work. Delicate, intricate work. Soon, very soon, she hoped, the learning systems would have enough parameters to automate the process.

Marta had custom-designed the scan-scope's gene manipulation system herself, and built most of it by hand. She knew the limitations of the system as well as anyone. It was an excellent machine, but if the project had to rely on manual tagging—let alone manual decryption—they'd never get done. Even with Georg working alongside her, there was infinitely more work than two operators could do. And, of course, Georg was not working alongside her. She glanced at the other scan-scope, and the vacant operator's chair in front of it. It was hard to imagine any circumstances under which he would be there again.

From behind her came the sound of a crash and a thud and a sort of rattling gallop. "Mommy? School session's over! Aren't you finished *yet*?"

Marta turned around to see her eight-year-old daughter in the corridor, standing in the doorway of the lab, breathless from running. Marta smiled. "Just closing down now, Moira," she said. "Give me just a minute. Did you remember to shut down the tutoring system properly?"

"*Yes*, Mommy," Moira said in a tone of exaggerated impatience. She fidgeted in the doorway for a moment, looked down at the floor for a moment, then asked, "Are we going back to Thelm's Keep soon?"

Marta shut her eyes for a moment to master her frustration. The child asked the same question every day. "I told you, Moira. Not for a while. I don't know how long."

Georg and Marta had shuttled back and forth between the science labs on Lesser Western Continent and Thelm's Keep on Largest Continent for the last few months, towing Moira along with them. But after the Thelm's three eldest sons died, and Georg tried to escape, and things got distinctly ugly between the Thelm and the High Thelek, Marta had found lots of good reasons to stay on Lesser Western. There had even been rumors—reliable rumors—that the High Thelek was going to challenge the Thelm himself to a duel. It seemed safer to be far away from the political storms. "I know it's not as exciting here as at Thelm's Keep," Marta said.

"It's lonely. There aren't even *Pavlat* kids to play with here—and Pavlat kids aren't all that much fun, anyway. Will there be humans moving in here soon, now that the barracks are nearly done?"

"That's the plan," Marta said. But would the plan ever happen? In theory, they were just about at the point in the work where they would be ready to shift over from pilot programs and testing to full-scale operations. Hundreds of genetic technicians and cryptographers and other specialists had already been recruited, and were literally waiting for the call—but with Georg under arrest, Marta didn't see how that call could go out.

But *Moira* wasn't bothered by any of *that*. There was a plan. It would work. More humans would come. They would bring their kids. She wouldn't be lonely anymore. Short, simple, straightforward. And Marta didn't see how to explain about the complicated parts. Starting with how Daddy had been arrested and convicted and might never see them again. "It'll all work out, I'm sure," Marta said, feeling not the least bit sure of anything.

"Good," said Moira. "I hope they hurry up."

"For right now, I have just a couple of more things to do, so you go and play for just a bit, all right?"

"Okay. I'll go over to the high-bay and say hello to Allabex and Cinnabex. Meet you there!"

"I'm not sure they'll want to be disturbed just now—" But Moira had already vanished from sight. Another slightly quieter crash signaled that Moira had already bounced through the main door to the outside, and the nearby high-bay lab.

Well, that was her daughter. Marta looked at the empty chair next to her again. *Their* daughter. Very much *his* daughter, for it was easy to see a lot of Georg in Moira.

Georg. Georg, captured while trying to escape. Georg, moldering away in the Thelm's Keep, in the city of Thelm's Keep. Georg, on the other side of this weary planet of Reqwar, determined that his death should do some good if his life no longer could.

Marta accepted those choices, even, as a staunch member of Pax Humana herself, agreed with them, and believed she would have made them herself. But even so, it was hard for her not to feel a jolt of resentment. She even indulged in a moment's sinful fantasy of all that could have been theirs—could have been *hers*—if Georg had been willing to submit, to obey the custom.

But no. Best not to think on that. Marta reached up to the chain around her neck and the Pax Humana pendant that hung from it, the outstretched hand of Peace, Help, and Hope. All three were in short supply on Reqwar. And the Devil himself knew how harshly they had all been punished for trying to bring in fresh supplies of them.

* * *

Three or four Reqwar workers were putting the finishing touches on a barracks building as Marta came outside into the cool pearly-grey light of an overcast afternoon. Reclamation Genetics, Inc. had set up its main labs in the central plains of the Lesser Western Continent, half a world away from Thelm's Keep and Thelmhome and Thelm's This and Thelm's That on Largest Continent. But they were in roughly the same latitude, and the climates were broadly similar. The weather in one place was just as dismal as in the other.

Reclamation Genetics had taken over the site of an abandoned manor home. None of the original structures had been in good enough condition to use, and all of them had been demolished. The trees surrounding the grounds of the old manor were still there, though they looked wan, sickly, and faded—as did nearly all the vines and creeper and trees and grasses within eyeshot. The dying plants added a gloomy air to the appearance of the lab compound—quite appropriate, given the situation.

The work-ending bell chimed, and the Reqwar Pavlat workers instantly started putting away their tools. One of them was assembling a wall section, and not only stopped halfway through getting the fastener in, but literally stopped his power-hammer in mid-stroke.

Marta tried to keep her annoyance from boiling over. They were, after all, lucky to get that much work out of the Reqwar Pavs. Not only were Pavlat's Medical Restriction Laws strict enough to forbid any

Pavlat from working on the actual genetic decryption work—it had taken a special dispensation from the Thelm himself to allow local Pavlats merely to do construction work on buildings related to genetic engineering. It was bad enough that all the edicts and restrictions were irrational and close on suicidal. But it was far worse to see that the workers they had fought so hard to get were mainly concerned with doing the absolute minimum labor possible under the terms of their contracts. *Whose planet are we trying to save, anyway?* Marta stalked away from the building site.

The scene that greeted her in the high-bay lab building did little to improve her temper. The high-bay lab had been built in part to house large and out-sized items that needed to be sheltered from the elements—but mainly it was there to house the Stannlar themselves—for the two of them, Allabex and Cinnabex, definitely qualified as outsized.

A Stannlar Consortium consisted of thousands of smaller creatures that lived together inside the tough, translucent exomuscular skin that gave a Consortium's main body its distinctive, if ever-changing, appearance. At present both Stannlar were in their more or less default shape: a streamlined teardrop two meters tall, three meters across, and five meters long from the tip of the bulging forward sense cluster to the guard talon on the base of the pointed tail. Allabex was currently an attractive translucent green, while her split-clone twin was an intense opaque blue.

The exoskin was itself a living being, and did more than just hold all of a Consortium's local biological, electronic, and bioelectronic components together. It provided protection from the outside environment, supported various embedded sensing and communications organs and components, and managed locomotion, among other things.

A Stannlar could swap various living sensory organs and electromechanical sensors in and out of its sensing cluster, but both Cinnabex and Allabex were wearing a fairly conventional array at the moment: two pair of black button eyes, a pair of trumpet-shaped ears that could swivel, widen, and contract as needed, olfactory bulbs nestled under the ear-stalks, and a bright red oval sound-making membrane—in effect a living loudspeaker—set into where the forehead would have been, if the forward sense cluster had actually been a head.

A conventionally configured Stannlar Consortium resembles a giant slug, but that was an extremely misleading comparison. One annoyed Consortium heard the slug comparison one time too many and observed that the average human came a lot closer than a Consortium ever did to leaving a trail of slimy debris in its wake.

Stannlar reproduced only rarely, and generally did so by a split-clone process—though other procedures were possible. But there was something else about Stannlar that most humans found more disconcerting then how they reproduced. They were far more put off by the Stannlars' semi-independent subcomponents, the ones capable of exiting and reentering the main body of the creature. They came in all sorts of shapes and appearances, but tended toward bright colors and rounded forms. Some walked, some slithered, some hopped, and some even rolled. Some were biological, some robotic, and some combined the two. They resembled nothing so much as so many bath toys come to life.

Stannlar subcomponents were absolutely central to the whole plan to decrypt and reset the genetic kill switches in the various life-forms on Reqwar. Once their various researches had collected enough data both about the decrypt algorithms and the proper methods for counteracting and resetting the genetic kill switches, Cinnabex and Allabex would, in effect, turn themselves into living factories, manufacturing subcomponents capable of independent existence, and capable of duplicating themselves through split-cloning, and bearing in their bodies organs that would produce the kill-switch reset organisms appropriate to a given environment.

The subcomponents would be shipped all over the planet, into every ecological zone. They would multiply, and deliver the resets where they were needed—in part by being bred to tempt the palate of carefully selected species that would serve to spread the reset organisms further. The independent components and the reset organisms would have their own kill switches, of course. The sixteenth generation of the components would be incapable of split-cloning, and would simply die out—or be gobbled up—after a time. Similar processes would be built into the reset organisms.

Some humans had been known to run screaming from the sight of Stannlar subcomponents emerging from a Stannlar's body, going about their independent duties, then returning, but Marta was used to all that. What made her lose her temper was the sight of Moira crouched over a sort of toy farm made out of bits of old packing cases and spare parts. Six or seven subcomponents were corralled into it, inside a miniature paddock. The subs were diligently trying to escape and get back to work, but Moira was catching them and putting back the ones that got too close to getting away.

Neither Stannlar was making the slightest effort to get Moira to stop. Either the subs were out on low-priority tasks, or else one or both of the Stannlar had sent the subs out with the express purpose of entertaining Moira so she wouldn't bother them.

But that was beside the point, and Marta was furious.

"Moira! Let those subs get back to work this instant! You know perfectly well you're not supposed to bother Allabex and Cinnabex when they're working!"

"But Mommy—"

"Really, colleague Marta, it is all right—" Allabex began, her voice booming a bit at first before she adjusted her speech membrane properly.

"No it isn't!" Marta snapped. "Moira! Outside! Now!"

"But—"

"Now!"

Moira scowled, then shrugged, turned, and ran outside.

"Marta," said Cinnabex, shifting about to face her sensory cluster direct at the human, "Allabex released those subcomponents specifically for Moira to play with."

"Moira shouldn't be disturbing your work by asking you to make games for her, or interfering with components that have other duties."

"She—she didn't ask," Allabex said. "I released them and prepared the little holding area for them before she arrived."

Marta opened her mouth—and forced herself to close it again before she said something unwise. There was something so absurd about it all. Her husband arrested, recaptured after escaping, convicted, and condemned. The whole project—and likely the fate of this planet—imperiled. The endless delays in getting their facilities up and running. Labor problems. Contract problems. Technical glitches. All that, and much more, had been stress that she could handle, if only just barely.

And then she had to go and snap—because she saw her daughter playing with the subs—and it turned out that *she*, herself, Marta, was in the wrong. It was frustrating, humiliating. She felt like a fool for being so angry—but she was angry all the same.

She glared at Allabex, then at Cinnabex. Her hands balled into fists. All the waiting, all the fear, all the uncertainty of the past days seemed to bubble up inside her, eager to burst out. "Now I'll have to go apologize to Moira," she said, barely managing to control the frustration in her voice. She turned and walked out of the high-bay, in search of her daughter.

\* \* \*

The two Stannlar watched the human female Marta Hertzmann depart, then turned to face each other. They communicated, using a pseudoetheric frequency, rather than by means of anything as awkward as speech centers.

Cinnabex began: *"You are more skilled than I at dealing with humans. You must go to her at once and speak the things that are required."*

Allabex: *"That would not be wise. Better to wait a brief time period for her emotional intensity to diminish."*

Cinnabex: *"My detectors show that an aircar with an official designation of the type used by couriers is on an approach vector. It is likely we are about to receive an update on Georg's case. We must obtain Marta's consent to send the agreed message before she receives this latest report."*

Allabex: *"I confirm the aircar's approach. But you assume that the courier will bring bad news."*

Cinnabex: *"Has there been any other sort since we arrived on this benighted planet? I will leave it to your judgment how long to wait until Marta Hertzmann will be rational enough for the needed conversation— but do not delay a moment longer than you must. Obtain her agreement before the courier's news injects additional variables that might alter the case."*

Allabex: *"I signal reluctant agreement."*

Allabex summoned in all of her subcomponents—including the playthings she had generated for Moira—and settled in to wait for the length of time she had computed as appropriate.

\* \* \*

Shortly thereafter, Allabex found herself moving about the grounds of the lab complex next to a moody and largely silent Marta Hertzmann. "There is no change in his status, then, friend Marta?" Allabex asked, once she judged that the silence had lasted long enough.

"No! Why should there be? How *could* there be, when he hasn't changed his mind, and the Pavlats haven't changed theirs?"

That would appear to be one of the questions that Marta Herztmann asked without expecting an answer. "I see," said Allabex. Her English-language module advised her that this was an appropriate neutral response meaning "I understand," frequently used by humans when they did not understand at all.

"The situation cannot remain as it is, friend Marta," Allabex went on. "And, I would submit, it is incumbent upon us to change it, as I greatly doubt the Thelm's people will do so."

"That much is obvious," Marta said. "The next obvious point is that we have precious few options for changing it."

*Georg could fulfill his obligation as the eldest son of the Thelm*, Allabex told herself, but she dared not make that suggestion to Marta again. Allabex—ten times Marta's size, twenty times her weight, all but indestructible, all but immortal, felt greatly intimidated by Marta's temper, her outbursts, her passionate *anger*.

"Moira!" Marta called out. "Settle down! And don't get so far ahead." Moira was her usual fifty meters in front, and showing no more signs than usual of needing to settle down. It had not taken Allabex long to note that Marta tended to speak harshly to her child whenever she herself was upset.

"She'll be all right," Allabex said reassuringly. "There is nothing dangerous up ahead."

"That's not the point," Marta said. "She needs to know to obey me, for when there *is* something dangerous."

*Why should Moira rely on the danger-sensing skill of a being that has gotten her into a situation this perilous?* Allabex asked herself.

Moira turned around and raced back toward them. The little girl laughed as she ran, but even someone as nonhuman as Allabex could tell there was something forced about the laughter.

She pitied Moira, and even felt something approaching empathy for the little girl. From her studies, she knew that human children, given the chance, were herd animals. But Moira Hertzmann had grown up shuttling from one off-planet project to another, on worlds at the far fringes of human civilization, with almost no human contact beyond her parents, let alone with any other children.

Her loneliness even drove her to try to recruit Allabex, of all beings, as a playmate. It had been humbling indeed to discover that thousands of years of personal and stored experience, effortless access to infinities of information, left Allabex wholly incompetent to manage imaginary tea parties or travel via nonexistent propulsion systems to entirely notional planets where events that contravened physical law were easily accommodated as being caused by magic.

Moira stopped a meter or two in front of her mother and Allabex and stood up straight, holding her hands behind her back. "Can I saddle up, Allabex?" Moira asked. "Please?"

"Not again, Moira," her mother protested, with a sidelong glance at Allabex.

"It's all right, Marta," the Stannlar said. It was one of her best child-entertaining tricks. She lowered her body to the ground, and set one section of exomuscle shifting, rippling, re-forming itself into a set of child-sized steps, leading to a newly created saddle-shaped depression about midway along Allabex's length. She extruded two knoblike handles, just forward of the saddle, for the little girl to hold on to. Moira scrambled up and plopped herself down into the saddle almost before it had finished forming.

"Now Allabex and I were just going for a nice, quiet walk," said Marta. "Don't start wheedling for her to gallop with you or anything. Just a nice, gentle ride this time, all right?"

"All right, Mother," said Moira, a hint of disappointment in her voice.

It occurred to Allabex that Marta was more likely to control her temper with Moira close enough to listen. Allabex decided to take advantage of the girl's presence and risk returning to the subject at hand.

"Getting back to what we were discussing," she said, "we are agreed that things cannot stay as they are, that the Thelm's people are not going to alter the situation, and that it is therefore up to us to alter it."

"I suppose that's all true," Marta conceded, with none too good a grace.

"Then the only issue is how we are to change things. Perhaps merely shifting location would be something useful." *In other words, it would be a very fine idea to get yourself and your child off-planet before things go utterly wrong.*

"We're staying here," Marta said, her voice hard and flat, ending all possible discussion. "We are going to go on with our work."

"It is impossible for us to go on with our work with Georg in his current situation," Allabex replied, trying to make her voice just as firm. "Leaving aside the fact that, should he gain power, the High Thelek would like nothing better than to be rid of us. Even ignoring the great inconvenience to Cinnabex and myself if our present bodies were destroyed, there are other issues. We require not only Georg's expertise and experience to do the research work itself, we also need his legally binding approval in order to get funds released, to disburse payments, to order equipment, and so forth. We are not even clear whether Stannlar law, human law, or Reqwar Pavlat Thelm-word would apply to the case—and plainly it would be unwise to risk any appeal to the Thelm's justice at this juncture. Furthermore—"

"All right!" Marta snapped. She paused, and then spoke again, in a tone of voice that was more tired, more sorrowful than Allabex had ever heard from her. "All right. Your point is taken. The Reqwar Pavlat will not move. Georg will not move. I will not move. But someone *must* move, and soon, if we are to avoid absolute disaster and the wreck of all our work."

"Then we must continue our search for an outside force, of some sort, that will break up the present impasse." Allabex chose not to tell her of the Kendari agent that she had confirmed was working with the High Thelek. She saw no reason to inflame the situation further until it was absolutely necessary.

"I agree," said Marta. "But I haven't the slightest idea where to start."

"I think I do," said Allabex. "I think it is time to contact Pax Humana and reverse your previous instruction advising them not to attempt any intervention." *Indeed, it is long past time.* Allabex had never fully understood why Marta had insisted that the PH not involve itself. She had given her reasons, but Allabex did not find them convincing. "I grant that, as members of PH, you and Georg must be most careful to avoid involving them in a dispute over a mere business venture. But I would submit that is now moot. An innocent man—a man who is a member of Pax Humana, and who represents all that is best, most noble—" *and, perhaps, most foolish and foolhardy*

"—about the organization is facing execution. Even if, as seems likely, it would embroil us all in a whole series of legal and political controversies, those controversies, and the publicity they would produce, offer us the best chance of breaking things open, of forcing the other parties to modify their positions."

Marta frowned, even scowled, then, at last, nodded. "All right," she said. "I've been holding on, hoping for something to change. I agree that bringing PH in will cause no end of turmoil. But now, short of a miracle dropping out of the sky, Pax Humana is the only chance we have."

"Agreed," said Allabex, far from happy to have won her argument. Allabex dreaded the Paxers. They were sure to create endless trouble. Georg had once said the Paxers worked from the heart, not the head, reacting with emotion, not with rationality or logic. Also according to Georg, the PH tended to listen closely to themselves and not much to anyone else. A request for help or a warning or a query from an outsider was likely to be ignored or explained away. A call for help from a member would be regarded in an altogether different light. If Marta sent a message, Pax Humana HQ would listen and respond—indeed, they would likely overreact.

Allabex couldn't help but wonder if the Paxers would all be like Georg, or, perhaps, all like Marta— a most alarming idea.

"If I have your final consent, then," Allabex said to Marta, "I will use my internal signaling system for the job and contact the Reqwar QuickBeam sender."

Marta grunted in a noncommittal fashion. "I take it you have already composed a suitable message?" she asked, seemingly taking offense at Allabex being prepared ahead of time.

But Marta would have to try harder than that to pick a fight. "Yes I have," Allabex said placidly. "A brief and factual report of the full situation, requesting assistance in your name." She quite deliberately did not offer to let Marta review it.

Marta did not respond for a moment, but Allabex resisted the urge to ask again. Silence, she judged, would be more effective.

It took a few seconds, but at last Marta gave in. "Very well," she said at last. "Send it."

"I shall," Allabex said. She stopped walking, both to allow her to concentrate more fully on the task, and also to make it easier for her internal signaler to lock on to the appropriate relays. She had just started to bring the signaler online when Cinnabex linked to her on a pseudoetheric link.

Cinnabex: *"Alert! Data scan from incoming aircar shows it is military. Transponder data request refused. Identity, affiliation, and mission of person or persons aboard unknown. Vehicle appears to be bypassing landing field and going for direct vertical landing near your location. Intention uncertain."*

Allabex: *"Alert received. Sending thanks for warning."*

Was the attack they had long feared finally about to come? Had the High Thelek and his allies finally tired of their indirect approaches?

"What is it?" Marta asked, noticing the shift in Allabex's stance. Even Moira sensed that it was a serious moment. She slid down off Allabex without any need to be prompted. Marta took her by the hand, and repeated her question. "What is it?"

Allabex did not answer at once. Instead she swiveled about on her base and reared up her fore end slightly to give her long-range tracking sensors a better look at the incoming vehicle.

"Allabex," Moira said, her high child's voice plainly worried. "Why won't you tell us what it is?"

There! She had a lock on it. Coming in fast and hard—but not all *that* fast. The course did not seem to be following any attack pattern Allabex could recognize. No. The pilot was just trying to get to his destination and land quickly. "My apologies to you both. I had to concentrate my attention for a brief time. There is an aircar approaching. It should be visible to you in a few moments. It appears to be military, but I judge that it is not likely to be a threat."

"How can you tell it's no threat?"

"Because we are still standing here alive and talking," Allabex replied. "The weapons that are usually carried on that vehicle could have destroyed us already." Allabex was still attending mainly to the task of tracking the vehicle, and it was far too late before she realized her words were not likely to comfort a nervous human mother. "Apologies for putting that too plainly," she said hurriedly.

By then she had a full scanning lock on the vehicle. Its weapon systems were not only inactive, but quite ostentatiously "cold," rigged in such a way that even a basic and hurried scan could establish the car's weapons were not functional.

"There it is!" Moira said excitedly, pointing at the sky.

"I see it," said Marta.

Almost at the exact moment the aircar became visible to human eyes, it began to decelerate violently, coming to an abrupt halt in midair about a kilometer away. It hovered there a moment, hanging silent in the sky, before sidling downward and forward. It sprouted a set of landing jacks and set down about three hundred meters away from them. A hatch opened. A Pavlat stepped out—a tall male. Allabex recognized him as Unitmaster Laloyk Darsteel of the Thelm's Guard.

Darsteel was old enough to be called a "surviving" male, past the age when it was socially required of him to engage in reckless and dangerous sports or military service. He was tall, even for a Reqwar Pavlat, wiry and muscular. His bluish-grey body skin and light brown facial skin both had the slightly glossy texture that spoke of good health and well-being. He was dressed in a one-piece red-and-grey flight suit that must have been custom-tailored for him. Everything about him was smooth, clean, elegant, precise. It was obvious from the expression on his face that something important had happened.

Marta stood beside Moira, watching Darsteel approach, but Allabex moved forward to meet him and, not incidentally, to hear what he had to say out of Marta's earshot.

"There's a new development," Darsteel said, as soon as Allabex was close enough for normal conversation.

"Please," said Allabex. "Tell me at once." *In other words, tell me before you tell Marta, in the event that she is upset by the news.* It was often useful to have at least a few seconds to think before Marta had a chance to wade into a situation.

Darsteel glanced past Allabex at Marta, and gestured assent. "My office received a routine confirmation of a report sent to the Thelm's chief of staff. The Thelm's message to the human government agency has received a reply—in the form of a ship with two lawkeepers aboard. They are en route now."

*That* was news that would require more than a few moments to consider, but one response was obvious. Allabex erased the message for Pax Humana from the send queue and powered down her internal signaler. Perhaps there would be no need to send for Pax Humana. Perhaps these lawkeepers would break the deadlock.

How would Marta take the news? Allabex did not turn around but instead opened a set of rear-facing eyes to look at her. It was clear that Darsteel's arrival had upset her. Allabex watched as Marta knelt and seemed to try to calm Moira—who had been perfectly all right until that moment. Moira immediately burst into tears.

It seemed an apt metaphor for what Allabex feared

from the Paxers: good intentions that caused far more harm than good. If these lawkeepers did nothing else, they had given Allabex an excuse for *not* summoning Pax Humana, and that was certainly something.

"Let us hope these lawkeepers can find a way to resolve the situation, then," said Allabex. "Only a few moments ago, Marta Hertzmann said our only hope would be a miracle dropping from the sky. Perhaps that is exactly what these human officers will be."

Darsteel flattened his ears back and frowned. "A pretty thought, Stannlar Allabex. But if we know they are coming, soon so will everyone else." He looked toward the sky, as if searching for the human lawkeepers—or for those who would most assuredly hunt them. He shook his head in worry. "The *real* miracle will be if they survive long enough to land."

# SEVEN ∙ **BROX**

Brox 231, Senior Inquirist of the Kendari Inquiries Service, activated the door controls and the hidden panel slid open. He felt remarkably silly, being reduced to the use of concealed doors and secret passageways, but such was the way of things on Reqwar—especially when living under the High Thelek's roof.

Before he went through, Brox paused a moment to double-check the misdirection gear, and thrummed his tail against the floor in a satisfied sort of way. Rather than recording his clandestine departure, the monitoring devices aimed at Brox's suite would be transmitting a convincing view of Brox sprawled out in his sleep-sling, snoring loudly. The watchers would be treated to a dull and quite noisy night's observation.

Brox trotted through the panel and turned around to make sure it closed properly behind him. The corridor was narrow, and a tight squeeze for a long-tailed, long-necked, four-legged being like a Kendari.

When standing or walking, a Kendari was about ninety centimeters high at the shoulder, and about two and a half meters long. One well-known xenophobic human had once described a Kendari as a cougar's body and legs spliced to a shortened kanga-roo's tail, an overbrained wolf's head, and a pair of chimp arms sprouting from the base of the neck, all of it covered in reddish-brown body felt. But Kendari were powerful and graceful beings, not collections of cobbled-together parts.

Even so, contending with stairs, ramps, corners, chairs, tables, and tall, narrow secret passageways de-signed for elongated bipeds was a dreadful nuisance. But Brox had been in among the Reqwar Pavlat long enough that he had stopped noticing such aggrava-tions.

Brox came to the end of the corridor and came face-to-face with a blank concrete wall. He did noth-ing but simply stand there and wait. After a few mo-ments, the concrete slab slid silently to one side, and Brox stepped through into what appeared to be—and in point of fact was—a disused storeroom, normally reached through a door in the wall opposite.

Nostawniek, his Pavlat contact, was there, waiting for him. "Greeting to you, oh noble Brox 231 of the Kendari," Nostawniek said as he fanned his ears wide and flattened them, and then made a low and sweep-ing bow. They were the formal Reqwar Pavlat words and gestures of greeting to a person of great seniority, status, and rank. Only the wry look in Nostawniek's eye revealed that he was mocking the very manners he was displaying to perfection.

As a professional intelligence officer, Brox viewed the hidden meeting place and the concealed doors and secret passageways as too clever, too elaborate. Brox had simply instructed Nostawniek to set up a way for the two of them to meet without being seen. He hadn't expected the Pavlat to get creative. But then, Nostawniek wasn't an intelligence professional. He was a gifted amateur who sincerely believed that making the High Thelek the Thelm was the best thing for Reqwar, and that backing the Kendari in general and Brox 231 in particular was the best way to do it.

Nostawniek was a Pavlat, but not, as he made sure everyone knew, not a *Reqwar* Pavlat. He had been born and raised on the Pavlavian home world, and it was only the accidents of fate—and several failed business ventures—that had stranded him on Reqwar. He was on the short side for a Reqwar male, a trifle over two meters tall, with a stocky, well-fed frame that was likewise unusual. He was dressed in the dusky blue-and-brown formal tunic of a high-ranking servant in the High Thelek's service—which was one of the things he was. He was also Brox's well-connected—and well-paid—informant.

"Greetings," Brox said wearily, as tired of Nostawniek's jokes about court etiquette as he was of the etiquette itself. "Have you got it?"

"Right down to business, then?" Nostawniek asked.

"If you would," Brox said. "It's been a long day." *They're all long days here.*

"And you would like to do a bit of authentic sleeping, rather than letting your misdirection generator do it for you. Very well," Nostawniek said. "Understandable. Here it is." He produced a data wafer and handed it to Brox. "A complete and authenticated— and quite unauthorized—copy of the full report on the accident. And note that I refer to an 'accident' and not 'incident' or 'event.' But see for yourself."

Nostawniek set up a portable data display system, then stepped out of the way to let Brox insert the data wafer and work the controls himself. "I've set it up to show the general view first," said Nostawniek.

Brox stepped up to the system and activated it. The display panel came to life and showed a flatview video sequence of an aircar flying through a canyon, the images apparently shot from the forward-view camera of an aircar just behind the lead vehicle. The aircar on-screen flitted between the rock outcropping, twisting and rolling as it soared past spires of stone, closer and closer to the canyon walls.

And then it got too close. It crashed, slammed into a jutting ledge of rock, exploded in a blue-white fireball. The trailing aircar, the one taking the pictures, veered off at the last possible moment, barely escaping destruction.

"Flight recorder data," Nostawniek said, and brought up another display. He pointed at one particular spike of data. "A gust of wind at just the wrong moment," he said. "That's all. Irvtuk didn't allow any margin for the wind shifting—and he paid for it."

"I need to see more," Brox said.

"Of course," said Nostawniek. "This is important. You have to be sure."

That was beyond question. All three birth-sons of Lantrall, the Thelm of all Reqwar, had died in one crash—a fact that was just too remarkably convenient for too many people—especially for the High Thelek. The problem was that it was suspiciously *tidy*. Brox had to make twice sure and thrice sure and double sure again that it *had* been an accident.

Brox felt a certain ambivalence, a certain mild regret, that the Thelm's three birth-sons had died, but he couldn't work up any more emotion than that. They only mattered because they were the heirs to the Thelmship. None of the three had been particularly likable or talented in any way. It was very sad that individuals had died prematurely; but *these* particular individuals weren't really anything much, no more than careless playboys, really. In the end, they didn't matter at all, aside from the fact that their absence created a void, and a political crisis.

Furthermore, they had lived and died in a culture that expected, almost *required*, young males to prove themselves by taking great risks. Getting themselves killed was, more or less, no more than what was expected of them. Brox studied the data in every detail, Nostawniek walking him through it all. The flight recorders, the pattern of damage to the aircar, the eyewitness accounts all agreed. Luck be praised, the evidence was absolutely irrefutable. It was pure pilot error. Irvtuk had been a fool, and misjudged a wind gust, which threw the aircar into a canyon wall. It was a freak accident that simply could not have been prearranged. End of story. "I am satisfied," Brox said at last. "The High Thelek has, perhaps, been guilty of many things, but he is innocent of the deaths of the

Thelm's sons. We must see to it that multiple copies of this evidence are preserved so as to refute any conspiracy theory that pops up in the years to come."

"Speak frankly in this matter," said Nostawniek. "You have seen Reqwar politics at work. You might be an alien here, but in some ways you understand the locals far better than I ever will. Why does this information matter so much?"

"In the short run, I doubt it does. If—or, so it would now seem, *when*—the High Thelek ascends to the Thelmship, no one is going to dare question him on this matter. But, you tell me. Suppose he *had* killed these three foolish drones. Suppose there was some proof of his guilt—or even, a suspicious absence of proof that it was accidental?"

"That's my point. I don't see how it could matter."

Brox gestured out at the world of Reqwar. "Somewhere out there is the infant son of the son of the widowed daughter of the uncle of some noble family or another. Or perhaps the infant I am talking about isn't even born yet. It almost doesn't matter. In the time between the death of Irvtuk and his brothers, and—if I dare to whisper a treasonous phrase—the eventual death of the present Thelm, just the right sequence of people will be born, live, and die in just the right order to make *that* infant, and no other, the person with the best claim to the Thelmship.

"Perhaps in law that child's claim will be stronger than the Thelek's—quite likely, as the Thelek's claim to the Thelmship is a rather weak one, if one considers the technical rules of inheritance rather than political reality. Or perhaps this imaginary heir will have a claim that is only relevant if the Thelek is disbarred from the succession—for example, for committing the crimes of murder and treason."

"Treason?"

"What else would you call killing the heirs to the throne?" Brox asked. "Suppose a month, a year, five years after his ascent to the Thelmship, our High Thelek becomes unpopular?"

Nostawniek nodded. "Then once your hypothetical heir grows up he could dust off the proof against the High Thelek, claim to be the legitimate Thelm, and start a civil war."

"Read your Reqwar history," Brox said. "There's no need for the hypothetical heir to grow up, or even approve of the attempt to overthrow the new Thelm. Seven times out of eight, it's been someone *else* who stirred up rebellion on *behalf* of the alternate heir. There are lots of ways it can get very nasty very fast.

"The Kendari Inquiries Service would not wish to be involved in such matters. Beyond all that, I will tell you quite frankly that there are many in my service who feel that, as a matter of policy, *and* of morality, we should have nothing to do with such political murders."

"But now you know it wasn't murder."

"Precisely. This will make it vastly easier for my superiors to maintain their support for the High—"

There was a sudden low, beeping noise from a device on Brox's utility harness. He glanced at the device and cursed in eloquent Kendari Maximum. "A Quick-Beam message," he said briefly.

He put away the signaler, stood up on all four legs, and made for the entrance to the hidden passage. "No one sends QuickBeam messages without a strong reason," he said. "We must meet again, tomorrow, in the same manner and at the same time, in case this message involves matters we must deal with," he said.

Nostawniek bowed again and fanned his ears. "We can talk more of blasphemy, murder, and treason then," he said. "I look forward to it."

\* \* \*

Eight hours later, after an all-but-sleepless night, Brox found himself in a familiar situation: The High Thelek was keeping him waiting.

*One brief shining moment*, he told himself. For one brief shining moment, after he knew the High Thelek had no part in the death of the three heirs, but *before* he had unbuttoned the QuickBeam message, all had been well. For those few golden minutes, the way ahead had been clear.

*But perhaps all will still be well. This was a complication, not a disaster.* But where the dark devils was the Thelek? The waiting was unendurable.

Brox had, thus far, managed to avoid pacing up and down the length of the Thelek's large and grand private office, and was pleased with himself for that. But then he caught himself in the act of slapping his tail on the floor—a far-too-obvious sign of impatience. He set his tail down on the floor and willed it to stillness, planted all four feet square and motionless, folded his arms, pulled his neck back, and brought his jaw down. It was the stance of watchful and alert readiness. Brox had no difficulty in being watchful, alert, and ready. Patience was the difficulty. Patience with High Thelek Caldon Saffeer and his endless plots and intrigues—and with the endless delays they caused. That was the challenging part.

But then, the death of the three heirs had turned everything so completely upside down that even Brox could scarcely blame the High Thelek for having a lot of details to attend to. Simply canceling all the plots and schemes that had suddenly been rendered meaningless was likely a full-time job. But that did not make the endless waiting any easier.

And there was no doubt he was being watched. Most members of the Reqwar Pavlat nobility disapproved of surveillance on principle, especially in their own homes. Not the High Thelek—quite the contrary, in fact. Brox felt as if he were an actor giving a performance in a show that never closed, never ended. The audience was always there—and often made little effort to conceal itself. It was often embarrassingly easy to spot the cameras. Brox could see two in the room he was in without moving his head.

For all Brox knew, the High Thelek's people had penetrated the misdirection equipment in his suite of rooms, and all of his other covert systems and activities, and they were simply letting him play at spies as part of some deeper game the High Thelek was playing. If so, there was nothing Brox could do about it. He *had* to have his own sources of information.

But that was a separate matter from the sloppily obvious and arrogant way the Thelek's security service monitored him. If the High Thelek had wished to send the message that he didn't entirely trust Brox, he could not have found a more effective way of doing so.

But turnabout and turn again was justice for all, as the saying went. Brox did not trust the High Thelek in the slightest. Thelek Saffeer always kept his promises. Of that Brox had no doubt. But Thelek Saffeer's promises were always so overburdened with qualifications and loopholes that the promises were not in fact worth keeping.

The only thing that made it all worthwhile was the glittering prospect, the prize, almost in sight, there at the end of it all: the planet itself. A new Kendari world. It would be slow and careful work, of course. Partial and indirect, behind-the-scenes control, limited settlement rights in return for technical and financial assistance. But get one foot in the door, let your tail get a good brace, be ready to work—and sooner or later both hands can pry that door open, fling it wide.

First, however, he had to handle the Thelek and his endless plots. Brox allowed himself a long, low growl and trotted over to the vast glass-walled window and the view of the city of Thelm's Keep, far below.

The High Thelek's home was situated high up on a hillside, looking down into the valley that held the city of Thelm's Keep, and perhaps more significantly, the Keep itself, from which the city derived its name.

Brox had often wondered at the reason Thelek Saffeer had built his home in such a place, with such a view. Was it some need to look down, quite literally, at Thelm's Keep, the home of the lord of all Reqwar? Or was it to give him a convenient view of what he hoped and expected to be *his* Keep, sooner or later, once this or that of his plots had raised him to the rank he obviously thought was his due?

At long last the door at the far end of the long, wide room slid open. Brox wheeled about to see the High Thelek bustling in, shedding his outer garments, and tossing them off behind him, trusting in his servants to catch them all before they touched the floor—a service they expertly performed. He went straight to his work space and dropped heavily onto his work stool. "Ah, Brox, there you are," said Saffeer, with a casual glance at his visitor. "Won't keep you waiting much longer. Just a few minor details to arrange."

"Take all the time you wish," Brox said in his good, if somewhat ponderous, Reqwar Pavlat. As if the Thelek would do anything else anyway.

"Thank you," said the Thelek. "Won't be a moment."

They were "alone," Brox noted—aside from the four servants hovering about the Thelek, making any number of small and completely unimportant adjustments to his stool, his desk, his clothing, bringing in unasked-for refreshments for the Thelek—though nothing for Brox—and generally fussing about, trying to look busy themselves in order to make the Thelek look important.

All these shows, all these games, and for what? To impress Brox 231? If so, they had the opposite effect. As Brox's uncle, Brezzen 2234, was fond of saying, anyone who had to *try* to impress someone else probably wasn't going to succeed.

Which brought Brox back to a question he had been puzzling over for some time. Which of them was the patron, and which the client? On the face of it, a high-ranking noble of an ancient, proud, and powerful race like the Pavlat was clearly in the superior position. The agent from the intelligence service of an upstart race like the Kendari, an agent normally kept well out of the public gaze for fear of causing unrest, was plainly the inferior. Except it was not so.

The High Thelek glanced at some reports as he sipped his whrenseed tea and tapped at one of the screens. "When you've got a moment, my dear Brox, this is a matter I'd like your opinion on. One of my, ah, business associates is seeking financial advice. You're good with that."

*In other words, some nephew of yours has run up some debts—gambling, probably—that you can't or won't cover yourself.* "Always happy to oblige, my Thelek." *Yes indeed,* Brox told himself. *Always happy. Because you just about are "my" Thelek, bought and paid for.*

The petty little money troubles of Thelek Saffeer and his myriad relations were a symptom of something bigger: The Reqwar Pavlat were poor, not only by Elder Race standards, but even by Kendari standards. Even humans would have considered many aspects of the local economy backward.

The High Thelek, of course, was quite a wealthy person—if one considered his material possessions. But Brox had managed a detailed and covert examination of the Thelek's finances, and come to the conclusion that Saffeer was rich in debts and had gone past the point of merely counting on his expectations. He was absolutely *relying* on ascending to the Thelmship as the only possible means for him to pay his creditors. He was a long-odds gambler, deep in the hole, betting everything on what had, not so long ago, seemed like the longest possible odds. Not now, of course. Now, insofar as Brox understood the local politics, it was all but inevitable that High Thelek Saffeer would ascend.

But a Thelek with all his debts paid would be a Thelek upon which the IS could apply only limited leverage. The worst the IS might do would be to threaten to expose his financial dealing and reveal that he had in effect mortgaged Reqwar to the Kendari. But that was not merely a double-edged sword, as the human expression put it. It was a sword with a handle made of sharpest thornwood. Even to grasp the weapon would be to do damage to oneself.

When it came to assisting with a client's debt—or, more accurately, manipulating the client by controlling his debts—one had to use care. There was an art to such matters, requiring a sensitivity to the traditions and psychology of the species in question, the local culture, and the individual. In the present case, Brox had judged it best to pretend that the IS had trouble arranging payment of such large amounts, that there was trouble in converting currency, that things had to be done slowly if they were to be done quietly. He paid off just enough to keep the Thelek's various enterprises from collapsing altogether, and enough more to allow him a few extravagances—such as this handsome new house—to ensure that he became and remained dependent on Kendari cash.

By applying light pressure here and there, by agreeing to take on this debt or provide this house or that spaceship or those weapon systems, always in exchange for a little more access, a little more freedom of action, the IS could see to it that the Kendari would become ever more firmly established on this world, even as the outmigration of Pavlat continued and even accelerated.

The High Thelek finished whatever bit of work he was doing—or, just as likely, whatever bit of busy-work he was pretending to do—and handed it to one of the quartet of hovering assistants. He made a hand gesture that was a signal for them all to leave and they bustled out as busily as they had bustled in.

"Now then," the High Thelek said, leaning back on his stool into what seemed like a most precarious position to Brox. It always seemed to him that bipeds were on the verging of toppling over. "I am not going to be put off any longer. Before we get to this 'urgent' news of yours, I want to hear some good news as regards the genetics repair plan."

Brox repressed a cringe. It was, of course, precisely the one topic he wished to avoid. He had no news at all, which, in the current circumstances, was the same as very bad news indeed. He had no choice but to keep on stalling. "There has barely been time for messages to go back and forth since the last time you asked, and the last time I sent a query," he said, more or less truthfully.

Of course, since the Thelek had been asking the same question over and over again for months now, it made very little difference *how* long it had been since the last time he asked, but never mind. The High Thelek was one of that odd breed of mind, the sort that lived by playing fast and loose with the truth himself, yet seeming incapable of catching others when they did the same to him.

"These things take time," Brox said, repeating what he had told the Thelek so often before. "We must not only find persons who seem capable of the work. We must study their technical and professional credentials carefully, before we approach them, to ensure they can do all the required tasks properly. And, of course, it must all be done as quietly as possible, to avoid attracting attention. Obviously, this far from our main operations center, I am not privy to every detail of the process, but I can tell you that every candidate is studied carefully." *At least, that would be the case, if we had yet located any candidate organizations at all.*

Somehow, sooner or later, he was going to have to start getting the High Thelek used to the idea that it might be Kendari scientists doing the job. Brox couldn't help but wonder how he was going to convince Saffeer that Kendari were wonderfully skilled in deciphering encrypted genetic material.

There were a whole series of crash programs under way on Kendal as Kendari scientists struggled to teach themselves what they needed to know, but it would be better, far better, if it didn't come to that. The IS was doing all it could to find an Elder Race genetics and terraforming concern willing and able to do the job for a sensible price—but it hadn't happened yet, and it would be most awkward for the planet in general and Brox in particular if they failed.

However, it was not yet time to face those worries. And there were a number of surefire ways of distracting the High Thelek from all such awkward issues. "Our technical people back on Kendal are working that side of the problem, sir. Their advice—and mine—is that our time would best be spent getting ready to move in fast and take over the human-Stannlar operation as soon as Georg Hertzmann is, ah, removed from the equation, shall we say." *And let's ignore the fact that the operation would be utterly useless without the Stannlar themselves, since they are planning to serve as their own bioreactors and breed their repair organisms in their own bodies.*

Brox could see instantly from Saffeer's expression that he had gotten the Thelek's attention with that happy thought. And, more to the point, Brox had distracted him from the awkward question of finding their own genetics team.

"Yes," said the High Thelek. "Getting Hertzmann

out of the way. Can't happen soon enough for my tastes."

"Nor mine," said Brox. He hesitated a moment, not wishing to admit ignorance to the High Thelek. But that was foolish. He was, after all, an alien, and if there was one area in which the High Thelek might actually have expert knowledge, rather than merely claiming such, it was regarding the laws of dynastic inheritance and ascendancy. After all, Saffeer had spent most of his adult life studying them with an eye toward how they might be used to his own advantage.

"Sir," he began, "forgive me if I walk us back down a length of road we have traveled already, but can it truly be the case that there is no way for Georg Hertzmann to resolve his problem? Does he truly have no direction of escape?"

"Only the way he has sworn not to take," said the Thelek. "And at this point, he has sworn not to take it so loudly and so often that I doubt the people or the nobles would stand for it if he reversed himself." The High Thelek smiled, but it was a cold and unpleasant expression. "*I* certainly would not stand for it," he said. "No. Herztmann's choices now are down to which way he dooms himself—and, as best I can see, he has already made that choice."

"There is no imaginable unforeseen circumstance that might save him?"

The High Thelek shrugged. "I suppose it's possible that if exactly the right forty-three impossible things happened just the right way—if *I* died, and *all* the other heirs presumptive and potential and so on died, *and* the Thelm outlived us all, that might change things. Outside of that sort of absurd situation, Hertzmann has no hope at all."

"I thank you for that reassurance," said Brox. "However, this brings me to the urgent news I received by QuickBeam last night. The Kendari Inquiries Service has intercepted some interesting messages. It seems the Thelm's office sent a message that was received by a human police agency called the Bureau of Special Investigations, or BSI. You'd call them lawkeepers. The message as received was badly translated and hopelessly garbled, and possibly misdirected. The lawkeepers saw that Hertzmann was a member of Pax Humana and asked the Paxers for information. Pax Humana headquarters included the text of the BSI query, and the message as received by the lawkeepers, on the daily update they send to all their various offices, noting that Pax Humana headquarters had decided 'not to reply to the BSI query, and to maintain policy, as per on-scene advice, of taking no action at this time regarding the Hertzmann case.'"

"Why not? I thought that crowd of busybodies lived to interfere whenever possible."

"The message noted a previous signal from Marta Hertzmann to Pax Humana, summing up the situation but warning that any action on the part of the Paxers would only make things worse. I suspect that is why."

"How do you come to know all this?"

"The Kendari Inquiries Service cracked Pax

Humana's encryption years ago. We read their daily headquarters reports before some Paxer offices get them."

"Could it all be faked? Some sort of deception plan?"

"Highly unlikely."

"But I have no doubt both you and your friends back home are working to confirm it."

Brox did not reply directly. He had no desire to discuss his sources of information with High Thelek Saffeer. "It shouldn't be hard to check," he said. "The text we intercepted clearly states that two lawkeepers have been dispatched here and are on their way. If they arrive, we know the message was legitimate."

"Human lawkeepers?" the High Thelek echoed in surprise. "What in the stars would they want to come here for?"

"It would appear they were summoned here by the Thelm, apparently in connection with the Hertzmann affair. But if, as you say, there is no hope for him, I don't see what they are likely to try to do."

Thelek Saffeer frowned and folded his ears flat back against his skull. "Nor do I," he said. "Nor do I." He looked at Brox. "I have next to no experience with humans. We haven't had much reason to concern ourselves with them."

"There is no reason why you should," Brox said. *And no reason I'd want you to have any unneeded dealing with our competitors.*

"True enough," said the High Thelek, "but they have a reputation as troublemakers—and Hertzmann has certainly lived up to that reputation. I doubt they are here to do us any good."

"You have just said there is no possible way out for Hertzmann," Brox said. *In any event, I've distracted you from the problem with finding someone to decrypt the gene blocks.*

"That is far from the same as saying there are no possible problems for me—for us," Saffeer said. "Perhaps, for example, the human agents are here to *arrange* some absurd set of circumstances for the benefit of our dear Georg Hertzmann. A sudden rash of more accidents, a few assassinations, and a few nobles who suddenly decide to vacate titles by departing the planet—as a result of threats, or bribes, perhaps."

"I think that is all highly unlikely," Brox said, cursing himself. He had failed to take the Thelek's streak of paranoia into account. "That is a great deal more than two human agents working alone on a strange planet could accomplish." *Or two agents, or twenty agents, of any species.* But that was beside the point.

"Perhaps," said the Thelek. "But is there even the slightest chance they are coming here for my benefit, to do me good?"

It was hard to miss that the Thelek didn't even bother to correct "me" to "us" the second time out. "Granted," said Brox. "But it is likely their reasons for coming have nothing whatever to do with us." He placed the slightest possible emphasis on the last word, but Saffeer didn't seem to notice.

"Then perhaps they will not be looking toward my

people as a possible source of danger. That could be helpful."

Brox felt his hands go cold and his mouth go dry. "Helpful in what way, sir?"

The High Thelek ignored the question. "How soon are they expected?" he asked.

"It's difficult to be precise, of course, interstellar travel being what it is," said Brox. "In two or three days, I would expect. Certainly not sooner."

"Very well," said the High Thelek. He turned and looked out the great window-wall, down at Thelm's Keep, far below. "Time enough, then, to contact my friends and followers elsewhere on the planet and alert them to be careful. It would be most unfortunate if, through some misunderstanding, the human ship was prevented from landing. An overzealous subordinate might well fire on their ship, for example, thinking that was what I wanted. There might be all sorts of unexpected results."

And Brox knew there was nothing he could do. He had, quite accidentally, put an idea into High Thelek Saffeer's head—generally a quite difficult thing to do. But once an idea was lodged in there, it was all but impossible to get it back out.

The humans might cause trouble. Therefore, the humans were going to meet with an accident.

An accident as phony as the one that had killed the Thelm's sons was real, but, no doubt, just as fatal.

# EIGHT·**JUMP**

Jamie continued his research, studying the culture, the history, the politics of Reqwar—and the language. The high-tech, high-speed language-learning systems that the BSI had were effective, but exhausting.

By their third day out, it was plain to Hannah that, left to his own devices, Jamie would do nothing but study the files, research the background of the case, and slog through the data morning, night, and noon, with as little time off as possible for eating, sleeping, and personal hygiene, until they arrived.

That was basically what he *ought* to be doing—it was basically what *she* was doing as well—but experience had taught her the value of pacing herself, of taking a break, and of getting some sort of rest.

It would do no good for him to arrive at the crime scene short on sleep and brain-fried. She needed an excuse to get Jamie to ease up for a little while—and she had one, ready-made.

She went to Jamie's cabin, knocked on the door, then slid it partway open and stuck her head in. "Time to knock off for a while, Jamie," she said. "Transit-jump in about ninety minutes. Drag yourself through the shower, get yourself into fresh clothes and meet me in the galley in fifteen minutes. We'll down a quick meal and catch the show."

"What show?" Jamie growled. He was seated, almost crouched, at the worktable in his cabin, three monitors running at once. Two backlit data tablets sat in front of him, each screen crammed with meticulous notes and diagrams plus a standard BSI issue paper notebook, also filled with notes. It was plain he didn't *want* to be dragged away. "I got up in the middle of the night for my first transit-jump, from the Solar System to Center System. I went to the party. Then I blinked, and missed it. I mean literally. I closed my eyes for a split second, and when I opened them again, the starfield was different. Nothing else had changed. I got a free glass of bad champagne because it was my first transit-jump. It gave me a headache. The other jumps I've done were all just about as exciting."

Hannah laughed. "You won't get any champagne this ride—but you might get a much worse headache. You've done *calibrated* transit-jumps, on some of the best-surveyed routes around. This ride is going to be just a little bit wilder. I doubt there have been twenty human ships to Reqwar, ever. We'll be doing prime survey work ourselves—or at least the *Hastings* will be doing it for us."

Transit-jumps were meant to be precisely targeted events, but precision was impossible when the exact mass and position of the target star was not known. Typically, a transit-jump aimed for a point 10 billion kilometers from the target star. Things could get rough if the actual arrival was farther out than that—

and a *lot* rougher if arrival was significantly closer in, or if it was disrupted by some uncharted mass—perhaps a minor planet or comet—that happened to be close enough to throw the grav-gradient tuning off. Coming in at an unexpectedly high or low relative velocity could also cause problems.

Because all the stars were orbiting about Galactic Central, and moving relative to each other, the distance between any two given stars was always changing, and the distance and relative velocity between most pairs of stars was not known to anything like the precision required to ensure a smooth transit-jump.

The rule of thumb was: If the error was one one-millionth of the actual distance, the transit was survivable. If it was one-billionth, the transit would be at least relatively smooth, or at least not too violent. If the error was on the order of one-trillionth of the actual distance, the transit would be unnoticeable if you weren't looking out the porthole when it happened.

The run from Center to Reqwar had only been made a handful of times. There was enough data that they were well inside the one-in-a-million range, but it would take a lot of blind luck to get them anywhere near the one-in-a-billion. One-in-a-trillion wasn't even worth thinking about.

"Freshen yourself up," said Hannah. "Meet me on the command deck—and get ready for a bumpy ride."

* * *

Jamie felt a good deal better after a wash-up and a half-decent meal. It was pleasant to get his mind off his research for a bit. He strapped himself into his chair on the command deck, ten minutes before transition, almost looking forward to that bumpy ride—and if there were a few fireworks thrown in as well, fine. He glanced over at Hannah and grinned. "So," he said, gesturing at the starscape outside the view dome, "what's this going to be like?" he asked.

"I haven't the faintest idea," Hannah replied. "Transitions are like snowflakes—no two are exactly the same. On calibrated runs like Earth to Center, the differences show up in about the twelfth decimal place, but they're still there. On poorly charted routes, believe me, you *know* the differences are there. In fact, what I experience and what *you* experience might be significantly different."

"Isn't that supposed to prove that telepathy or psychic energy or whatever exists, and that different people were getting different signs and signals, or something?"

"Nope. They tested the effects, and spoiled all the good stories. They didn't detect any noticeable effects on measurable brain waves—but they *did* confirm that the various field gradients are steep enough to make the view from one chair totally different than the view from another. It's a real effect. What I see as blue puppy dogs floating slowly past might look like red chickens flying rapidly in the other direction to you, because you're two meters away. No one can predict it. So I hope you like surprises."

Jamie glanced over at the countdown display. Three minutes and a few seconds left. He shut his eyes. Not enough time to go and do anything. All he could do was what he was doing already—sit there and wait. It was the first real chance he had had in a while to just stop and take a little time for himself. He savored the feeling.

But that small luxury wasn't his for long. An alert tone went off, and the words INCOMING QUICKBEAM MESSAGE lit up on the main display.

"Oh, great," Hannah muttered. "Perfect timing."

"What's the problem?" Jamie asked.

"QB messages and transit-jumps don't mix," she said. "Even besides the transit-jump power-down, the transit-jump itself can jam reception. If we don't complete reception before the jump, and we miss the end of the message, we might be out of luck. Even if we miss just a chunk of the message during transit, that could be trouble, if they've used some sort of monolithic encryption."

"I thought they resend QB messages a few minutes later for just that reason," Jamie said.

"They do—when the sender pays for it," Hannah said. "If someone is sending on a budget, or decided to risk sending one long signal once with no backup, instead of sending a shorter one twice, or if we've already managed to miss the first transmission, we're out of luck."

A monolithic encrypt meant the decrypt was an all-or-nothing proposition. No part of the message could be decrypted unless all of it was in hand. Getting only the first portion of the message would leave them not with half the text, but with a partial message that could not be decrypted at all.

QuickBeam messages were faster than light. However, the actual transmission rate was maddeningly slow, and highly susceptible to all sorts of variables. The relatively small and low-power receivers that could fit aboard a small ship like the *Hastings* could only handle a very slow transmission rate. It was like having a cross-city phone conversation with a man who talked very slowly. The message signal crossed the distance almost instantly—but if the person on the other end spoke at the rate of one word a minute, reception could still take a while to complete.

The on-screen indicator showed they were receiving the message at the glacial rate of one byte per second. The transmission rate edged up to 1.5 bytes per second, 1.8., and even as high as 2.1 before edging back down to one byte per second, and even a hair below.

Jamie glanced at the countdown clock. Two minutes until transit-jump. "Come on, come on," he muttered at the QB receiver.

The message might be any number of other things, but it was just barely possible it might be from Bindulan Halztec—*if* Bindulan had decided, for whatever reason, that a message from Jamie Mendez was a top priority and he answered it at once.

But that was a long shot. Jamie was starting to feel a little foolish about wasting BSI time and money on the nonsensical idea of a message to his old boss. He had been a stock boy, after all. Jamie had been a good worker and a courteous subordinate, and Bindulan had been kind, even respectful, to him—but that was no reason to think he had some sort of claim on Bindulan.

Ninety seconds until transit-jump. A new message appeared on the displays.

INITIATING PRE-TRANSJUMP POWER-DOWNS

The *Hastings* was shutting herself down as completely as possible, so that power surges would have fewer places to crop up and less chance to do damage. A whole series of subsystem names started to scroll by under the main notice.

COMMAND DECK LIFE SUPPORT . . .
SAFE
POWER-DOWN COMPLETE
MAIN DECK LIFE SUPPORT . . .
SAFE
POWER-DOWN COMPLETE
ENVIRONMENTAL THERMAL CONTROL SYSTEM . . .
SAFE
POWER-DOWN COMPLETE

The ventilator fans died, and Jamie was disconcerted, not so much by the silence as by the realization that he had been surrounded by their low hum for days without hearing it. Other systems switched off, each subtracting its previously unnoticed whir or tick or hiss from the background noise of a working spacecraft. "What about the message retrieval system?" Jamie asked, his voice sounding oddly loud in the suddenly too-quiet command center.

"Checking that now," Hannah said, scrolling through a status page on her left-hand screen. "One of the last systems to be cut out, and the first to come back on," she said. "It shouldn't be off-line for more than a few seconds."

"Suppose we need the QB receiver on for those few seconds?"

"Then we're out of luck. Suppose we did have the QB receiver on for those few seconds and it fused into a solid lump, or blew up, or caught fire?"

There wasn't any good answer to that. He glanced at the QB retrieval indicator, and swore under his breath as the reception rate briefly dropped to .5 bytes per second, before climbing back up to to the dizzying heights of 2 bps.

"Hang on," said Hannah. "Lights and nonessential displays next—then acceleration compensation and gravity control."

"Tell me the main thrusters are off," Jamie said. If they were still accelerating at twenty gees, or whatever fearsome rate it was, and the compensators went out—well, then, they'd most likely be dead so fast they wouldn't notice it happening.

Hannah chuckled—but double-checked her displays. "Yes, the thrusters are off. Acceleration zero. We can't tell, thanks to the compensators, but the auto-sequencer cut the engines out ten minutes ago. Believe me, there are all sorts of interlocks to make sure we don't do a transit-jump with our main engines firing."

"Yeah," Jamie muttered. "Nothing can possibly go 'worng.'" The cabin lights died and his insides did a few quick backflips as the grav system cut out and left them in the dark and in zero gee. Jamie had little experience in zero-gravity environments, and it was a struggle to keep his stomach from registering a violent protest.

Only a few displays were still lit, glowing in the darkness, but Jamie only had eyes for the one still blandly reporting that a message was incoming. Less than a minute to go. He told himself there was very little point in staring at the display, and forced himself to look away, out the viewport. The glory of the starscape outside the darkened spacecraft showed in all its splendor, so close and real and vibrant it seemed to be just a few centimeters outside the hemispheric dome of the command center viewport.

Jamie felt overwhelmed by the waves of emotion that seemed to wash over him. The simple beauty of what he saw left him in joyous awe, but that was swept aside by wonder, and even fear. The universe was so impossibly *big*. How did humanity in general—and Jamie Mendez in particular—dare to imagine being capable of dealing with it, of going out into the stars and accomplishing anything of any value at all? And he *was* going out, to a world where few humans had ever been, to deal with a situation he was certain he did not understand, and after only a few days of study

that he was equally certain had left him quite unpre-
pared.

A chime sounded, and drew his attention back to
the status display.

MESSAGE RECEIVED AND STORED
MENDEZJ_BHEMP DECRYPTION KEY REQUIRED

The changed message seemed to pop up on the
screen so suddenly that Jamie had to stare at it for a
moment, just to be sure it was really there. "So it is
from Bindulan," he said in a low voice.

"What's MENDEZJ_BHEMP?" Hannah asked.

"My employee contact code from Bindulan
Haltzec's Emporium—BHEMP," he said. He reached
for the keyboard, eager to type in his decrypt key and
find out what Bindulan had to tell him. Bindulan had
come through for him. Bindulan knew something
worth telling, and he was passing it on.

"Hold it!" Hannah called out.

Jamie paused with his hands over the keyboard,
and at that moment the QuickBeam status display—
and the whole QB system—went dead.

"Good," said Hannah. "If you had started keying
in your decrypt key and the system shut down, it
might have read your partial code as being the complete one and rejected it for being wrong. That could
have lost us the whole message."

Jamie pulled his hands back from the keys. She was
right. Some messages were set as one-try-only. Get the

decrypt wrong, and they wouldn't just refuse to open. They'd erase themselves completely.

"Transit-jump in ten seconds," Hannah announced calmly. Even in the dim illumination coming off the few remaining system displays and the glow of starlight through the view dome, Jamie could see that Hannah's body language was a lot more on edge than her voice. She was gripping the arms of her chair hard enough to dig her fingers into the padding, leaning forward, straining against her safety belt as she stared at the transit-jump countdown clock.

Jamie could see the clock as well as she could, and his fingers were dug just as deep into the arms of his chair. It could be anything at all out there. *Anything.* Five. Four. Three. Two. One—

The clock reached zero and died.

The universe vanished altogether. Nothing. There was nothing at all. And not just beyond the viewport. The ship itself, the command center, the chair he was sitting in—even, Jamie realized in horror, his own body—were gone. He tried to gasp in astonishment, but his voice, his mouth, his throat were not there to do the job. He tried to move his head, but he had no head.

He strained to move, to blink, to look somewhere else, to look anywhere at all, but his head wasn't there, his eyes weren't there. *There* wasn't there. He could not see feel hear smell taste sense anything. Time and space were gone.

Time not there. *How long have I been this way?* he asked himself. It seemed to have started not so long ago, but how was he to be sure? Perhaps his thoughts themselves had been speeded up, or slowed down. Had it been a half second? A minute? A year? *How long will I be like this? Will I be like this forever?* It was hard not to imagine such things. *What happened to the ship? What happened to Hannah?* She had warned that a transition could be wildly different for two different people sitting in the same compartment. Maybe the universe had vanished for her as well—or maybe it was only Jamie.

Maybe, somehow, the transition had done some very permanent and terrible damage to his nervous system, severing every connection between his mind and the outside world. Perhaps days, weeks, months had already passed, and his body lay in some intensive care ward somewhere, while the doctors struggled to find a way to reach his mind, put it back in contact with his body—or else had to decide whether or not to pull the plug and let him die.

Or perhaps he *was* dead. Perhaps *this* was death, and death was a mind caught forever in simple and eternal nothingness. How long, he wondered, until he went mad? How would he be able to tell? Or perhaps the state of death itself would prevent him from going mad. Perhaps his mind would be locked forever in its present state, incapable of any change.

Yes, it must be death. He had heard all the old stories about a light or a tunnel—and there it was! Straight ahead of him, coming closer—

Light! He could see! And it was not a mere spot of light, it was the outside universe rushing back at him—or was he rushing back at it? Suddenly he was *in* it, flashing through it, the stars and galaxies and dust clouds and the wide dark voids and planets and light and heat and cold and dark hurtling by—

And it stopped.

And he was back where he had been, sitting in the copilot's chair, staring at the countdown clock.

The ship systems began to power themselves back up—calmly, quietly, without any fuss, as if all was right and normal with the universe.

"Did—did everything just go away, and then come back? I mean, everything?" he asked. "Did that just happen? Did it happen for you?"

Hannah answered, in a voice that seemed quiet, even subdued. "*Something* just happened. No. No it didn't. *Nothing* happened. I've—I've never been in Nothing before."

"Other people have?" Jamie asked.

"I've heard of it," Hannah said. "It's pretty unusual. Mostly what you get are the stars looking weird and distorted, or space looking blue instead of black, or a gravitational effect or something. The effect is *outside* the ship, with the ship staying more or less the same. But that was *inside* the ship."

"That was inside *us*," Jamie said. "Whatever just happened got between our brains and our bodies, or something."

"Maybe," said Hannah. "Maybe we just got flipped into some side universe where our kind of nervous system doesn't work, then flipped back. Or we just got stuck between two femtoseconds for a while."

"How could that possibly be? That doesn't even make sense."

"Fine," Hannah said. "*You* come up with a better explanation." She checked the nav boards. "The main thing is that we're alive, we're all right—and we're where we're supposed to be. We've got what looks like a nice simple navigation solution for Reqwar. We're just about four days out."

Which gave them four days to find out everything they could about the place. Jamie refocused his attention on that point—and on one very promising source of more information.

The message control system switched itself back on, and prompted him to enter his decrypt key. He reached for the keyboard—and noticed Hannah very ostensibly looking the other way. In the BSI that was a piece of basic etiquette. If everyone in an organization was trained to seek out hidden information, it was more than sensible for everyone to get into the habit of making it clear they weren't seeking out *your* hidden information.

Jamie finished entering the key sequence and prepared to temper his eagerness with patience. Even with modern ultrahigh-speed equipment, it could take several seconds, or even longer, to decrypt a long or complex message protected by an especially tough encryption system. Some messages were sent such that the decrypted message was itself an encryption of an inner message, and there might even be another layer inside that one.

He sent his decrypt key to the message system. A red box appeared on the display, with the words PLEASE STAND BY: PERFORMING DECRYPTION on it. But the red box turned green almost instantaneously, and displayed the words DECRYPTION COMPLETE.

"*That* message couldn't have had much encryption," said Hannah, who plainly felt no compunctions about looking at a status report screen. "I take longer than that to remember how to spell my own name."

"Yeah," said Jamie. "I was kind of thinking the same thing."

The decrypt had taken the briefest fraction of a second. For a message to get unbuttoned that fast, it would have to be in a brainlessly simple code, *and* be an extremely short message. This message qualified on both counts. The actual message, without header or routing info, was all of nine characters long when encrypted, and a whopping twenty-one characters long once it was unbuttoned.

The stats display showed that the message had been sent in the simplest possible merchant's code, meant not to conceal data but to reduce transmission time, a standard number substitution system, where a given number represented a specific word. In other words, Bindulan had sent a very short message containing information that he felt no need to conceal. Jamie flipped the display to show the message itself. It read "123-4-458." The decoded version was just below it.

"*That's* all the advice he could give me?" Jamie felt sick to his stomach. He hadn't realized how much faith he had already started to put in Bindulan's wisdom, even in the few brief minutes since he had learned the message was from him. Now the bottom had dropped out. Now they were on their own again.

"What?" Hannah asked. "What is it?"

Jamie realized that Hannah was still dutifully not looking at the display, being careful not to read his mail. "Go ahead," he said. "Take a look. A lot of good it will do you. Or us."

"Wonderful," said Hannah as she read the message. "How in the dark stars of hell are we supposed to do that *now*?"

But, like most simple and impossibly impractical advice, the message offered no guidance on such mundane details. On the bright side, it was at least clear and to the point.

It read, in full:

REFUSE THE ASSIGNMENT

# NINE ▪ **RISK**

Zahida Halztec at least had the good fortune to receive her QuickBeam message at a civilized hour. It came in late afternoon, at just the hour a young unmarried female Reqwar Pavlat of high rank, such as Zahida, might well be expected to remain at home in hopes of being there to receive visits from her prospective suitors.

But there were no suitors, and were not likely to be any, other than the dreadful bore her parents had dug up. Zahida had grown very used to whiling away the afternoons—and the mornings, and the evenings, and the long, dreary nights—since she had dutifully obeyed her parents' summons and returned from off-planet.

The front salon's message center chirped at her, and she hurried over to it, glad for any diversion. She sat down and decrypted the message. It was from her great-uncle Bindulan Halztec. Well, eager for *almost* any diversion. Her mother had warned her before Zahida had gone to Earth and met him that Bindulan had a genius for stirring things up, then getting out of the way "as fast as bad new travels by QuickBeam." She began reading, and learned just how right her mother had been.

And just how strong were the ties of family obligation. She knew, long before the end of the message, that she would do what Uncle Bindulan asked.

* * *

"I must ask that you leave now," said Unitmaster Darsteel to the determined young female who stood before him.

"You must allow me to see him!"

"I must do no such thing, Lady Zahida," Darsteel replied. "In fact, the thing that I must do, under these circumstances, is *keep* you from seeing him."

Unitmaster Laloyk Darsteel had felt worn-out and frustrated even before Lady Zahida Halztec burst in on him. The flight back and forth to the human-Stannlar camp had been long and grueling, and Marta Hertzmann had been far from gracious or appreciative when informed of the human lawkeepers' pending arrival.

Things had scarcely improved since his return. A routine check of the message-routing service showed that the report on the human lawkeepers had never reached the Thelm's office, let alone the Thelm himself. Someone, somewhere in the maddeningly intricate and interlocking bureaucracy that was the Thelm's household, had both the power to filter the information that reached the Thelm himself and the desire to keep him from knowing certain things. There was no telling who was doing it, or who they were serving, or to what purpose. But plainly someone wanted the Thelm ignorant of the whole affair. That, in and of itself, was enough to convince Darsteel that the Thelm needed to be told.

But Darsteel could not march up to the Thelm and report directly to him without being arrested, and, more than likely, handed over to the very persons who had blocked the information in the first place.

Then this impossibly belligerent female of the minor nobility had barged into his office. "Please," he said again. "Understand. The rules forbid it. You must leave."

The Lady Zahida Halztec drew herself up to her full height and breathed in deeply. "No," she said. "I must speak with the Thelm. If need be, I will invoke the right of Noble's Risk to do so."

Darsteel looked at her sharply. "I beg of you not to make that claim," he said. "It is no empty formality. The Thelm takes his obligations in this matter most seriously. If he cannot, in good conscience, swear an oath that it was right and proper for you to seek the audience, then your execution *will* be carried out. There is no possibility of clemency. The Thelm is forbidden to show mercy under the claim of Noble's Risk. You will be killed, in the manner prescribed by law. It has happened, and recently."

"I am fully aware of all that," she said. "But I must bring certain information to the Thelm, and do so at once. If there is no other way, then I shall choose the Risk."

"What is this information?" Darsteel asked. "Is it something someone else could bring to the Thelm on your behalf?" He fully expected to be told no, to hear some absurd story about secrecy, and oaths of silence, and all the other weary nonsense.

"The information is this," said the Lady Zahida. "Two human lawkeepers are on their way here, having been summoned in the Thelm's name, but very likely without the Thelm's knowledge. They are unknowingly traveling into grave danger, and the Thelm will be greatly dishonored if they come to harm. It does not matter in the least who tells him these things, so long as he is told." She looked straight at Darsteel. "Do you not feel that warning the Thelm of danger to his own honor merits the Noble's Risk?"

It was precisely the information he had been burning to report himself. Darsteel almost found it hard to return her gaze. "I will help you draft the legally binding written claim of the right of Noble's Risk," he said.

\* \* \*

At first, Darsteel had no qualms at all about sending the Lady Zahida on her way. Once she left, he started working through his mountains of paperwork in a fine and happy mood. There would be no risk to her under the Thelm's roof. Not if the Thelm was just and honorable. The Thelm had to know, had to be told.

It was not until many hours later that it dawned on him just how many other dangers the Lady Zahida might be bringing down upon herself. For there were other people besides the Thelm with the power—if not the legal right—to have noble females killed.

\* \* \*

The Thelm's Private Audience Chamber was on one of the topmost levels of the Thelm's Keep, a grand chamber that took up nearly all of the level, with wide windows that looked out over the great valley all around. Now, in the nighttime, there was little to see but the lights of the small city, also known as Thelm's Keep, below, and the lights of the stars overhead. But even that illumination was washed out by the brightly lit interior. The Thelm liked the place blazing with light—another of the almost un-Pavlavian eccentricities for which he was famous. Those same wide windows were open at the moment, and even if they failed to provide a view, they certainly provided a draft.

Zahida Halztec had dressed hurriedly, in a formal mode suitable for an unmarried female of her years. Her modest tunic and demure pantaloons were deep blue in color, with designs in silver embroidered on the chest and sleeves. All very classic and tasteful—but woven of very thin, even sheer, cloth. She knew her costume suited her well, and was appropriate to the occasion—but she wished mightily that she had remembered what she had read about the Thelm's habits and worn something *warmer*.

Lantrall, Thelm of all Reqwar, stood before her tall and erect, wearing a male's robe of semiformal cut, taupe in color, with an absence of decoration that was almost severe—but his garment was richly made of the finest material. Thick, warm material.

She stood before the Thelm, forcing herself to courage and dignity, marshaling all the skill of argument and logic that her long years of training in the arts of noble etiquette and debate had bestowed. "I come, honored Thelm," she began, speaking the first words of ritual as she bowed low in perfect courtly form, her arms spread wide, palms open, the upper and lower thumbs of both hands perfectly vertical. "I come to do you all honor, and to bring you news you must hear."

"Rise up, daughter of Reqwar," Thelm Lantrall intoned. "Rise up, and then, pray—sit down." He spoke the last two words in a much more everyday voice, far less formal and grandiloquent than the first part of his speech, even with a note of humor.

He indicated the lower of two seating cushions in one corner of the room. He could see that she hesitated and gestured more emphatically. "Yes, yes, go ahead. Be seated in the presence of the Thelm, who will remain standing. The Keep will not crumble to bits because of it. Society will not collapse. But you will speak more calmly and more quietly, and with less infernal ceremony, if you are seated. I prefer to move about while I listen."

"Very well, Thelm of Reqwar," Zahida said, feeling even more uncertain than she had a moment before. She levered herself down onto the cushion to sit cross-legged.

"So," said the Thelm, turning his back on her

and facing the southwest window, "you have been most persistent in seeking a private audience with me and have prevailed upon one of my most loyal and reliable subordinates to make it happen quickly. Unitmaster Darsteel clearly feels that what you have to say is of the utmost importance, even urgency, as he allowed you to take the Noble's Risk." He turned around and looked at her sternly, and both his ears swiveled forward toward her in a way that indicated annoyance, even anger. "And you are here, at least in part, as the clanswoman of a dishonored exile."

Here was the dangerous moment, where the truth must be spoken—though the truth might kill her if the Thelm's whim so commanded. She must be especially careful not to refer to Great-uncle Bindulan by name. One simply did not use the names of dishonored exiles—even those exiled on questionable charges—in front of the Thelm of all Reqwár. "Forgive my disagreeing with you, Great Thelm, but my clansman was merely *accused* of dishonorable action. It was later proven—after he was forced to exile—that he in fact *had done* nothing dishonorable. The legal basis for his exile collapsed, and the sentence was commuted. But the stain on his name could not be removed without the cooperation of his accusers, who refused to admit their own shame in willfully making an invalid charge. My relation then elected to remain away from the Pavlat worlds and became a voluntary expatriate."

It was the official family party line. All of it was

precisely and literally true—and all of it wildly mis-leading. Uncle Bindulan had in fact refused to fight a duel, and been accused—indeed found guilty—of cowardice. It developed that the Pavlat who had challenged him was badly intoxicated at the time and later claimed he could not even remember the incident. Bindulan had refused to accept a challenge from a Pavlat in a diminished mental state, and also claimed he would have found it dishonorable to fight an opponent who was so inebriated he could not operate his weapon. It would have been, he said, murder, not an affair of honor.

Except it was never clear just how drunk his challenger truly was, or whether his challenger really couldn't remember it all. It was also possible that his challenger had realized after the fact that a claim of intoxication would allow him to avoid a charge of making an improper challenge.

And, drunk or sober, the Pavlat who had challenged Uncle had shown remarkably bad judgment: Uncle was a crack shot, and no doubt would have dispatched his challenger no matter what condition the fellow was in.

None of that mattered, however—or was allowed to matter. The charges against Uncle were confirmed and he was forced into exile at lightning speed. The rapidity with which he was found guilty stood in stark contrast to the years, the decades, it took to get the conviction overturned and the case thrown out.

And there was one other minor point that had its

part to play in the story: his challenger was one Caldon Saffeer, the younger son of a minor noble family with a tenuous connection to the house of the High Thelek. But a whole series of unexpected events—deaths, scandals, marriages, adoptions, even a divorce—had disqualified a whole host of other claimants, and the upshot was that young Caldon Saffeer had ascended to the title of High Thelek, ranking only behind the Thelm himself.

Even one so daring as Uncle Bindulan had felt it would be unwise to risk a homecoming when it might embarrass someone as high-ranking, and as ruthless, as the High Thelek. To call his exile "voluntary" was putting quite a bold face on things indeed.

But it would not do for her to say all that before the Thelm. "As you know, Great Thelm, the later details of the case would have proven somewhat awkward to a great noble. It was, in part, to save the noble grave and needless embarrassment that my relation elected to stay away."

"I have heard versions of the story from both families in the past, of course," said the Thelm. "I would observe that both sides choose their facts very carefully, and use even greater care in how they present their versions of events. Such as choosing to continue in exile due to one's kindly concern over embarrassing the scion of a great family—who is also a deadly enemy."

Zahida sat up straight, and forced herself to be calm. "Permit me to suggest that choosing one's facts and phrasings carefully is an ancient, honorable, and common skill among our people—and a necessary one, given how long our memories are, and how our families remember for us, after we are gone." She felt both her hearts thumping wildly, and with good reason. She was taking her life in her hands to say such things.

The Thelm smiled grimly. "Our noble families are so intertwined one with the other, both by alliance and enmity, that we *need* polite fictions if we are to be able to function at all." He gestured to indicate both of them. "This audience could last until dawn, each of us naming a slight or a failing committed by my ancestor against yours, or the other way round." He fluffed his ears out and let them drop back into the relaxed position. "Too much history," he said. "That's our problem. Far too much history." He stood in thought for a moment, then turned back to her.

"I will now tell you a secret—or at least a fact that is not yet common knowledge. You will likely learn it at a later time anyway, and if I do not reassure you now, you will then likely be quite alarmed, fearing that I might have taken offense at the words you have just spoken. You must know that my own relations with the High Thelek Caldon Saffeer recently deteriorated to the point where there was some serious possibility of *our* fighting a duel to resolve the matter."

Zahida felt her hearts suddenly pounding against her spine-shields. She would not have dared speak of Bindulan's troubles with Saffeer if she had known such a thing. The Thelm was right. He might well have thought she was mocking him in some complicated, subtle, very Reqwar Pavlavian way, as if she had said to the Thelm *my uncle paid the price of exile, but you avoid the duel with no consequence.* Besides which, even an oblique reference to the Thelm in a duel was a reference to the Thelm's possible death. "I—I had no idea," she said numbly. *The Thelm seriously contemplating a duel*? How could that be? Or was it merely one of the Thelek's hyper-involved schemes, a bluff that had gone a bit out of control?

"I am sure you did not," said the Thelm. "But now that you do know, I would ask you to keep the knowledge quiet—though I am sure it will quickly spread far and wide. And be confident that I have not taken offense. But you are here on a matter of some urgency, and you are no doubt straining at the lead, wishing that your Thelm would stop talking and let you get on with it." He gestured for her to speak, and began to pace up and down the room.

She paused in a vain attempt to calm herself, then spoke. "Great Thelm, my great unc—my relative in exile sent me a message. Two human lawkeepers, agents of what they call the Bureau of Special Investigations, are on their way to Reqwar."

Thelm Lantrall stiffened, straightened up, and turned to face her. "On their way here? Now?"

"Yes, Great Thelm. In response to a message—a message that was far too short, and was badly translated and extremely garbled by the time it got to BSI.

My relation speculates that it was sent by the High Prosecutor's Office."

"I knew that the message—or at least *a* message— was sent. But no one told me they were coming," he said quietly, and turned his back on her again.

Zahida knew he had not been told. No doubt some underling indebted to this or that family opposed to the Thelm had misfiled the message "accidentally." That sort of game was played all the time. What shocked her was that the Thelm had simply *admitted* that no had one told him. He had made no effort, in front of a complete stranger of only middling rank from a suspect family, to make it seem otherwise. He was in effect admitting there was no longer any point even in *pretending* he was in control.

"But why send lawkeepers?" the Thelm asked, after a few moments' thought. "The facts in the case are painfully clear to all. Certainly nothing needs to be investigated."

"The message does not ask for lawkeepers, but for a negotiator," she said. "I have not seen the original version, but, at a guess, the message was translated two or three times into intermediate languages as it was passed along, losing detail and precision each time. My relation believes the message started out as a request for official witnesses to whatever punishment was decided, but the term 'witnesses' was somehow mistranslated to 'negotiators' along the way. The message was delivered to the BSI, the lawkeepers office— an office that also handles such things as negotiating prisoner escorts and exchanges. He speculates that the humans assumed the message was intended as a request for such services."

"I see," said the Thelm. "In short, the usual level of care and attention to duty was applied in this case."

"Yes, my Thelm." There seemed little else to say to that point, but there were other issues to raise. "Uncle Bin—my relative—believes that good may come of all this. By chance, he is personally acquainted with one of the agents who is on the way, and gives a very positive report of him. My relative believes there is at least a hope the BSI agents could resolve things cleanly, honorably, and in a manner that would satisfy the various parties—at least to the point where they wouldn't complain too loudly."

"How that could be?" the Thelm asked. "These agents are members of a well-intentioned but not particularly overcompetent Younger Race—not magicians or master diplomats. I have the greatest respect for Georg Hertzmann, as should be obvious. But it should be equally obvious that he is an exceptional human—and *he* has found no way out."

"I agree the chance is small that the humans might find a way—but the chance is there."

"I concede your point," said the Thelm. "And, exile or not, I have always respected the judgment and opinions of Bindulan Halztec." He smiled at her. "You see, I spoke his name, and *still* the Keep did not crumble away into dust. But you sought this audience with great urgency. All of what you have said is important, yes. But what of it is of such immediate importance that you undertook the right of Noble's Risk?"

"Great Thelm, the human agents are on their way now, and have been summoned by your government, in your name—though without your knowledge. We do not know *why* they are coming—but we hope, and it is just barely possible, that they can find a way out of our problems. But are there not, Great Thelm, those who have considered the changed circumstances regarding your hypothetical successor?"

*Hypothetical successor* was the proper euphemism for the heir to the Thelmship, as it was improper to refer to the death of the Thelm except in the most indirect way possible. Zahida was starting to remember why she had stayed away from court so long. The need to speak so carefully was simply exhausting. "Might there not be those who would learn of the human lawkeepers' arrival, and fear that they might represent a *threat* to hopes, however improper, that had suddenly been raised?" *In other words, the High Thelek is going to try to kill them before they can land and reach territory you control directly*, she thought. *Wouldn't it be nice if I could just say that?*

The Thelm's expression told Zahida that she had managed to shock him once again. "Yes," he said. "You are right. Quite right. These humans have been summoned in our name and are likely flying into danger." He thought for a moment, then looked to Zahida. "Honor requires that they be protected. It is clear you have given this some thought. What do you propose that I do?"

"First, honored Thelm, it might be wise to do nothing." *Something we've all gotten very good at.* "It is at least possible that those who might wish them harm are not yet aware they are coming. Any attempt on your part to alert forces to defend the humans could well serve to alert those who might wish to harm the humans."

"Agreed," said the Thelm. "At the same time, we must be ready to act if we should learn they *have* found out about the lawkeepers. But act in what way? Honor requires that we protect those summoned in our name, but I cannot risk open confrontation with High Thelek Caldon Saffeer right now."

It was still another admission so bald and frank that it shocked Zahida. "I do not understand," she said.

"I shall speak plain and rough, so as to be clear," the Thelm replied. "If it begins, where does it end?" he asked. "What if I call out a guard of defense for the humans and send them to the spaceport to await their landing, and the High Thelek finds an excuse for not recognizing the guard force's authority—or what if he simply claims that mere humans are not entitled to such an honor? What if his operatives prevent my guards from entering the spaceport, and my guards quite rightly insist—and then one side or the other fires a weapon? What happens then?"

Zahida abandoned her caution of speech. If the Thelm could speak "plain and rough," so could she. "Then there will be a fight, and one side or the other will win, at least for the moment," she said, "and the nature of the outcome might well determine if the fight will stop then and there—or if it will widen."

"Exactly," said the Thelm. "If it escalates, and keeps on escalating, if no one can call a halt, then it *could* set off a civil war. I might be deposed, or the High Thelek might be brought low, and never rise again—or perhaps both things could happen, and some new power center would come into being."

"But," said Zahida, "all of that is unlikely. The *most* likely outcome is that your force will defeat the Thelek's, in part because you'd send a strong force, but also because at least some of his troops will be unwilling to draw arms against the Thelm. Precious few of *your* soldiery will be unwilling to draw arms against the High Thelek. There is a risk of one of several bad outcomes if you send a force and it fails, but the force is far more likely to succeed.

"Further, if you do not take the risk, if you do *not* send a guard of defense, because you fear it *might* fail—then the High Thelek has won already, because the danger of offending him has taken precedence over doing what honor requires." Zahida drew in her breath and dared not move. The words she had spoken were all true—she had no doubt of that. But nor did she have any doubt that they could also be her death warrant if the Thelm was of such a mind. She still was under the threat of Noble's Risk, after all.

"You speak in dangerous ways, daughter of Reqwar," said the Thelm. "There have been higher-born than you silenced for speaking far less than you have."

"I know that full well, Great Thelm."

"So be it. 'A dangerous answer is the child of a deadly question.' But it would be wise to go no further down that road." He flicked his ears forward and back, dismissing the topic and turning toward another.

"The danger of inaction is greater than that of action—but alerting our enemies needlessly is the greatest danger of all. Furthermore, we do not yet know when or where the humans will arrive. Nor do I wish to deploy armed soldiery first. If our enemies do not have forces deployed, but saw ours on the march, that might be all that was required to tip the balance and send their militia into the street."

The Thelm considered for a moment. "I will order a guard of defense to be prepared," he said, "but quietly. It will be next to impossible to do it quickly *and* quietly, but I will do what I can. Once they are organized, I can hold them in readiness at their barracks, ready to deploy. We must hope the humans do not attempt a landing before the guard is ready and trouble does not start before the guards can be deployed."

"But, honored Thelm—what if they *do* arrive sooner? Suppose trouble *does* begin without warning?"

"Then a guard of defense will not be of any use."

"But what would be useful?" she asked.

But before the Thelm could speak, the answer came to her, clear and certain. It was something old, half-forgotten.

But something that just might save their future.

# TEN ▪ **WORK-AROUNDS**

Twenty-four hours after completing their transit-jump, Hannah and Jamie had just about recovered from the twin shocks of the jump itself and Bindulan's disconcerting message. Their incentives for coming in as quietly as possible seemed to be getting stronger with each piece of information they dug out about the complex, violent, faction-ridden politics of Reqwar. Jamie and Hannah did not know who had summoned them, or why, or if their pending arrival had been kept quiet, or if the whole planet knew about it. All they could do was hope they had been summoned by someone with good intentions, and try to avoid undue attention from the opposition—whoever that turned out to be.

And all those hopes went out the window the moment the *Hastings* entered parking orbit above Reqwar and cut her engines. Hannah and Jamie were both strapped in on the command deck, eager to see what happened next—and also eager to get the best possible view of the planet.

Reqwar hung in space before them on the other side of the big main view dome, a world of wide blue oceans, dotted with islands and island continents.

The waters around the larger landmasses were bright green, tinted by the Reqwar equivalent of algae mats anchored in the shallower waters. Most of the landmasses were lifeless browns and greys, with patches of faded green showing where the Pavlat settlements were.

They passed into the nightside of the planet and saw the dim lights of two or three small cities. Cloud cover was at about the same levels as on Earth, but Hannah knew from her reading that one odd feature of Reqwar was the degree to which cloud decks could simply park themselves over a given piece of real estate for weeks or months at a time.

They had expected to wait until they had a direct line-of-sight link with the planetary capital, then attempt to contact the local government quietly, without attracting needless attention.

It didn't happen that way. Within seconds of their engines shutting down, the *Hastings*'s autonavigation system received a hail from a groundside station and automatically entered into negotiations as to approach and landing procedures.

The *Hastings* was programmed to speak all of the more common standard machine-to-machine languages used by the Elder Races' various navigation centers. Hannah watched as the *Hastings*'s nav system attempted to contact Thelmhome Spaceport and work up a flight plan.

Hannah was not particularly surprised when the autonav system kicked the problem back to her as being outside its competence. But she was taken aback when she saw what the problem was. "That doesn't make much sense," she muttered. She keyed in a few commands for the autonav to translate into the local navplot system and transmit to traffic control. The response she got didn't satisfy her. She tried a time or two more, then started swearing under her breath.

"Have a look," she said to Jamie. "This make any sense to you?"

Jamie brought up the navplot Hannah was studying on his command display. "*That's* the ground track they want us to follow?" Jamie asked in astonishment. "That's a glide path three-quarters of the way around the planet. Didn't you tell them we'd be coming in on a ballistic lander?"

"The autonav system told them that, and they gave it this plot, so it bumped the problem up to me. I told them the same thing, but all they said was that we are required to follow the indicated route. No exceptions allowed, because this was their standard approach path, period."

Jamie studied the plot for a moment, then let out a low whistle. "No it isn't," he said. "It's their standard setup for an ambush," he said. "That trajectory will give every region run by a faction opposed to the Thelm's government a chance for a potshot at us."

"You mean the regional factions have independent militaries? I thought Reqwar had a unitary government."

Jamie laughed hollowly. "Yeah. It does. Just like Earth."

Hannah grunted and nodded. UniGov did its best

to pretend it really was united, and really was a government, and really represented all of humanity in its dealings with the various alien races. Still, it didn't fool many humans and probably fooled fewer xenos than the UniGov diplomats would like to believe. If Reqwar was no more unitary than UniGov, than it wasn't very unitary at all. "Point taken. But what makes you think our entry approach is an ambush?"

"A lot. Based on all the murky and dated info we have, it *seems* as if the main political debate of present times is between those who want to keep things as they are and those who say it's time to change at least a little. Call them Staticists and Dynamists. And anything new, or any outsiders—like us—represent change, and therefore danger, to the Staticist. And— well, I'll have to show you the rest."

Jamie worked the display controls. The globe repainted itself to show the landmasses in blues and reds of varying intensity, along with some splotches of grey. "That's an overlay of our approach ground track with a political map of the planet. Grey is no data. Blue is Dynamist territory, red is Staticist."

Hannah didn't say anything. She didn't need to. Jamie pointed at the screen. "We've got fourth-hand, third-rate intelligence reports that put good-sized military installations here, here, here, and here," he said, pointing at four areas that were very clearly marked as Staticist. Their assigned flight path took them directly over all of them—three of them with empty ocean to the east of their ground track, so that anything that got hit would almost certainly fall beneath the waves, rendering the evidence conveniently invisible. "The same semireliable intell says two of those sites are there for the express purpose of shooting down hostile spacecraft."

"So what happens if we *don't* fly that entry path?" Hannah asked. "If we just flew the sort of short ballistic-entry approach our lander is designed to make?"

"Best guess? We'd get called an imminent threat and get shot down on final approach. At last report, the main spaceport was under Thelm's Law—but it's in sort of a salient, a thumb-shaped piece of land that's surrounded on three sides by the High Thelek's land—and the Thelm is Dynamist, but High Thelek Saffeer is a heavy-duty Staticist."

"Wait a second," Hannah said. "There was something else that didn't quite make sense until now." She brought up a close-in detail map of the spaceport, showing their final approach and assigned landing area. "Would you bet your life that there's still Thelm's Law at the spaceport?" she asked grimly. "My guess is that there's been a change in management. Why else tell us to land where there won't be witnesses?"

Jamie could see it as plainly as she could. Their assigned landing point was ten kilometers away from the normal set-down zone, and even farther off from the terminal itself. "That's about as isolated as you can get on the spaceport," he said. "Far enough off that you wouldn't have to worry much about blast debris in populated areas. Or chance witnesses."

"Right. My bet would be that your High Thelek friend is in control of the spaceport these days. He's painted a target on the ground and told us to land on the bull's-eye. So, if we fly the assigned approach, we'll beat the hell out of our lander and probably get shot down before we ever *get* to final approach," said Hannah, staring at the screen. "If we *don't* fly it, we'll probably get shot down. And if we *do* manage to land, we'll be sitting ducks. Got any suggestions?"

"Well," Jamie said in an apologetic tone, "I do have one. But you might not like it."

*That we quit and go home right now?* Do what Bindulan suggested and REFUSE THE ASSIGNMENT? She couldn't blame him if he did suggest such a thing. It would be impossible to do their work without at least a minimal level of cooperation from the locals. If instead the locals were looking to kill them at once— and they weren't even exactly clear what they were supposed to be doing on arrival—there would come a point when there would be no point in persevering. "Go on," she said cautiously. If he did suggest bailing out, she had no idea how she would reply. After all, she had pretty specific orders to come home alive, or at least bring Jamie home alive. She liked to think it came to the same thing.

"Well, if they have any sort of file on the BSI—and they ought to—they'll know we have a reputation for being lousy pilots. And *I'm* no pilot at all."

"No, you haven't had the training yet. What's your point?"

"Well, no offense, but maybe we should play up to that reputation."

"What do you mean?" Hannah asked.

"Maybe you should fly the assigned approach route," Jamie said, "but just not very well."

# ELEVEN • ENTRY

The *Lotus* lifted off from her docking stand on the upper deck of the *Hastings* and came about to the proper attitude for her deorbit burn. Hannah moved the *Lotus* about two hundred meters away from the *Hastings* and then took her hands off the controls. The *Hastings* came about to a new attitude and fired her main engines.

Hannah watched the *Hastings*—and their ride home—boost out of view toward a more distant and safer orbit, then turned toward the controls of her own little ship with something less than complete confidence. The *Lotus* was a far more cramped and spartan craft than the *Hastings*. The pilot and copilot chairs would have been a tight fit even without pressure suits. In the suits, they barely fit at all.

Hannah was, in theory, qualified to fly such landers, but she had flown only one actual landing in one—and that under far less challenging conditions than they now faced. But there was no sense spending too long with her doubts. This would *have* to be a largely manual entry. It was all on her.

"All right," she announced as the countdown clock moved toward zero, "here we go."

The *Lotus*'s autosequencer fired the main engine, right on spec for attitude, thrust, and duration, leaving them exactly in the groove for entry. That was all well and good—but the rest of the flight was up to Hannah.

"Okay," Jamie said, watching the tactical plot, his voice coming to Hannah through her suit radio. "Site One coming over the horizon *now*."

There was silence in the ship for a minute or two, but then an alert tone went off.

"We're getting painted by triphase radar," Jamie announced as he silenced the beeper. "*That* sure ain't traffic control. Definite hostile intent."

"Might be time to make my first mistake," Hannah said. She brought the *Lotus* about to a new pitchdown heading and fired the translation thrusters, introducing a navigation error into their previously correct heading. "Oh, dear." She smiled. "I've corrected for an error that wasn't there in the first place. Now I'll have to correct in the opposite direction."

"They've locked on," Jamie announced.

The *Lotus* jerked hard sideways and shuddered violently as Hannah deliberately overcompensated for her phony error. Two warning lights came on, and three distinct audio alerts started beeping.

"Lock lost," Jamie reported. "I think we have them confused."

"Wonderful," Hannah replied, fighting the controls. Confusing the opposition wouldn't be all that much help if she managed to get them killed while doing it.

With a bang and a rattle, the *Lotus* let it be known that she had hit the top of Reqwar's atmosphere. Almost immediately, two more audio alarms popped on, warning of too-rapid temp increases. The *Lotus* was a tough little ship, but she couldn't hold up to all that much overheating. Even the flight path they had been instructed to take would have been rough on the lander—and the flight path they were currently on would be harder still on the hardware.

"Time to do a skip-out," Hannah called out. "Hang on a little bit harder."

"They have lock again," Jamie called back. "Do it before they get a weapon on us!"

Hannah gritted her teeth and pulled back on the joystick, shifting their angle of attack. Suddenly the *Lotus* was pulling twice as many gees, eyeballs down, pressing them hard into their seats with crushing force. More alarms instantly began hooting—then cut out, as the overloads went away, at least for the moment, and the gee forces slacked off. The *Lotus* had literally bounced off the top of Reqwar's atmosphere, and was heading back out into space. The temperature alerts shut down and the strain gauges slid back into the normal range.

Suddenly the cabin of the lander was strangely quiet. But it was nothing but a lull before the storm. Things were going to get a lot worse before they got better—if they *ever* got better.

"Tell me we're out of range of Site One," Hannah said. She brought the *Lotus* about to a normal entry heading again. They were near the top of their atmospheric skip, and just about to head back down again.

"Lock lost," Jamie said. "Site One still has us above their horizon, but not by much. The real question is how closely they're working with Site Two."

"We'll find out," Hannah said. Site Two was the one that had worried Jamie the most. The *Lotus* had to do an almost direct overflight of the site, and it was one of the pair of known military installations specifically designed for shooting down hostile spacecraft, with defense responsibility for a whole continent. If Site One passed on all its data to Two, and did it fast enough, then Two would have ample time to reaim their weapons—whatever those weapons might be. The out-of-date fourth-hand intell that was the ultimate source for their planning data hadn't gone into too many details on that point.

Hannah checked attitude one more time and shifted in her flight chair. This second entry was going to be the trickiest part of the whole operation. As expected, the skip-out entry had thrown off their whole preprogrammed flight plan, and tossed a heap of complications into the mix.

In order to make it to an on-target touchdown, they were going to have to stretch their high-altitude flight path as far as possible. That meant no fun and games with maneuvers in the next phase. Later, if they got that far, Hannah could throw in some evasive action. For the moment they would have to fly arrow-straight, right on down the line, just begging the bad guys to get in some target practice. So maybe it was time to stop worrying about an on-target touchdown.

"We've lost line of sight on Site One," Jamie announced. "We should be over the horizon for Site Two in thirty seconds."

Unless they weren't. Suppose they got there a little bit sooner? The whole idea of their entry plan was to be unpredictable, to do things that a race of careful and conservative beings would not expect. All right. They were supposed to be slowing down and descending in order to make their entry, and the techs watching their screens at Site Two knew that as well as Hannah did. So why not speed up and go higher?

Hannah grabbed at the controls, swung the ship around through ninety degrees, and gave the main engines a good swift kick of thrust directly toward the zenith, then another ninety-degree pitch-over to point their nose straight toward the horizon, and pulsed the engines again for another short sharp jolt of power. Then she swung the ship about one more time, putting the *Lotus* back into her proper stern-first attitude for atmospheric entry. Anyone using the last tracking data to take a potshot at them was going to be aiming in what had just become the wrong place. Maybe she had just saved them—or she had just doomed them by setting up a entry profile the ship couldn't survive.

She looked over at Jamie. He was staring at her in wide-eyed, speechless shock. Hannah silently dared him to protest. Instead he nodded, once, very slightly, then turned back to his tactical plots.

"We've got a debris cloud rising toward us," he announced. "Many targets, all sizes from off-scale low to a meter across, radiating out from one point at about eighty-three kilometers altitude, and almost exactly over Site Two."

"Great. What's all that mean?"

"They loaded a pile of junk—bits of metal, chunks of concrete, even just plain old rocks—into some sort of canister. They launched it straight up at suborbital velocity, so it would go up, then drop back down. They blew the can up while it still had lots of upward momentum. The debris cloud will get up high enough to hit us, then all fall back into the water. They're hoping we'll fly into the junk and hit something. They're trying to get us with a covert, deniable weapon. It'll look like we rammed into a piece of orbiting junk instead of being deliberately shot down."

Hannah's gut went cold. "And will we hit something?"

Jamie studied their tactical plot. "Thanks to that last stunt of yours, I don't *think* so. We're going to skirt the upper limit of the cloud, instead of flying right through the center of it."

What was the greater risk? Boosting again to fly a bit higher, but fouling up their entry path even more—or staying as they were and hoping to dodge between the outer fringes of the debris cloud?

Higher seemed safer to her—if she could bring the *Lotus* about to the right attitude fast enough and then get her back to the proper entry angle again in time.

She pitched the lander's nose back toward the zenith and started the setup for another quick burn to boost them just a trifle higher and dodge the top of the debris cloud. At best, she had only a couple of seconds to do what—

*BLAM-BLAM!*

Cabin lights died and the ship was tumbling, pitching, lurching in all directions. Alarms started hooting. There were crashes from the lower deck. Smoke spewed into the cabin, blinding them. Emergency lights cut in but they were dim and hard to see in the blue-black smoke.

*Hit*, Hannah told herself. She felt her suit starting to stiffen around her as the air was sucked out of the cabin, leaving only vacuum behind. *We must have taken a hit.* Maybe two. She felt foolish that it took her any time at all to reach a conclusion that obvious, but the shock had thrown her off.

Hannah forced herself to be calm, to think. Never mind about the vacuum. Their suits would protect them, at least for the time being. Another danger came first. If the *Lotus* were still tumbling at entry, they were going to be burned to a crisp. She needed attitude control, fast.

She reached up to the upper right side of her control panel and flipped open the safety cover on a switch marked STOP ALL ROTATIONS—EMERG USE ONLY.

She snapped her finger down hard on the switch under the safety cover. Instantly, the ship's automatics set to work, ignoring all other problems or inputs, and simply used every possible system to stop all movement through roll, pitch, and yaw as quickly as possible. Thrusters fired wildly, slamming Hannah and Jamie around in their seats. The autos worked far faster than a human ever could, and the thruster firing steadied down in surprisingly short order, canceling out roll, pitch, and yaw within a few terrifyingly efficient seconds.

A light came on under the STOP ALL ROTATIONS light, announcing—a bit smugly, to Hannah's way of thinking—ATTITUDE STABILIZED.

All well and good—but the autos had left the ship with her nose pointed directly at her direction of travel, precisely and exactly the wrong way around for entry into atmosphere. However, it didn't stay pointed that way for long. The nose started yawing about almost at once, and the ATTITUDE STABILIZED light started to flicker, then went out. Hannah quickly switched off the tumble-stop before it could start correcting things again in the wrong direction.

They were losing cabin pressure. A hole had been knocked in the ship. It had to be the air jetting out that was causing the yaw. She took a moment to try to find the hole—and it wasn't hard to do. By craning her neck around, she could see not one, but two holes in the inner hull, directly opposite each other. One was big, maybe five centimeters across, framed by jagged daggers of metal that jabbed out into the cabin. That had to be the entry hole. Opposite it was a smaller, neater-looking hole. Some sort of opaque gas or smoke was spewing in from that hole, whirling around inside the cabin, then jetting out the larger hole. The exit hole must have punctured some sort of high-pressure gas or fluid line. Either more of the stuff was

gushing out into space through a corresponding punc-
ture in the outer hull, or else whatever had hit them
had failed to smash all the way through on the way
out, and the outer hull was still intact on that side,
leaving that opaque gas with no place to go but into
the cabin.

In a sense, it didn't matter. They were in plenty
enough trouble even if there was only one break in the
outer hull—and besides, for all she knew, the *Lotus*
had taken half a dozen other hits in the same split second, in all sorts of places they couldn't get at. The
lower deck, the propulsion system—anywhere.

But she could at least do something about their yaw
problem—and maybe the smoke, too. She flipped the
safety off another switch marked CABIN PRESSURE
EMERG to reveal a selector switch that could be
pointed to various commands, with a big red button
marked ACTION under the knob. She twisted the knob
to LIFE SUPPORT SHUTDOWN and stabbed down on the
button. A tiny screen came on next to it and started
counting down from five seconds. She had to hold the
button for that long before the system would accept
the command. A sensible safety feature—unless you
were getting close to the top of the atmosphere, and
five seconds seemed like an awfully long time. The
count finally crawled down to zero, and the indicators
for the ship's life support all suddenly went red.
*There*, she told herself. *Now the ship wouldn't try
pumping more air into the system.*

Next she had to get rid of the smoke-filled air they
already had. Hannah instantly twisted the selector to

PURGE CABIN AIR and punched the ACTION button
again. Whatever committee of engineers decided such
things had set this one to a three-second countdown.
The count went to zero, then an indicator lit up saying
PURGE VALVES OPEN—but she knew that already. The
sudden roaring noise in the cabin, very loud at first,
then fading away, told her as much. She didn't worry
about making the yaw motion worse. The purge
valves outlets on the outside of the ship were posi-
tioned so that the air jetting from each was canceled
out by the jets from the others. There was still that
opaque gas leaking into the cabin, but it was being
drawn off by the air purge system.

The yawing motion seemed to stop as soon as the
air purge was complete, and there wasn't any significant amount of gas or smoke to jet out the hole in the
hull, but Hannah didn't wait for a precision test. She
grabbed the control stick and fired thrusters to bring
the *Lotus* back into a more or less correct attitude for
atmospheric entry. The instruments all told her she
was on-attitude, but stars alone knew which systems
had been damaged and which were still working.
What if an attitude sensor had been knocked ten degrees out of true? Never mind. Not much she could do
about it. The view out the window showed her lined
up with the horizon, and that would have to be
enough. She had also added an appreciable amount of
altitude with her last burns before the impact. She
had not the slightest doubt that the bonus altitude
had saved their lives—for the moment. But it also

meant they were going to hit the atmosphere coming in high, hot, and long. But by how much?

Hannah glanced over at Jamie, wondering what sort of shape he was in—and discovered that he was watching her. As best she could see through the visor of his suit helmet, he seemed in control of himself, and he had just shown the common sense to keep still and refrain from shouting unhelpful advice at a pilot during an emergency. If anything, he seemed a bit *too* calm, considering the amount of trouble they were in.

She nodded toward the back of the cabin. "Box on the back wall marked EMERGENCY AIDS," she said. "Hull patch kits in there. Patch the holes—and do the one with the smoke dumping in first."

"Ah, right," Jamie said, his voice oddly matter-of-fact. "Okay." He undid his seat restraints and lifted himself very carefully off the seat, using every hand-hold he could find to move himself toward the rear of the cabin. He moved out of her field of view, and she turned back toward her piloting problems, which left her with more than enough to worry about.

As best she could see from the numbers, their attitude and velocity at entry were going to be just barely within the safety specs for the *Lotus*—and that was assuming the lander was basically undamaged, and she certainly wasn't making that assumption. If they were going to have any hope of reaching the ground in one piece, they were going to have to fly as gentle an entry as she could manage.

But did they still *want* to reach the ground? She could try for an abort-to-orbit, boosting the poor old

*Lotus* into some sort of minimal orbit to take stock there. They'd have the luxury of time to make decisions, and perhaps repairs.

But that could leave them marooned in orbit. Besides, they would still have to maneuver to try entry again, sooner or later, or else either try to reach the *Hastings* or have the *Hastings* reach them—thus bringing the main ship within easy range of their groundside attackers. "Jamie. How's it going back there?"

"Fine. The hardest part so far has been reading the instructions on the patch. Just about to slap it down—*now*."

She heard a grunt and a muffled thud relayed by his suit radio. The smoke and murk in the cabin began to thin out almost instantaneously. That had been quick work. But not quick enough. There was still another patch to go—the harder one, too. And they were short on time.

"Okay, that's it for the first one," Jamie said. "Once the last of that gas vents, you should probably close the purge vents again before we hit air."

Hannah had almost forgotten that. She most definitely did not went air vents open while they were slamming into superheated air at umpteen thousand kilometers an hour. "Ah, right," she said. "Get started on the second hole. But I don't think you can use a regular flat patch on the entry hole. There should be a can of expanding foam sealant in that kit," she said.

"Yeah, I see it."

"Okay, get started with that," she said. "But

meantime—I'm thinking about abort-to-orbit. And we have to decide *fast*."

"No," he said. "Anyway, *I* vote no. That'll just give our friends groundside more chances to shoot at us, once per orbit for each of them—and we'd still either have to boost out, or try to land again anyway. Besides, there might be damage to the *Lotus* that we don't even know about. What if our power systems got hit? I think that smoky gas stuff was power coolant. We might not even have enough thruster power left to *reach* orbit."

"Well, I'm voting against it too," said Hannah, "so I guess it's unanimous." But if they were going to try for a landing, she was going to have to clean up their trajectory. They were going to hit the top of the sensible atmosphere very soon, but the nav displays made it clear they were going in too fast. She was going to have to put the brakes on and correct their entry angle at the same time. And she was going to have to do it more or less by feel. No time for anything fancy. "Jamie," she said. "I've got to do another retro burn. I'm going to do it low-power to keep the stresses down, so it's going to be a long burn."

"Ah, okay," Jamie said. "Starting when?"

"In about thirty seconds," she said. "Brace yourself. We'll be braking at about a quarter gee."

"Good," said Jamie. "Doing this job with gravity has to be easier than floating around squirting sealant everywhere but the right place."

"Hang on," she said. "I'll give you a countdown from five." She checked her plots once again, tweaked her attitude, and prayed she had gotten things more or less right. "Braking burn in five, four, three, two, one, zero!" She throttled up the engine and felt weight return.

"Okay," Jamie said. "Try to hold that steady. That makes this a *lot* easier." She heard a series of grunts and what might have been muttered curses, then silence for a moment.

Jamie spoke again after one last series of muffled grunts. "All right," he said. "That's the foam sprayed in and around deep enough and thick enough to cover the entry hole. The patch kit came in a metal can. I squirted some expanding foam into that and shoved it down over the whole patch to reinforce things a bit. Best I can do," he said.

"Good," Hannah said. She immediately closed the purge valves. "Get yourself back over here and strapped in before anything else can happen."

"Right," said Jamie. He scrambled back into his seat, snapped all his restraints back into place, and started studying the tactical displays again.

"One thing," he said. "This cabin is now in vacuum. Just bear in mind those patches were designed to keep pressure *in*. Once we hit the atmosphere, the patches will be keeping pressure *out*. Any idea what will happen if they fail? Will it matter?"

"I don't know," said Hannah. "I haven't had a chance to think too far ahead." She checked her displays. "Coming up on three minutes into the burn. Shutdown in *mark*, thirty seconds."

And if she had it figured right, that ought to bring

them right down to something like a safe entry heading and velocity just a few seconds above the sensible atmosphere.

The engines died, and they dropped, however briefly, back into zero gee. Moments later, they began to feel weight returning as the *Lotus* entered the upper reaches of Reqwar's atmosphere one last time and started to decelerate. Almost immediately, the ride started to get rough. A low, thrumming vibration seemed to take hold of the entire ship, rattling Hannah back and forth in her seat. No sound could move through the vacuum in the control cabin, but that only made the shaking and shuddering seem more intense and somehow magnified the creaking and rustling and rattling that came from inside her suit.

There was a loud and intense *bang* that came from somewhere belowdecks, hard and sharp enough to get transmitted right through the padding of her seat. Hannah didn't even want to know what that might have been.

The gee forces were starting to build up as they piled into heavy air and started decelerating more rapidly. A red glow of superheated air began to surround the ship, cutting off their view of the outside world and painting the interior of the cabin a dark and lurid ocher. Hannah could not help but imagine what was going on outside their ship, just out of view. The *Lotus* was cone-shaped, flying blunt-end first for entry. Nearly all of the energy of entry would be absorbed or reflected by the heat shield in the base of the ship, but the upper hull would come in for its share of heat and stress.

The heat shield seemed to be working, protecting them from the terrifying frictional heating of their atmospheric entry—but what if it had been hit? What if it had been cracked, or a hole smashed part of the way through it? And the main heat shield wasn't the only danger point. If the upper hull was damaged much, that would do the job. The entry hole Jamie had just patched from the inside could burn through from the outside with no trouble at all.

All it would take would be a thin finger of superheated air streaming up from the blunt forward end of the *Lotus*, catching on the lip of the entry hole, heating the exposed edge, worming its way into the interior spaces between the inner and outer hull, heating the outer hull from the inside, weakening it, stressing it as more and hotter supercompressed superheated air pounded its way in, like a blowtorch slicing through paper, like a steel wedge splitting open a seasoned log, peeling back the outer hull, the inner hull, a hot spot forming under the patched hull, the patch itself melting, disintegrating, a tongue of fire stabbing through, slicing the *Lotus* open, tearing it to shreds, casting them out into the hellish fires of atmospheric entry incinerating the ship and its passengers so fast they would scarcely have time to know that it was—

*BANG! CRASH!*

For a split second Hannah thought it was all about to come true—but then she realized she wouldn't have had time to wonder if it had. She spotted a new flashing red indicator over her displays. CARGO NET 4 UNSECURED, it warned.

Hannah managed a laugh. A cargo net had come loose, and dumped a stack of supplies to the deck. *Wouldn't it be nice if all our problems were that minor?*

The shaking and shuddering began to fade away, and the gee forces were letting up. The red glow was fading away from the window. Hannah realized they had made it through the most violent part of atmospheric entry. They were merely in a gliding high-speed fall, still supersonic, still flying a good seventy kilometers above the ground, well below orbital speed and inside the atmosphere.

She allowed herself the indulgence of a sigh of relief. They were well away from Site Two, and not yet anywhere near Sites Three or Four. Besides, an orbital attack was one thing, and an airborne intercept or shoot-down something else—but an attack on a vehicle flying at their speed and altitude was a third and extremely difficult thing entirely. "Well, we made it this far," she said. "Now we just have to land this thing."

"Without being shot down," Jamie said. "But if I'm reading the tactical plots right, I might have some good news on that score."

"I could use good news," Hannah said, studying the ground track and glide path in her flight displays. "Tell me more." There was something there under Jamie's unnerving calm. An intensity, an *enthusiasm* for it all. He reminded her of a kid playing a game so intently he lost track of time, skipped dinner, stayed up late, and didn't notice he was getting hungry.

"Well, if I have this figured right, at the time we dropped below the horizon for Site Two, the *Lotus* was tumbling badly and venting gas. From Site Two's perspective, I *think* it would look like the *Lotus* was deep inside the debris field, not at the upper edge. With any luck at all, Site Two will score us as a kill, or at least a probable. *Maybe* Sites Three and Four will hear that and stand down."

"Maybe," Hannah said doubtfully. "I wouldn't bet my life on it."

"Me either," Jamie said. "But at least it's something. The other bit of left-handed good news is that the debris field attack makes it pretty clear they're trying for a deniable attack: one they can make without leaving evidence."

"What's so great about that?"

"It limits the *ways* they can attack. I don't think we'd be flying along right now talking things over if the people at Site Two didn't care about getting caught."

"That's all good news—sort of," she said. "But we'd be upping our odds if we could dodge Sites Three and Four, keep them from getting line of sight on us. *Can* we dodge them from where we are now, at our current speed and altitude?" Hannah asked.

"Site Three shouldn't be a problem. It's to the north, and we're already way off course to the south.

Site Four, though. It's just fifty kilometers from Thelmhome Spaceport. We're going to *have* to get near it if we're going to put down there."

"At the *spaceport*?" Hannah had assumed that all their wild maneuvering had thrown them completely off course. She brought up her terminal maneuver displays and saw a map of a big slice of Reqwar, with an elongated oval "footprint" overlaid on its center. The *Lotus* was designed to function as a lifting body, and could maneuver aerodynamically, within limits. The oval represented the range of locations it would be possible for them to reach under glide, assuming that they did not relight their engines before the final landing maneuvers—and Hannah wanted to use the engines as little as possible.

Until she studied that footprint, she had assumed they were going to have to put down in whatever clearing they could find. But, somehow, all their maneuvers seemed to have canceled out, and put the spaceport fairly near the middle of their footprint, about a hundred kilometers east of their uncorrected landing point projection. Beyond that, it was pretty clear that the spaceport itself was the only reasonably flat and unforested piece of land they had any chance of reaching. Hannah didn't much like the idea of dropping the *Lotus* into a stand of trees or setting down on a hillside or in the water, which seemed to be the only other choices they had. Hannah shook her head ruefully. "Okay, Jamie," she said, "you got it right. We don't have much choice in the matter. We're going to *have* to put the *Lotus* down at the space-port."

She was just starting to figure out how to do that when an explosion belowdecks shook the lander from stem to stern.

# TWELVE · **HAND**

Zahida gunned her open-top self-drive transporter down the highway toward the spaceport, dodging and weaving among the robotically controlled traffic, breaking every law in the book. She nearly missed the turnoff and swerved violently at the last moment, wheels squealing.

It was coming on toward evening, Reqwar's sun just touching the western horizon. A high wall of cloud shielded the sky. She glanced at the dashboard timepiece and swore. The humans had arrived in-system and started their descent days before they were expected. The Thelm's guard of defense was nowhere near organized or ready to deploy. Even the tracking center hadn't managed to function properly. They had promised to give her at least an hour's notice of the human ship's arrival, and they had barely managed fifteen minutes.

And without the guard of defense, Zahida and the pendant charm hanging around her neck were all the humans had left for protection. If she didn't get there in time, the humans likely wouldn't have more than fifteen minutes left to live.

She gunned the engine harder.

* * *

Hannah held on to the control stick as if—and be-cause—her life depended on it. The *Lotus* was still in the air, still flying under control—but just barely. It had taken all of her piloting skills to keep them from being knocked out of the sky.

*Something* in the lower decks had exploded with almost enough power to throw the *Lotus* on her side. Unless one of them went down to check, they weren't ever likely to learn more about whatever it had been—and neither of them even considered taking such a pointless risk.

At least Site Four hadn't fired on them. Maybe the *Lotus* had never gotten into range for them. Or maybe no one thought that a shoot-down from Site Four, so close to the capital and a city full of witnesses, would be "deniable."

"How close now?" Hannah called to Jamie, still hunched over his tactical display.

"We're still fifty kilometers east-southeast of our assigned touchdown point," Jamie said. "We have to keep backtracking."

"I don't know if I can hold this thing together long enough."

"Hang in there, Hannah. You've gotten us this far."

* * *

Zahida peered through the darkness. The spaceport was dead ahead. She was driving flat out—but then she saw something that made her slam on the brakes and come to a violent halt.

She stared up into the sky. There it was, just breaking through the high cloud deck, and difficult to see in the failing light. The little ship was coming in from the *east*, not the west. Plainly they had overshot. The Hard Spikes, a tall and cruel range of mountains, were not far off in that direction. It would have been near-on suicide to try to set down a lander there—but scarcely safer to do a full stop in midair, reverse course, and head back to Thelmhome Spaceport.

The little ship was getting closer. It was canted over hard in the direction of travel, losing altitude as it came in, hard and fast. Smoke was pouring out of at least two hull breaches, and tendrils of vapor were oozing out of three or four places in the aft section.

Every rescue and alert vehicle at the spaceport should have been out and rolling toward the BSI lander's projected set-down point—but none were in sight. No alarms sounded. That told her a lot. Zahida started up her vehicle again and drove as hard as she could toward the nearest field access gate.

The guards at the spaceport gate were gawping at the injured ship coming in, and paid the least attention to the vehicle blasting through the entrance at top speed.

It didn't occur to Zahida until she was through the gate that she could have stopped, shown the Thelm's Hand, and been waved through amid a flurry of respectful salutes—but that would have slowed her up, and she had no desire to risk running into some guard who wasn't particularly impressed by the mere sight of the Thelm's Hand.

*No, you'd rather run the risk of a bullet through your back.* She instantly felt a terrible itching sensation along her spine-shields, and hunched her head forward to reduce the target area—but no shots came whistling past her. Maybe the guards were too stunned to respond. Maybe they had received orders not to interfere with whatever happened and were taking that a bit too literally.

She drove as fast as she could toward the point where the foundering craft looked likely to put down if it didn't crash first.

Then the weapons fire began—but it was not aimed at her. The low *pat-pat-pat* of a medium-caliber electromagnetic slug thrower was coming from off to her left. She turned her head to look and saw streaks of fire in the sky. It was unguided tracer fire, one slug in ten treated with a special coating that flared on contact with air. Fortunately, the gunner hadn't come close to hitting the lander so far.

No doubt the High Thelek had ordered some underling to "welcome" the humans, with a wink and a flap of the ears to convey what sort of welcome he wished. That subordinate would have ordered *his* subordinate to give the humans "the proper sort of welcome," and *his* subordinate might order his people to "keep the humans out of trouble," and *his* subordinate might instruct his underlings to "see to it the humans were kept from ever causing trouble," until at last some security force squad leader came right out and ordered his gunner to shoot down the human ship with a gun meant for some other job. The investigators, if any, would trace the sequence of orders and discover it was all a most unfortunate mix-up, with each underling misinterpreting his orders and taking more drastic action than was intended.

And, of course, the electromag guns in the spaceport would all vanish almost before the human vehicle had finished crashing—and if anyone checked, it would turn out to be a long-scheduled plan to decommission surplus hardware, and merely a coincidence that they were removed at about the same time as the unfortunate accident. And, yes, they had been test-fired that day as part of the decommissioning process, and if a few stray rounds had somehow gotten mixed up in the wreckage, that meant nothing at all. Besides, it was a wholly unsuitable weapon for bringing down a spacecraft; therefore, it must have been an accident.

It took Zahida no longer than the time required for the first burst of tracer fire to streak across the sky to get that far in her thinking. It was all business as usual, the way the game was played.

Everyone would *know* that the High Thelek had ordered that the human ship be shot down. But that did not matter, so long as it was nearly impossible to *prove* that he had done so, and so long as he made it possible for everyone to *pretend* that he hadn't done so. As long as there was some chain of logic, some line of reasoning, however flimsy or improbable, that made it remotely conceivably that he had nothing to do with the crash, that would be enough. What was it Great-uncle Bindulan had written to her? *We have lost our every shred of honor by striving to preserve all* appearance *of honor.*

*But what honor, O High Thelek, in murdering those whom your lord has summoned to assist him?*

But the humans hadn't been murdered. Their ship had not crashed. Not yet.

She heeled the steering over hard to the left, and headed straight toward the sound of the guns.

\* \* \*

The cabin of the *Lotus* was a place of jolting shocks, weird, low, far-off noises and echoing silences that should not have been there. The cabin was still in vacuum. Hannah had been too busy to open the vent valves to allow outside air in. Besides, she didn't *want* the ship to suck in any of the clouds of smoke and swirling gas she could see through the viewport. She had enough problems without being blinded in the bargain.

With the cabin in vacuum, all the sound that came to her was what the headphones in her helmet passed along, plus whatever sound was conducted, dimly and muddily, through the vibration of her pilot's chair.

The alarm lights flashed silently, the ship bucked and shuddered and shook without a sound, and loose bits of the *Lotus* banged and flapped against the outer hull in all but perfect quiet.

Somehow, they had made it this far. They were only a kilometer up and about as far from their touchdown target. With just a little more luck they would—

"Jink to starboard! Incoming fire!" Jamie called out.

Hannah hit the port attitude jets hard, shoving the *Lotus* sideways. "What kind of fire?" she demanded.

"Mag gun," he said. "Iron or steel shot, probably. Whoever is doing the shooting isn't very good."

"Glad to hear it," she said.

"I think the smoke we're dumping has him a little—"

*WHUMP-bang! WHUMP-bang!*

The sounds shuddered dully through the fabric of the ship, through the pilot chairs, and into their suits. Hannah was surprised to discover she did not react at all at first, and allowed herself a split second or two of wondering if she had crisis fatigue; too many life-and-death dangers, one after another, had simply used up all her supplies of adrenaline. But a half heartbeat after that thought, the cabin was filling with smoke, her pressure suit suddenly wasn't anywhere near as stiff, and exterior sounds—loud, unpleasant sounds— began to stage a return. Dim and seemingly far off at first, then louder and louder, came the roar of air into the cabin, the hooting and shrieking of alarms, and an ominous clanking noise from the overhead bulk-head.

"The patches blew inward!" she shouted, as if Jamie hadn't noticed, or couldn't figure it out for himself. "What about that gunner on the ground?" she cried out.

"I think he's lost us in the smoke for the moment."

"Good! Let's not give him too much of a chance to find us. Are we over any part of the landing field?" She couldn't see a thing through the viewports—in fact she could barely see the viewports, or her own displays.

"Stand by," Jamie said, studying his screens. "Yes! Tactical shows us over the field—nothing but empty stresscrete under us."

"All right, I'm putting her down." She brought the ship back to vertical, throttled back on the main thrusters, and used the attitude jets to kill all of their horizontal motion, leaving them settling slowly toward the ground, only eight hundred meters below.

Hannah reached out, flipped the landing gear deployment switch—and instantly another hooting alarm joined the chorus. A big red light over the switch lit up with the words NEGATIVE DEPLOY.

Hannah flipped the switch on and off three or four times, but the light and the alarm didn't shut off—and she didn't hear the familiar and reassuring sound of the four landing legs extending out and down.

"No landing gear! No landing gear!" she called out. She checked the thruster-power indicator. It showed only about two minutes of power at current rate of expenditure—and less than that if they went into a hover and tried to get the gear extended. They were going down, and there was no way around that.

There was a way to do a no-gear landing. The lander itself might not be usable after such a stunt—but the *Lotus* wasn't going to be worth much after this flight anyway. The question was whether she was pilot enough to make a no-gear landing work.

"Coming out of the smoke again!" Jamie announced. "Whoever is on that gun will be able to see us in about five seconds!"

*And if he doesn't kill us in about ten seconds, we'll die in the crash in about ninety seconds*, Hannah told herself. *Unless I get a lot better at this, and do it fast.*

Just then, the gun started firing again.

\* \* \*

Zahida drove straight for the gun emplacement, trying hard not to think about what the electromag gun could do to her car—and to her.

A camera. She should have brought some sort of camera, to record everything and transmit it all to a remote recorder. She should have brought her own gear, and made sure the High Thelek's flunkies knew that she had it.

*That's what pocket comms are for*, she reminded herself. She drove one-handed, the car veering all over the landing field, as she pulled out her comm unit, and tried to think who or what to call that would be able to set up to record voice and image, and have the presence of mind to do it fast. *And someone you'd be willing to subject to the danger of holding evidence against the High Thelek.*

It was no good calling emergency services—like everything else in his territory, e-services were controlled by the High Thelek. Any recordings they made of the call would vanish at once, without anyone even having to issue an order for someone to misunderstand.

She would have to bluff, and bluff hard. Fake the call.

*Thap thap thap thap thap thap. Thap. Thap thap thap thap thap.* Streaks of light from the tracer rounds flew out straight over her head, heading toward the crippled ship behind her.

The gunner was firing again, in shorter bursts. She didn't dare take her eyes off the her driving long enough to look behind, but she swiveled her ears back and refocused them to tune out the sound of the gun firing and the bullets whizzing. She listened intently behind, but there was no sound of a crash or an explosion. Either the gunner was still scoring clean misses, or else the human ship was tough enough to absorb the further punishment of mag-gun fire.

She was close enough to the gun emplacement to make out the gun itself, and the gunner and two or three other members of the gun crew.

"Stop!" she cried out. "In the name of the Thelm, cease fire!" The gun crew were working under dim blue lights that preserved their night vision. Zahida deliberately aimed her self-drive straight at them and brought her driving light up to maximum, in hopes of dazzling them, and, if nothing else, ruining their aim for a few seconds. She stopped the car.

The gunfire stopped, at least for a moment—but plainly just so the crew could look up and see what was going on, who was shouting at them. The gunner himself peered through the glare of her driving lights and turned toward her. He swiveled the gun around as well, so it was pointing straight at Zahida. Her insides froze, but she forced herself to give no outward sign. There was something in the stance, the facial expression of the chubby little gunner, that said he was simply in the habit of pointing the gun at whatever he was looking at—and likewise something in his face that told her he wasn't especially bright. Another member of the gun crew flipped on a light of his own and pointed it at her.

She grabbed the Thelm's Hand on its thick and heavy gold chain and pulled it from her pocket. *Foolish female!* she told herself. *You should have thought to put it on properly to make a grander appearance. No time for that now.* She took her powered-up pocket comm in the other hand and held it so the camera was pointed out, toward the gun crew. She stepped out into the space lit by her driving lights and held up the Hand, forcing them to see it. "In the name of the Thelm, stand away from the gun! Cease fire!" The gun crew froze, surprised, uncertain—but not sufficiently impressed to obey unthinkingly. She lifted the Thelm's Hand higher. By ancient right, law, and custom, whoever held it had the power to extend the Thelm's personal grant of protection. Once Zahida declared that the Hand had been raised over the human lawkeepers, harming them would be treated as causing harm to the Thelm himself.

Perhaps a bit of grand and formal talk would make up for her failure to wear the Hand properly. "Know that the Thelm himself gave unto me this Hand of gold and steel, and commanded me to place yonder ship, and those aboard it, under the direct and lawful protection of his Mighty Hand. Stand away from the gun!"

The four gun crew members nervously shuffled back. "Cease all hostile action against the ship now trying to land, and against those aboard!" she half shouted. "Let those aboard pass freely, and do not interfere with them." She looked over the four crew members, and picked the one who looked the smartest. "You!" she called out, and pointed her pocket comm straight at him. She wasn't recording or transmitting his image—but he couldn't know that. "Use your comm system and relay those orders, given in the Thelm's name by one who bears the emblem of the Thelm's Hand, to all the other security forces at this spaceport, and confirm receipt of the message with your headquarters." He hesitated for a moment, and she shouted again. "Do it! I command in the Thelm's name. And when you speak, speak in proper form, as one should when speaking the true words of the Thelm."

*That* put some snap into his spine-shields. He stood up straight, pulled out his own pocket comm, made some adjustment to it, and spoke into it in a low clear voice. "This is Small Unit Guide Cantro Flen, Gun Crew 345. One who bears the Thelm's Hand commands me to relay to all units the order to cease all hostile action against the ship now trying to land and against those aboard. We are ordered to allow those aboard to pass freely, and not interfere with them. I request that Spaceport Central Security Office acknowledge receipt of this report."

He held out the comm unit for Zahida to hear the reply. "This is Spaceport Central Security Office acknowledging." Small Unit Guide Flen nodded, and slipped the comm unit back in his pocket. "I have done as you ordered in the Thelm's name," he said simply.

"Well done, Guide Flen," Zahida said, struggling as hard to hide her relief as she had to conceal her fear. "You have done the will of the Thelm, and so I shall report. Now I, too, must do his will. Fair evening and farewell." She bowed, very slightly, to them all, and quite deliberately turned her back on them to climb into her vehicle, start it up, and drive away. She pocketed her commlink once she was out of sight of the gun crew.

There was no point in trying to confirm that the orders given in the Thelm's name were being obeyed. There was no end to the tricks and the deceptions that Flen could have committed while pretending to obey. His call could have been as phony as her own commlink camera stunt. He could have called a quick-witted accomplice who had the sense to pretend to be the all-points channel and give a false acknowledgment.

She looked up into the darkening sky, toward the incoming ship—and instantly wished she hadn't. It was in even more trouble than she had thought.

# THIRTEEN · FIRE

Jamie barely noticed when the guns stopped firing. They had too many other problems to worry about. Hannah had just explained the landing plan in as few words as possible. He had a half dozen urgent questions to ask, but there was no time for any of them. He could see the thruster-power reserve indicator sliding down toward zero just as well as she could.

"Okay, double-check all your seat restraints," she said. "Make good and sure you're strapped in."

Jamie did as he was told, tugging on all the belts and buckles, wondering just how much good they would do. "Belts okay," he reported.

"Good," said Hannah. "Ready?"

"Yeah, all set." A lie, of course. How could anyone get ready for a thing like this?

"Here we go," Hannah said. "Just pray that it all works." She throttled the main thruster down, and let the *Lotus* drop faster toward what would be her final landing. "Stand by for evac hatch jettison," she called out. She flipped yet another safety cover off yet another for-emergency-use-only control, armed the system by twisting a knob, and then stabbed her finger down hard on the jettison button.

*BLAM-BLAM-BLAM-BLAM* and four fat triangular sections of the control cabin's hull, spaced at ninety-degree intervals from each other, suddenly blew off and were arcing away into the gathering darkness to crash onto the landing field. One jettisoned section contained the main viewport, and Jamie suddenly found himself with nothing but his pressure suit between him and the wind whipping past outside, howling and roaring at the frail and dying spacecraft that was going down for the last time.

They needed all four evac hatches blown off for a very simple reason. With no landing gear to hold the ship upright, they knew the *Lotus* was going to topple; but they didn't know which way. With all four hatches gone, the odds were good that at least one hatchway would be clear enough for them to get out.

The ship continued its powered fall, dropping straight down at a steady rate that conferred an odd stateliness on the crippled ship, even though they were still moving far too quickly for anything like a survivable crash landing. At a bare hundred meters altitude, Hannah throttled up as hard as she could to max power, and the engines screamed to life one last time. Jamie watched the altimeter and braced himself for an impact that didn't come—at least, not at once.

The *Lotus* came to a halt a bare eight meters above the ground. Hannah immediately throttled down hard to hover, before the ship could pogo back up into the sky. The ship lifted by only the slightest amount, not more than a meter or two. Hannah held the *Lotus* there, floating all but motionless, just above the ground, dumping the last of the system's thruster power, rather than risking its being released on impact in the form of a large and unpleasant explosion.

The ship hung there, hovering, for a handful of seconds that seemed like hours—hours in which yet another system could fail, or another faceless enemy could take a potshot at them, or something else could go wrong with their snakebit arrival.

One last alarm began to beep, then to blat, and finally to howl. Warning panels flashed on in blood-red letters, blinking with the warning THRUSTER POWER DEPLETION. The main engine cut out, then lit again just for a moment before dying completely. Then the *Lotus* dropped, and dropped hard, smashing stern first into the landing field with a resounding crash and a horrible shriek of metal tearing itself apart.

The tortured little ship hung there, teetering on its rounded base, for a second, for five seconds, for ten, until Jamie thought it was going to stay that way, balanced upright, for good and all. But then came another bang as something gave way, and the elongated cone that was the *Lotus* began to topple over backwards.

The ship fell slowly over with a long, horrible, grinding, crashing noise that seemed to go on forever, gathering force and speed as it went, until finally the cabin level smashed into the ground with a deafening roar. Jamie and Hannah were flat on their backs. The forward evac hatch, where the main viewport had been, was suddenly over their heads. Cracked and grimy sections of the landing pad's concrete were visible through the two side hatches. A geyser of dust and debris and bits and pieces of wreckage engulfed the cabin, mixing with the clouds of smoke and gas and steam billowing out from a half dozen wounds on the ship.

"Time to go!" Hannah called out, and Jamie needed no further urging. He undid his restraints and half fell, half climbed down from his perch and climbed down onto the control panels and displays that now formed the floor of the cabin. He stumbled backwards through the smoke and dusk to the rear lockers of the cabin, knelt, and pulled them open, stopping for a moment to kick clear a pile of debris that was jamming one locker door.

He pulled out the emergency packs, the weapons packs, and the two small personal packs and dumped them at his feet, then turned around to see Hannah's feet just disappearing out of the forward evac hatch, directly overhead, the only one of the four that was completely clear of wreckage. Her head reappeared a moment later, and her arms reached out for the big, awkward, heavily padded containers. Jamie grabbed them by their handles, one after another, and heaved them up to her.

"That it?" she asked after the last one came up.

"Yeah," said Jamie, then turned and looked at the open lockers. "No. Just a second." There were two or three other smaller packs in there. They had probably been sitting in the emergency lockers since the *Lotus* was shipped from the factory. He had no idea what they held, but whatever was in them was meant for use by humans and to be useful in an emergency. He grabbed whatever had a strap he could throw over his arm or shoulder and scrambled up out of the evac hatch, Hannah hauling him up and out onto the hull.

The moment he was clear of the evac hatch and out on the chewed-up hull of the ruined *Lotus*, Hannah started throwing the equipment and emergency packs away from the ship. Jamie tossed the last two packs clear. They proceeded to scramble down off the ship, working toward the blunt nose of the lander and sliding down from there. Hannah was ahead of Jamie and hit the ground first. She made a beeline for the closest of the scattered packs, scooped up a bunch of them, and started running away from the *Lotus*.

Jamie scooted down the last section of the ship's nose, sitting down and moving feet-first, steadying himself by leaning back and putting his hands down palm first on the hull. He made his way far enough toward the nose to slide down the rest of the way and drop to the ground. He landed heavily, clumsily, falling backwards, banging the back of his helmet against the lander's nose. He scooped up all the packs Hannah hadn't grabbed, and started trotting off after her, struggling to arrange the various straps and handles as he moved.

He instantly discovered that a sealed pressure suit made a lousy runner's outfit. Still, he was glad to have it on. The clouds of undoubtedly toxic smoke and dust were still swirling around everywhere, and he had no wish to breathe any of it.

He ran after her, making the best speed he could, gaining on her slowly. He caught up with her, matched pace with her long enough to grab the pack that was the most awkward for her, then upped his pace again and passed her.

It didn't take more than a few seconds more for his sides to start aching and his suit to start overheating. He would have cranked the cooling up to maximum if he had had a free hand to reach the controls. The suit's visor started to fog up. One of the escape packs was banging into his right leg with every step, throwing him off-balance. And he must have twisted his left ankle somehow in the drop from the *Lotus*, because it was sending a jolt of pain up his leg with every step.

Jamie gritted his teeth and kept moving. A few more moments of pain and exhaustion would be a fair trade for staying alive. He leaned forward, determined to keep on going—

And fell off the edge of the landing pad, tumbling into a drainage ditch that ran along its edge. He landed hard on his left side in a tangle of arms and legs and equipment bags and straps, banging up his ankle again. Before he had a chance to unsnarl himself from his possessions, Hannah came crashing on top of him, and seemed to land with her entire weight directly on the spot on his right leg that had been slammed around already.

They thrashed around in the darkness for a

moment, struggling to organize themselves and catch their breath. It was plain that it would make no sense to try going much farther in the dark over what seemed like rough ground ahead without making some sort of plan first—and it didn't seem likely they'd find anyplace that would afford better cover against a blast if it did come.

At any rate, they seemed to have gotten clear of the smoke. Jamie decided it was just about time to open his visor. They were going to have to start breathing local air sooner or later, anyway. He rolled over on his back to get both arms clear, then reached up and undid the visor's safety releases, then the inner latches. There was a soft sort of *chuff* as the pressure equalized with the outside air, and Jamie pushed the visor up.

The first thing that struck him was the smell—no, the *multiple* smells—that seemed to rush in at him from all directions. Something like fresh grass, cool night air, and a nasty cocktail of unpleasant burning-chemical smells. A patch of smoke slipped out of the way, revealing the cold and clear light of stars, strange stars, spangling the darkness overhead in a sky never seen from Earth, or Center, or any human world.

This world wasn't just new to him. It was all but unknown to humans. The gigabytes of data they had waded through boiled down to less actually useful information than would fill a modest datapad—and none of it was going to do them much good in a muddy ditch deep in hostile territory. They were in trouble—big trouble.

*So it's time to start thinking about how to get out*

*of it*, Jamie thought. He rolled over on his stomach and looked toward Hannah as she opened her visor. Jamie left her to it, and belly-crawled up to the edge of the drainage ditch to look back at the *Lotus*—or, rather, the remains of the *Lotus*.

It would have been a lovely and dramatic sight if it had had nothing to do with him. The long, tapered black-and-white cone that was the *Lotus*, toppled over on its side, was framed by the gathering darkness of night and the light of all manner of fire. There was a dim glow visible from the crew cabin, and tendrils of smoke eddying up through the evac hatches. A jet of flame spurted up now and then from somewhere on the back side of the ship, silhouetting it against the red-orange bloom of light. A smaller, steadier fire was alight in the cracked-open stern, burning with a deeper red, almost the color of dying embers.

A gouge through the hull revealed an angry, white-hot flame burning amidships. Smoke spewed forth from a dozen wounds, and the wind blew it about, obscuring and revealing the ship as a whole, and each of the separate fires, from one moment to the next. The smoke caught and blocked the light, changing its color from moment to moment as it reflected and then obscured the various patches of fire.

Hannah belly-crawled up beside him. As they watched, some pressurized tank in the aft end blew up with a loud *BANG* and a flash of light. The next time the smoke parted, the *Lotus* was still more or less intact, but with a new hole torn in the stern. The whole ship had been rocked sideways by the blast.

"I wouldn't want to bet on it, but I don't *think* the whole ship is going to explode," Hannah said in a whisper. "It looks like all the volatiles are cooking off and burning instead, with maybe a few more storage tanks popping off from the heat."

"Good, I guess," Jamie whispered back. "Though I wouldn't want to be any closer when the next tank blows."

"Oh, I'm right with you," Hannah said. "I'm not going back toward it. But I think we're pretty much safe where we are."

Jamie pulled his head back down and rolled over onto his back, signaling for Hannah to follow. Hannah moved back down into the ditch and turned on her side to face him. "We won't get killed if the ship blows up," he said, "but we're not safe from whoever was shooting at us. We need to get out of here before someone comes poking around. Got any ideas?"

"Nothing that isn't obvious," said Hannah. "Try to repack the gear we saved so we can move more easily. Be glad we landed at sunset, take advantage of the darkness, and hope they don't use good night-vision gear to look for us. Take advantage of this ditch to move—that way, I guess, away from the main terminals. Get out into the forest, find someplace to hide, try to figure out who on this planet—if anyone— *won't* shoot at us. Make contact with them—"

"And then try to find out what, exactly, we were supposed to do here, and why stopping us from doing it means they need to kill us."

"Right. Then all we have to do is the whatever-it-is and figure out some safe way to get home."

Jamie let out a weary sigh. "Sounds real simple," he said. "Might as well get started." He slid down farther into the ditch and started gathering the padded gear bags together. He reached for the weapons bag first. "Can you keep watch while I'm working here?" he asked, in as loud a whisper as he dared.

"Quiet!" she hissed back, in a voice that made it clear she meant it. He looked up. He could barely see her silhouette against the darkening sky, but it was obvious, just by the angle of her head, and the way her arms had tensed up, that she was watching something. Something dangerous.

Almost before he knew it, Jamie had the weapons pack open, and was pulling out hardware. He was careful to close up the pack properly when he was done. If they had to make a sudden run for it, he didn't want to do it with half their weaponry spilling out of the pack as they moved.

He headed back up the slope of the drainage ditch on his belly, cradling a multigun rifle on his forearms and moving on his elbows and knees. Hannah pointed to what she had spotted, but there was no need. A headlight, or what looked like a headlight, was moving toward them. He caught just a glimpse of the new arrival as it moved in front of some lit-up structure on the horizon. One vehicle, a big car or a small truck, was headed straight for the crash site from the far side of the spaceport. Jamie powered up the night scope on the multigun and looked through it.

"Good-sized open-frame vehicle," he whispered. "No armor or weapons visible. Nothing that looks like rescue or fire gear. One occupant visible. Probable Pavlat female, but not certain. Wearing what looks like conventional civilian dress for a young adult female Pavlat, but not working clothes. Semiformal, say. Nothing that looks military. No official-looking markings or placards or anything like that on the car. No attempt at evasive driving. She'll be at the *Lotus* in about thirty seconds."

"Okay," Hannah whispered back. "We crashed ten minutes ago, and they probably don't think we survived the crash—I don't quite believe it myself. So probably they didn't have any prearranged deception plan to fool crash survivors. Therefore, she's almost certainly what she looks like she is, and not some plan to fool us for whatever bizarre reason. So what is it that she looks like?"

Jamie, still watching through the night scope, gave a minuscule shrug. "A tourist?"

"A witness," Hannah suggested. "A verifier. Sent to make sure it was a nice, violent crash and we didn't make it out alive."

Jamie wasn't convinced. According to all the sources on Reqwar culture he had studied, young females were regarded as worthy of protection and young males were far more expendable, close to cannon fodder. It would be unlikely in the extreme for the Reqwar Pavlat to send a high-caste female in to do something as low-status and high-danger as checking to see if there were any survivors aboard a crashed spacecraft.

That seemed an awful lot of explanation to get across to Hannah in whispers while lying flat in a drainage ditch, and Jamie didn't try. But there didn't seem to be any other obvious explanations. "Maybe," Jamie conceded.

"Let's hope that she finds that brightly burning spacecraft very convincing. It'd be nice for us if she decides we didn't get out, and we're both safely dead."

"Then we'd better hope something else—that she doesn't notice that the evac hatches are all blown."

But that hope didn't last long. The vehicle roared up at high speed, and came to a halt between the *Lotus* and their hiding place in the ditch.

The driver of the vehicle reached down and picked up something that proved to be a very powerful handlight. It stabbed a shaft of light through the smoke and lit up the side of the ruined ship in dazzling brightness. The light beam searched up and down the wreck until it came to rest on the evac hatchways, then worked slowly over the hull toward the nose. The handlight was far too bright for the multigun's night scope, and Jamie flipped over to daylight mode. He studied what their visitor was looking at—and cursed. "Footprints," he said. "We left footprints and handprints and all kinds of smears and marks as we got out of the ship."

He looked over at Hannah's suit, then down at his. Both their suits were filthy, stained and spotted with all the dirt and dust and smoke and soot that had filled the cabin. He looked at the glove of his suit and was shocked to see how much crud was still on it— and that was after it had left big smeary marks all over the nose of the *Lotus*.

He went back to watching through his scope. The stranger was still working the light down the length of the hull. The light paused at the spot near the hull where Jamie had slid to the landing pad, then it played over the ground. It was impossible to see what the light was pointing at—and impossible not to guess what their visitor was seeing. If they had left footprints and handprints on the lander, they must have left them on the ground.

He swung the scope back to watch their visitor. He could see that she was still pointing the light at the ground. She got out of the vehicle and moved a trifle closer to the fire. She knelt, pointing the light at the ground between her feet, then walked a bit closer to the wreck. A subdued *whump*, a jet of fire that stabbed up from the upper evac hatch startled her, and she backed off a bit but kept at what she was doing. Very plainly, what she was doing was tracking their footprints away from the spacecraft.

Hannah could see it as well as Jamie without the aid of a night scope. "Our tracks can't go on too long," she whispered. "We'd have walked off whatever dirt and soot was going to come off before we went fifty meters."

"She won't need more than ten meters," Jamie replied. "Even if she's never seen a human footprint before, she'll see them moving in a straight line, directly away from the fire. Straight toward here. And even if she can't tell a running print from a walking print, there's a burning spaceship right there. She'll be able to guess we were moving fast, and that we probably wore ourselves out, and that we can't have gotten far, and that—"

"We've got to get moving," Hannah said, cutting him off. "Now." She slid down into the ditch and set to work pulling on gear bags. But there was something that kept Jamie watching. Something wasn't quite right. Their visitor had no arms or armor, and had come alone. There was no sign that she was in communication with anyone, though of course she could be wearing a headset, chatting a mile a minute with her controllers. Maybe she had hidden weapons. But he didn't believe it.

There was something in the way she stood, the way she moved, that showed she was new to tracking and searching. And it went further than that. He felt quite certain that she was not hunting them. Not exactly. She was *seeking* them. But he wasn't going to bet his life on a vague impression.

He was just about to move back down into the ditch when he saw her start walking, moving along, plainly following their footsteps. She stopped dead and looked up from the ground, straight in Jamie's direction but without pointing the light. He fought against the impulse to duck. Pavlat eyes weren't that much more sensitive than human eyes, he was far away in the dark, and her night vision must be all but useless at the moment, because she had been using the dazzlingly bright handlight. But he still felt like a jacklighted deer, caught in a car's headlights. He studied her through the scope. There was something in her expression that told him she was not so much *looking* in his direction, as *thinking* about what might be in that direction.

She seemed to reach some sort of decision. She shut off the handlight, went back to her vehicle, climbed in, and drove forward, almost silently, with no other sound than the hum of the wheels on the roadway. Even that sound died as she paused at about the line of their footprints and looked out along their line of travel, as sighting along a landmark.

Then she started up again, and drove off, moving, not toward them, but *parallel* to the edge of the landing field and the drainage ditch. Jamie watched her go in the night scope, feeling relieved and a little bit bewildered.

"She left?" Hannah asked, from close up enough that Jamie almost jumped out of his pressure suit and his skin, all at once. He had been watching their visitor so closely he hadn't even heard Hannah coming back up beside him.

"Ah, well, ah, yeah," Jamie said, trying to settle himself down. He kept watching the vehicle's driving light move smoothly off down the landing field, turning to the left a bit as it followed the edge of the field.

But then the headlight went out. Through the night scope he saw the vehicle take a hard right turn, right off the edge of the landing field. Then the vehicle dropped out of sight as suddenly and completely as if it had fallen down a rabbit hole.

Or a drainage ditch.

Then Jamie understood. Too late, perhaps, but he understood. She was cutting off their line of escape. She would drive into the ditch, then drive back down its length, forcing them to climb out one side or the other, out into the open, where they would be easy to catch, or kill.

*But why turn her headlight out?* he wondered, even as he scrambled down to join Hannah. If she was trying to flush them out, she'd want them to see her—and she'd want to be able to see them. Never mind. "Grab it all, and get out of the ditch, now!" he cried. "Up the side away from the landing pad. Her car's coming, and we need to be out of the ditch and flat to the ground before she gets here!" *And just pray that she drives right past all the chewed-up dirt and mud and grass we've made by thrashing around down here.* It seemed a pretty forlorn hope, but it was all they had.

The two of them, overburdened and thrown off-balance by the gear packs, dropped into the soggy bottom of the ditch. They had been on the landing-side slope of the deep ditch until then. It was only as they tried to move to the other side that they discovered the bottom of the ditch was filled with malodorous squelching mud. It turned to glue the moment it touched the boots of their pressure suits, but when they tried to scramble up the opposite side, it served as a first-class lubricant that sent them sliding back down into the muck.

Dumping their gear and scrambling up the opposite slope more or less unimpeded was not an option. They needed that equipment. Besides, a heap of abandoned supply packs would be a signpost impossible for her to miss. They were going to have to move slowly, methodically, carefully, if they were going to get out of there—but there was no time for that before their visitor came barreling down on them.

They were just barely starting to make progress, stabbing their gloved hands into the soft earth to make their own handholds when they heard the sound of the vehicle's wheels squelching and splashing along through the mud, moving slowly, coming carefully.

*Moving slowly, lights off*, Jamie noted. *Why, when she's trying to flush us out?*

Without any conscious thought on his part, he stopped climbing and had the multigun rifle back in his hands and the night scope to his eyes. There she was, just coming into view around a corner of the ditch, driving slowly and carefully through the muddy bottom of the ditch. Coming slowly, but coming straight for them. They were trapped. Utterly and absolutely. She would drive up to them, and they would have the choice of surrendering at once or making some pointless run for it.

Except—

*Shoot!*

It was a blindingly obvious thing to do. There she

was, literally right in his sights. All he had to do was dial in the sort of ammo he wanted to use, and then—

Except—*why is she alone why isn't she using some sort of comm to coordinate with another team why isn't she using night-vision equipment why*—

Never mind. She's coming straight for us. Her friends chased us halfway around the planet trying to kill us. *Shoot.*

She was getting closer. His finger was on the trigger. He had his target point, right on her throat, had the shot sighted, locked, and tracked. He dialed in GUIDED JET ROUND on the ammo selector. All he had to do was pull the—

"BINDULAN SENDED ME!" she called out. She stopped her vehicle, and through the night scope he could see her peering into the darkness, straining to see. "I mean, Bindulan *sent* me." A pause. "Hello? Is you—*are* you—dere—there? My English rusted—rusty. Understanding me? Bindulan sent me!"

Jamie froze, and held his trigger still, absolutely rigid. The slightest wrong move, and the weapon would fire. It would do no good at all to point it somewhere else with the tracking system live, and with a guided round in the chamber.

"What's she talking about?" Hannah hissed at him. "Who is that? Bindulan is your contact in—"

"Quiet!" Jamie snapped back. "My weapon's hot. If I twitch the wrong way, I'll kill her, whoever she is." He eased back his trigger finger, flipped on the safety, deselected all ammo, powered down the tracking system, and shut off the night scope as well, just to be on the safe side. He checked over the weapon one last time. Then and only then did he allow himself to succumb to the shakes. *I could have killed her I could have killed her Bindulan sent her I could have—*

"Hello? You there? Bindulan sent me—and we have to get out quick!"

The voice roused him, and he turned to Hannah. "Do we buy it?" he asked. "Do we trust her?"

Hannah was about to speak, but before she could reply, the voice called again. "Is you Jamie Mendez and Anna Foxson? Is you? We got to go now!"

Strangely enough, Hannah managed to find a way to laugh at that. "*Now* I'm sold," she said. "Someone might have guessed or found out you contacted Bindulan, though I don't quite see how. The bad guys might even have known enough to call us by name. But getting my name *wrong*—somehow, that's pretty convincing." She turned toward the voice, and called out in a voice calculated to carry, but not too far. "We're coming! We're coming." She scrambled to her feet, grabbing whatever gear she could, and slogged back down the slope toward their visitor's vehicle.

Jamie couldn't follow. Not at first. Not after he had come so close to taking that shot. He shut his eyes, swallowed hard, and forced himself to breathe deep, once, twice, three times. Then he forced his eyes open, reslung his weapon, gathered up the gear bags Hannah had left behind, and trotted along behind her.

He caught up with Hannah just as she reached the vehicle. Their visitor—no, their rescuer—was standing up in front of her seat, her hands still on the controls. Without the benefit of his weapon's night-vision equipment, he couldn't see much of her. All he could tell for sure was what he had guessed already: she was Pavlat, female, youthful, and dressed in a style that denoted a person of high rank.

"Good, come, quick, now," she said, gesturing toward the inside of the vehicle. "I am Zahida. Bindulan be my great-uncle." Her English was sketchy, but something in the way she spoke gave Jamie the impression that she was more fluent than she sounded—just out of practice. Her accent was actually quite good. He placed it as American Southern California, with an overlay of Hispanic influence—pretty close to his own, for that matter.

"Thank you for—" Hannah began.

"Later! Later! Now we go!" said Zahida, cutting her off.

The vehicle was a big open-topped affair, with a perching stool for the driver—more a padded back support for a standing driver than a place to sit down—and the rest of it just an open bed with a padded floor, and a padded waist-high panel-wall wrapped around its edge. They tossed in their gear bags and climbed aboard—and discovered that the floor and side panels were a great deal more comfortable than they looked. It was more like sitting on a big couch than a truck bed.

"Hang on," Zahida said, "because now we go."

There didn't seem to be much to hang on to, but Jamie braced himself as best he could for a sudden lurch forward—then tumbled into Hannah and half the luggage when they gunned in reverse, back the way they had come, the flat-truck bouncing and crashing and splashing along as it straddled the bottom of the ditch.

"Sorry for that!" Zahida called out over the noise. She swiveled her perch stool around, and the control panel came about as well—though she didn't seem to make any use of it. The vehicle was driving itself, running its last route in reverse. "Much less deep behind," she went on, "but hole—hole?"

"Ditch?" Hannah suggested.

"Yes! Ditch I think is deeper going on first way. Better to go back." Zahida fluffed her ears out and flattened them against her head, and, using a human gesture, shook her head ruefully. "My English is got way too rusted."

Jamie didn't much care about the banging and jostling. They were down. They were on the ground. They had been picked up by someone they might imagine trusting. Not safe, exactly—but at least they had some hope of staying alive long enough to—

A flare of light, from nearby.

*WHUMP—WHUMP—WHUMP.*

More flashes of light, not as bright, and more dull, flat, booming noises, and echoes of the first blast bouncing around in the ditch and around the whole spaceport.

"*Gralz talkrit fitz-palp!*" Zahida said, or at least that was what it sounded like. Jamie certainly hadn't learned those words of Pavlat from the speed-learner, but it didn't take much to guess they weren't generally used in polite society. "They are here now already," she announced. "Now we got problems." She brought the flat-truck to a jarring halt, then drove forward a bit, slowly, turning the vehicle a short way, carefully easing them up out of the landing-field side of the ditch. "We need to see," she said, just edging the top of the flat-truck up out of the ditch.

And there was plenty to see. They were about three hundred meters from the remains of the *Lotus.* The whole of the lander was engulfed in flame, all of the smaller blazes merged into one grand inferno. Nor was it hard to see what had caused the change. Two military ground vehicles were parked between them and the ship, and Pavlat on both vehicles were using short-range low-caliber mortars, lobbing round after round of incendiaries into the blazing wreck.

"Destroying the evidence," Hannah said.

"Yes," Zahida agreed, and said nothing more, plainly entranced by the flames.

Jamie looked away from the blaze and at his companions—and realized with a start that he could see them quite plainly. *If any of those guys happen to look this way, with those nice bright flames lighting us up*—"Friend Zahida! Please! Get us back down out of sight!"

"What? Oh! Yes!" She shifted to reverse and backed them slowly down the rise, plainly worried about losing traction in the soft and muddy ground. Jamie gave thanks once again that the Pavlats liked their vehicles quiet. Not that it was likely to have made much difference, with the roaring of the fire and the noise of the incendiaries going off.

They almost got out of sight in time—but not quite. Jamie heard the faint and distant cough of a semi-silenced mortar firing from in back of them. He turned and looked over his shoulder, and saw a third military-style vehicle coming up, still far enough away that they could see the dim reddish flash of another round being shot off a second or two before the sound of the mortar being fired could reach them.

The upcoming vehicle must have spotted their silhouette against the fire. The sound of the second mortar round being fired reached them at almost the same moment that the first round came howling in, off to their left. It slammed into the bottom of the drainage ditch and exploded with a roar, the incendiary charge sizzling and popping angrily, though there wasn't much chance of its being able to set a mud puddle on fire.

But a round like that could certainly set *them* on fire if it managed to hit Zahida's flat-truck. It took less than half a heartbeat for Jamie to see that it was up to him to deal with the situation, if for no other reason than he was the only one with a weapon to hand.

"Get us away from this part of the ditch again!" he shouted at Zahida, trying to find the words that would explain things clearly even if her English was rusty. "They see us against firelight, know we are in this part of ditch."

Zahida understood instantly, reversed them back, then gunned the truck forward again to get away from where they had been seen. She steered the car back down into the center of the ditch and started driving into the darkness and gloom.

But that wasn't the way to escape. Driving along in the ditch couldn't keep them safe for more time than it took the locals to shine a light down into it. Besides, she would have to drive slowly and carefully along a muddy trench, without her lights. Their attackers could drive a lot faster with their lights on, up on the concrete of the landing field. The bad guys could easily outflank them, chase them down, and surround them.

They couldn't run fast enough to get away. They had to fight back, knock out the three vehicles on the spot, then get out of there fast, before reinforcements showed up.

But the days full of cram-study aboard the *Hastings* had taught him that there were times when all-out attack was perfectly legitimate, even obligatory—and other times when the only honorable course was to sit there quietly and die—with dishonorable action subject to severe and nasty punishment. If he got it wrong—well, he had also learned about how the Pavs meted out justice. There were worse ways of dying than a nice clean firefight in a spaceport ambush.

He had to ask, and never mind how strange the question might seem. "Zahida—I must know." He gestured toward their attackers. "They shoot at us, try to kill us. It is allowed, legal, and honorable for us to shoot back, defend ourselves?"

Zahida looked back at him from her driver's seat, her ears fanned out to their maximum extension, a plain sign of astonishment. "But, yes. Of course. This is no inheritance duel! And they violate the Thelm's Hand. Yes, if you have gun, we shoot back!"

"I have gun," Jamie echoed grimly, glad that Zahida clearly had no idea how he had almost *used* that gun. He didn't follow the references to inheritance and the Thelm's Hand, but that could wait. "Stop your flat-truck," he called to her.

"What? What for?" Zahida said. "We need to run, get away. We shoot back if they catch up with us."

"Not *if* they catch. *When*," Jamie said sharply. "They are faster and have friends. We fight, *then* run."

"Who fights them? With what?" she demanded. "You? With *that*?"

Jamie didn't need to know much about Reqwar Pavlat culture to understand the meaning behind the way she gestured at his multigun. Suddenly he was angry—at her, at whoever was shooting at them, at the murk and confusion over what they were supposed to do on Reqwar, and even at the BSI for dumping him into this mess. And even at himself, for what he had nearly done to Zahida—and what he was about to do to the three assault cars up on the landing field. "Yes," he said, his voice hard, cold, holding the anger in.

"If he says he can, he can," Hannah announced flatly. "Do what he tells you to do, and we all live through this. Stop the vehicle."

Her tone of voice made it plain she meant to be taken seriously. Zahida hesitated momentarily, then brought the car to a sudden halt. "Now what?" she asked.

Jamie looked back the way they had come. The ditch was too deep for him to see over the edge, but he could see where the glow from the burning of the *Lotus* was brightest. He pointed toward the glow. "Reverse, and as soon as we're at a spot where you're sure you can do it, get us up out of the ditch and back on the landing pad."

"Go back there and they kill us!"

"Go forward and they kill us just as much," Jamie said. "But if we go back and *fight* them—maybe we have a chance to live. Go back, go back up to the landing pad. Don't stop moving. I will drop off the truck. Drive in a circle around the burning vehicle," he went on, gesturing with both hands to make sure she understood, rusty English and all. It was no time to try out his speed-learned Pavlat standard for the first time. "Not a perfect circle." He moved his index finger in a jittery wheeling pattern. "Go back and forth, make it hard to track you. As you circle, you will be hard to see as you go in and out of light and dark, in and out of smoke. While they are watching you, I will shoot at them. Understand?"

She stared at him, motionless, expressionless, for one, two, three heartbeats, then spoke. "I understand." Without waiting for further orders or explanations, she flipped them into reverse and went back the way they had come.

Jamie shifted over to the forward corner of the flatbed, off to one side of the driver's stool. The flat-truck bounced and shuddered and splashed through the ditch as he struggled to get his suit helmet off. He'd do a lot better shooting without it. Finally, the helmet came free, and he tossed it down into the bed of the truck. He steadied himself as best he could against the back supports and shut his eyes, trying to steady his emotions as well.

The flat-truck hit a bump big enough that it nearly threw him clear earlier than planned and brought him back to the present moment, where he very definitely needed to be.

"Here we are going!" Zahida announced as they came to a stretch where the ditch was a bit shallower. She veered the flat-truck hard over to the left and shifted it back into forward. It slammed into the slope and slithered and swiveled upward, wheels skidding and drive engines straining hard enough that they could actually be heard. Then, suddenly, they were up and over, the front end of the flat-truck crashing down onto level ground.

Time froze. Nothing was in motion, and there was no sound. The assault vehicle that had fired on them was heading for the spot where they had shown themselves. The other two assault vehicles had turned away from the ruins of the *Lotus* and were converging on the same point.

The *Lotus* was a pillar of pure fire, a torch tearing into the sky. Smoke billowed out from the wreckage, and the wind whipped it around into knots and tendrils that vanished and reappeared and shifted and shifted again moment by moment.

There were no other vehicles visible, or any other lights closer than halfway to the horizon. Maybe, maybe, maybe, if they were able to knock out these three assault vehicles, they'd have a chance to escape.

Zahida's flat-truck bounded through another pothole, and the illusory moment of frozen time was gone. Sound, speed, motion, smoke, smells all seemed to come alive again, all at once, as she aimed her flat-truck straight for the *Lotus* and gunned the engine.

Jamie barely had time to judge his drop. He went over the side and landed hard on the ground, just shy of the paved landing field itself. He rolled sideways and came up in the approved prone-firing position. His weapon was in his hands and the ammo selector set to PENETRATING EXPLOSIVE ROUND before he had fully come to rest.

He didn't go to the night scope at once but instead stayed with ambient light as he checked the scene. The headlight of Zahida's flat-truck came on, throwing new light and shadows on the landing pad. She was bearing down on the *Lotus*, veering just slightly away to the right, setting up to drive around the wreck in a tighter circle than Jamie would have suggested.

She was definitely drawing the attention of all three assault vehicles. All of them had been streaking toward the ditch, but now all three slowed down and turned to meet her. The one closest to the ditch, the one that had fired on them already, came to a complete halt.

And none of them had taken the slightest notice of

Jamie. That was the whole idea. He had three targets, spread out over about 180 degrees of view, none of them moving fast.

He had to pick which one to go for first. The one closest to the ditch had come to a dead stop. If he missed with his first shot, all three vehicles would be alerted and start to do evasive driving—and all three would be shooting back. Jamie made a snap decision. Kill the easy one, the sure thing, first, and be sure of only two enemy vehicles coming for him over a ninety-degree field of incoming fire, instead of risking three vehicles over twice as wide a field. Jamie brought the night scope up to his face, put his finger on the trigger, exhaled, and fired at the motionless vehicle in the moment between two heartbeats.

The multigun kicked back violently, and the heavy-caliber round slammed into its target. The penetrating round burrowed deep into the assault vehicle and exploded, instantly touching off secondary explosions as the truck's power supplies overloaded and stored ammo blew up.

Jamie shifted to his left. The two remaining assault vehicles were still coming round in their turns, one of them nearly all the way about and the other pointed straight at him. The one that had completed its turn was more of a threat to Zahida and Hannah, although it was a harder target. He aimed his weapon again and fired. He scored another hit deep in the engine compartment, but this time there were no helpful secondary explosions. Either his luck wasn't as good the second time out, or else the crew of that vehicle was more careful about storing explosive ammo.

It didn't matter. Even if the second AV hadn't blown up, it had caught fire. Jamie used the night scope's image-enhancement mode to see one crewman fall off, a second drop to the ground, drag himself clear, then collapse—and a third who was clearly visible, slumped over and motionless in the cab of the burning vehicle. Jamie knew, in that moment, that it would be that image, that memory, that would stay with him.

The cough of a mortar round being fired brought him back to more pressing concerns. Without thinking or looking, he rolled right, fast, three times, four times before—*BLAM!*

The mortar struck and exploded right where he had been. They must have commanded its autotargeting system to locate the source of the weapons fire and shoot back at it. It had been plain foolishness on Jamie's part to stay in one place long enough to fire two shots at different targets. He had almost been inviting them to triangulate in on him.

The dirt and rocks and mud and bits of exploded mortar rained down on him, and he felt as if someone had just kicked him in the head—which was near enough to the truth. He heard the hissing and sizzling of an incendiary round trying to set fire to wet earth. They hadn't had time to switch to explosive rounds, and that had saved him. A high-explosive shot the size of that incendiary would have killed him for sure— and dug a crater big enough to bury him.

He looked up, and saw that the remaining AV had given up any thought of chasing Zahida and was bearing down on him. He was too shook up by the near miss to set up a precision shot quickly. He fired an unaimed penetrator round in the general direction of the last remaining AV. It struck the ground and blew up about a hundred meters shy of the oncoming vehicle. The blast didn't do any damage, but it did throw up a nice cloud of dust and smoke that would shield him for a second or two. It also distracted the AV long enough for Jamie to shift position again, settle in, preaim his weapon, and wait for the last enemy vehicle to punch through the wall of smoke and head straight for him. But he instantly regretted firing that shot, even if it did do him some good.

The multigun rifle was a superb weapon, but it had a distinct disadvantage. In order to make room for all the gadgetry, and to allow it to fire multiple types of ammo, it could only load a limited number of each type of round. Jamie was down to his last penetrator round. The multigun would automatically default back to standard rifle rounds the next time he fired. He would have the choice of firing standard rounds in hopes of getting lucky and hitting something vital, or else of spending three or four precious seconds to shift over to explosive rounds that would be the next best thing after the penetrators.

Better, far better, to make the next shot count. Get settled. Stay calm. Be ready.

The last assault vehicle broke through the smoke cloud, headlight bright, moving fast, coming straight for him—or straight for where he had been, which was close enough. He could see someone beside the driver with what looked like a plain old-fashioned automatic rifle—which could be a lot more deadly than a self-ranging mortar in the current situation.

The driver was swerving back and forth, trying to make the AV a harder target to hit, but he was already too close. Jamie couldn't have missed if he had wanted to. And Jamie very much wanted to score a hit.

He fired, and nailed the AV, the penetrator smashing into the front power housing and exploding there, snapping the front axle. The AV's chassis crashed to the ground and the whole vehicle flipped over on its side. Jamie almost jammed the ammo selector by trying to flip to explosive while the defaulting system was still dropping back to standard rounds. It took him six seconds, not three or four, to make the switch, and another two to aim and fire the explosive round—and something less than a half second more to realize there had been no need to fire it at all. The AV was burning almost as brightly as the *Lotus* even before the explosive round hit. No one in it could possibly be alive. But then the exploder hit, and went up with a loud and useless bang—and there was barely an assault vehicle there at all.

He set down his weapon, pushed himself up out of the approved position for prone shooting, and knelt on one knee for a minute, trying his hardest not to feel anything, not to think anything. Zahida's flat-truck was squealing out from behind the *Lotus*'s funeral pyre, and came charging back in his general direction, slowing down to dodge the bits and pieces of burning wreckage that littered the area. A handlight came on and started sweeping through the darkness, looking for him.

He scooped up his weapon, got to his feet, and called out, just making a noise, no words at all. The light turned toward him, spearing him in its bright beam. Behind its glare he could hear the sound of the flat-truck coming forward.

"Yes," said Zahida. "Yes. You did it."

Jamie said nothing, but simply climbed aboard and dropped himself into the truck bed. Hannah gave him a quick once-over, shining the light over him, satisfying herself that he hadn't been hit or injured. "All right," she said. "All right." She shut off the light, and Jamie could see her, though only as a shadow in the fire-rippled darkness. She turned to Zahida and spoke. "It's time to go," she said, and turned back to Jamie. "Thanks. You saved us." She turned to Zahida. "And so did you," she went on. "They would have hunted us down for sure if you hadn't gotten here first."

"Their friends still might, if we much stay here," said Zahida, and started her flat-truck going again, rolling smoothly down the landing pad. "We must go. We reach the fence and cut it and be in the forest quick. Then I shall take you to some place safe and quiet."

*Safe and quiet*, Jamie thought. *That sounds like a*

*nice change of pace.* "Let's go," he said. "I'll like to get away from all this."

Zahida said nothing, but turned back to her controls, speeding them all off into the sheltering darkness.

# FOURTEEN · REUNION

Lantrall, Thelm of all Reqwar, sat in the rear seat of his ground vehicle and watched as his security agent examined the displays one last time. Then the agent checked the area personally with the use of an infrared scanner. He turned on his swivel chair and faced the Thelm—without standing. Others might make the foolish mistake of attempting to stand in the presence whilst in a closed low-roof ground vehicle. This agent did not. Protocol gave way to practicalities in matters of security, and attempting to stand in the car would have reduced his ability to protect the Thelm.

… *To protect the Thelm*. It seemed as if everything else revolved around those words. There had been a time, or so the story went, when the Thelm of Reqwar had no need to worry about his own security. The people were happy, the High Thelek and all the other notables were united in support of their Thelm. There had been none who would wish the Thelm ill, let alone try to do him harm.

In those days, if they had ever truly been, the Thelm had walked freely among his people without an escort of any kind. The present Thelm doubted most strongly that there had ever been such days—but even if there had been, they were long gone.

"The area appears secure, my Thelm," the agent said.

*Ah, yes*, Thelm Lantrall thought, *but in these days, how many things are what they appear to be?* "Very well," he said. "Then I shall go in."

"I do not judge that wise, my Thelm," the agent said.

"Your judgment is noted, and appreciated," the Thelm replied. "Nonetheless, I shall go in." He allowed himself a rare moment of levity—dark levity, perhaps, but a jest all the same. "After all, old friend, I go to visit my son. Is that not the one circumstance where it is thought improper for me to be protected?"

"Very true, sir. But the situation is—unusual."

The Thelm nodded sadly. "Yes," he said. "It is. And that is why I judge it as both safe and necessary that I pay this call." He gestured for the guard outside to open the door, and the guard did so.

Thelm Lantrall stepped out into the fine, cool night. If he had listened to his guards, he would never venture outside Thelm's Keep—or, for that matter, would never leave his own quarters inside the Keep. But acceding to their wishes would make it impossible for him to govern.

And, of course, such was the goal of certain elements in his security services: to make the Thelm a virtual prisoner of his protective detail, to prevent him from acting, to control whom he saw and what news he received. There were times when it seemed they were coming close to achieving that goal. But not now. Not tonight.

Not all of his security people had been subverted. There were still many who could be trusted. The challenge came in ensuring that no security agent in the pocket of the High Thelek had a chance to report in soon enough to stop the Thelm from doing what he wished, on the grounds of "security."

The Thelm had waited for a night when a particular team of security agents would be on duty in order to pay this visit—agents who weren't in the pay of the Thelek. The High Thelek would find out sooner or later, of course. But at least he would not find out soon enough to prevent the meeting.

The Thelm walked forward, into the light—and there was light aplenty. The reports were that his host for the evening had searched all of the town before selecting an old sculpture gallery that was the available structure with the fullest view of the interior from the outside. He had then enhanced that view by illuminating the grounds and the exterior of the house in such a way as to keep the interior clearly visible as well. He wanted to be seen, and wanted everyone to know where he was.

He had, by all accounts, succeeded in that. The local authorities had been obliged to erect an automated defense perimeter around the building to hold off the often-hostile crowds that formed during the day. After dark, no one was there except the hovering patrol robots left to watch by night.

One advantage of the automated patrol system was

that unlike flesh-and-blood guards, robots were never startled by the appearance of someone unexpected. The Thelm was, of course, on their basic list of authorized persons, and therefore was allowed to pass without comment.

He ventured through the grounds and up to the entrance. He reached out to press the annunciator, and was not particularly surprised when the door slid open before he could do so. After all, if the idea was to allow anyone—including those hostile to the occupant—to see in, it was only to be expected that the occupant had been careful to arrange matters so he could see out.

The figure that opened the door was, very briefly, in shadow. "Father Lantrall" said the familiar, oddly accented voice, "I am most pleased to see you. Please come in."

The Thelm of all Reqwar did so, and stood to one side as his adopted—and sole surviving—son closed the door and turned to face him.

Georg Hertzmann looked terrible, but that was to be expected. He had been through a great deal and had doubtless been getting less sleep than humans required. But appearance was one thing, and manners were another. Georg bowed in precisely the proper way, bending to exactly the proper angle, and straightened up. "I bid you welcome, my father, Thelm of all Reqwar," he said in his careful, nearly perfect Pavlavian.

"I thank you, my son," said the Thelm. "It is good

to see you. We have not been together since you, ah, tried to depart."

"No, sir. I wished to come to you, but under the circumstances, it would have been neither wise nor possible for me to attempt it."

"No, of course. I understand. And so, now, I come to you. I wish for us to speak together."

Georg gestured to a room at the end of a corridor. "I am glad. I think we would be more comfortable through there, sir."

"Thank you," said the Thelm, and led the way, as protocol required.

If the room was "more" comfortable than the rest of the building, then that comfort was relative. The room was empty, but for a single, severe, straight-backed human chair, and a single Pavlat-style stool. It was obvious the room had once been some sort of gallery display space, and was walled almost entirely in glass. The room was brightly lit, so that the occupants would be plainly visible to anyone outside. That was, after all, the point, but nonetheless, it left the Thelm distinctly uncomfortable. An odd reaction, considering that the whole point of Georg's choosing to live there had been to make the Thelm feel safer.

The Thelm set himself down on the stool and gestured toward the human chair. "Please," he said, "sit."

Georg did so, and looked up at him intently. But protocol required that he speak no more, unless the Thelm spoke in a way that required an answer, and Georg had always been most careful about protocol. But there was, of course, a way around the rules. "I bid you speak, if you wish it, and say what you like," said the Thelm.

"Father, I am sorry," Georg replied on the instant. It was clear the words had been at the ready within him, perhaps for a long time. "I have failed you, and caused you endless trouble."

"Nonsense. It is we, our people, who have caused all the trouble, our own and yours as well. It is not only off-worlders who view some of our customs as misguided, even barbaric. And I should have been forethoughtful enough to see the looming danger. But when I took you as my adopted son, I intended none of this. I had three other sons by birth, all older than you. I did not foresee that all three would—would . . ."

He stood up, unable to speak further, unable to sit still. Georg began to rise hurriedly, but the Thelm gestured for him to sit. "Please," he said. "Stay where you are. Don't go bouncing up and down simply because I wish to stand."

Georg paused a moment, and then settled himself back down. "As you wish, sir," he said. The room was silent for a moment. "Sir, if I might speak further—"

"Yes, yes, please! Speak! Talk to me! We might not have many more chances, you and I. Don't fuss about protocol. Not inside the family."

*The family.* Lantrall was struck by a disturbing thought. His other sons gone, his wife long dead, the heiress-apparent some great-great-niece of his wife, completely under the thumbs of the High Thelek— aside from Georg Hertzmann, aside from this strange, quiet, brave, determined, well-meaning, intelligent, naive half boy half man—aside from this *human*—the Thelm realized that he had no real family at all.

This odd alien, so close to a Pavlat in appearance and so different. The strange coloration and hair patterns, the unsettlingly mobile face muscles, the motionless ears, the unsightly and fragile knob of flesh they called a *nose* there in the center of the face, the hands with the lower thumbs missing, the feet each with one toe too many. And yet, this, this *creature* was his son, in every legal and moral sense of the word. And stranger still, he felt closer to Georg, more fully in the proper relation of father to son, than he had with any of his sons by birth.

Georg hesitated, then spoke. "I—I only wished to express my sorrow at the loss of your three—three *other* sons. The aircar accident that took all their lives was a terrible tragedy."

"It was idiotic," said the Thelm, sharply. "They should never have all gone on the same hunting trip, let alone in the same aircar, precisely *because* Irvtuk's show-off piloting could place us all in this intolerable situation, just as it has done. I know your human phrase, 'do not speak ill of the dead'—but the fact remains that the dead have done ill—very ill—by us. That aircar crash altered the fate of this entire world, in ways of which we cannot yet be sure. And yet, by all reports, all three of them behaved as if there was nothing at stake but their own lives."

"Nonetheless, sir, I grieve."

"Do you? You know as well I do that none of them liked you much, or approved of your adoption.

Thought it was all some foolish bit of symbolism and nothing more." The Thelm surprised himself by talking so angrily, but then wondered why in the world he was so surprised. His three sons by birth had grown apart from him long ago, had come to view him as nothing more than a means to an end, a card to be played when the time was right—and that time had been coming soon when they died. *That* was the true reason he had made the grand and unexpected gesture of adopting an off-worlder, an alien. Georg Hertzmann did not see Thelm Lantrall as a useful tool, a valuable token that could be exchanged at a profit; but instead viewed him as a leader with the daring to waken his people and his world, to move them forward out of the slumberous shadows where they had been for far too long. *Of all my sons, only Georg ever saw me as a father.*

"Whether or not they believed it was mere symbolism, Father, I know that was not the reason."

"Of course not," said the Thelm. There was a moment's awkward silence. So many things they should speak of, and so many things that neither dared to say. But there were things, *useful* things, he could report. "I come with news. When you were first, ah, prevented from departing, I ordered that word be sent to your government. Far too late, I learned that, either by design or by incompetence, the message was translated and sent by a clerk who scarcely spoke Reqwar Pavlavian, let alone any form of English. It was badly garbled. Nonetheless, UniGov dispatched two agents of their Bureau of Special Investigations."

"The BSI? But there's nothing here to investigate."

"True enough. We did not ask for BSI agents. But that is what we were sent. And, I might add, it seems highly doubtful that the agents could possibly discern the actual reason they were summoned from the message."

"Why *were* they?"

"We wanted diplomatic witnesses to the execution," the Thelm said bluntly. "To see that all was carried out according to proper law and ritual, so that there could be no later complaint. And to negotiate the proper procedures and rituals for escorting, ah, the remains home, and to perform that escort duty. But, I am pleased to report, that is all beside the point. We did not ask for law-enforcement agents, but that is what we received—and, despite the best efforts of the High Thelek and his friends, they actually survived their landing at Thelmhome Spaceport."

"It was a bad day for you—for us—when the High Thelek managed to claim the fealty of the spaceport," Georg said.

"Agreed. But at least that little transaction forced him to tip his hand. We knew from then on to watch him—and knew from then on that he was watching us. But to return to the present issue, I have been advised that there is at least some chance that these agents, with a non-Pavlat viewpoint, might be able to find a way out of our problems."

"Father Lantrall, with all due respect, *I* have an outside, non-Pavlat perspective, and a very strong incentive for finding a way out of all this—and *I* haven't come up with anything. I don't dare hope that some-one else can find a way."

"Point taken. But allow me the luxury of hoping on your behalf."

"Yes, Father Lantrall. Of course. I meant no offense—but quite honestly, I do not see what magic answers they might bring."

"We shall see. In the meantime—there is another matter. A thought that recent events brought to my mind. With all the protection and security provided to you, there was one safeguard that I failed to employ. I will employ it now."

The Thelm hesitated a moment, suddenly not sure how Georg would react—and just as suddenly realizing that how Georg reacted mattered a very great deal to him. He almost did not dare take the risk. But no. It was too late to go back. Besides, he felt quite urgently the fatherly impulse to protect his child, and he had no other way to do so. Even if the gesture was pointless, or even ghoulish, it was all he could offer.

He reached up to his neck and lifted off a chain made of fine threads of specially treated silver, steel, and bronze, symbolizing beauty, strength, and wisdom woven together. The metal that gleams, the metal that shields, and the metal made by skill, craft, art, and experience.

The pendant hanging from the chain was a stylized Pavlat hand, held open with both the inner and outer thumbs spread wide, in the traditional gesture of benevolent protection. The hand itself was carved from a piece of the hull metal from the first Pavlat ship to land on Reqwar.

It was meant to be a far grander and more impressive Hand than the ones Zahida Halztec had convinced him to give to her. The cases were different in any event. Thelm Lantrall had granted to Zahida the *authority* to extend the Thelm's Hand. He had not placed Zahida herself under that protection.

However much the Hand he now held was meant to impress, in plain cold fact it was a rather ugly little trinket. It was the weight of overblown symbolism, the provenance of the material from which the Hand itself was made, and the fact that it was given from the Thelm's flesh-and-bone hand that gave the object whatever value it had.

No. That was not true. Not at all. The value it had was that it might save Georg's life. If it did that, if there was even the *chance* that it could do that, then it could be the most ugly, overblown, intrinsically worthless object on the planet, so far as the Thelm was concerned.

He held the chain high over his head and spoke in a loud, clear voice that, somehow, was not as certain or as powerful or as confident as he intended.

"Be it known and published throughout this world that I hereby extend, directly and personally, the Protection of the Thelm's Hand over Georg Hertzmann, adoptive son and heir of Lantrall, Thelm of all Reqwar. Whosoever harms this same Georg Hertzmann, or compasses harm against him, shall be judged as having harmed the Thelm and shall pay the full and heaviest penalty for that crime."

Even to the Thelm, the grand words of ritual seemed faintly absurd when there was no one there but the two of them. But the words of the pronouncement had meaning and value, and were legally binding in the moment they were spoken.

All that remained was to place the chain around his son's neck and speak the final words. "Arise, Georg Herztmann," he said. Informality was all very well for a family chat—but not for the Extension of the Hand. If Georg had remained sitting, then the Thelm would have been obliged to bow or even kneel slightly in order to place the chain properly, and that would never do.

Georg stood, and Thelm Lantrall placed the chain around his neck. It was only then that he remembered that Georg already wore a pendant—the Pax Humana Hand. There was something comforting about that idea—two hands, one Pavlat, one human, one extended to protect, the other offering help. If only it were that simple.

The Thelm moved back a step or two before intoning the last words of the ritual. He spoke with greater conviction than he had a moment before, a conviction that he truly felt. "Now it is done. Now none will dare to harm Georg Hertzmann, so long as Lantrall, Thelm of all Reqwar, shall live." *Except, of course, those responsible for enforcing the sentence already handed down against you for the crime of which you stand convicted.* There was nothing the Thelm could do to protect Georg from *that* peril. Perhaps placing the Hand on his adopted son could do nothing but ease Lantrall's own guilt and shame, if only by the merest trifle. But if the High Thelek got impatient for Georg's death, or, if, by some miracle, a way out *was* found, then perhaps putting Georg under the protection of his Hand would have some practical use.

Georg bowed low, straightened up, and looked upon his adoptive parent. "Thank you, Father Lantrall," he said, a storm of unreadable emotions playing across that strange and alien face. But his feelings, and the Thelm's, were unimportant. None would dare to harm Georg Herztmann without the law's consent so long as Lantrall lived. That was the main thing.

And therein lay an irony so deep, so vast, that no possible single emotion could do it justice.

# FIFTEEN • MINDER

Jamie Mendez leaned across the windowsill and glared out the hexagonal window of Room Four of the Biped Wing of the Standard-Grav-Standard-Air Floor Number Two of Hotel Number Two.

He looked down across fabulous downtown Thelmhome. He was not impressed. Thelmhome was a small, tired, worn-out place. Somehow the entire city looked as if it needed a coat of paint. Thelmhome was immediately adjacent to Thelm's Keep, and to about twenty other things and places with the word "Thelm" in them.

Jamie turned from the hexagonal window to look around the hexagonal cream-colored room he was sharing with Hannah. Or maybe hexagonal prison cell would be more to the point, because even though they could go through the oddly impractical hexagonal door, and even take the hexagonal elevator down to the hexagonal entrance level, that was as far as they could go. Jamie had considered charging through the guards down there and making a break for it, if only for the pleasure of seeing something that didn't have six sides to it. But they weren't allowed out of the hotel unless they had an escort, and the escorts were really quite good at keeping themselves unavailable.

All the room's furnishings appointments were cream-colored, and, if at all possible, hexagonal: the tables that were too high, the perching stools that were wrongly proportioned, the bowls they ate out of. Even the foods in the bowls, no matter what they tasted like, were cream-colored.

If there had been a way to make the various bland-flavored pastes hexagonal, Jamie had no doubt the hotel cooks would have done it. Hannah and he had to eat the stuff to conserve their own emergency stores, but the local cuisine was not up to the standard of BSI field rations—and that wasn't saying much.

But it wasn't just being cooped up, or the bizarre room, or the bland food. It was that none of the murk and muddle seemed to worry Hannah. She had been out in the field plenty of times when her instructions amounted to little more than "solve whatever the problem turns out to be," but he wasn't used to it.

"So how long are we going to be here?" Jamie asked.

"I have no idea," Hannah replied placidly. She was leaning over the table, sketching on a large pad of paper. It was a view from the pilot's seat of the *Lotus*, looking down through the viewport at Thelmhome Spaceport. Jamie had no idea whether she was doing it for her own amusement, to pass the time, or whether she intended it for use in some sort of evidentiary report, if and when they got out of this.

"What the devil is keeping Zahida?" he asked. "What's she planning to do with us—or to us?"

Hannah looked up from her sketch and gave Jamie a wry smile. "See previous answer," she said. "No sense asking me when I know as little as you."

"Sorry," said Jamie. "You're right, I know. But I'm just not used to this sort of thing yet."

"If you're going to be a BSI agent, you'd better learn that patience is a job skill."

"Well, I haven't quite developed it yet."

When Zahida had promised to take them to a place of safety, Jamie had imagined some rustic campsite hidden deep in the forests. But Zahida had different ideas about safety. In a forest camp, they could have disappeared without a trace. In the middle of the city of Thelmhome, that would be much more difficult to arrange.

And so Hannah and Jamie found themselves ensconced in comfort, or at least relative comfort, at the imaginatively named Hotel Number Two, as public and visible a place as one could hope to find, with instructions to wear their Thelm's Hand medallions at all times, just to be on the safe side.

Jamie did not feel "hotel" was the most precise description of their temporary home. After two days in the place, he concluded that Hotel Number Two could have been more accurately named "Medium Security Storage and Confinement Facility for Potentially Troublesome Aliens." But, as Hannah pointed out, that might not be good for business, or easy to fit on a sign.

The Pavlat obviously viewed aliens as an unpleasant necessity, best kept out of the way and out of sight, but close to hand in one place for ease of control. Hotel Two was where all that was accomplished. Hotel Number One was evidence that Reqwar Pavlat xenophobia extended to their own species. It was directly next door, catering to off-world Pavlat, with the idea of keeping *them* all safely penned up as well, so as to prevent the spread of dangerous un-Reqwar ideas.

It took a day or two to learn even that much, while they were very politely but firmly confined to Hotel Number Two. Meanwhile Zahida flitted in and out, checking on them and reporting on the status of an important meeting she was working to arrange— though she was vague on what the meeting was for, or with whom it would be. Jamie and Hannah got the distinct impression that Zahida thought someone else might be listening in.

All she would tell them was that they would need to see the parties in question before the agents did anything else—which left them with no clearer idea of what they were expected to do, or ought to do.

Getting themselves more or less organized and settled after losing everything in the crash kept them somewhat occupied. Clothes were less of an issue than they might have thought. There were one-size-fits-all-but-not-very-well coveralls in one of the emergency packs, which gave them something to wear besides the long-john-style garments worn under their pressure suits. Better still, on the morning after their arrival, Hotel Number Two's Technical Service Department delivered what appeared to be human-style, hand-tailored clothes: undergarments, socks, semiformal working clothes, and even fairly credible shoes. The clothes fit so well that Hannah concluded that (a) Tech Services' database on human clothing was a lot better than their information on human food, (b) Tech Services had done body scans of both of them, probably while they were sleeping, and (c) Tech Services didn't really care if Hannah and Jamie knew how closely they were being observed.

Jamie crossed to the table and refilled his hexagonal cup with coffee. That was the one minor miracle that made it all bearable, somehow: Tech Services had found a way to synthesize something very close to real tea and coffee, and was willing to provide both in unlimited amounts. The trouble was, of course, unlimited amounts of coffee was not the best idea if one was already restless and agitated.

Jamie set his cup down untasted. "I can't take it anymore," he said. "I'm headed up to the General Room." They spent much of their time in the General Room, which was something like a hotel lobby, but not quite, mainly because there was precious little to do in their own room.

"Suit yourself," Hannah said, as she worked on shading in a corner of her drawing. "I'll see you back down here when you can't take it anymore up there."

Jamie couldn't quite find the right words to reply. He settled on a low growl, pulled open the hexagonal door, and stomped out into the hexagonal corridor.

* * *

Hannah did her best to put on a good show. She sketched. She napped. She wrote letters to family that she knew perfectly well she might never be able to send. She was not as calm and at ease as she pretended to be for Jamie's sake, but she was, after all, the senior partner. It wouldn't do for her to start pacing the room. Better to let Jamie blow off as much steam as he could, while putting up a placid front herself. If patience was a job skill, waiting was even more of one.

But there were things she had to tell Jamie at the first opportunity and they dared not talk in the room. They couldn't even risk writing notes to each other—not when they were using pens and paper provided by Tech Services. T.S. might have embedded nano-sized motion detectors in the pens or put pressure sensors in the paper. If so, they could literally play back every movement of the pen, or reproduce every mark on the paper exactly. Even if they hadn't gone to that much trouble, Hannah was sure there were also cameras hidden in the ceiling. Tech Services could simply read over their shoulders.

The necessity of silence, and the urgent need to talk, kept her anxious, in spite of her calm exterior. But real conversation would have to wait until they were able to take an afternoon stroll around the city, away from the insultingly blatant surveillance of Tech Services. Until then, there was little to do but continue her drawings. She sighed and studied her rendition of the *Lotus*'s control panel, then started reworking the perspective on the left side of the sketch.

* * *

The chance to get out came on their third day. Hannah came back into the room after yet another completely pointless prowl around the General Room to find Jamie rushing about their room, getting himself ready—though ready for what Hannah couldn't quite tell. "What's going on?" she asked.

"We've been assigned an escort!" Jamie said, pulling clothes from the cupboard. "We've got permission to go outside. We can leave in"—he checked his wristaid—"eight minutes."

"Let's not keep them waiting," Hannah said. The two of them had some practice with a shortage of privacy. They carefully turned their backs on each other and started changing clothes.

Hannah had thought about this moment, when they were finally allowed out, and planned it out in some detail. She was determined to wear nothing but garments they had brought with them, and never mind if her badly fitting coveralls gave a poor impression of BSI agents to the local populace. Her newly made, locally made clothes were not to be trusted. Tech Services could have easily woven any number of subminiature mikes and transmitters into their nice new outfits. It was a problem that the BSI had faced before, and their BSI-issue clothes actually had jamming circuits and other countermeasures literally woven into the fabric.

She got into her human-made stuff as fast as she could. She even went so far as to wear the big ungainly boots from her pressure suit instead of the much better locally made shoes. "I'm done," she said. "Ready for me?"

"All set."

Hannah turned around—and was more pleased than surprised that Jamie had likewise changed back into nothing but human-made gear. She hadn't dared to warn him, for fear T.S. would overhear and take further steps. She smiled at him. "Those coveralls aren't much," she said. "But on you they look good."

*   *   *

It was a vast relief to get out of the hotel and walk the small and tired city of Thelmhome. Never mind that the sky was gloomy, or that the streets and buildings were shabby, or that the locals glared at them with something between belligerent curiosity and pure hostility, or that their escort—supposedly their guide, but very obviously in fact their minder—was a steady sixteen paces behind them, watching every step they took.

The minder did not speak English, but instead relied on a speech generator that would more or less translate to and from Reqwar Pavlat, or else respond to keyboard commands. To Hannah's amusement, every speech that came out of the generator started with "Honored sirs." As Jamie pointed out, that was at least 75 percent wrong. Only one of them could possibly be a sir, and neither of them was being honored all that much. Their minder was constantly hurrying up to urge the honored sirs to go this way or that way, or suggest the honored sirs look at this shop or not bother about this one. They decided to return the compliment and called their minder Honored-sir.

At least they were out, under an open sky, without anyone trying to kill them. Better still, Zahida had sent word that she had finally arranged their meeting for that very night. There was the prospect of learning the score, of knowing enough to take action, in the very near future.

And at last they could talk. There were, no doubt, dozens of ways for Hotel Number Two's Tech Services—or whoever Tech Services worked for—to listen in on them, even if they were walking in the open. All it would require would be for Tech Services to try hard enough. Hannah, however, had a very strong hunch they wouldn't bother. The whole setup had the feel of a place where the local security thugs tried to watch and listen to *everything*, simply as a matter of routine. It was meant to intimidate as much it was intended to gather information—and probably both those motivations took a backseat to sheer habit. The local spooks watched and listened simply because they had always done that to aliens, and always would.

The flaw in that approach was that it gathered in too much data. It was impossible to evaluate it all quickly—especially when it was in a completely alien language. In all likelihood Jamie and she would be off the planet—or have gotten themselves killed—before the collected material could be translated, analyzed, and put to use.

But there was no point in taking chances, or in

making it easy on Tech Services. The two of them stuck to entirely inconsequential topics of conversation until they came upon a very busy and very noisy demolition site, where some decrepit old structure was being taken down long after it should have been. The work crews were going to have to hurry if they were going to tear it down before it collapsed of its own accord.

It was impossibly loud directly in front of the worksite, but it faced on a sort of bedraggled park, full of half-dead plants. The other three sides of the park were formed by low buildings that produced a splendid barrage of echoes for every boom and crash from the demolition site.

In the center of the park was a small stand of trees and overgrown decorative shrubbery with a path leading into its interior, a small and private space just right for a moment's quiet relaxation—except for the building being torn down next door. So far as Hannah was concerned, it was near to ideal for a private chat. They could talk normally without much need to worry about eavesdroppers, and their minder could stand outside the copse waiting for them for as long as he liked.

"¿Habla Español?" Jamie asked. It was a sensible tactic; the Reqwar Pavlat barely had facilities for dealing with English, let alone any other human languages.

"*Un poquito*," Hannah answered in the same language. "Closer to Spanglish, really. We can switch back and forth when I don't remember the words.

That might even make it harder for them than just staying in Spanish. But don't think it will stop them if they *really* want to know what we say."

"*Comprende*. There could be a high-power distance mike on us right now, good enough so *they* can hear me better than *you* can," Jamie said.

"That's about right." They both knew that even if Tech Services couldn't understand their conversation, they could still record it, then sell the recording to the Kendari Inquiries Service—and the Kendari IS could and would translate it all and add the transcripts to their databases. Hannah sometimes wondered just how thick the IS file on her was. She had not the slightest doubt that the IS had already started a file on Jamie.

Even if the Kendari learned nothing about *this* case in time for it to do any good, they might pick up something about BSI procedures or even on Hannah's and Jamie's attitudes, beliefs, and habits of thought. The Kendari might pull out those files ten years later, while trying to figure out how to deal with Agent Mendez or Agent Wolfson in some other context.

"So we should not talk at all?" Jamie asked.

"*Podemos hablar. Necessito hablar.*" We should talk. We *must* talk. "But no matter what precautions we take, the risks are there—*Comprende?*"

"*Comprendo.*"

"*Mucho bueno*," said Hannah. "Because we need to get a few things straight *e nostromos habemos solo um rapiod tempo*." We won't have much more time. "Honored-sir is going to find some excuse or other to come in, or else he'll discover some security problem that means we have to come out. So let me get to it." She looked at Jamie, hard, for a moment. "We don't know what's going on, but they wouldn't have tried to kill us if the stakes weren't high. Maybe it's the genetic reclamation job. If Georg Hertzmann's taken out of the equation, maybe that job collapses and the whole ecosystem dies. We don't know.

"I've never met Georg Hertzmann. All I know is what I've read in the files and reports, and what we've learned about what he's doing out here. *Ele é simpatico, no?*" He's easy to like, isn't he? "And he's in trouble. I want to be on his side. Help him. And I'm guessing you feel the same way."

Jamie shrugged. "*Certo. Nostromos estamos aqui para ajudar-io. E nuestro job.*"

"No, it isn't," Hannah said sharply. That was what she was afraid Jamie would think. They *weren't* here to help Hertzmann. It *wasn't* their job. "We're here to help the *human race*. The most useful and important thing we can do is to convince the Elder Races that humans are worth troubling themselves with, and to convince them that we play the game fairly. We look out for our people, but we *don't* shield them from justice. If a human does wrong, we don't pretend otherwise. We're *not* defense attorneys here to get Georg Herztmann off on a technicality. We're *not* here to save him—but to act in the best long-range interests of the human race. We're not just cops, not just investigators. We're out here not just to solve crimes, but to represent humanity to a universe full of intelligent species, most of whom don't care about us at all, and some of whom are actively, dangerously, hostile to us. Whatever job we were summoned here to do, remember the job is first, and helping out our fellow humans comes second, by a long shot. *Comprende?*"

"*Comprendo*," Jamie said. "*Pero*—"

And then their minder bustled into the copse. "Excuse-me-honored-sirs-but-there-is-danger," his speech generator burbled, all the words run together as if he had only had to push one button to get the whole preprogrammed announcement to run—which was probably the case.

Jamie shut his mouth, shook his head, and opened it again. "Right on schedule," he said to Hannah as he stood up. He turned to their minder and nodded wearily. "Right," he said. "Terrible, terrible danger," he said. "Let's go. We must flee at once. Thank you so much, Honored-sir, for saving our insignificant lives."

But Honored-sir's speech generator didn't seem to have any button he could push to respond to that.

\* \* \*

Honored-sir the Minder boldly led them clear of the completely undetectable danger and back to Hotel Number Two. There was an unusual amount of hustle and bustle around its entrances when they got back. There were three large and very grand ground vehicles parked outside, with drivers in formal livery standing in the Pavlat equivalent of parade rest in front of each one.

A small crowd had gathered, and there was an

excited buzz of conversation. Jamie and Hannah didn't even bother to ask Honored-sir what it was all about. The obvious way to find out was to head directly up to the General Room on the top floor—where the answer was instantly apparent. There were two beings, a Pavlat and—infuriatingly enough, a *Kendari*—dining at the best table in the room. Indeed, at the moment, the *only* table in the room. Everything else had been cleared away. The normal hum and bustle of the General Room had given way to almost complete silence, though the room was far from empty. A large and respectful crowd of Pavlat, all of them hotel employees as best Hannah could tell, were standing three and four deep behind a rope barrier, staring at the diners.

*Where are all the guests—all the xenos?* Hannah asked herself. At a guess, they had all been told to stay away—or all simply had the *sense* to stay away. *And what in the name of the dark sky devils is a Kendari doing here?*

Whatever was going on was plainly for their benefit. Jamie and she had been allowed straight on up and in, with no word of warning, no mangled order from Honored-sir. Suddenly Hannah understood why they had been allowed out of the hotel in the first place, and why Honored-sir had detected terrible danger at just the moment he had. It was theater. They had been cleared out of the way to set the stage, then, once all was ready, had been summoned back to play their parts in whatever artificial drama this was.

"It's a setup," Hannah whispered to Jamie as they moved forward into the room. "Watch yourself."

"How about watching out for that Kendari having a nice lunch with the High Thelek himself?" Jamie whispered back.

"*What?*" Things had just gotten taken up a notch. "The High Thelek? Are you sure?"

"Either that, or I was wasting all my time memorizing those Pavlat faces and insignia on the ride here."

"Don't get cute," Hannah said tersely. "We need to play this totally straight. He's here for our benefit. I just don't know why." She paused, and looked about the room, just as the crowd parted to let them through, and an obsequious attendant opened the rope barrier and gestured for them to step inside. "Okay," she said, looking straight ahead at the table, smiling faintly, "I've got the field experience and you did more study on Reqwar politics. Which one of us does the talking?"

"I haven't the faintest idea," said Jamie.

"Me either," said Hannah. "We'll make it up as we go."

"Ah, there you both are," High Thelek Saffeer called out. "Come, Agent Wolfson. You too, Agent Mendez. Please, join us."

Senior Inquirist Brox 231 watched nervously as the two human agents approached the table. He glanced over at Thelek Saffeer. The fool was positively radiating confidence, utterly sure that he had already won, that the game was over before it began. The High Thelek had of course known that the humans suspected their Pavlat-made clothes were bugged, and that therefore it was to be expected that the humans would wear their own clothes, however absurd-looking, when they wanted a private chat. The Thelek, Brox knew, had deliberately used that knowledge to arrange for this meeting to take place when the humans were badly dressed. What sort of creature would go to that effort merely to make an opponent look bad?

"Welcome, welcome to you both," the Thelek said.

"Thank for welcome," said the younger of the two humans, the male. Mendez, that was the name. The Thelek had spoken in Reqwar Pavlat, and Mendez had at least done his best to answer in the same language.

"You are of course the brave human lawkeepers Mendez and Wolfson," said the Thelek. "I am known to you. I present Brox 231, of the planet Kendal." It did not escape Brox's notice that the Thelek did not identify him as an Inquirist of the Kendari Inquiries Service. On the other hand, the humans were not likely to assume he had come to Reqwar as a tourist.

Both humans turned to Brox, and nodded very slightly. "My partner and I greet you," said Agent Wolfson, likewise in Pavlat, very stiffly and correctly. *And we don't much like seeing you here*. They didn't say it, but they might as well have done so.

"Please," said the Thelek. "Sit down, join us."

The two humans exchanged a quick glance, a half nod that Brox would not have caught at all, if not for the training he had received on human nonvocal communications. The humans were unsure of their ground, but confident enough about each other to go forward without discussion. Brox felt sure the Thelek hadn't spotted any of that. He was taking a terrible risk with a face-to-face meeting if he couldn't interpret human reactions better than that.

The two humans took to their seats at the two more or less human-style chairs set at the six-sided table, between Brox and the High Thelek. There was no food or drink set at their places, and their chairs were equidistant between Brox and the High Thelek so that they had to sit at the angles of the table, rather than at the sides. All that was theater, of course, and Brox had no doubt the humans were receiving the message that the High Thelek was sending. *We have placed chairs suited to your species, so you know you were expected. We have not arranged a comfortable place for you, or a meal, however, so that you will know you are not worthy to eat with the High Thelek, though Brox the Kendari has received that honor.*

Brox had to wonder why the Thelek had chosen to bring him along to such a public occasion after keeping him hidden away for so long. Certainly part of it was to put him on display in front of the humans, but why do it so publicly? Reqwar Pavlat didn't care for *any* non-Pavlat sentient beings.

Was the Thelek hoping to play off against the current tension by trotting out his alliance with a species that was perceived as being antihuman? That would be giving the Thelek a great deal of credit for subtlety. Saffeer worked almost entirely by instinct and impulse.

And what part was Brox to play here? Was he on display as Saffeer's partner, or advisor, or spy? Were the humans supposed to think he endorsed everything Saffeer said? And would the humans read it the way Saffeer wanted? Had it crossed the High Thelek's mind that the humans might see Brox as his keeper or his instructor? Probably not. The Thelek's imagination might not be much, but his ego was massively strong.

"Ask what is occasion for you us be here?" said Mendez, still struggling with Reqwar Pavlat.

Brox could see that the High Thelek was baffled by the question. He would be willing to bet that it had never occurred to the High Thelek that his guests might not speak his language fluently. He had brought no translation equipment along. "Perhaps it would be wise to use another form of speech," said Brox, speaking for the first time. He turned to Mendez and spoke in middling-fair English. "I doubt Thelek know any human tongue, but he does good talk in Lesser Trade Speech. You talk it?"

It was the female, Wolfson, who answered—in Lesser Trade Speech. "Lesser Trade Speech will be fully acceptable," she said, but then she glanced at her partner. "I believe Agent Mendez is somewhat less practiced in Lesser Trade, but he will at least be able to follow the talk."

Mendez instantly demonstrated he could do more than that. "Notable High Thelek," he said in quite good Lesser Trade, "I politely ask the reason for our meeting here and now."

The Thelek cocked his head to one side and spread his ears out in an expression of relaxed confidence. "To welcome our human guests, and to provide you with useful information."

"Notable High Thelek," said Mendez, "forgive the rudeness, but your allies and subordinates tried most hard to kill us, many times, during our arrival. Your people have spied on us constantly in many ways since we came to Hotel Number Two. I must ask: Why the attacks and spying, and why, now, such a very fine welcome?" Mendez gestured at the table, taking in both the meals in front of Brox and Saffeer and the blank places before the humans. Even the Thelek would be hard-pressed to miss the implied sarcasm.

Brox could not but admire the courage of this young Mendez, though perhaps his judgment was somewhat impaired.

Or perhaps not, for the Thelek did not seem disturbed. "Circumstances change, young human," said the Thelek. The word "young" was mildly insulting in Lesser Trade, as it was in nearly all the languages spoken by the Elder Races. "New information arises. But, most importantly, we meet *here* today, in a place where the Thelm's Law is in effect. Here I enforce *his* commands, and he has commanded that you be kept safe. In my own lands, which, as of quite recently, include the spaceport, I rule by the grant of the Thelm's Will—but I am left entirely to myself in interpreting what his Will would be if he ruled where instead he wills me to rule."

"Even if he does the exact opposite in places where he expresses his Will directly?" asked Agent Wolfson.

"Just so," said the Thelek.

Wolfson touched the pendant at her throat. "Then the Thelm's Hand is of no protection in the lands that you rule by grant of the Thelm's Will?"

"Oh no, that is quite a different matter," said the Thelek. "In effect, the Thelm's Hand places you inside a bubble of Thelm's Land that travels about with you. You are under his direct rule wherever you go, and under his protection."

"Then what of those who fired at our vehicle *after* we landed, after the spaceport security personnel had been told we and our ship were under the Thelm's Hand?" Mendez asked.

"Ah, that was a flaw in procedure," said the Thelek. "Zahida Halztec was empowered to place the two of you under the Thelm's Hand. She was in no way empowered to place your vehicle, or any other inanimate object, under his Hand."

"No doubt the assault car drivers consulted with the best legal authorities before firing on our ship," said Hannah.

"Unlikely, I grant—but my people are well schooled, and well trained—and the power to extend the Thelm's Hand to an object, rather than a person is not valid unless properly published. They *could* have looked it up from the scout cars' data systems. But, as there were no survivors, it is impossible for us to know."

"Your well-trained assault car teams fired on me, directly, when I was well away from the ship," said Mendez. "And I can tell you they made no effort whatsoever to check if anyone was still aboard the craft before they fired at that inanimate object. If we had still been inside, our bubbles of Thelm's Land would not have been much protection."

There was a sudden hint of steel behind the geniality as the Thelek answered. "There are often unanswered questions. You are alive, and now under the Thelm's Hand and Law, both because of where you are and because of the pendants you wear. I would gently suggest that you leave it at that."

"Noble Thelek, I will," said Agent Mendez. "But I am grateful to hear you confirm that we are now and shall remain under the Thelm's Hand, which, needless to say, you honor in all respects."

"Yes, yes, of course," the Thelek said hurriedly, obviously not seeing the trap that had been set.

But Mendez's partner saw it plain, and she snapped it shut on him. "Does not the protection of the Thelm's Hand extend to surveillance and privacy?" she asked. "Has there been some oversight on the part of the attendants here at Hotel Number Two? We are trained to watch for watchers, as it were—but I can tell you the watchers here have not required much skill to detect."

A moment's silence grew longer, and longer still, before the Thelek could reply. "Yes, of course," he said again, quite meaninglessly. He gestured toward the silent crowd that stood observing them all. "As you can see, my popularity is strong. Some subordinates are overzealous, too eager to please me. They seek to anticipate my wishes—and they do not always guess my wishes correctly. I will see to it that surveillance of the two of you on the part of employees of Hotel Number Two will stop."

One would think the human Mendez had spent his whole life comparing the Thelek's promises against his actions, judging by the way he pounced on the glaring loopholes in Saffeer's words. He spoke carefully, shifting to Spoken Greater Trade Writing Language for the purpose. "Forgive me, noble Thelek, for use of the more formal version of speech, but my skill in Lesser Trade Speech sometimes is not complete. I might have missed part of that. Are you promising that, effective immediately, there will be no more listening, watching, datalifting, or other covert information retrieval directed against us, by any person in your employ or under your direct or indirect command? And that there will be no literalist or tortured interpretations of that commitment?"

"I did not say—but, well, yes, of course. All that goes without saying it."

"But now it has been said," Mendez replied. "And all is made clear, to all present."

His command of Lesser Trade Speech might or might not have been limited, but his use of Spoken Greater Trade Writing was highly skilled. Even the High Thelek would have a hard time finding a hole in that promise, given in front of a herd of witnesses he had invited himself.

Brox looked over the BSI agents. The Thelek—and Brox himself—had underestimated these two. But if these humans thought that scoring a point or two would win them the game, then *they* would be underestimating the High Thelek—to a most dangerous degree.

And the Thelek undertook to demonstrate that immediately. "But these are things of the past," said the Thelek, making a dismissive gesture. "I have come here now to do you a service—to provide you with vital information that no one, not even your great friend Zahida Halztec, has seen fit to give you. Indeed, so vital is this information to your work, I was not even aware you did not have it until just today: I assumed it had been provided to you. It shows that you were not wise to trust in a person of such poor pedigree. She is the grandniece of the traitor Bindulan Halztec—an exile of such degraded reputation that it is forbidden to so much as utter his name in the Thelm's presence."

"We'll bear that in mind if we ever meet the Thelm," Mendez said. "Please go on."

"You should know that I have an intelligence service that rivals your own fine organization. And as I am sure you do know, much of the work in intelligence concerns itself not with what is secret, but rather with what is freely available and yet unexamined. Thanks to my private service, I have seen, as you have not, the original version of the message sent to the human government, as well as the mangled version finally delivered to your superiors."

*Private service indeed!* Brox restrained the temptation to growl. Brox and his secret informants were the only intelligence service that had brought Saffeer any useful information on the subject. And yet he was forced to sit here and listen to this nonsense. Was that why he had been brought here, or at least one of the reasons? To force him into a situation where he dared not deny the Thelek's near lies, so that he would be forced to stick to the story in the future?

"Can we take it that there was some significant difference between the two?" Wolfson asked.

"Oh, yes," said the Thelek, "a very great deal of difference indeed. But it was the *absence* of information that told me the most, and is the greatest of reasons that, as I have said, circumstances have changed."

*In other words, why he no longer feels as if he needs to kill you*, thought Brox.

"So," asked Mendez, "it is the change in circumstance, and *not* the awesome respect all hold for the Thelm's Hand over us, that keeps us alive?"

Anger flashed in the Thelek's face, and his ears darkened in color as they folded back hard against the back of his head. Brox marveled at the risks the humans were taking—but then thought to wonder if they *were* risks. The Thelek, after all, had acknowledged publicly that he was not going to harm them, and that he now considered them inviolate.

"Do you question my honor, young human?"

"Noble Thelek," Mendez replied, "I do not believe there is the slightest question concerning your honor."

It was not at all clear to Brox if High Thelek Saffeer saw the double meaning in that answer. But what was starting to become clear was that, in some way, the Thelek *needed* the humans. Even so, Brox had no doubt that the Thelek was already imagining tragic accidents that might befall them the moment their usefulness was at an end.

But of what use to the Thelek *were* the humans? Brox looked to Thelek Saffeer, and it was if he could read the answer in his face, as sharp and legible as words on a datapad: The Thelek planned to use the humans as a tool to further humiliate and isolate the Thelm. The Thelm, Brox had learned, was pinning his hopes on the humans. Let them raise those hopes. Let the hopes distract the Thelm from pursuing other options, on the off chance there was some way out for

the Thelm and Hertzmann that the Thelek had not
blocked. And then let the humans fail, as fail they
must, and dash those hopes altogether.

And, once they had failed—*then* would come the
unfortunate accident.

But the Thelek, of course, said nothing of such
matters. "I am glad to know my honor is beyond
question," said the Thelek, in the aggrieved tones of
one accused unjustly.

That was the amazing thing to Brox. The Thelek
truly *did* believe his honor was unstained. In his mind,
dealing in half-truths, deceptive implications, and
misleading assumptions was quite proper so long as
he did not tell out-and-out lies.

"But I return to my point," the Thelek continued.
"Circumstances have changed—for we now know
more about your mission here."

"I see," said Agent Wolfson, in a carefully neutral
voice. "What is it that you now know?"

The Thelek laughed in triumph. "That you yourselves do not know what it is!"

Neither Mendez nor Wolfson spoke, or moved
in any way. The absolute failure of the two humans
to respond was, in itself, a most eloquent response.
Perhaps *this* was why the Thelek had told Brox to attend, because he knew that Brox had trained to read
and interpret human expressions, and could report
his findings later. If so, then he would have much to
tell the Thelek. The Thelek had scored a hit, and no
doubt.

"You could not *possibly* know," the Thelek went

on, "based on the message that you received. And it is time, past time, for you to learn the truth—for it is far, far past the point at which you could do anything to change the situation. And, for no other reason than because it pleases me, I will tell you that I know what will happen to you next.

"You will be met in your room by Grand-Niece-To-Traitor Zahida Halztec. She is there now and quite unaware that I am in Hotel Number Two. She will take you to a meeting she has been working with such diligence to arrange with the Stannlar Allabex and Cinnabex, and the humans Georg and Marta Hertzmann. Niece-Traitor Zahida believes she has kept the meeting very secret, but now you see the success of that."

*And so much for all of the covert monitoring I arranged*, thought Brox. *Now they will know to be even more careful, to check for Kendari-style listening devices and the like*. But it was too late to stop the Thelek.

"Once you have arrived at this secret meeting, they will very sadly explain that Georg Hertzmann is not guilty of murder. They will tell that you are *not* here to arrange his transport home to serve out his sentence in a human prison." The Thelek paused, and smiled, and his ears fanned out wide, and blushed pink with pleasure. "They will tell you that he is, in fact, the adopted son of the Thelm, and heir to the Thelmship—something else the Niece-Traitor has failed to mention. The problem is that he is also guilty of a crime—of treason, in fact. He is guilty

260 ROGER MACBRIDE ALLEN

of failing in his duty. And his duty, my dear humans, was to follow the strict and unyielding law that requires him, absolutely *requires* him—to kill his father."

The two humans did not respond—at least not in words. But their stunned silence told Brox all he needed to know.

Even the Thelek could read humans at least well enough to know that he had scored again, and scored greatly. "Furthermore," he went on, "there is a time limit involved, and time is growing short. He *must* be the cause of death for Lantrall, Thelm of all Reqwar, before sunset at the Thelm's Keep four days from now—or else he must die in the Thelm's place. You were sent for in order to witness his execution."

And Brox knew the rest, and felt sure the humans could guess it. *And when Hertzmann dies*, thought Brox, staring at the triumphant High Thelek Saffeer, *there will be none left who can stop Saffeer's ascent to the Thelmship*.

It was the goal that, he, Brox, had been working for all this time. It would be the moment when he won, when the humans were denied a triumph, when history would mark the first step toward the Kendari claiming this world.

But in that moment, Brox looked upon the Thelek triumphant, all masks pulled aside to reveal the vortex of scheming ambition that was all there *was* of Caldon Saffeer.

Brox found himself wondering if making Saffeer into the Thelm of all Reqwar would be such a good idea after all. Saffeer was the sort of being who could never be truly satisfied. And that begged the question: When all his schemes were complete, when his ambitions were achieved—then what would he want next? And from whom would he take it?

# SEVENTEEN • **THELM**

Cinnabex drew her forward end to its full height and swiveled her forward sense cluster to face each being around the table in turn. "I thank you all for coming," she said. "Affairs are coming rapidly to a head. There is a great deal our newly arrived visitors must learn quickly."

That much was certain. Jamie felt starved for information—and also a little bit betrayed. How had the High Thelek known what was going on? Jamie and Hannah moved forward through all the events he had predicted, like characters in a dream knowing what came next but unable to do anything about it.

Zahida had indeed been waiting for them in their room. She had summoned them to a meeting she had arranged with precisely the attendees that the Thelek had predicted. Jamie could almost imagine that the High Thelek could have told them what the seating arrangements were going to be.

The idea of a nighttime meeting in a warehouse had instantly summoned a thousand positively ancient clichés into Jamie's mind. The decrepit old structure at midnight full of dark, hulking, abandoned machinery. Broken windows, the sound of water dripping from some leaking pipe that was hidden in the shadows.

The reality was a meeting that started right after dinnertime in a clean, well-lighted, well-maintained building. They were in a large, high-ceilinged warehouse space that took up nearly all of its interior. A small windowless office space had been built against one wall of the main room, and its one door stood slightly ajar.

It was clear why their meeting place had to be in so large a building: The warehouse was where the Stannlar lived when they were in town, and, after all, Stannlar were big.

Jamie found himself wishing he could have taken the time to savor the moment, the experience of seeing two Stannlar right in front of him. Few humans ever saw even one. And in a sense he was seeing more than two—for there seemed to be a constant stream of components of all sorts emerging from their Consortia, going off on various errands, then reentering the Stannlars' main bodies—and, unless Jamie wasn't keeping track of their movements as well as he thought, a few of the little starfish-shaped ones were shuttling back and forth *between* the two main bodies of the Consortia. It was a disconcerting sight.

He shifted his attention to the Hertzmanns. Georg Hertzmann—tall and handsome, with a studiously neutral, even stoic expression on his face. Even to Jamie's eyes, he seemed awfully young to be at the center of all this. And if Hertzmann had been found guilty of treason, why the devil was he allowed to attend secret meetings at night?

How could Hannah and he possibly accept that any human being could be found guilty of *not* committing a murder, then witness his execution, and finally return to Center as if nothing had happened? No. The best interests of the human race included protecting its honor, and to leave Georg Hertzmann to that fate would heap dishonor on all humanity. And Caldon Saffeer ascending to the Thelmship would not likely be good for Reqwar or human involvement on Reqwar.

Jamie glanced over at Hertzmann's wife, Marta Hertzmann. Her expression was defensive, defiant, angry—and she was doing a completely hopeless job of hiding her own fear. How exactly did she fit into things?

"Before we go any further," Hannah said, speaking in Lesser Trade Speech, "we have to tell you that the Thelek knows everything." She quickly described their meeting with Saffeer and Brox, and how accurately the High Thelek had predicted what would happen next. No one around the table seemed particularly surprised by any of it.

"You can bet it's that Kendari Inquirist," Zahida said. "Brox is good. He's very good, and he's developed a lot of contacts—and my guess is he's also just done a lot of good research work."

"I also have to say they had listening devices in our room," Jamie said dourly. "We tried to be careful—we *were* careful—but it's at least possible we gave them some sort of lead, enough for a really good Inquirist to work with."

Hannah laughed bitterly. "I don't see how we could have, given how little we knew—how little we still know—about what's going on."

"That was a large part of the decision not to brief you immediately," said Zahida. "There seemed no point in giving Brox more material to work from."

"But the bugging, the surveillance, is at an end now," said Cinnabex.

"You put that much faith in the Thelek's promises?" Hannah asked in surprise.

"Hardly," Allabex said. "We put our faith in Stannlar jamming equipment." She extended a pair of pseudopods toward the BSI agents. Jamie took what appeared to be a featureless golden coin about three centimeters across. Hannah received a similar coin. "Keep those about your person. Ingest them, tape them to your torsos, wear them as pendants, implant them. Do so however you wish, but keep them close to you, and they will ensure that, whatever device the Kendari or the Thelek's people point at you, it will fail to pick up anything."

"Never mind about the ingesting part," Georg said with a small flash of humor. "I keep having to remind Allabex that things like that might work for Stannlar, but not for humans. I keep mine in here," he said, patting the breast pocket of his tunic, "and it works just fine."

Jamie realized that, somehow, a line had been drawn, sides had been picked, and everyone here was simply assuming the BSI agents were on their side. It might even be true. And while he was entirely prepared to believe that the Stannlar coins would block any Kendari bugging, he was going to assume until it could be proved otherwise that the gadgets would also serve as convenient listening devices for the Stannlar themselves. So long as he didn't say anything he didn't care about the Stannlar twins hearing, it wouldn't matter.

Hannah pocketed her coin with a smile, then got down to business. "Before we go any further—or anywhere at all—my partner and I need to know more. A lot more. We've been getting bits and pieces of the situation. We need someone to start at the beginning and explain what is going on around here."

Marta Hertzmann opened her mouth to speak, and Zahida did the same, but it was Cinnabex who spoke first, cutting off the other two in deferential tones. "Perhaps it would be best if this were explained by one outsider to another," she suggested. "Georg has already told us he would prefer to let someone else do the talking on this point. Marta, of course, has strong emotions about the case, which might make it difficult for her to explain things with enough objectivity. Lady Zahida is also quite close to the situation, both in terms of the politics, and, forgive me, in terms of the ah, biology. I mean no offense."

Zahida shrugged, imitating the human gesture, and sat again. "I am not offended. It might even do some good for me to hear a xeno perspective on this."

"Go ahead if you want to," Marta said, in far less gracious tones, and took her own seat again.

"Excellent,". said Cinnabex. She turned back to Hannah and Jamie. "I suggest we start with the *biological* background to the problem. Georg has remarked to me more than once that humans and Pavlat are almost *too* similar in outward appearance, similar enough that all parties constantly make the mistake of assuming that the two are more alike than they are."

Cinnabex nodded to Allabex. "My split-clone and I are convinced that the primary cultural difference is rooted in a few seemingly trivial biological differences, most especially that regarding the birth ratio between males and females."

"What in the stars could *that* have to do with my husband facing execution for not committing murder?" Marta demanded.

"Stannlar like to take the long view of things," Georg said evenly.

"There's taking the long view—and there's going too far," Marta replied in a half mutter.

Cinnabex went on smoothly. "Birth ratio, we believe, has everything to do with Georg's predicament. Both species usually have one birth per pregnancy, and pregnancies are usually widely spaced. However, there are differences. In human births, males and females are born in roughly a fifty-fifty ratio. Of equal significance, the life expectancy between various human populations varies widely, but, within each population, there is an all-but-inviolate rule: No matter what the average life span for the overall population, women on average live slightly longer than men. One other feature of human biology is of interest. Humans can suffer mental deterioration due to age—and this affects both sexes in more or less similar numbers. However, this is the exception, not the rule. It is quite common for old men and women to retain clear minds and sharp memories until death."

*That* not particularly fascinating bit of news had Zahida sitting bolt upright. Glancing at her, Jamie sensed that they were on the edge of something big, something at the center of it all.

"I should emphasize that in all this I speak in generalities, and there are exceptions to all these statements." Cinnabex paused, and swiveled her forward eye pair about the room. "But consider how profoundly a change, even a slight one, in any of these biological facts would have altered human cultural and political development. If women outnumbered men five to one, would marriage customs be the same? Would the common tradition of the eldest son inheriting all power, wealth, and property on the death of the father have developed if male births were rarer, or if males lived half as long as females?"

"Wait a moment. Did you say the eldest son inherits power *and* property?" Zahida asked. "What do the daughters get?"

"Basically, nothing, under those rules," said Hannah. "But it only really mattered back when most countries were ruled directly by kings. They aren't, anymore."

"But Reqwar is," said Jamie. "What is the Thelm, if not a king?"

"That is a key and vital point," said Cinnabex. "But I call upon my split-clone, Allabex, to speak of the Reqwar Pavlat."

Cinnabex settled back, while Allabex raised herself up a bit, and directed her speech generators, forward eyes, and main ears at the assembly.

"Thank you, Cinnabex," said Allabex. "The prime thing," she began, "is to remember we talk of the *Reqwar* Pavlat, the Pavlat that inhabit this world of Reqwar. Genetically, they are virtually indistinguishable from the Pavlat of other worlds. Culturally—forgive me, Lady Zahida, but they are throwbacks."

"Believe me, I know that much," said Zahida. "That's why I left here in the first place—and why I wasn't too happy when the family said they needed me to come back."

"Very good. Your attitude means I won't have to try so hard to be polite about things. As Cinnabex said, both cultures have a lot of traditions and ways of doing things that can be traced back to pretechnological times. Reqwar was founded, a very long time ago, by Pavlat who wanted to go *back* to the old ways, even pretechnological ways. They banned certain technologies—including certain types of medical assistance and pretty much all forms of genetic engineering. That's the main reason for Cinnabex's, Georg's, Marta's, and my coming here, of course. The Reqwar Pavlat don't know how to restore their ecosystem, so we're here to do it for them."

Allabex looked around the table. "There are also bans on quite straightforward and simple medical processes that are used on other Pavlat worlds to, shall we say, adjust the natural state of affairs."

"You hear that phrase a lot on Reqwar," Zahida said bitterly. "The 'natural state of affairs.' As if being natural was always for the best. A good many deadly poisons are entirely natural."

"So they are," said Allabex absently. "But the point is that, the technical and cultural adjustments made on most Pavlat worlds were long since undone on Reqwar."

"Can someone explain how that plays into the current situation?" Jamie asked.

"No problem," Zahida said bitterly. She held up one hand, extended both thumbs, and counted on three of the four remaining fingers. "There are three big effects of banning modern medicine. One, male births are about three times as common as female births. Two, males live about fifty percent longer than females, if you don't count violent deaths and accidents, which kill off a large fraction of young males. And three, without treatment, males that live past about one hundred and twenty Pavlat years always go senile, in a very slow and gradual way. Females never go senile."

"A very clear summing-up," said Allabex. "There are simple medical procedures to select gender before birth, to extend the lives of females, and to prevent the onset of senility. All three processes are listed in the large number of illegal medical procedures on

Reqwar. They are not practiced at all in the general population here.

"However, any basic statistical analysis of the upper orders, the nobility, on Pavlat makes it plain that both female life extension and male senility prevention must be quite common, though done very quietly. You will find that both male and female members of the upper classes are often very cautious about revealing their ages—for fear that they will be accused of using proscribed medical practices."

Jamie mentally reviewed his briefing materials, and noted that the current Thelm was something like 130 Pavlat years old. No one, of course, would ever admit it, but the inescapable conclusion was that he must have been taking antisenility treatments. *Maybe he's even been taking them without knowing it, because he doesn't want to know. Maybe some ultraloyalist in the kitchen has been putting the treatment in his whrenseed tea without telling him. It would be awfully convenient to keep oneself ignorant about a thing like that.*

Allabex spoke. "Any analysis of human traditions concerning ascension to power and inheritance will show the rules are not meant to protect individuals, but to preserve property and power, and retain them in the family. The Reqwar Pavlat rules are quite different, but have the same effect. There is a surplus of males. Even among the ruling families, they are treated as 'cannon fodder,' to use an unpleasant term. There are endless border squabbles, turf wars, incursions, raids, and so on between the various ministates that aren't supposed to exist, but do. There is a great deal of banditry in the rural areas, and the battles against the bandits produce a more or less constant level of casualties on both sides. Young males are expected to show bravado and daring, to demonstrate their manhood and courage by seeking out dangerous sports and activities. The accident that wiped out the Thelm's sons by birth was by no means unusual. Dueling is popular."

"And females are rare and precious jewels," Zahida said with heavy sarcasm. "My brothers were all expected to go out and get themselves slaughtered in the grand old style to thin the herd. I was supposed to stay home and wait for my marriage to be arranged. I got tired of waiting. I left." She looked around the room defiantly. "I went to lots of places, including Pavlat worlds where they perform a variety of female life extension treatments, most of which leave no medical trace, aside from your not dying early. But there are laws about that here, as Allabex has said. So I won't say more.

"At last I was called back here, as I knew I would be, sooner or later. Family duty. After all, I am a precious jewel—who can be bought and sold, for the right price. I am to be married off to a certain older son with a powerful father and a rich mother, and inherit certain properties of great value. Assuming it all works out, I will benefit from the bargain as well. *I* will do the inheriting. I will own the property and control it."

"Quite right," said Allabex. "The son inherits the

title and the political power. The *wife* of the son inherits the property, and the revenue from the property, on the death of the son's last surviving parent—which is nearly always the father. But it is the historical fact of commonplace male senility, and the cultural solution to the problem, that mainly concern us."

Jamie thought it through out loud. "The Thelm—or the Thelek, or the land-thelm, or just the rich land-owning father—would outlive his wife, and the estate would be entailed during his lifetime, going to his eldest son's wife at the death of the father. But the old boy would just hang around, staying alive forever, but getting a little bit more out of it all the time. He would *control* the land, but not own it outright, and wouldn't have the mental capacity for the job of managing it. There would be infighting and maneuvering to get real control of the property—a regency, or whatever. The son might die violently, and might or might not leave a male heir, a grandson. And the *grandson* might marry and have children, and—well, after a while, there would be lots of rival claimants and factions and family feuds and on and on.

"And as the old boy lived on and on, but had less and less ability to manage things, and the situation got worse and worse, someone might decide it would be a mercy to put him out of his misery—and get the title and the property safely into the hands of the next generation, who had been waiting a long time."

Hannah nodded eagerly. "And after a while, mercy killings of senile old vegetables would get to be a pretty common tradition. It would become an institution, a standard ritual."

"Yes!" said Allabex eagerly. "Now you are indeed starting to see. It *did* become an institution."

"A barbaric one," Hannah said. "Forgive me for saying so, but the moment it became medically possible to prevent the senility—"

"It was too late by then," Zahida said sharply. "Pavlat don't like change. Among the ruling elite, the obligation to kill one's incompetent father had long since come to have the force of law. Reqwar was settled by Pavlat who *really* hated change, and who settled an entire world for the sole purpose of living the way things used to be—or at least the way they imagined things once were. I don't disagree with you. It *is* a barbaric survival. But part of why it survives is that it hardly ever happens anymore."

"Why not?" asked Hannah.

"I was coming to that," said Allabex. "As Lady Zahida has noted, the obligation took on the force of law. It was formalized, codified, regulated. The eldest son was required to kill his father in order to protect the title and the property. But the son was only obliged—or even permitted—to do this after he himself had reached adulthood, only after his father had reached the age of one hundred twenty Pavlat years—and only after the son was married."

And the last piece of the puzzle fell into place for Jamie. "I get it! For the last few hundred years, or even thousands—or maybe longer—lots of members of the nobility have all very quietly gotten antisenility treatments, so there hasn't been any *reason* to kill the father." He thought a moment longer. "And so long as the eldest son *remained unmarried*, he would not be required to kill his father. So eldest sons—probably even most younger sons—wouldn't marry while their fathers lived."

"The funeral wedding, it's called," said Zahida. "The son marries as soon after the death as he possibly can, with the entailment of property shifting onto the son until he marries, so as to ensure the inheritance and protect the property. Very often the funeral and wedding actually take place in the same ceremony."

"The process tends to make sons marry later in life," said Allabex, "and thus lengthens the time between generations. And *that* serves to prevent a situation with three or four or five generations all waiting for the patriarch to pass away."

"So there have been very, very few cases in the who-knows-how-long of a Thelm's son actually having to kill his father," said Hannah, "but at the base of the whole system, the thing driving it, is the *threat* of being required to kill your father. Everything else has been set up to *avoid* that duty."

"And the Thelm's three sons by birth were all unmarried," said Jamie, "probably mostly because of the law we're talking about—but Georg, the adoptive son, had a wife and daughter when he was adopted. And I'll bet no one ever thought that would be an issue."

"Stars in the sky," said Hannah. "So *bang*! in one

split second of bad piloting, the other three sons are wiped out, and Georg, as the sole surviving son, is therefore the eldest, and he *is* married—"

Every eye in the room that could be brought to bear was turned on Marta Hertzmann, and Jamie had the feeling the Stannlar would have pointed their stern-facing eyes on her too, if they could have managed it.

Georg did not respond. He had scarcely spoken all evening. He stared straight ahead, at nothing at all, his face a perfect blank, his hands folded in front of him.

Marta returned their gazes, one after the other, her expression angry, defiant, and miserable. "And so that's the way it is," she said. "If Georg fails to kill the Thelm, he is guilty of treason and will be put to death. If he *does* kill the Thelm—he *becomes* the Thelm. He will step over the corpse of his adopted father, and rule this planet—in complete violation of every oath he ever swore to Pax Humana." She was quiet for a moment, then looked to Jamie and Hannah. "There's the case you've got, if you can call it that. The only mystery, so far as I can see it, would be finding out if there is a way out of this mess. If there is, I haven't found—"

She stopped talking, for suddenly there was the sound of a door swinging open, then footsteps, moving smoothly and confidently toward them. They all turned to look, and saw the door to the warehouse office standing open and a tall, splendidly dressed Pavlat walking toward them. Zahida was instantly on her feet, and so were all the humans. Even the Stannlar managed to raise themselves up a bit.

"Forgive me, all of you," said the Thelm of all Reqwar as he came toward them. "I pray, let there be no ceremony—as I have chosen a most unceremonious entrance."

"Honored Thelm—my father," said Georg, bowing very slightly. "I am—we are *all* honored by your presence."

Marta managed a sort of a curtsy, and Zahida bowed in what was very clearly the approved manner for one of her rank. Concluding that no ceremony meant "some ceremony" in the present context, Jamie did his best to duplicate Zahida's bow, and managed it about a half heartbeat after Hannah.

The Thelm acknowledged them all, and moved smoothly to the table, where he remained standing—as did everyone else. "Lady Zahida did me the kindness of arranging for me to be present—quietly—so I could hear what you had to say. The Thelm too often hears what people *wish* him to hear, or what people believe he wishes to hear. I felt the need to hear your views spoken frankly, as they would be without my being present." He turned toward Cinnabex and Allabex with a slight smile. "I expect your antisurveillance device *is* quite effective against electronics and other technical means—but it can't stop someone in the next room from listening in."

Zahida looked at the others and shrugged apologetically. "The Thelm asked to be here and to listen to the discussion. Making those arrangements was part of what made this meeting hard to set up. I ask that you forgive me for this small deception."

" 'It's easier to get forgiveness than permission,' " Hannah said in a wry tone of voice. "We take no offense."

Jamie muttered some sort of agreement, and the others made similar little speeches—all doubtless doing what Jamie was doing, frantically thinking back over what they had said, wondering if they had made any remark that might greatly offend the Thelm.

Jamie could not help but stare. It was strange to be in the presence of the ruler of a whole planet, especially one that he had been studying intensively, even coming to admire in one way or another, for the last ten or twelve days.

The Thelm acknowledged their bows and curtsies with a modest smile. Then he let his smile fade away and let his voice and expression turn serious. "Thank you," he said. "Thank you all. It is a strange and complex crisis—really a whole series of crises and accidents—that has brought all of us together tonight. I think it might be wise if I summed up the situation as I see it at present. If we all agree as to where we are, perhaps we can better seek out the way ahead—even the way out.

"We are caught in a game—a deadly one. The obvious issue, the immediate issue, is of course whether Georg will live or die. That is of great concern to those of us here, but to the people of Reqwar, there is a larger question. Who shall be the next Thelm of all Reqwar after I am gone? Will it be my adoptive son,

Georg Hertzmann? By law and tradition, his claim is unimpeachable—except that he refuses to kill me. There is also the issue of his not being born a Reqwar Pavlat, but instead being adopted into my family—and, in effect, into my species.

"Georg never sought the post of Thelm, does not want it, and will only accept it out of a sense of duty—and a sense that he must protect the planet from its fate under the other claimant, my distant and estranged kin, the High Thelek Caldon Saffeer.

"But this is not merely a game of who-wins-the-planet. Georg, his wife Marta, Stannlar Allabex, and Stannlar Cinnabex had nearly completed the task of establishing their laboratories and just started arranging for trained technicians to be brought in when this crisis erupted. I am no expert on this point, but as I understand it, various components and subselves of the Stannlar themselves are integral parts of the laboratory. The laboratories cannot function without them, and the subselves cannot operate—or even survive—without the main beings of which they are parts at least remaining on-planet.

"If our Stannlar friends are forced to leave the planet, the labs will not be able to function. If Caldon becomes the Thelm, he will be obliged to throw the human-Stannlar team off the planet and will likely bring in technicians selected by the Kendari, who have been backing him.

"The Stannlar would not remain if Georg were executed, for several reasons. I will note but one. They are, after all, here performing tasks that Reqwar

Pavlat are forbidden to undertake. Might some zealot, inspired by Georg's death, find some forgotten, antique law, some technicality regarding the ban on genetic engineering? Could they be found guilty of violating such a law, be forced to meet the same punishment as Georg? If Georg was put to death, they would quite understandably fear for their own lives."

Allabex nodded her forward sensory array gravely. "Being executed would be a serious inconvenience for us both. Reconstituting ourselves so soon after the split-clone process might well be difficult, expensive, and even dangerous. Neither of us would wish to risk it."

*Being put to death is more than an inconvenience to those of us who don't run off full backup copies of our mentalities once a week*, Jamie thought.

"Just so," said the Thelm. "You would leave. If the High Thelek has his way, you will be forced out before you have the chance to leave voluntarily. He will bring in technicians under his control. And they will not have the expertise, the experience, the data, or the skill of the present operation. According to the estimates from our Stannlar friends, there is close to a zero percent chance of their successfully decrypting the necessary genetic material in time. In short, resolving this crisis will likely decide whether the terrestrial ecosystem of Reqwar survives or not.

"So," he said at last, "there is the situation as I understand it." He turned his attention toward the two BSI agents. "Lawkeeper Mendez. Lawkeeper Wolfson. You were brought here through muddle, confusion, and perhaps even deliberate dereliction of duty on the part of my translation and communications staff. I am looking into that. But only a fool rejects a gift of great value because it can be put to better use than the giver intended. That brings me to the question I came here to ask: Can you do what none of those here have yet been able to do? We are hoping against hope that you have a sufficiently different perspective, that you can see what we cannot. Having heard the situation, understanding the stakes involved—can *you* come up with a way out of this horrible mess? If so, as Thelm of all Reqwar, I do not command you to speak—I beg you to speak."

Jamie felt his stomach tie itself into the tightest knot imaginable. He turned and looked at Hannah. He desperately wanted to speak with her first, to get her advice, to hear her thoughts. But he was face-to-face with the ruler of the world, the ruler he had been reading about and admiring ever since he drew this assignment. He felt compelled to answer, and to speak the truth. "I think I might," he said. Even before the words were out of his mouth, he knew he should have kept silent. He should have spoken later, or not at all. But by then it was too late.

Far, far too late.

There was a general murmur of happy surprise and disbelief in the room, and Jamie held up both his hands in front of himself, palms out; a gesture of warning. "Not a very good idea, or a pleasant or satisfactory one," he cautioned them, "but perhaps it would at least be another way out. And there may be reasons I don't know about that will make it impossible. Will you allow me at least a little time to think on it?"

"Yes. Yes, of course," said the Thelm. "But only a little time—for that is all that we have left."

# EIGHTEEN • LIFE

Hannah looked around the table, and at the individuals ringing the table. It was one of the most absurd and ghastly moments in her professional life. All the individuals looking at Jamie were suddenly illuminated with new hope, new enthusiasm.

But Special Agent James Mendez, BSI, didn't look hopeful. *He* looked scared to death—and Hannah sincerely hoped that it was Senior Special Agent Hannah Wolfson that he was most afraid of.

She stared at her partner—her very young partner—in shock, horror, and more than just a dash of rage. Her first impulse was to drag Jamie out of the room and beat some sense into him, but that would have to wait for later. She forced herself to focus on what was going on in front of her.

"I must return at once to Thelm's Keep," Lantrall was saying. "I slipped away very quietly, and I wish to return before too much notice is taken of my departure." He turned to Jamie. "When you have taken the time you need to think, Lawkeeper Mendez, we will all be most eager to hear your idea. For now, however, let us talk of your comfort." He fanned his ears at Jamie, then at Hannah, in what the briefing data said was a gesture of informal welcome. "'My roof shall be your nightshield,'" he said, in a tone of voice that made it plain it was some sort of quotation or formal statement.

"I—I beg your pardon?" Hannah said, still too distracted to focus properly.

"'My roof shall be your nightshield,'" the Thelm repeated, a faint hint of impatience in his voice.

"It is a formal statement of invitation," Georg said quietly. "You are asked—technically, commanded—to accept the Thelm's hospitality."

Hannah was quite certain from the way he spoke that it was very much a command and by no means a mere technicality. "Oh!" she said. "I see."

"Just so," said the Thelm drily. Probably he had expected Hannah and Jamie to accept with unbounded gratitude, rather than fail to comprehend at all. "You shall sleep tonight—and all nights, until you depart for home—at the Thelm's Keep. Your possessions have already been removed from Hotel Number Two, and by now should already be unpacked in your apartments in my home."

"We thank you most heartily for your hospitality," said Hannah. It would be a relief to be out from under the Thelek's microscope. But would the Thelm's people be any less enthusiastic about monitoring them? And being moved into the Thelm's Keep would be another point of pressure on the two of them, pushing them toward the Thelm's side in his struggle against the Thelek. Sleeping under his roof was something close to a statement of alliance—and of course the Thelm knew that.

That the move was involuntary almost made it worse; it meant they were not truly players in the great and deadly game the Thelm had spoken of—they were game pieces, to be moved around at will, used and discarded as best suited the player who controlled them. It was not all that hard to imagine all Reqwar involved in a civil war, and humanity pulled into it on one side or the other, because of where she and Jamie happened to be sleeping.

But what choice did they have? With their clothes and gear already moved out, they could not go back to Hotel Number Two, even if they had so desired, and they had to sleep somewhere. "It is a great honor that you bestow upon us," said Hannah.

To her relief, Jamie had just enough wit left to chime in. "We thank you for this boon, and for extending to us the comforts of your home."

The Thelm smiled, clearly pleased that the two thick-witted humans had finally managed to understand. "You are most graciously welcome," he said. "You shall travel there with me now, in my private aircar."

"Again, we thank you most gratefully for this further honor," Hannah said.

At that moment, the big doors at the end of the warehouse slid silently open. The Thelm's private vehicle came inside, as quiet as a whisper. Two security-agent types popped out of it and stood at the ready.

There was a brief flurry of farewells. Georg was going to a different destination, and would depart at a different time on a different route, for the sake of security and of keeping a low profile. The Stannlar were going to stay where they were. Everyone else was to travel with the Thelm back to the Thelm's Keep.

Marta and Georg stepped into the office warehouse for a private good-bye, and came out again after a minute, arm in arm, reluctant to be parted once again. The others did their best not to watch, and to offer the couple some sort of time by themselves.

"One thing—well, one of many things I don't understand," said Hannah to Zahida, taking her off to one side and speaking in a low voice. "Not to be rude or anything, but Georg is accused of what amounts to treason."

"Go further," Zahida said. "He has to all intents and purposes been found *guilty* of treason, based on his own sworn statements that he refuses to do what is required. The finding will become permanent if, ah, no change in the situation has taken place before the statutory time period expires in about four days."

"All right, then," Hannah said, making up her mind to be blunt about things, "why is Georg Hertzmann wandering around free? Why hasn't he been locked up?"

Zahida looked at Hannah sharply, then laughed. "Forgive me. To a Reqwar Pavlat like me, the answer is so obvious that the question would never enter my mind. He is free so he will be able to go ahead and— so he can do what is required if he so chooses," she said, correcting herself in midsentence. It was clear that even Zahida thought it best to be careful about what she said. "He has until the time period is expired to 'fulfill his obligation as the eldest son,' as I believe the law reads. Obviously, he has to be at liberty in order to carry out that obligation."

"Obviously," Hannah said, feeling a trifle dizzy. "But he wants to make it as clear as possible he is *not* going to commit the—ah, act." If Zahida was being careful in talking about the Thelm's death, Hannah decided she would do likewise. Was there some law against it, or just a strong tradition? "So he moves out of the Keep and into a glass-walled building and invites the world to keep an eye on him."

"Exactly," said Zahida. "You're starting to understand how we think around here."

"Oh, good," said Hannah.

"*Is* it good?" asked Zahida. "I was about to add, 'if you call that thinking.' But come on. The loving couple has finished their good-byes. Let's get everyone but Georg into the Thelm's car before they start up again."

* * *

The Thelm's aircar took off—and the Thelm started in on Jamie almost before they had leveled off. "I must say again, Lawkeeper Wolfson, Lawkeeper Mendez, how pleased I am—we all are—that the two of you did indeed come to us."

"We are delighted to be here," Hannah lied politely.

"Good, good." Thelm Lantrall hesitated, then

went on, addressing Jamie rather than Hannah. "Forgive me, Lawkeeper Mendez, if I do not indulge in many pleasantries, but things are not very pleasant for any of us just now. The point is, while I very much appreciate the fact that you need time to think things through—and have had next to no time to do it—I wonder if perhaps it might be helpful if you told us *something* of your thoughts on a solution, however imperfect, to our problem. Perhaps one or more of us could help guide your thinking in some way."

*I'll just bet you want to be helpful,* Hannah thought. *And it doesn't have the least thing to do with pressuring him to speak now, would it?* She could hardly blame the Thelm for asking, but she wanted desperately to keep Jamie quiet until she got him alone—but they were there in the Thelm's own private car, traveling to his home, to live under his roof—and, as she had reminded Jamie herself that very afternoon, a BSI agent was supposed to be part-diplomat. What was she supposed to do? Order the Thelm of all Reqwar to be silent? The Thelm probably had it figured that Hannah would want a chance to corner Jamie, and was deliberately leaning on him before she had the chance.

Jamie shifted uncomfortably in his seat. "Before I do that, Great Thelm," said Jamie. "It would be helpful if I asked you a question or two about the legal situation, if that is permitted. We are strangers here, and cannot know all. I might quickly learn whether my idea is of any use."

"Of course, of course," said the Thelm, most earnestly. "Please, go on."

"First off, you are an absolute monarch, or very near to one, and yet it is quite apparent that you cannot protect Georg in the present case. Could you explain that?" Jamie asked.

"A good point. For the very reason that it would invariably put fathers in judgment over their sons, cases concerning mandated parricide are automatically removed from the jurisdiction of any land-thelm or thelek or High Thelek or whatever who would otherwise have the right to lessen or cancel a lawful sentence. I am specifically excluded from granting mercy in such a case as this.

"The Court of High Crime has sole jurisdiction over Georg's case, and I cannot interfere. If I *tried* to interfere, that would be construed as treason after the fact. *After* the fact because the sovereign cannot commit treason against himself. Therefore, in the moment I committed an act deemed treasonous, I would cease to be the sovereign. I would be executed in the same moment as Georg to prevent the survivor of the two of us from claiming that the death of the other removed the legal basis for the charge against the survivor. In other words, if he was killed first, I might claim that my attempt to save him was moot, and therefore my treason was moot, and therefore I was again sovereign. If I was killed before Georg, he might point out that leaving me alive was his crime, now rendered moot, and—well, you see the point."

"I do indeed," said Jamie. "I apologize for bringing up such unpleasant topics."

Everyone else in the car was clearly uncomfortable with the repeated mention of the Thelm's death, but the Thelm was not. Zahida's behavior in their chat at the warehouse made it clear that it was at the very least bad manners to discuss the death of the reigning Thelm. But for all of that, it was the *duty* of the Thelm himself to make arrangements for his own death. It made for tricky conversation.

"Let us talk of perhaps less unpleasant hypotheticals," said Jamie. "I understand that Georg attempted to escape, hoping to avoid the mandated duty that way. It seems that it would have been very convenient for all concerned if he *had* escaped. Why was that prevented?"

The Thelm chuckled. "I ought to flap my ears in indignation and waggle my finger at you for asking why I didn't break my own laws. But you have already seen enough of subordinates being helpfully incompetent and dutifully misunderstanding their orders. However, if Georg *had* escaped, had managed to vanish, leaving me with no immediate heir, and the High Thelek next in line for the Thelmship—then right now we'd have a full-blown civil war on our hands.

"Things have calmed down for the moment—but things might well get very dangerous again, very quickly, if Georg were to, ah, meet his punishment in four days. There are many of my people who would not stand for the High Thelek being next in line to take over. They might well see violence as the only way out. And the High Thelek might judge, and judge rightly, that his only chance to triumph, or even to survive, would be a bit of preemptive violence on his part.

"Beyond all that, Georg misjudged the political situation quite badly when he chose which way to run. At the time my guards caught him, he was headed straight for the border of lands belonging to a certain local landowner who had shown great loyalty to the High Thelek—and great skill in misunderstanding orders correctly. Georg would not have survived a day in his custody."

"Would the same problems apply to Georg's openly going into exile?" Hannah asked, hoping to divert the conversation away from whatever Jamie's bright idea was. The Thelm was clearly in a mood to talk. Maybe she could string him along until the car landed. Maybe then she could find some way to grab Jamie and talk to him alone for five minutes—for half a minute—before any more damage could be done. "I have heard and seen references to a law that seems to say that nobles who depart the planet without leave from the Thelm are stripped of their titles. Wouldn't that apply to Georg?"

"No, and for two reasons," said the Thelm. "First, the same law that takes him out of my jurisdiction of mercy removes him from my jurisdiction of permission, and for similar reasons. If a noble leaves the planet without my permission, I am not *required* to strip him of his titles, lands, properties, and wealth—but I can if I so choose. I have the discretion, and use it, on a case-by-case basis. The knowledge that I could slows the departure of our wealthier citizens, believe me.

"But this must not be applied to the heir. Say that Georg was opposed to one of my policies, argued against it, and planned to reverse the policy when he came to power. Say that I grew weary of his complaints, and, perhaps wanted to protect my policy. All I would have to do would be to force him off the planet by whatever means I wished, fair or foul, or perhaps just wait until he went on a holiday somewhere, declare that he had departed without leave, then debar him from the succession. The law prevents such abuses.

"The second reason is that Georg could come *back*, despite being debarred, weeks or months or years or decades later. Our history is full of exiles who return, have people flock to their cause, and stir up no end of trouble for the Thelm of the day." He smiled. "I will deny it if you quote me publicly, but that more or less describes how *my* great-great-great-grandfather came to the Thelmship.

"And if Georg were exiled," the Thelm went on, "he would not even need to come back in order to become an automatic focus point for dissent against my rule, or that of my successor, whoever that might be. He would not even need to take an active part in the dissent. He could even publicly denounce the dissenters, and it might not matter. His mere existence would be a temptation to plotters and conspirators as long as he lived—perhaps longer. They would only need to say that he was secretly with them, or some such nonsense. Forgive me for even mentioning this, my dear Marta, but if Georg were exiled, and then died, you, or even his daughter, Moira, might become some sort of involuntary rallying point or bargaining chip."

Jamie nodded. "That all makes sense," he said. "But I think—I *think*—none of it presents any impediment to my not-very-pleasant or satisfactory solution. Am I correct in assuming that the political situation has now stabilized somewhat? The facts on the ground might not be greatly changed, but emotions are now not running as high?"

"A fair summing-up."

Jamie leaned forward toward the Thelm and spoke intently. "I assume you still feel it vital that the High Thelek not be your successor."

"Yes, that is essential."

"Very well. So, if I have it straight, the reason exile is no good is that Georg *might* come back. Someone could claim to be revolting in his name, clearing the way for his return—even if Georg had nothing to do with the revolt. But if Georg left the planet, under circumstances where it would be *impossible* for him to return, and that was made clear to the public—would it be possible for you to arrange an alternate successor? Perhaps by adopting a suitable young noble? Forgive me if that is a distasteful suggestion, but I do not know your ways well enough to know what is and is not proper."

The Thelm thought. "If Georg departed in such a

way that he could *not* return—though I don't see how that can be assured—and if things were done quietly, carefully, slowly—then yes, it might be possible. The High Thelek would make no end of trouble, getting that near the prize, then being pushed away—but perhaps he could be bought off. Name him the Regent-Designate during the young heir's minority, if I picked someone young."

Jamie leaned farther forward, his voice eager, caution forgotten. "Then maybe, maybe, it is possible. My idea is Penitence."

Hannah cringed, and her insides tied up in knots. *Oh, Jamie Mendez, you bloody fool.*

Everyone else in the passenger compartment, even Zahida, reacted with surprise, even alarm, but the Thelm merely frowned and looked puzzled. "I don't quite see how Georg's expressing sorrow and regret will solve the problem," he said.

Jamie was puzzled in turn for a moment, then understood the point of confusion. "What? Oh! No, no, forgive me, noble Thelm. I used the Lesser Trade word, when I should have used the English-language place name, *Penitence*. It is a place so well known—perhaps I should say notorious—among humans, or even anyone who has spent time with humans, that I forgot that you would not know of it."

"Penitence is a penal colony," said Hannah, her voice stiff and precise. "It is used instead of capital punishment by most human governments."

"Without going into a lot of detail, it has been designed so that it is difficult to get to—but impossible to leave," said Jamie.

"It is also a hellishly nasty and dangerous place," said Marta, speaking for the first time since they entered the car. "It might not technically be a death sentence to send Georg there, but you would almost certainly be sending him to an early and unpleasant death. That it is used *instead* of a death sentence should tell you a lot."

Hannah swore under her breath. Mendez was a fool twice over for having made the suggestion while Georg's wife was there to hear it. But too late now.

"It isn't a good place to be," said Jamie. "I won't pretend it is. I said my solution wasn't very good. But surely, noble Thelm, it is better than Georg's being executed, or his being forced to kill you. And, of course, it would have to be a voluntary exile. He would have to agree."

Zahida winced visibly, and Hannah cursed. How could he have so little sense that he spoke *that* bluntly of the Thelm's death in the Thelm's presence?

But the Thelm did not seem to notice, or care. He was thinking, considering. "What of his family?" the Thelm asked. "Do you propose sending them, as well? Or do you propose sundering husband from wife, father from daughter, for all time?"

"Noble Thelm, to be honest, I have not had the chance to think that far."

"It is even possible, permissible, to send the family there?" asked the Thelm.

Jamie shifted uncertainly, and glanced to his right, where Marta sat, speechless with fear, rage, doubt, anger.

*And who could blame her?* Hannah asked herself. After all, just a few moments before, the Thelm had been pointing out that Marta or their daughter Moira might potentially become a focus of dissent if Georg were removed from the scene. Obviously, it was the Thelm of all Reqwar doing the talking and the thinking, not loving and indulgent Grampa Lantrall. And *was* he even wrong to consider exiling them, as well? If they went away and could never, ever, come back— then they would be as good as dead, insofar as serving as a rallying point for dissent.

Jamie's face grew pale as he spoke into the silence. "It is possible and permissible, under some circumstances, noble Thelm," he said. "I will not attempt to make things sound better than they are. Penitence is a rough and wild place, settled by murderers and worse. But there are fortified towns, defended places, where the settler-prisoners—and the descendants of settler-prisoners—struggle to make a decent home for themselves. If this thing was done, I am certain that arrangements could be made to land Georg Hertzmann, and, if it came to that, his family, in such a defended town. It would be a matter of landing enough materials, equipment, and supplies with each person in order to compensate for accommodating new mouths to feed, new backs to watch."

Hannah shook her head. What the devil else was Jamie going to commit the human race to? She had to speak. She knew better than to disagree with her partner in the midst of outsiders, in the presence of the Thelm, but she could at least point out the difficulties. "I must emphasize that the road to Penitence is strictly one-way," she said. "Going there would be a life sentence, a permanent exile, for whoever was sent. Leaving alone the question of what is and isn't physically possible, there is a moral element, an ethical element, that will have a strong effect. I can tell you for certain that the United Government of Humanity and the people of Earth and the human worlds will not like these ideas. It would be bad enough to send someone there as a punishment for *not* committing murder. It would be far worse to send someone there as punishment for being *related* to someone being punished for not committing murder. Speaking personally, I cannot advise sending a child there under any circumstances."

"Can you advise that a son be required to kill his father?" the Thelm demanded. "Can you advise that a father be forced to stand by and permit the execution of his son—for the crime of letting that father live? Can you advise that I require *all* the fathers and sons and mothers and daughters of Reqwar to live under the rule of an unprincipled, unthinking opportunist like the Thelm whom Caldon Saffeer would become, and be required to suffer his government, and the political upheavals and ecological collapse it will likely cause if he succeeds me?

"Shall I spare one or two or three individuals of the necessity of living in an unpleasant place, and instead allow starvation, food riots, planetary climate failure, and the death of Reqwar? You frame it as my choosing this or that for my family, for those that I love. But it is a choice between death and life for my people, my world, whatever the consequences for individuals. And if that is the case, then I will choose *life*—life for my people, life for my son who would otherwise die, life for his family, albeit life in a cruel place—and yes, my life as well."

There was silence in the passenger compartment of the Thelm's car as Thelm Lantrall thought through the new idea, the dangers and the possibilities. It was Marta who dared to break in on his thoughts. "Father Lantrall!" she said at last. "Please! Do not do this! Find some other way, some other place to send us."

The Thelm, lost in his thoughts, looked up sharply, an irritated expression on his face, quickly covered by a kindly smile that was not entirely real. "Stay calm, wife of my son. Of course we will pursue other possibilities. As Lawkeeper Mendez points out, even he has had next to no time at all to think this through. There may well be other ways, other places. But time is short." He looked back at Jamie, and his expression grew serious again. "If—*if*—we were to do this thing, many things would have to be accomplished first. Legal arrangements, announcements to the public— that side of the business—leave all that to me."

"Yes, noble Thelm," said Jamie.

Hannah frowned. *Don't worry, Jamie. The Thelm will also take care of browbeating Georg into saying yes, and then browbeating him into taking his family along. It will be harder—much harder—to bully Marta into going along with it, but I'll bet he can do that, too.*

"Very good," the Thelm was saying. "I promise there will still be work enough for you to do. I assume you would have to contact your government, make whatever arrangements are required at this Penitence place for new arrivals, get various approvals."

*And now, somehow, suddenly, we aren't his allies anymore. We're his subordinates, his staff,* Hannah thought, then spoke out loud. "That would be the start of it." Maybe the paperwork angle would be the way to stop this thing. Emphasize those difficulties as well. "Frankly, honored Thelm, I doubt all the arrangements could be made in four days' time— especially if we have to work through QuickBeam messages, and all the time-zone changes between here and the various offices and departments that would be involved."

"No, I understand all that. But if we—if you— could make a *start* on all that, a good, substantial start, then I believe that would be enough to bring before the Court of High Crime and arrange a stay of execution. And, of course, Georg would have to be held in custody, once the remainder of the time period allowed for his killing me had expired..." The Thelm was lost in thought again for a moment. Hannah felt as if she were watching a master game player studying his board, considering how best to move his pieces— what to sacrifice and what to protect.

Then he came back to himself, just as the car was

approaching the Keep. "Pardon me," he said. "There is suddenly a great deal to think about. I would be most appreciative, Lawkeeper Mendez, Lawkeeper Wolfson, if you could get started on making those arrangements—on a contingency basis, of course. And, needless to say, if you, Lawkeeper Mendez—if any of you—come up with a better solution, come to me, personally, with it—at any time of day or night."

But Hannah could see, clear as day, that his mind was made up. The contingency was already reality, as far as the Thelm was concerned. He would make it happen. In his mind, it had *already* happened. He was probably running through possible candidates for his designated heir.

The car drew to a halt in the courtyard of the Keep, and instantly a guard had the door open and the Thelm was out of the car and being escorted inside.

Hannah, Jamie, Marta, and Zahida got out of the car and watched the Thelm walk toward the main ceremonial entrance of his Keep.

"You shouldn't have given him that idea," said Zahida to Jamie. "Now he'll latch on to it, and never let go. I know exile. I know how hard it is, how little choice even a 'voluntary' exile really has. But now that the Thelm is focused on it, even if someone comes up with another idea, another solution—he'll want to stay with this one. No matter who gets hurt."

Hannah looked at Zahida, and was startled by the anger in her face as she watched her Thelm retreat into his Keep. "No matter who," she said again.

The ornate doors swung open ahead of the Thelm. He stepped through them, and they swung shut again, with a low, solid boom that echoed across the courtyard.

The Thelm was back in his Keep.

# NINETEEN · **DEATH**

The two agents were alone. Hannah looked around their quarters in the Keep with the eye of a practiced traveler, seeing what sort of place she'd be calling home for the next little while. "Well," she said at last, "whatever else has gone wrong today, at least our accommodations have improved." Jamie didn't answer. He just slumped in a chair and stared at nothing at all.

Hannah ignored him for the moment. If he felt bad, he should, and she was in no mood to play cheerleader. Instead, she indulged herself in a brief exploration of their apartments.

There was a large common room, a proper washroom, and, best of all, two small but private bedrooms. The main room was large, with polished stone walls and heavy planked-wood floors, and high, arched ceilings. There was only one tiny window per room, each about eighty centimeters high by forty wide, almost too high to look out of. The window had sturdy steel bars, too narrow to get through, set into the interior sides of the window frames. Skillful interior lighting kept the rooms from feeling claustrophobic despite the small windows. The rooms were appointed with quite credible human-style furniture;

more or less real chairs, tables, and beds. Everything was a copy of a copy of a copy, but that didn't matter.

A late supper had been waiting for them in the common room when they arrived, plates filled with better food than anything they had seen thus far on Reqwar. However, neither of them was in much of a mood to enjoy a good meal. Hannah sat down to eat regardless. Jamie took his cue from her and started in as well. They ate in silence. Hannah forced her food down out of a sense of duty, because agents in the field ate when they could, because they never knew when the next meal might come. Jamie seemed to be eating with about the same attitude. The two of them worked through the food in front of them without saying anything much.

But Hannah knew she had some other duties beside keeping herself fed—such as a duty to herself and to the mission to say what had to be said. It couldn't be avoided any longer. She finished eating, set down her utensils, and leaned back in her chair. "Zahida was right," she said. "You should never have given the Thelm the idea of using Penitence."

"I know," Jamie said quietly. "It was a mistake. A huge mistake. I knew it was the wrong move before I was finished saying I had an idea—but it was already too late by then."

Hannah felt a brief and irrational annoyance at Jamie for denying her the argument she was all set to have with him. She was sorely tempted to pick the fight anyway, just so she could give him a good yelling-at. Stars and Space knew he deserved it. But it could

304 ■ ROGER MACBRIDE ALLEN

accomplish nothing—and would almost certainly interfere with their ability to deal with the situation. Better to be cold, analytic, brutally logical. "You fouled up," she said. "Hugely. Massively. I'm not going to try to make it look pretty to you, now, or in the mission report—if we live long enough to file one. You've done very well, otherwise, on this mission. But you could have just created a disaster. Interstellar incident stuff. It's going to take some *really* good work, from both of us—plus a run of luck—in order to undo the damage this has done."

"I know," Jamie said. "I know."

She resisted the temptation to beat on him harder. There was too much at stake. "So what do we do now?" she asked. She looked down at her utensil. It wasn't quite a fork, but it served as one—but you had to be careful with it, or the side-pointing prongs would stab you on the inside of your mouth. And what the devil were the side-pointing prongs *for*, anyway? So many things were like that here—almost, but not quite, like what you expected—and the differences could easily turn around and bite you.

"I don't know," Jamie replied. "It would be nice if at least one of us could dream up another way out. Is there any other place in human-controlled space where you can go in, but can't ever get out? A place not as bad as Penitence?"

Hannah laughed bitterly. "That sounds like a straight line for a joke about whatever city or town you don't like much. But no. I don't think there is. That's what makes Penitence a semiplausible solution, if you don't think about it too hard," she said. "It's a *real* one-way trip. No one has ever come back. If we can give the Thelm *that* part of it, some other way than exile to a penal colony, then he'd be glad to forget Penitence."

"Death's the only guaranteed one-way trip that I can think of just at the moment," said Jamie.

*But would it have to be Georg's death?* asked a nasty little voice in the base of Hannah's skull. She didn't want to listen to such ideas. She stood up from the table, collected her plate, and carried it to the small gallery to one side of the common room. "Oh, well," she said. "They wanted us to pull a rabbit out of our hats, and you did. It's just a mangy, ugly, bad-tempered rabbit, that's all."

"So let's hope we can reach in again and pull out a nicer-looking specimen—is that it?" Jamie asked ruefully.

"Best suggestion I can come up with right now," Hannah said. She knew she ought to yell at Jamie more, and longer—but they were both exhausted, and anyway, she doubted he could feel much worse about things than he already did. "I suggest we get some sleep and start trying to come up with our nicer-looking rabbit tomorrow. It's been a long day. Let's see what we come up with in the morning."

"All right," said Jamie. "I'm too tired to think straight anyway—and that looked a lot like a regular human-style bed in my room. I'm going to sleep on the problem."

"Good," said Hannah. "But do me a favor. If you

come up with any other brilliant suggestions, clear them with me first, okay?"

Jamie's face reddened, and he nodded, his eyes cast down. "Okay," he said, "I promise I will. Believe me, I'm not going to pull *that* stunt twice."

"Then let's both go get some sleep," said Hannah. "I'll finish tearing your head off in the morning."

\* \* \*

Immediately after Georg Hertzmann made his farewells, Allabex and Cinnabex secured all entrances to the warehouse, recalled their subcomponents, completed all short-term tasks and interim backups, then ended all other volitional activity in order to consult with each other intensively.

Allabex: *"Events are moving to a crisis. The arrival of the two human investigators has acted as a catalyst."*

Cinnabex: *"Things would be happening rapidly even if they had not arrived. Georg Hertzmann either must fulfill his obligations within four days, or else be put to death. Events would move to a climax even without the agents."*

Allabex: *"Granted. Nonetheless, they have already altered events significantly, to the point where we have no reliable basis for prediction."*

Cinnabex: *"I do not concur. While short-term events are difficult to predict, there is no longer any plausible medium-term scenario in which Georg Hertzmann returns to work with us. Our project will therefore likely lose the political support, the techni-*

*cal expertise, and the human business contacts that he provided. Further, it will be far more difficult to recruit the human technicians upon which our plans rely. It is also increasingly likely that we will lose the contribution made by Marta Hertzmann. However, as her part in the project is nearly complete, this is not as significant an issue."*

Allabex: *"[Pause]. You are correct. My analysis focused far too much on the short term, and on the fates of individuals."*

Allabex: *"Without the benefits that Georg Hertzmann could bring to the project, it cannot succeed as currently planned. If he is killed, then I believe it highly probably that our own continuities of existence could be endangered. Furthermore, there is increased stress on and danger to the terrestrial ecosystem with every passing moment. Soon it will reach the point of irretrievable failure—if it has not done so already. Irrational beings might blame us for the failure—and there is no shortage of irrational beings here. I believe we must commence our emergency plan at once. We must act now and not wait until the Hertzmanns are removed from the scene and we ourselves are in peril."*

Allabex: *"[Pause]. [Pause]. I signal most reluctant concurrence."*

Cinnabex: *"Let us begin at once."*

\* \* \*

Jamie got between the covers in his nearly-like-a-regular bed, and found himself staring at the ceiling.

His almost offhand suggestion was likely to uproot an entire family, sentence them all to life in a hellish place, and perhaps change the course of history on Reqwar. It was terrifying that a few words from a glorified police officer could change things that much. Might some future careless choice or act of his, something he never even thought again of afterward, perhaps wasn't even aware of doing—change everything for some group of total strangers and innocents?

Maybe Pax Humana's ideas about nonviolence didn't go far enough. Maybe noninterference would be safer. Or even nonaction. Sit still, do nothing, say nothing, take no chances, take no blame, let someone else deal with the mess. Absurd and impossible, of course, but quite an attractive idea to Jamie at the moment. He left it at that as exhaustion won its fight with worry, and he dropped off to sleep.

\* \* \*

Half an hour after getting to bed, Hannah relearned something she knew all too well already. Life was completely unfair. She could tell by the low, peaceful snores coming from the other small bedroom that Jamie, guilty of causing all sorts of trouble, was deeply and completely asleep, while she, guilty of nothing at all, was utterly and irrevocably awake.

She cursed silently to herself. *As long as I'm awake, I might as well start paying for Jamie's sins.* She had been staring at the ceiling, mentally drafting a signal to BSI HQ, trying to find an acceptable way of asking if they could please make a reservation for two adults and one child on Penitence. She might as well get up and do it for real. She toyed, for a moment, with the idea of making Jamie draft the request himself in the morning. But somehow, forcing Jamie to write the thing, even forcing him to do long-distance battle with the bureaucrats, didn't really seem quite in proportion with little Moira Hertzmann's having to spend the rest of her life in a living hell like Penitence. Such a trifling punishment wouldn't fit the crime. It would do worse—it would trivialize the crime. Besides, this was the sort of drafting she was better at than he was. She got back out of bed and got to work.

\* \* \*

A few minutes later she was standing in the small galley area of the main room, getting some coffee made while she mentally struggled to find some way to say what needed to be said. The devil of it was that what the Thelm had said was all true—if the cost of saving a world from climate collapse was the exile of three people to an unpleasant situation, then surely that was an equitable bargain. But what if Georg wasn't willing to cooperate? The assumption inherent in Jamie's idea was that he would be a willing sacrificial lamb. And Jamie's idea had been to send him, alone. Georg Hertzmann *might* be willing to accept that, in order to save Reqwar from the Thelek, and from the Kendari's inept genetic engineering. But what if, instead of one man nobly and willingly sacrificing himself, they had to pack off three unwilling, violently protesting victims? How would *that* play on Reqwar? Or on Earth, or Center? Or with Pax Humana?

And, of course, they only had the word of the Kendari's competitors that Kendari-hired gene engineers would fail. Hannah had been up against the Kendari enough times to know they played rough, and played to win, enough to know that she didn't much like them—but that didn't mean they were bad at genetic decryption.

For that matter, Jamie's idea assumed that the human-Stannlar collaboration could or would go forward without Georg's presence. Suppose the work simply couldn't go on without him? Or what if the Stannlar *could* do the work, but refused to do so if their partner was exiled?

There seemed no end to the holes in Jamie's clever little solution. All of those flaws, and more, would occur to her superiors as soon as their signal arrived. She and Jamie would have to be prepared with answers for all of them. It was going to be a long slog ahead, and an uncertain result.

The coffee was finished. She poured herself a cup and went to the window, reaching through the iron bars to undo the catch on the glass window outside. She swung the window open to get some air into the room. It was a cool, crisp night, the air full of fitful breezes that seemed to rush up out of nowhere, promise to do great things, then vanish before they accomplished much of anything.

She took a sip of her coffee—and frowned at the flavor. No, not the flavor. The flavor was all right—it was the aroma of the coffee that was off. It smelled overcooked, even badly burned. No. Worse than that. Like burned wood and plastic—

With a start, she realized that the smell wasn't coming from the coffee at all, but from the open window, the tendrils of wind-carried smoke whipping past the window.

Smoke! In the instant she realized what must be happening, an alarm began to hoot, letting off a bloodcurdling mechanical scream that made most human-made alarms seem like background noise. She rushed for the door of Jamie's room to roust him out—but the alarm had done the job of waking him. The bedroom door swung open and Jamie stumbled out, carrying his shoes and still pulling his pants back on.

"Fire!" Hannah cried out, before he had the chance to ask what the alarm was. "Fire somewhere close. We've got to get out of here."

The main lighting died just as they stepped out into the corridor, leaving the two of them stumbling forward as best they could until a set of lurid green emergency lights kicked in. Hannah spotted a flashing sign just ahead, and decided it must lead toward the exit. She went that way, Jamie behind her, with the wisps of smoke in the corridor growing thicker and heavier, minute by minute.

They literally bumped into one frightened Pavlat, and soon encountered a crowd of them—servants of the Keep, technicians, specialists, all of them headed in a fast and orderly way toward the exit. Hannah was surprised by just how many Pavlats had been in the Keep to start with.

They merged into the stream of foot traffic and allowed themselves to be carried along by it. Hannah reached out and grabbed Jamie's arm hard, determined that the two of them not be separated in the crowd.

Then suddenly, they were outside, in the night and the dark, with the wind whipping by them, and the sharp cold air stinging their skin. The main lights were out, but more emergency lighting was powered up outside, providing just enough illumination to guide them well clear of the Keep.

Smoke and flame billowed out of the windows of one of the Keep's upper stories, throwing an angry yellow-red light on the crowd below. The steady green emergency lighting and the flickering, leaping reds and oranges of the fire seemed to do battle with each other as one, then the other colored the crowd, the landscape, the night.

The massive building was made to resemble a large outcropping of rock, or perhaps a small hill, and the belching fire and gouts of smoke looked like the eruption of a miniature volcano. The fire itself was making noise, but not anywhere near as much as the alarms that still shrieked, or the cries and moans of the crowd. Even with Hannah's far-less-than-perfect grasp of Reqwar Pavlat, she understood what the Pavlat in the shocked and stunned crowd were saying to each other.

Jamie heard it too, and turned to look at her,

shouting the news she already knew in her ear. "That's the Thelm's private study up there," he told her. "And the Thelm hasn't been seen since the alarm."

*And he won't be, either*, Hannah thought, a sick certainty twisting her stomach into knots. One look into Jamie's eyes told her that he had reached the same conclusion she had.

But guesses and assumptions would do them no good. Her agent's reflex for isolating the facts in a crisis situation took over. Hannah noted the time, estimated how long it had been since the alarm, noted the weather, the wind direction, anything that was measurable.

She scanned the crowd, noting who was there, who was not. She spotted Zahida ten or twenty meters off, standing by herself, wrapped in her sleeping blanket, her face dull with shock. And there, Marta and a little girl, a human girl who had to be Moira. Moira was in tears and shock, clinging to her mother. A man in street clothes, but in stocking feet, knelt to pick her up and hold her tight. Then Hannah blinked and forced herself to think. This was a Pavlat world. There *were* no human men here—or precious few. Hannah realized with a start that the man was Georg Hertzmann, wearing the clothes she had last seen him in. The darkness and the weird shifting light had made him all but unrecognizable.

Suddenly, three flying machines, moving in formation, dropped out of the sky and stopped dead in midair, right at the level of the fire. Spotlights came on from somewhere on the ground, and aimed themselves at the fliers. They looked like nothing so much as giant flying Easter eggs lying on their sides, painted in patterns of clashing iridescent green and fluorescent orange.

Suddenly, hatches opened on the forward ends of each flying egg, and jets of white smoke or gas blasted at the flames. Cold gaseous carbon dioxide, at a guess, serving both to cut off the air supply to the fire, and to cool off whatever was burning enough to keep it from reigniting once the $CO_2$ dispersed. Wherever the jets of white vapor struck, the flames shrank back like a living thing. The flames came back when the vapor dissipated, but not as bright, not as hot, not as big, not as strong.

The flying eggs moved about to stand on all sides of the burning tower, then drove in toward the fire, blasting away with their gas jets, driving the fire back, forcing it down. Other nozzles appeared from other hatches, and fired bright yellow foam in short precise shots into the flames, slapping down the surviving stands of fire.

One of the eggs nosed its way into one of the shattered windows, deliberately plowing its way through, and the sound of broken glass and protesting metal was plain to hear. It vanished into the interior, the glow of unseen flames still visible. A huge cloud of vapor erupted out of the ruined windows, then another, and another—and a sudden belch of dark black smoke erupted from the interior as the last of the fire was quenched.

The eggs stayed where they were, occasionally firing another shot of yellow foam whenever the flames threatened to flare up, but the fire was out. The sirens stopped sounding, the normal outdoor lighting came on, and the emergency lights shut off. The roar of the crowd had died away with the roar of the flames, and all that could be heard were muttering whispers, a few quiet oddly human sobbing sounds, and occasional low, keening cries made all the more heartrending because they were so alien.

The show was over. Hannah felt an absolutely overwhelming urge to get up there, to what she was assuming was a crime scene, immediately. She had to get there *now*, *this moment*, before the fire authorities could tramp over things, before evidence damaged in the fire could crumble and collapse into nothing. *Before two or three different competing sets of cops can start to argue out who has jurisdiction, who they're working for, and what that person will want found. Before they have a chance to misunderstand their orders correctly.*

She realized that she had never let go of her grip on Jamie's arm. He took her by the hand and shouted in her ear again. "We're wearing the Thelm's Hand Pendants. Maybe those will be enough to get us up there." Good to know that her partner was thinking the same way she was.

"Let's go," she said—but there was another hand, neither human nor Pavlat, tugging at her other arm.

She pulled back, spun about—and was astonished

to find herself nose-to-snout with Brox 231. "You do not trust me," he said without any preamble.

"No," said Hannah, after she had recovered from her surprise. "We have no reason to do so."

"And I have no reason to trust you," he said. "We back different sides, have opposite goals. But what has just happened puts this planet on the edge of chaos and civil war. That serves no one at all." Brox reached out his arms to encompass the three of them. "But even if we cannot trust each other—perhaps all of us together can trust—all of us together."

"A joint investigation?" Hannah asked.

"What about the local cops?" Jamie demanded.

"There barely are any, and it will take them hours, if not longer, to get organized." Brox looked from one of them to the other. "I have been here much longer than you. I can tell you there is not a hope in the universe of the local police authorities dealing with the crime scene properly. We must do it ourselves."

"So you assume it is a crime scene," said Hannah.

Brox flicked his head back dismissively. "I am not a fool. This was no accident—though the history of this world is written in convenient accidents and botched or suppressed investigations. I tell you it will cease to be a crime scene—or at least a crime scene of any use, if it is not secured *now*, by all of us."

Brox looked at both of them, and spoke further. "The High Thelek does not know I am here," he said. "And he would certainly object if he did. I do not even know if he is yet aware of what has happened— though he wouldn't have to do more than look out his window to find out. Once he *does* find out, he will start scheming about ways to take advantage of events. I tell you plainly that the ultimate goal of my government is to install him as Thelm, then to use our relationship with him to establish a major presence on Reqwar. And I will tell you plainly that the Thelek's instinct for plots and schemes will serve him very badly indeed in these circumstances." He gestured up at the tower. "Whatever is up there must be protected, recorded, witnessed, preserved. If it is not, and if what I fear has happened—if what we *all* fear has happened—then murk and doubt and uncertainty and suspicion will poison everything. The air will be thick with conspiracy theories, and with genuine conspiracies.

"The troubles we have seen so far will be as nothing. This world will slide into civil war, and that war will bring on a final collapse. You have not been on this world long—but surely you have been here long enough to know that what I say is true. And now only truth, facts, evidence, proof, certainty can save this world from that fate. Please. Let us do this together, for everyone's sake."

Hannah hesitated. This was way beyond her pay grade, her level of authority. She wasn't even sure she knew who, if anyone, in UniGov had the power to authorize a joint investigation with an agent of a hostile xeno agency on a third-species planet that had no diplomatic relationship of any kind with humanity. But that was what being a BSI Senior Special Agent was all about. She caught the eager hunter's look in

Jamie's eye and saw him give the slightest of nods. That was enough for her. "All right," she said. "We do the crime scene together."

"You'll need me," said another voice from behind her. Hannah turned and saw Zahida there. "I know the language, know the rules, know some of the officials—"

"No," said Jamie. "No, Lady Zahida," he said, using her title for the first time that Hannah had ever heard. "You must not come. For the safety and security of all—including yourself—you must not get near that chamber."

Zahida opened her mouth to protest—but then the full import of what Jamie was implying hit her, full force.

*That's right, Zahida. You're a suspect. A prime suspect. We can't risk it being you who 'accidentally' muddles the evidence.* But there could be no harm in helping her save face. "Jamie's thinking like an investigator, Zahida," she said, deliberately *not* using her title. "There's no physical evidence of your being up there during the crime, because you weren't there." *Or at least we'll go with that assumption for purposes of this conversation.* "We couldn't answer for the consequences if you inadvertently left misleading physical evidence behind by going there now."

Zahida's eyes widened as her ears contracted back against the sides of her head. "Oh," she said. "I hadn't thought of that."

"Do it another way," said Jamie. "A way that helps us and protects you. Find us a cop. A local, honest cop. One from the right jurisdiction. Someone junior enough to have some initiative, and senior enough to give orders and have them obeyed."

"And someone who might actually be interested in having the case solved," Brox said drily. "That by itself will limit the field quite a bit."

Zahida's eyes brightened. "I know just the one," she said. "And he ought to be here, now."

"Find him," Brox said, and stabbed a finger toward the ruined top of the Keep, where tendrils of smoke were still eddying out into night sky. "And tell him to take us—there."

The night was turning cold, and the wind was picking up again. The area around the Keep was lit up nearly as bright as day, and the roiling clouds overhead were dimly visible from the ground. Huge weird shadows would loom up on the Keep whenever someone walked in front of a powerlight. Now and then a whiff of smoke, or steam, or burned wood, or some stranger smell born of fire, would waft past.

The crowd was thickening up, and edging in toward the Keep. Unitmaster Laloyk Darsteel told one of his officers to have the barriers pushed back again, then turned back to the fire officer, struggling to keep his temper. The fool was behaving as if this was some brush fire out in the hill country, not a possible assassination.

"The fire is out," said Darsteel, "and we need access to the room where it started, and need it *now*. You've done splendid work, but you must move that fire floater out of the interior at once, so we can have room to work. *And before it can smash the evidence to kindling or dissolve it with firefoam residue*, he thought. But there was no need to rile the fire officer up. "You can keep your fire floaters on watch outside the Keep. If there is a flare-up, they'll be close enough to handle it."

The officer hesitated, then nodded. "Very well."

"Good!" Darsteel decided to press his luck, so long as the man was agreeing. "And I want you to hang some tarping over the broken windows. If a storm brews up, we don't want the wind and rain in there."

"It will be done," said the fire officer, saluting smartly.

Darsteel had other reasons for wanting the fire floater out and the tarps in place. The fire floater that had nosed into the Keep had a remote camera. So far, the only ones to have seen the view it provided were the fire officer—who was, fortunately, a person of no imagination whatsoever—and Darsteel himself, who had plenty of imagination. He had no desire to let anyone else see the grisly scene just yet. With the floater out of the interior, and the tarps shielding the view from anyone else who tried to get a flying camera up there, the odds on keeping things more or less private, at least for a little while, were much improved.

Cameras. For a fleeting moment, Darsteel indulged himself in the wish that the Thelm had taken the High Thelek's example in one way, at least. The High Thelek's home was reputed to be a forest of cameras and snooping devices, inside and out. If the Keep had been like that, it would have made the investigation vastly easier. It might even have made the crime impossible to commit.

Most Reqwar Pavlat, including the Thelm, disapproved strenuously of interior surveillance. Cameras and security should not intrude into the living areas, into one's private life. It was an extension of how the Reqwar Pavlat felt about their flesh-and-blood guards. The protectors should stand on the outside, ready to defend against exterior threats, not stand on the inside interfering with those they were meant to protect. It would be unseemly for the Thelm to have his every move observed, as if his life were merely some performance put on for the guards' amusement. A laudable sentiment, no doubt—but it left Darsteel with no inside cameras, and no imagery at all of any part of the Keep's private living areas.

Darsteel forgot about the fire officer and moved on to the next problem. Two other police organizations—the Thelm's Keep City Constabulary and the Thelm's Valley Rangers—already had officers on the scene. Sooner or later an official from one or the other of them, someone of higher rank than Darsteel, would show up and claim jurisdiction over the crime scene. Inevitable. Law of nature. Lawkeepers from other security services were likely on the way. The only way to avoid complete jurisdictional gridlock was to have the situation under firm enough control before the high-rankers showed up, and then make them feel involved enough to protect the arrangement that had been made. And the best way to do that was to involve their people.

Darsteel ordered three-lawkeeper static posts all around and inside the Keep, assigning one lawkeeper from each service to each post. If they spent most of their time keeping an eye on each other, then they would keep each other honest. Darsteel posted the most reliable teams he could at the entrances to Thelm Lantrall's Private Audience Chamber, with orders not to admit anyone at all unless Darsteel himself was present.

Whether or not he could make that stick he didn't know, but he had to try. He might not have the legal authority to command in this situation—but *someone* had to take charge, and fast, before things got completely out of control.

Just as he was ordering that more powerlights be aimed at the Keep's upper stories to give the crews hanging the tarps more light, he spotted the Lady Zahida Halztec pushing her way through the crowd, trying to get to him. He shouted orders to let her through the barrier.

She headed toward him on the run. "Unitmaster Darsteel!" she called out as soon as she was close enough. "The aliens! The alien investigators!"

"What?"

"The humans and the Kendari. The off-worlders want to offer their services to you in an immediate joint search of the crime scene. A joint investigation."

Darsteel was so relieved he almost smiled. "I'd be mad to turn that offer down—unless they start asking for favors or conditions." His own experience in managing a major crime scene was all but nil, and he did not trust most of the lawkeepers who would likely try to move in and take over if he didn't have a legitimate investigation of his own launched at once. The odds on drawing a chief investigator more interested in enhancing his own status and/or reaching the conclusions most likely to keep his patron happy were far too high. "Let's go see what sort of deal they're trying to make."

\* \* \*

If the off-worlders were aware of how urgently Darsteel needed their expertise, they didn't show it. He had expected them to demand rights of control over the investigation, or else to insist on some completely unrelated favor in exchange. Instead, somehow, he found that *they* were deferring to *him*. Maybe they needed an honest investigation as much as he did. Maybe it was just that the humans and Kendari did not trust each other. The fact that they distrusted each other could prove useful to Darsteel. It might serve to cancel out whatever opposing biases the two species would bring to the case.

Knowing they were not interested in demanding conditions made Darsteel willing to impose a few of his own. "If—if—I agree to let you join me in the crime scene investigation," he told them, "you *must* first agree not to touch or disturb anything, but merely to observe. You must examine without making any physical contact, aside from walking around the room."

"Agreed," said Brox.

"Fine with us," said Agent Wolfson.

"I have two requests," Brox said. "For our mutual protection, I suggest none of the four of us be allowed into the crime scene unless all of us are there. Second, I would ask that in future, any evidence shown to the humans be shown to me at the same time—and any evidence shown to me be shown to them in similar fashion."

"I was about to ask for the same things," said Wolfson.

"Very well," Darsteel said, trying to mask his eagerness with a show of reluctant agreement. He would have trained and experienced professionals examining the evidence, and full access to whatever they learned—and their mutual distrust was a superb guarantee that they would not start plotting together against him. "I would suggest we collect whatever equipment we can, and get started at once." *Before some higher-up can cancel the arrangement.*

* * *

It took time to get organized, and to improvise solutions to some fairly basic problems. Brox had his own isolation wear and had it brought to him. Brox was also able to produce some lights and cameras, and Darsteel came up with a few bits of hardware as well.

The crime scene gear Hannah and Jamie had brought to Reqwar had been destroyed in the *Lotus.* The emergency packs they had managed to grab after the crash were full of survival gear, not investigative equipment. However, Darsteel was able to scrounge together some Pavlat-style sterile foot coverings and yellow-colored isolation garments that would more or less fit humans. He also provided them with bright pink Pavlat-style surgical masks and hoods and

326 ■ ROGER MACBRIDE ALLEN

six-fingered rubber gloves. None of the Pavlat gear fit
the humans properly, but it would get the job done.

They were a motley crew at best in their bulky, vari-
colored, mismatched, ill-fitting iso-suits. None of the
rest of their gear was anything much, and it wasn't all
they would have wanted, but it was all they were
going to get. They were as ready as they were going
to be.

* * *

The Thelm's Private Audience Chamber was a big
room, taking up just about all of one floor of the
Keep, and it was a burned-out wreck. The ancient
stone walls, and the scarcely less ancient wood-plank
floors and ceiling were badly scorched and damaged,
but still appeared to be sound. It was mainly the
room's appointments—the richly embroidered sitting
cushions, the handsomely carved perching stools, the
wall hangings and tapestries, the worktables—that
had burned.

But that was all incidental, the mere loss of property. What had brought them there was the dead
Reqwar Pavlat—the dead Thelm—on the floor.

"The Thelm is dead," said Hannah Wolfson,
kneeling by the body, looking into the lifeless, staring
eyes. "Long live the Thelm."

But that was the question, of course, Jamie
thought. With Lantrall dead, and the planet teetering
on the brink of disaster, who *was* the Thelm?

Jamie, Hannah, and Darsteel focused on the victim, but Brox seemed happy to let the others study the

corpse. He looked the body over for a few moments, then began studying the room itself.

The corpse lay on its back, on an elaborately embroidered carpet, almost in the center of the room. The body was barely burned at all, though its clothing was blackened and charred on the chest. Blobs of fire retardant that had yet to disintegrate were splashed about on the carpet and the corpse. It looked as if the fire had been closing in on the center of the room. If the fire had gone on much longer, it would have incinerated the corpse, destroying whatever information might be derived from the condition of the body. The investigators had been lucky on that score.

The corpse had not been lucky at all. Its limbs were splayed out, its arms and legs thrown wide. The face was contorted into an expression that seemed to speak of shock, anger, fear—but that expression might be some side effect of the Pavlat equivalent of rigor mortis.

The carpet that the body lay on had burned along one edge, and in a few patches here and there, but the rest of it had not sustained much damage. There was a scorched but mainly intact table next to the carpet on which the body lay. It had been pushed over on its side somehow, and the bottles it had held had all been knocked over and emptied. Their contents had soaked into the carpet, in and around several of the most intense scorch marks.

It was instantly obvious that it was not the fire that had killed the Thelm. There was a gaping wound in the center of the corpse's chest, the flesh around it burned and scorched. Near the wound, the clothing was burned and blackened, and there were twists and bits of metal visible in the chest cavity. It looked very much like a fairly slow-moving projectile had struck the victim in the chest and exploded.

There was a weapon in the two-thumbed, four-fingered left hand of the victim; it was an elaborately carved and decorated pistol of some sort, almost certainly handmade, and the corpse was holding it as one would to fire it. One finger was on the trigger, and by the looks of things, the corpse had a firm enough grip on the pistol that it would possibly require post-mortem surgery to remove it. The pistol was badly damaged, though not, it would seem, by the fire. The barrel of the weapon had burst. The breech end of the firing tube was threaded, so that an endcap could be screwed into place—but the threading had been sheared off, and there was no endcap to be seen.

Jamie knelt there in his rustling bright yellow iso-suit and stared at the lifeless face. *The Thelm is dead.* It was impossible to take it in. The Thelm had been alive and vigorous, full of schemes and plans, with a kind word for everyone, and perhaps a knife in the back for some, just a few hours before.

Unitmaster Darsteel knelt next to Jamie and stared solemnly down at his Thelm for a long time. "I had seen him, many times," he said. "I had always hoped to speak more than a word or two of greeting with him, to offer myself for his service at any time or place. Now it is too late."

"Then do him the last service of helping to find his murderer," said Jamie.

"Murder!" Darsteel said in shock. "But it is suicide! He was distraught over the loss of his birth-sons and the crisis of his adoptive son. The gun is in his hand! He fired at himself."

"Quite right," Brox said, sarcasm dripping from his voice. The Kendari was standing by the wall at the far side of the room, examining something there. "Hours after being seen in very good spirits, enthused over some new scheme, he comes up here, shoots himself in the chest, then knocks over the furniture, empties all the bottles in his drinks cabinet onto the floor, sets fire to the room in several places, then collapses on the floor and dies of the wound that should have killed him instantaneously."

"How can you tell he shot himself—or was shot—*before* the fire started?" Darsteel asked.

"Two things," said Brox. He extracted a handlight from his shoulder tool harness and directed it to a ragged pattern of irregularly shaped and sized pits and holes in the wall. "One glance at the wound makes it clear that the projectile that hit him shattered. It might even have had an explosive charge. Unless I am very much mistaken, these holes are the impact points for fragments of the projectile that hit the Thelm, passed through his body, and lodged here in the wall. If you come here and look carefully at the holes, you will see that bits of cloth—and what might be small portions of the Thelm's skin—were torn loose from the Thelm's body and have lodged with the fragments."

Darsteel moved carefully over to the spot in the wall and studied the area Brox indicated. "I see," he said. "But how do fragments in the wall prove the fire happened after the shot was fired?"

"They don't—but the cloth and skin fragments do. The wall is badly burned. The bits of cloth that protrude from the holes have been thoroughly charred. But the bits lodged *in* the wall by the projectile fragments have not been burned at all. Conclusion: They were lodged in the wall before the fire started. Furthermore, the wall itself has been badly damaged and weakened by the fire, practically reduced to charcoal—yet the holes produced by the fragments are sharp and angular, and the fragments have not penetrated far. The impact points would not look like that if the fragments had struck a wall that had been weakened by fire."

Darsteel studied the section of wall carefully. "I follow your argument, and grant your logic. But it might be that the materials used here are outside your experience and are misleading you."

"Possible, but unlikely," said Brox. "And in any event, my second proof is clear enough that I can see it from across the room and saw it with one glance at the Thelm. If you examine the carpet under the Thelm, you will see it is blackened and discolored everywhere but *under* him. I expect that when the body is removed, we will find an area of more or less undamaged carpet forming a perfect outline of his body. Also, there is fire debris—ash and soot and bits of the ceiling that fell and so on—scattered about on the carpet, and on top of the Thelm's body—but there does not appear to be any *under* his body. The obvious conclusion is that he fell to the floor, and was lying motionless in that position, when the fire started."

Darsteel returned to the side of the body, and studied what he could see of the area under the Thelm. "You're quite right," he said. "It's very clear, now that you point it out."

"There's more," said Jamie. "Look at the weapon again. It's badly damaged. It malfunctioned, drastically, somehow. The breech, the end of the gun closest to the shooter, is destroyed. You can see that the breech end is threaded on the outside. If you look at the Thelm's chest wound, you can see shattered fragments with about the right curvature, and they have what looks to be the corresponding threading on the inside. Those have got to be bits of the endcap from his pistol."

"And look how he's holding that pistol," said Hannah. "Straight out, away from his body. With a barrel that long, he couldn't possibly have held the gun in that way and pointed the weapon at himself. If he had wanted to shoot himself with that gun, he would have held it in both hands, in the center of his chest, with the barrel pointed *at* him. He fired the weapon, yes—but he did not intend to shoot himself. He fired it—but instead of the round flying out of the weapon away from him, it shot backwards, shearing off the endcap and smashing the round and the endcap into his chest."

"But who or what was he shooting at?"

"I haven't the faintest idea," Hannah said. "But unless I'm judging things wrong, and Pavlat are stronger than I think, and their arms and wrists and fingers bend in ways I don't know about, he died trying to shoot at someone else."

"No," said Darsteel. "Looking at it all more carefully, I believe you have it right. But—"

"But what?"

"Well, with the weapon in his hand and all that— are we meant to *think* it was a suicide? The things you point out show that it was not. But perhaps this is a botched attempt to *fake* a suicide?"

"It could be," Jamie said doubtfully. He studied the pistol that Lantrall held in his hand for a moment. It had an oddly long gun barrel for a hand gun, more than thirty centimeters. The gun barrel started flaring out from about the halfway point, widening out toward the muzzle, so that the gun barrel resembled an elongated funnel. There was also what looked like the guard of a sword just forward of the breech end of the barrel. "What can you tell me about that weapon? It looks more elaborate and decorative than just a regular target pistol or something. And the firing mechanism is strange."

"It is one of a pair," said Darsteel. "Dueling pistols. Rocket-gun single-shot dueling pistols."

"Rocket-gun dueling pistols?" Jamie asked in surprise.

"It's a fairly common way to make such guns," said Darsteel. "It fires a small projectile powered by a miniature solid rocket motor."

"It seems like a strange way to build a practical weapon," Jamie objected. At least it explained the flared funnel-shaped barrel, and the guard around the barrel's breech ends. They were both there to protect the shooter from the rocket's exhaust jet.

"They aren't *meant* to be practical," said Brox. "Rocket guns have to be fairly big. They have a distinct shape. They are meant for a particular upper-class ritual, the duel. They make a lot of noise and smoke. They're used to settle affairs of honor at a moment's notice. They're meant to be grand and dramatic." He shook his head. "A lot of nonsense, if you ask me."

"That might be," Jamie said with a faint smile. "But I take your point. He turned back to Darsteel and pointed at the gun in the Thelm's hand. "Any idea where that came from?"

"As I said, it was one of a pair. I was part of the team that inventoried the valuables in this room a few years ago. As I remember, they were displayed in a case over there on that show table."

Jamie glanced over at the table. Several large chunks of collapsed ceiling and other debris had landed on top of it, collapsing its legs and burying whatever was on top of it. He wouldn't be getting a look at whatever was left of the case and its contents for a while yet. Not until they started cleaning the place up. "Would loaded weapons have been left on display in the Thelm's office?" Jamie asked. "Prepped, loaded, ready to fire?"

Darsteel hesitated, and then nodded. "Yes," he conceded. "Loaded weapons. As Inquirist Brox noted, with some sarcasm, one must be ready to settle affairs of honor at a moment's notice. There are various safety mechanisms, of course. But they are easy to switch off."

"I'd like to see a duplicate of the weapon, or as close to it as you can come," said Jamie. "Plus a sample of the ammunition it fired, and maybe some kind of quick briefing on how the weapon works."

"Certainly," said Darsteel.

"And if I am reading this right, we'll need to confirm that what we're seeing in the wound are fragments of the endcap. And we'll have to examine the projectile as well, of course. Forgive me if I offend, but I do not know your laws. Will there be a postmortem examination of the Thelm? Some cultures would prohibit it."

"I am certain that there will be such an examination," said Darsteel. "And I will see to it that it is done properly, with no attempts to shade or 'correct' the evidence. Shall I see to it that you get the report as soon as it is complete?"

"That's what I was about to ask for," Jamie said.

"Wait a moment," said Hannah. "I want to get this straight. The gun—*two* guns, probably—were in the room, loaded and accessible?"

"Yes."

"So anyone who got into this room could have

picked up one of those pistols and taken a potshot at the Thelm at any time?"

"We've just got through proving he must have fired the gun himself, presumably unaware that it would blow up, or fire backwards, or whatever it did," Brox protested.

"Hannah's not saying that someone else *did* shoot at him," said Jamie. "She's just asking if it would have been possible." He turned to Darsteel. "So—were there two guns there?"

"Yes," Darsteel admitted reluctantly. "Obviously that was most unwise," he went on stiffly, making a remarkable understatement, "but that was how it was."

"Maybe that *was* how it was," Hannah suggested. "Maybe he *didn't* shoot himself. Maybe someone who knew the gun would malfunction held the gun backwards, shot him with it that way, and then put the gun in his hand."

"That sounds about as probable as my theory that he shot himself, then started the fires," Brox said acidly.

"It would be impossible," Darsteel said flatly. "His hand is in the clasp reflex position. It's a common Pavlat reaction to shock and surprise. The hand can't possibly be forced into that position after death."

"Clasp reflex?" Jamie asked. "What's that?"

"The Pavlat hand," said Brox. "It is formed in ways useful to the arboreal ways of the species from which the Pavlat evolved. When closed around something—a tree limb, a gun butt, whatever—it has a relaxed-lock reflex, so that it holds on effortlessly, and it requires a deliberate effort to make it let go. Many arboreal species on Kendari have it, and on Earth too, I expect. It allows a creature to lock its claws closed when holding on to a branch, and, for example, to sleep without danger of falling. And, of course, danger stimulates the reflex so that surprise or shock would cause one to hold on all the harder."

"Yes," Hannah said. "Lots of birds on Earth do something like that when they roost for the night." She leaned over the dead hand and the weapon it held, shining a bright handlight on them, studying them as closely as she could. "So what you're telling me is that he has that gun in a death grip. He had to be alive for the reflex to kick in—and no one could possibly open his hand after death."

"That is correct," Darsteel said.

"Well, I'm no expert on what postmortem injuries look like on a Pavlat—but it sure looks to me as if someone *tried* to open his hand. You can see the scorch marks from the rocket projectile's exhaust on his wrist—more proof he fired it himself—but there's something else. Scratches and discolorations. They're faint, but they are there."

"What?" Darsteel cried out, the shock plain in his voice. He leaned in next to Hannah and studied the hand of his Thelm. "You're right," he said. "But why? For what purpose?"

Hannah made no reply. Jamie had his own ideas, but kept his mouth shut.

Brox had been quietly continuing his search of the room, moving his body gracefully through the tight spaces of the chamber. "I have found something of interest," he announced in a voice of studied neutrality. "It is a tight fit back here," he said. "Let me back out. I would suggest that you come in one by one. And I need not repeat the vitally important point that nothing be touched."

A large decorative plant had been toppled over, just in front of a service door opening onto a corridor that allowed the servants and serving robots to come and go without using the main hallways and stairs. It would be just barely possible to use the door with the plant blocking it, but the plant had fallen in such a way as to create a tight spot between it and the wall with the door. Darsteel went to look first, let out a muttered oath, and backed out quickly—and for some reason he was instantly interested in Hannah's feet, and Jamie's as well. Hannah went next, and came out looking at the two nonhumans with wry amusement. "Agent Mendez and I are in the clear on this one," he said. "Definitely not my style. And not Agent Mendez's size."

Jamie went in after her, and instantly understood. It was a shoe print—but a print made by a human-style shoe, and a largish one at that, far larger than Jamie's size. No nonhuman could have been expected to be able to read the print beyond spotting it as human-style. But Jamie could, and did. It was unquestionably a human shoe, a man's shoe, for the right foot.

And, to the best of his knowledge, aside from himself, there was exactly one male human being on the planet.

All of a sudden, it would seem that Georg Hertzmann had some explaining to do.

They took detailed pictures of the Thelm's body, of the weapon, of the scratches on the Thelm's hand, of the shoe print, and of the impact damage caused by projectile fragments, along with a whole series of general views of the room. They hunted and they studied, but if the Thelm's audience chamber held any more surprises, none of their party spotted them.

All of them were exhausted, physically, mentally, emotionally. Dawn was not far off, but the endless night wasn't over for them. Not yet. There was some talking to do, some decisions to make. The four of them stripped off their iso-suits, and, at Darsteel's suggestion, they went to the BSI agents' apartments to talk around the big round table in the common room.

Brox started things off. "This is a disaster," he said flatly as he sat down on his haunches on the floor and folded his arms on the table. "I tell you plainly that I have not the slightest idea who will succeed Thelm Lantrall under these circumstances—the High Thelek, or Georg Hertzmann, or perhaps even some distant alternate heir. The laws of succession are extremely complex. But if this case is left unsolved, in the grand old Reqwar Pavlat tradition, whoever *does* succeed will not have sufficient support from enough quarters to be able to rule this planet. The present hostilities and suspicions will seem like an era of peace and mutual trust."

Hannah had barely heard the last part of what Brox had said. Georg Hertzmann, Thelm of all Reqwar? She had been viewing that as an interesting oddball theoretical possibility that might be politically useful as part of some plot or conspiracy. Could it really happen? Was it about to happen? But this wasn't the time to bring up that sort of question. "All right," she said. "Then we, those of us here, have to solve this murder, and do it fast."

"We have to do more than that," said Jamie. "There has been a political murder. We can't assume there won't be more killings. We can't exclude the possibility of a conspiracy, a coup. And the conspirators might still be at work—and watching. I would advise that we work on the assumption that we are being observed. Any number of groups or individuals might want to keep an eye on us."

"A sensible assumption," said Brox. "But let us not be paralyzed by our own precautions. I would suggest that we start discussions—and I would suggest that our first task should be to assemble a list of likely suspects. I would be interested in hearing the thoughts of my colleagues on that point."

*In other words, you want to see our cards before you show your own*, Hanna thought.

"With what we've just discussed in mind," Jamie went on, "I won't mention names out loud. I'll write them." He took out a pen and a piece of paper and jotted down a list of suspects.

Hannah caught Brox's quizzical, amused expression as he watched Jamie work. No doubt he thought writing on paper was hopelessly old-fashioned. Let him think what he wanted. It beat all the "modern" techniques when it came to easy and reliable security. No power sources to monitor or code impulses to intercept, no forgotten backup copies that didn't get erased.

Jamie finished writing, then shoved the paper across the table to Darsteel.

"I would strongly suggest that everyone on that list be placed in protective custody at once," Jamie said. "As a safety precaution, in case one of them turns out to be a suspect instead of a potential victim, I would also advise that they not be allowed to talk with each other. Don't let them return to their homes before picking them up—just in case their homes contain concealed dangers, the way the Thelm's chamber did. In fact, I would suggest that each of their homes be checked very carefully for traps while the owners are in protective custody."

Darsteel looked at the list, then slid it across the table to Brox. "A sensible idea," Darsteel said blandly. "But what if an overzealous police commander misinterpreted this suggestion and ordered the persons listed here to be kept away from each other in order to prevent conspiracies from forming, or to prevent those on it from talking together and getting their stories straight? And an overzealous police commander might even let that check for traps and weapons degenerate into a full-blown search for evidence."

"Well, if that happened, it certainly would be unexpected," said Jamie.

"Be prepared to be surprised," Darsteel said drily.

"Let me see that list," Hannah said. She read it over and looked up at Jamie. "You're casting your net pretty wide, aren't you? There are a few names I wouldn't have included."

"I can guess which ones," said Jamie. "But I have my reasons—though I don't want to go into them here, when the walls might have ears."

*And you might have to talk through a few points you don't want to discuss with Brox in the room.* "There's also a great big hole in this net—and it's such an obvious one that I'm going to risk discussing it out loud. I'm certain it's a name that's occurred to every one of us already—and to everyone else on the planet as well. We might as well talk it through. Why isn't the High Thelek on the list?"

Jamie shrugged. "Acceptance of political reality. We're not going to be able to get him to go into protective custody or do a search of his property. That doesn't mean I didn't think of him. Obviously, he stands to gain from the Thelm's death. For no other reason than that, he ought to be considered a suspect."

"*Is* it obvious?" asked Brox. "Again, I will not insult your intelligence by pretending I don't have a vested interest here—but I tell you again quite honestly, I for one haven't the faintest idea who succeeds under these circumstances. The Thelm is murdered by a person or persons unknown, but his son lives, guilty of treason for a reason that is now obviously moot. Do *you* know, Darsteel? Does *anyone* know?"

Darsteel turned his hands palms up. "I have no knowledge," he said. " 'The son rules what his wife receives from his father.' That little catchphrase is all one usually needs to know. But, needless to say, I will find out."

"There *is* someone who does know," Hannah said. "Whoever committed the murder. I suppose there is just some bare chance that the Thelm was killed at this exact moment for some totally unrelated reason. Maybe someone with an old grudge even picked a moment when we'd all assume it was a political murder—but I doubt it. Whoever did this did it *because* of how it would affect the succession. He or she was trying to pick the next Thelm. And with all due respect, Brox, that goes double for the High Thelek."

Jamie took back the paper from Hannah and wrote something else down. "This might be hard to check on, or it might be dead easy," he said, "depending on how closely the Thelm's security people watch his guests. But it would be useful to know if you find it out." Jamie paused for a moment. "And one other thing. Two items that need to be searched for and found. I'll write down where I think the first ought to be. If you find the second—that ought to break the case wide open."

Darsteel took the paper, read over the additions that Jamie had made, then folded it without showing it to Brox or Hannah. "I think it would be best for all concerned if those instructions were kept as closely held as possible," he said.

"I would like to know what he wrote down," said Brox.

"And I would like to keep this case under some sort of control," said Darsteel. "If there is a leak of this information to the High Thelek, we will know it cannot have come from you."

Brox looked irritated, then shrugged in resignation. "Very well. I will not press the point," he said. "But there is one other aspect of the evidence we must discuss. I've done some fire-crime cases in my time. I have neglected to emphasize one point, because it was obvious to me, and I treated it as a given. However, it might not be evident to the unpracticed eye. I can tell you flat out that the fire in that room had nothing to do with the actual attack on the Thelm. Oh, they were done by the same person, at the same time, of course—but I think we're *meant* to believe that it was sparks or debris or some such from the rocket-gun shot that started the fire."

"That's not at all uncommon," said Darsteel. "The rocket-gun projectiles do tend to ignite things."

"But this time they didn't," said Brox. "Something else did. There were several scorch marks on various unburned surfaces—the carpet the Thelm was on, for example. It was damaged by the fire, but it did not burn. I am almost certain those scorches were caused by someone aiming a pocket firestarter directly at those surfaces at full blast. When that didn't work, that someone used some sort of accelerant—a líquid that burns fast and hot—and splashed it around the room, and set fire to that. Some places it managed to ignite whatever it was on, and there are other places— such as that apparently fireproof carpet—where just the surface layer is charred or melted. Those are places where the accelerant itself burned up, but nothing else did."

"So the fire did not start as an incidental or unintended consequence of the rocket-gun shot. The assailant set the fire in a separate act, *after* the murder," said Darsteel.

"As we discussed earlier, I think we can assume the Thelm would have objected if the fire was set while he was still alive," said Brox.

"That begs a couple of questions," said Hannah. "Presumably, the fire was set in order to conceal or destroy something—evidence of some sort. But what *was* it supposed to destroy—and did it manage to do the job? Is the whatever-it-was still here?"

"I don't see any way of answering that question just yet," said Darsteel.

"But it does make me think of something else that needs checking," said Jamie. He took another sheet of paper, scribbled for a moment, and handed the note to Darsteel.

Darsteel read it with a puzzled expression. "I assume you know this is a bad time and place for making jokes," he said.

"I do know that," Jamie said. "That's a serious and important request. And don't forget—I want to see a duplicate of the weapon and the ammunition that killed the Thelm—and yes, dummy ammunition will do fine."

"If you are serious, I will make the inquiry. And you will get the gun and some dummy rounds. But, speaking of pocket firestarters—" He folded the two notes together once, then pulled a starter from the pocket of his blouse and set fire to the paper. Darsteel let the notes burn almost completely before dropping them to the table. "It will all get done," he said to them all.

Hannah smiled as they watched the last of the paper burning. Another demonstration of the advantages of the simple, the low-tech, approach to security. It was far from the first such proof. It was only a few hours ago, after all, that the Thelm himself had simply sat quietly in the next room and thus defeated security gear as sophisticated as—

Suddenly she sat bolt upright. "Burning devils!" she said. "Jamie! The Stannlar coins! They could be listening gear as well as jammers."

Hannah pulled hers out of her pocket and threw it on the table. Jamie scrabbled in his breast pocket, extracted his coin, and threw it down next to Hannah's.

"You've got to destroy those," said Hannah to Darsteel.

"What in the worlds are they?" the Pavlat asked. "What is the matter with both of you?"

Hannah explained as quickly and as briefly as she could what the coins were and where—or rather who—they had come from. "We haven't had any chance to test them in any meaningful way," said

Hannah. "So we can't know for sure if they *are* jammers. They probably are—but they could be listening devices as well. The Stannlar are good at electronics, and they supposedly use a whole range of pseudo-etheric wavelengths no one else even knows how to detect, let alone use."

"So there is at least a chance that your noble Stannlar allies have heard everything you have said and done these past several hours?" Brox demanded.

"Possible, yes," said Jamie. "But not very likely."

"Why do you think it unlikely?" Brox demanded. "Because the Stannlar are so good and noble? In my experience, they regard individual sentient beings as being about as expendable as those ghastly little subcreatures they are constantly unleashing and retrieving."

"I think it unlikely because that's a mighty small coin into which to fit a full jamming system, plus a concealed microphone, plus a pseudoetheric transmitter, plus a power source," Jamie said irritably.

"Quiet, all of you!" said Darsteel, scooping up the coins. "I will see to it that the devices are destroyed at once. However, my task has just been made that much harder. Now I must work on the assumption that the Stannlar have heard everything we have said and done." He glared at the humans. "I hope there will be no further errors of this sort."

Jamie looked at Hannah, then back at Darsteel. "Today has been a bad day for mistakes," he admitted. "But we'll do our best."

"I am glad to hear it," said Darsteel. "But I can't

count on your not making further mistakes—or on your absolute discretion. I must take precautions." He held up his hand, gesturing for them all to remain quiet. "Before you can swear mighty oaths that everything will be kept confidential, let me be blunt. When my superiors finally get organized enough to demand to know what I have been doing, I cannot tell them I have relied on the promises of aliens for the security of the investigation. Not if I want to keep my job—or perhaps even my life."

Darsteel turned to Brox. "I must *know* as a matter of certainty, and be able to tell them, that it was physically impossible for you to warn the Thelek, your patron—who you have at least tacitly conceded is a suspect—of what evidence is being sought."

He turned toward the two humans. "And I must be certain that *you* cannot warn your fellow human Georg Herztmann of what might be coming. *None* of the three of you will leave these apartments until I decide otherwise. Nor will you communicate with anyone except me, face-to-face, whenever I see fit to come and make a report, or to consult with you. However, couriers might bring papers, materials, evidence to examine—as I see fit. Food and drink will be brought to you."

Darsteel paused, and went on in a gentler tone. "I apologize, but I expect you would take the same precautions if the roles were reversed. I doubt that it will be necessary to hold you here more than a day or two."

"But what about—" Jamie began.

Darsteel went right on talking, ignoring Jamie completely. "While we were examining the crime scene, my people fitted locks and bolts to the outside of the door, then entered here and removed all personal articles, on the off chance that one of them might contain a concealed communications device or the like. You two humans will find coveralls in your respective rooms. They are cut to fit a Pavlat, but they ought to do for now. You will change into them and turn your present garments over to me, once again on the chance that your present garments conceal listening devices or communicators."

Jamie opened his mouth, ready to argue, but Hannah held up her hand to quiet him. "We accept—under protest, but we accept." She turned to Jamie, who still didn't look happy. "We don't have many cards to play here," she said to him quietly. "I think we might do better by going along."

Jamie shrugged and nodded wearily. "Sure. Why not? We don't have anything much left in the way of usable hardware, anyway."

"We'll cooperate," said Hannah, "but only on the condition that Brox is required to turn over all *his* clothing and gear." *Which will probably hurt him more than us. He actually has functioning police equipment.*

"I was about to instruct him to do that," Darsteel said.

"And *I* protest," said Brox, half-rising.

"Protest if you like, but you have no choice but to

comply. You will turn over your clothes and equipment and remain here."

"But there is no accommodation for a Kendari. Everything is built to suit humans!"

"We will provide suitable bedding and so forth," Darsteel said. "You can sleep here in the common room. It will be up to you—to all of you—to make the best of it."

"Why can't I be placed in a separate apartment?"

"Because I have no time and precious few subordinates I can trust, because the Spirit of Reqwar alone knows how many others I may need to lock up tonight, and because half the Keep is still off-limits for use because of the fire!" Darsteel half shouted. "I have enough to deal with as it is. Do not make my night harder or longer than it will be already."

Hannah regarded their host with interest. She had no doubt the temper, the anger, the exhaustion were real—but somehow she had the sense he was *using* his emotions just a trifle. All his reasons were valid—but that did not mean they were his *only* reasons. Darsteel had to know of the rivalry between the two species, how improbable it was that they would willingly plot together. If the humans and the Kendari were all locked up in one place, he could save on a few guards. The two species would simply keep watch on each other for him.

Brox glared at Darsteel, but sat himself back down at the table—though it was hard to miss the tip of his tail twitching furiously. "Very well," he said calmly. "I understand the need, and accept the inevitable—but I do not like it, and I give you fair warning that the Kendari authorities will register the strongest possible protest. There may well be consequences for this act."

"I will take that risk," said Darsteel, and he stood up to leave. "Orderlies will be in soon to collect your clothing and bring in food, water, replacement clothing, and bedding."

He bowed gracefully, in perfect form, and left. The door swung shut behind him, and they could hear the bolts being slammed home.

The room was deathly quiet for a moment, but then Hannah spoke. "Well," she said brightly, "what shall we talk about?"

Allabex and Cinnabex both stopped all motion and activity when it happened. First signal number HB2XR7 from Special Agent Mendez's device died, and then, seconds later, the signal from number X3477B, the unit given to Senior Special Agent Wolfson. They both *sensed* each signal die, like the touch of a hand being withdrawn, a song cut off in midnote. They waited a moment, to see if the devices given to the Hertzmann family would go as well—but no, for the moment at least, those three remained online.

But the two sudden silences sent a message as clear as any words spoken aloud. Fear and distrust were spreading, strengthening. Events were moving toward a crisis.

Without a word exchanged between them, the two Stannlar returned to their preparations with redoubled speed.

*  *  *

Hannah had meant her question to be ironic, but Brox 231 was in no mood to parse the subtleties of human wit. He knew exactly what he wanted to talk about, loudly and forcefully. He wanted someone to get him a proper sleep-sling, and something to eat, and some sort of civilized arrangement for Kendari sanitary needs.

Fortunately, someone on Darsteel's staff had already had the sense to contact Hotel Number Two, which had at least some Kendari-suitable gear in stock, including a complicated-looking hammock arrangement that Brox conceded was more or less acceptable as a sleep-sling, and a remarkably compact, portable, fully hygienic and completely self-contained refresher unit suitable for Kendari. Getting that and his sleep-sling into their suite and setting it all up took most of an hour. The new equipment filled up most of the common room, but they would all be able to manage. Somehow.

But once it was done Jamie could shut the door on the outside world, and sleep, uninterrupted, for the first time since his arrival on Reqwar, on something more or less like the beds back home—even if the mattress was too hard and the sheets were somehow slippery and scratchy at the same time.

Simple exhaustion should have had him dead to the world the moment his head hit the pillow—but instead his eyes snapped open, and his mind started racing. What had happened? Who had done it? And why?

Better to start at the beginning, with the solid facts. They knew that the gun in the Thelm's hand had malfunctioned in spectacular fashion, and very likely had been sabotaged. The Thelm died with his finger on the trigger, and several of the fragments he had seen in the wound looked the right size and shape to be part of the missing endcap of the gun.

There was no plausible alternative to the conclusion that the Thelm had fired the gun, and that the wound was caused by the shot he fired. So, in a very limited sense, the Thelm *had* killed himself. But it was all but impossible to believe he had done it deliberately. His attitude and behavior mere hours before were anything but suicidal. Besides, Brox had shown that the fire had been set deliberately, *after* the Thelm had been shot and killed and had fallen to the floor. Suicides can't set fires after they die.

But who or what had the Thelm been shooting at, and why? To Jamie, at least, it looked very much as if the Thelm had been manipulated into shooting at whatever-it-was, in order to cause the gun to malfunction and kill him.

Look at it from another angle. *Who benefits?* It was the most basic question in any criminal investigation. Answer that question, and you'd almost automatically have a solid list of suspects. The devil of it was that who benefited depended on who had done the killing. The simplest case was that, if Georg did it, then by all the lunatic, barbaric, old-stone-age laws of Pavlat, *he* would benefit by becoming Thelm—and, just incidentally, by not being executed, or exiled.

But the murder as planned required very specific preparations—for example, rigging the gun and planting it. Georg had manifestly *not* been carrying out any such plan, but had been doing his best to be visibly far away from the Thelm, and visibly sitting there in his glass house, not doing anything to prepare for killing anyone. *Except he was here at the Keep last night*, Jamie reminded himself. *And that shoe print was there.*

But the guns had been on display—and the business about being ready to deal with an affair of honor at a moment's notice, absurd as it seemed, was probably all the reason a Reqwar Pavlat Thelm would need to keep loaded weapons in his study. The guns could have sat there more or less indefinitely. There might have been a risk that the Thelm would want to get in a little target practice—but he would not have used the ornately decorated pistols on the show table for that. The guns could have been rigged—and planted in the Thelm's audience chamber—months ago—or the day after Irvtuk and his brothers died. So it had to be conceded that Georg had motive, means, and opportunity.

*Except*, Jamie had to keep reminding himself, *it's not only legal for him to kill the Thelm—the law requires it. But it had to be that the law had some sort of provision for cases where the father died of natural causes—or at the hands of someone besides the son—before the deadline. What were the rules covering those cases?*

And if Georg decided to kill Lantrall, he wouldn't skulk around. He would want it known, *need* it known. Georg would not kill with a booby trap, or make it look like a possible suicide. What Georg would need would be absolute proof that *he* had personally and deliberately killed the Thelm.

If Georg had any sense, he would have marched right up to the closest news reporter and handed him a video recording of him committing the murder— and thus secured his claim to the Thelmship. Georg had motive, means, and opportunity to commit a *public* murder of the Thelm. But doing it the way it was done was exactly *contrary* to Georg's apparent motive. He might have decided to kill the Thelm to avoid execution or exile. But even in such a case, he could only be safe if he was very, very public about the murder. Unless or until they could come up with an alternate motive for Georg to kill the Thelm furtively, Georg was a problematic suspect.

What if Georg was a knowing accomplice—or had hired a contract killer? Jamie couldn't quite think what motive Georg would have for having someone else do the job—but never mind about motives for the time being. Just as a piece of legal theory, would *that* be a crime for Georg? Would it be a crime for the accomplice? Jamie could invent a plausible argument for either possibility, but he had a hunch that calling in an accomplice to do the dirty work would be considered dishonorable.

What if an unknown party carried out the murder *without* Georg's knowledge or permission? Then Georg would likely, but not definitely, benefit by becoming Thelm on the death of his father. Darsteel should be able to tell them for sure in the morning. But Georg was the *only* person for whom the murder would *not* be a crime. So the unknown person would be subject to arrest and punishment.

Tentative conclusion: The murder was definitely and indisputably a crime only if Georg has nothing to do with it, and clearly *not* a crime only if Georg definitely and indisputably did the killing, and did it entirely by himself.

But there was another weird angle: Since the murder was definitely and indisputably a crime *only* if Georg had nothing to do with it, any attempt to frame Georg for the killing would *benefit* Georg by preventing his death or exile, and by making him Thelm—and *also* protect the real culprit from punishment.

Jamie turned to the question of who *else* might benefit. In other words, who else would have a motive for killing the Thelm? Anyone who *didn't* want the Thelek to be next in line for the Thelmship would have a motive to kill the Thelm—and to do so as soon as possible. If the Thelm *didn't* die before Georg was executed, and before the Thelm had any chance to come up with a way to establish an alternate heir, then the High Thelek would be indisputably next in line for the Thelmship. Thelek Saffeer would become Thelm Saffeer once the Thelm did die, in a week or a century.

Therefore, anyone who wanted to prevent the Thelek from becoming Thelm would have a reason to kill the present Thelm immediately, *before* the last four days of the time period expired and/or before the Thelm could find a suitable replacement heir. The only problem with that idea was that an awful lot of people didn't want the Thelek to become Thelm.

They'd have a long list of suspects if they went by that motive.

And then there was the whole category of motives that had nothing to do with the succession. Hannah had mentioned that someone with a grudge against the Thelm might choose this moment for revenge simply because everyone would assume the killing had political motives. What she hadn't mentioned was that their good friend Lady Zahida Halztec fell neatly into that category. She had certainly played the part of a good and loyal subject—but on the other hand, her family might hold a grudge against the present Thelm, who had not lifted a finger to prevent her great-uncle Bindulan's exile, or done anything much to clear his name.

And, edging back over into succession-related motives, the Bindulan clan most decidedly would not want the High Thelek to be Thelm. Family self-interest, even self-defense, might well serve to reinforce a revenge motive.

There was another element. The killer, or an accomplice, had to get to the dueling pistols and tamper with them before last night. Of all the suspects Jamie could think of, Zahida was the only one that he knew for certain had recently been in the Thelm's Private Audience Chamber. That she had gone there to save the lives of a certain two BSI agents made him less than happy to use that visit to help build a case against her, but those were the facts.

What about other suspects? The Thelm was the ruler of a faction-plagued world, and he had been in power for a very long time. It would be a miracle if he hadn't made some enemies along the way. There might be dozens of them, all eager to do him in.

If he wanted to cast his net even farther, Jamie could go look in the mirror. Darsteel hadn't just locked them up to keep them safe. It had to be that Darsteel was treating them as suspects. After all, they were in the Keep the night it happened, and it shouldn't have been too hard for Darsteel to imagine a motive strong enough to inspire the humans to murder the Thelm.

Jamie smiled to himself in the darkness. So either Georg did it, or someone else did. He decided to give it up for the moment and try again in the daytime. He quit staring at the ceiling, shut his eyes, and went to sleep.

\* \* \*

Hannah wasn't in the least surprised to come fully awake once again when she got to bed, her thoughts speeding along almost too fast for her to keep up with them. She'd been on too many cases not to expect it.

The Thelm's death must have, to a certainty, set chaos loose on Reqwar. *The High Thelek has to be jumping out of his skin by now*, she thought. And it must have been doubly bad for him to have his tame Kendari vanish into thin air. Hannah was entirely prepared to believe Brox when he said the Thelek did not know he had gone to the fire. But even if Brox had been lying, he vanished for sure and for real once Darsteel had gotten them all locked in together.

But the Thelek would not be the only one starved for information. Every land-thelm and thelek on the planet had to be wondering what the devil was going on, and who was going to wind up on top. Every small-time land-thelm who distrusted his neighbor would be wondering if the neighbor was going to take advantage of the confusion to strike now, when the central authorities were likely too distracted to interfere. And every small-time land-thelm who got that far in his thinking would start reflecting on the advantages of striking first . . .

It could be the case that civil war, a whole series of civil wars, had already broken out, that the whole Reqwar political system was unraveling already. But she was letting her imagination run away with her. With a little luck, there would still be time to calm the situation before it reached that state.

But the only way to calm it would be to replace uncertainty with clarity. And the only way to do that would be for one undisputed and universally acceptable successor to the Thelm to emerge. And the only way for that even to be *possible* would be to figure out who the devil had killed the Thelm, and why.

*Did* the means and timing of the Thelm's death affect the succession? If so, how? Were they looking in all the right directions for their suspects? Jamie's list of suspects had certainly erred on the side of inclusiveness. He had included the two Stannlar Consortia, for example. Hannah wished she had had the chance to ask him why—but with Brox right there, and Darsteel too for that matter, there hadn't been the chance.

But why *had* he included them? Perhaps simply because, mere hours after playing host to the Thelm in their converted warehouse, the Thelm was dead. Had the Thelm—or anyone else at the meeting—said or done something she had missed that would suffice as a motive? Or was it just that it would be awfully convenient to have their business partner made the king of the planet? Or might they have done it for some related, if more altruistic, reason? The Thelm himself had warned that the planet's terrestrial ecology would collapse altogether if the High Thelek took over, booted out the human-Stannlar team, and asked the Kendari to take over—or, rather, start over from scratch. Kill Thelm Lantrall, make Georg Thelm, and save the world?

The Stannlar did have a well-earned reputation for being rather casual about the death of an individual. Death, after all, was something that happened to insignificant components. The Consortium itself lived on.

It suddenly occurred to Hannah that this particular murder would have been absurdly easy for a Stannlar Consortium to commit. The whole case revolved around persuading or compelling the Thelm to fire that ridiculous dueling pistol, so that the rocket slug would shoot backwards, out the wrong end of the gun, and kill him. Well, what better way to scare him than with a nasty monster right in front of him?

One or both Stannlar could have sent any number of smaller components into the Keep, through any number of routes. The components could have met up in the Keep, then assembled themselves into whatever sort of size and shape monster would be most likely to scare the Thelm. Well, all right, subcomponents going "boo" was getting a bit outlandish, but she was casting about for possibilities, not probabilities. They might have used some other way to get the Thelm to fire that gun.

The Stannlar would have to sabotage the gun first, but that was true of every possible suspect. But, after the murder—that was the beauty part. The Stannlar components could start the fire in the room, making sure to destroy any bits of evidence they needed to get rid of—such as whatever it was they used to create that shoe print—then throw *themselves* into the fire. That would leave whoever investigated searching for an escaped murderer, when the murderer in fact no longer existed.

Suicidal for the components themselves, yes, but for the Stannlar Consortium of which they were a part, it would be a sacrifice, a degree of stress to the system, somewhere between a haircut and a blood donation. How much stress *would* it be? How would it show, and how much? If, say, both or either Stannlar suddenly showed signs of needing to regenerate, or seemed to have not quite as many components on view, that might well tell the investigators something. The signs might be subtle, or fleeting. They would have to check at once, as soon as Darsteel came in to talk with them in the morning.

She moved on to other questions. What, exactly, had Jamie asked for in that second note? Brox's being there was a dreadful nuisance. Though, it had to be confessed, Brox really was a decent sort. No. More than that. Downright honorable. Capable of seeing beyond short-term advantage for his side, of worrying about the long-term consequences for all.

She yawned. Good old Brox. Good man to stand by in a crisis. But he wasn't a man. Kendari. Got to watch out for trusting him. Yes, sir. She yawned mightily, shut her eyes, and stretched. Watch out for the Kendari, even the good ones...

And she slept, fitfully, nervously, her slumbers disturbed by dreams of trying to work a crime scene while a whole herd of miniature component-Kendari in tiny iso-suits endlessly split up and re-formed into all sorts of monster shapes, before turning into the Thelm, up and walking around with a gaping hole clean through his chest, then melting into a pair of earnest Stannlar who kept interrupting her measurements with eager explanations of how death was nothing to worry about.

And then the dreams faded down into the calm and welcoming darkness, and she slept.

* * *

Brox 231, as an individual, liked to believe that he was not much given to fretting in bed. He was, for that matter, a member of a species not much given to it either. His main problem was with the confounded excuse for a sleep-sling that they had brought in. The blasted thing had obviously been built by someone who had seen a picture of one once, but that was where its resemblance to a proper sling ended. It somehow managed to be too long and too short, too narrow and too wide, all at the same time. He finally gave up trying to adjust it and resigned himself to suffering with things as they were. He probably would have been better off simply curling up on the floor somewhere.

But Brox had always prided himself on being honest with himself. It wasn't just the badly designed, badly made sleep-sling—though that was a part of it. There was a great deal more going on to keep him awake.

He was only thankful that the humans and Darsteel showed no signs of realizing the real reasons he had left the Thelek's home without a word, the moment he had heard of the fire.

First and foremost, the Thelek *had* to know, backwards and forwards, the exact laws of succession under every possible set of circumstances. He had lived and breathed the ambition of ascending to the Thelmship for so long that it had all become second nature to him. But the instinct, even the need, to scheme and plot had also become second nature.

The Thelek would not be able to resist the temptation to find advantage in this catastrophe. Given half a chance, the Thelek would have sucked Brox into whatever plots he started to hatch. Brox wanted no part of such schemes and wanted the Kendari government to have no part of them.

If, as seemed quite possible, there was a way for the Thelek to ascend to the Thelmship legally, properly, and openly, Brox would do all he could to assist him. But if Thelek sought to achieve that goal by exerting pressure to suppress evidence, by encouraging witnesses to forget certain details, or encouraging them to remember other details in a more helpful manner, by altering documents or "correcting" evidentiary photos, or any of the rest of it, the Kendari government could not be involved. Not only was such nonsense stupid and dangerous, not only was it dishonorable—worst of all, it was doomed to failure. After all, the human investigators were there, ready and watching for all the usual tricks.

And of course there was the very real possibility that the Thelek had committed the murder. Oh, not himself. Of course not. That would not be the done thing. But as the head of a vast, complex, and murky conspiracy? Yes, absolutely. And the evidence all pointed to the sort of conspiracy the High Thelek would have come up with. A needlessly complicated way to do the murder itself, involving an upper-class obsession like dueling. Various indications of a botched follow-up, such as the repeated attempts to start the fire, and the odd scratches on the Thelm's hands and fingers. The attempt—however crude—to plant evidence implicating an enemy in the crime. Brox did not know for sure who had done the killing, but he had not the slightest doubt in his mind that the shoe print was faked, somehow.

It looked all too much like a High Thelek job. And if Brox had been there at the High Thelek's side in the aftermath, he would have gotten sucked into the explanations, the deceptions, the cover-ups that were likely being devised even now.

Far better to be safely locked up here in these apartments, literally caught in the middle, with a snoring human in either side room. Put that way, his current situation seemed quite satisfactory indeed.

Brox sighed, stretched out into the least uncomfortable position he could manage, and went to sleep.

Somehow or another, Jamie managed to be the first one up in the morning. He emerged as quietly as possible from his room, and slipped in and out of the human-style refresher without waking Brox. It was only after he emerged that he noticed a box on the main table. It had his name—written in very clumsily written Roman letters instead of Greater Trade Writing phonetics—scrawled on the side. He scooped it up and took it to his room to open. Inside was a rocket-gun dueling pistol, two dummy rounds, and a simplified manual with lots of pictures. That was helpful, as Jamie's ability to read Reqwar Pavlat was severely limited.

He set to work studying the gun. It took only a minute or two for him to understand its basic workings—but somehow, he got the feeling that it could tell him a lot more if only he gave it a chance. He sat there, thinking, for a long time. It was almost coming. Almost.

* * *

The other two were awake, in and out of the refresher, fed, and ready for the day by the time he came out again. There was a tray waiting for him, and he saw with regret that the food had dropped back from palatable to merely digestible again. But it was all he was going to get, and so he sat and forced it down, whatever it was, as best he could. Brox studiously looked the other way, apparently not finding the sight of a human eating all that pleasant.

"One of Darsteel's flunkies brought a message in for you a few minutes ago," said Hannah.

"What was it?" Jamie asked.

"It was sealed, and still is," she said, handing him a message tube. "It was addressed to you."

*And if we don't want Brox opening messages that aren't for him, we can't do it either.* "All right," said Jamie. He broke the seal on the end of the tube and fished out the note itself. He read it over quickly and summed it up out loud. "It's a quick update and an answer to one of my queries," he said. "It's date-stamped about ninety minutes ago. As of then, everyone on our list of suspects except the Stannlar has been removed from where they were staying and placed elsewhere, with reasonable but limited freedom of movement. There was no other good place to keep the Stannlar, and so Darsteel has left them where they were in the warehouse and posted guards all over the place. None of the suspects has said anything useful, and nothing remarkably suspicious was found when the places where they were living were searched. However, he does report that Georg's *left* shoe was found in Marta's quarters in the Keep. Not being all that familiar with human shoes, they tested it, and confirmed that it makes a print that is a mirror-image copy of the print found at the scene."

"Very interesting," said Hannah. "So that pretty much nails down the fact that Georg was here at the Keep *before* the fire last night."

*It does a lot more than that*, thought Jamie. But he wasn't quite ready to work on that side of the puzzle. "So it does," he said, and went no further.

"Brox and I have been talking about the timing of the crime," said Hannah.

"In reality, we have been doing our best to pass the time until the door opens up, and Darsteel brings us some *news*, and not just notes that tell us nothing we couldn't guess," said Brox. "Or, better still, until he lets us out of here."

"I'm not so sure I *want* to get out just yet," said Hannah. "Feelings are likely to be running a little high just now—and the locals have already tried pretty hard to kill Agent Mendez and me."

"I grant your point," Brox said.

"What's this about the timing of the crime?" Jamie asked. "You mean its happening so soon before the execution deadline for Georg?"

"That too," said Brox, "but we were mainly looking at events that happened *before* the murder, to see if any of them might have been the trigger, so to speak. Your arrival, for example. It might well be that someone in some faction feared that you might cause trouble for them. Perhaps someone who feared that you would suggest a solution to the Georg Hertzmann crisis."

Jamie and Hannah exchanged looks. Jamie was startled to realize that his suggestion about Penitence was only a few hours old—and that Brox had very likely not heard about it yet. But should he hear about it now?

"What do you think?" Hannah asked, engaging in a not particularly difficult bit of mind reading.

"I think he's played pretty much straight with us, and it won't stay quiet for long, anyway."

"That's about the way I figured it," said Hannah, "but I wanted to get your okay first."

"Might I ask what in the soul's dark forest you are talking about?" Brox demanded.

Jamie wasn't quite sure what a soul's dark forest might be, but he took the sense of the question. "I made a not-very-smart little suggestion toward the end of the meeting last night," he said, and quickly described his idea about sending Georg on a one-way trip to Penitence. Brox instantly understood its significance, and was not shy about sharing his opinion that Jamie had not been wise. He asked a series of sharp and detailed questions about how the Thelm reacted and what had happened next.

"This is vital new information," said Brox when he had heard it all. "It was a serious failing on your part not to report it at once last night."

Hannah let out a weary sigh. "You're right," she said. "But in our defense, we were a little busy with other issues. I don't even think it occurred to us that you didn't know it already."

"How could I have?"

Jamie resisted the temptation to laugh, or worse, answer that question. Brox could have known easily, through all sorts of means he might not want to talk about. "Let's just leave it there," he suggested. "We've told you now, and that ought to count for something."

"Anyway, for the sake of argument," said Hannah, "let's assume that Jamie's bright idea about Penitence was the motive."

"Let's not," Jamie said. "I don't want the Thelm's death to have been caused by my shooting my mouth off."

"It was not," Brox said flatly. "It was caused by a sabotaged rocket-propelled projectile blasting back into the Thelm's chest when the Thelm attempted to fire his gun, even though the Thelm had no intention of shooting himself. Whoever set the—what was the term you used?"

"Booby trap," said Jamie dejectedly.

"Whoever set the booby trap caused his death. You spoke—unwisely, perhaps, but out of honorable motives—to try to save the life of your fellow human. You cannot be responsible for another party's deliberately acting to subvert or prevent what you intended. The Thelm fired, most likely to defend himself against some unknown intruder—and yet he killed himself instead, as an unintended consequence of his own actions. It would be no more logical to blame him for his own death than to blame you."

Something in what Brox said brought Jamie up short. Somewhere in there, his subconscious was telling him, was a piece to the puzzle, a big one, and an important one. But where it fit, or what the puzzle would look like, Jamie could not yet see. "Thank you, Inquirist Brox," he said. "But getting back to the case, if we're looking for motives, and if my suggestion about Penitence *was* the motive, then we've only got two suspects. Zahida heard it, and so did Marta."

"You have *three* individual suspects," said Brox. "And, my apologies, one additional pair of conspiratorial suspects."

Hannah looked at him coldly. "Go on."

"The Lady Zahida heard your idea," said Brox. "Marta Hertzmann heard it. *And so did the Thelm.* Perhaps—perhaps—this looks like a suicide because it *was* one. The Thelm realizes that the only way he can save his sole surviving son, and his family, is to kill himself. For whatever reason, he has the booby-trapped weapon and *knows* it is booby-trapped. Maybe one of the two dueling pistols has been booby-trapped from the start, so that the Thelm could not lose a duel—even if he missed, his opponent would shoot himself in the chest."

"Unless his opponent happened to pick up the gun intended for the Thelm," said Hannah. "Then it would be impossible for the Thelm to *survive* a duel."

"A trivial objection," said Brox. "There are a thousand ways the pistols could have been marked. But let us imagine he had no way of knowing which gun was which. That might add a little of the absurd drama that our Reqwar Pavlat friends seem to need in their politics and personal life. The Thelm deliberately selects a gun without knowing which it is. He fires, not knowing if he is about to smash a hole in the wall, or through himself. Let the fates decide, or whatever other poetry you might wish to apply to a random choice."

"What about the shoe print, and your idea about an accelerant and a fire that started after the death?" Hannah demanded.

*And how about the fact that* you *found the shoe print while no one else was looking your way?* Jamie thought, his eyes on Brox. *You could have stashed the shoe in your iso-suit and made the print while we were all examining the Thelm's corpse, then disposed of the shoe somehow. It's still missing, after all.* But he didn't want to explore those ideas just at the moment.

Brox cocked his head to one side. "Those are flaws," he admitted.

"Easy ones to answer," said Jamie, glad for the chance to steer things in another direction. "As long as we're theory-spinning, let's say the Thelm sets the fires out of anger, despair, or whatever, *then* kills himself immediately, shooting before the fire can spread very much. He gives himself a Viking funeral."

"A what?" asked Brox.

"Viking funeral," said Hannah. "A human death ritual involving fire. Go on, Jamie."

"Georg comes in, sees what has happened, realizes he can do nothing—or is so disgusted or horrified he leaves in a panic—or perhaps he arrives after the fire has really taken hold and he can't get close enough to do anything. He manages to leave the shoe print, probably without realizing it. By the time he gets outside, a few minutes later, he decides that explaining all that won't make him look too good, so he keeps quiet."

"And what happened to his missing shoe?" Hannah asked. "Why was he in socks but no shoes after the fire?"

"Because the right shoe, the one that left the print, has some sort of fire marks or heat damage, or just smells strongly of soot and smoke. Maybe he accidentally stepped on a hot ember and melted the sole of the shoe. Whatever. It's marked in some way, but the left shoe isn't. Since the right shoe's condition is evidence he was there when he says he wasn't, he has to conceal it or destroy it. Maybe he just chucked the shoe into the hottest part of the fire.

"The main thing is, if he doesn't know that he left a shoe *print*, he doesn't know there is no point in hiding the shoe, if you followed that. Either he meant to get back to Marta's apartments and take the second shoe anyway, but never got the chance, or else he didn't think of it until it was too late. Wearing just one shoe would draw attention to the missing one—so he goes out during the evacuation in his socks."

"That more or less holds together," Brox conceded.

"Of course," Jamie went on, "if Georg *did* do it, instead of just finding the Thelm right after his suicide, and if for some reason he felt he had to conceal that fact, then we can play the postmurder events pretty much the same way." He turned to Brox. "But I want to hear about this pair of conspiratorial suspects," he said.

Brox lowered his arms, hands open, shoulders out—the Kendari equivalent of a shrug. "I was simply making a point, and a poor one at that. Each of you serves as an alibi for the other during the period of the murder—but who serves as an alibi for you *both*? The conversation in the car might or might have something to do with your motive. Perhaps the suggestion of Penitence merely started some later train of conversation between the two of you.

"Or perhaps the Penitence plan has nothing to do with it. Perhaps you realized that the human race could claim the rule of a whole new planet, merely by disposing of a single tiresome old alien and installing a human ruler in his place. Control over a whole planet is a strong motive for murder—especially for two police agents who also have orders to be alert to the political agenda."

Jamie felt himself getting angry, but controlled himself—just barely. Hannah saved the situation by speaking first. "It's an excellent motive for murder. In fact, I'd suggest it's possibly the strongest motive in all of human history. The trouble is, it never even occurred to either of us."

*Speak for yourself*, thought Jamie. It *had* occurred to him, as a bit of logical theorizing. But no, he hadn't acted on it, or mentioned it, and he certainly wasn't about to do so. "I'm not so sure it *is* that great a motive, just because it is so big and long-term and impersonal," he said. "Besides, Georg's becoming Thelm doesn't make this a human world. It just makes it more possible for humans to have some political influence down the road. The motive wouldn't be 'kill the Thelm and win yourself a world.' It would be 'kill the Thelm today, then if everything goes just right, and they don't throw Georg out right away, in ten or twenty or a hundred years, my people might have the start of a nice big settlement on one of the other continents.'"

"I merely offered a theory that others will no doubt think of," Brox said mildly. "But setting the human race on course to colonize a world would result in a positive rating in one of those Employee Fitness Reviews that you BSI agents seem to worship without end."

Hannah laughed. "Your point is made. I know quite a few agents who might kill for a high-positive EFR." But then her expression grew more serious. "But jokes and theories to one side, I will tell you in all frankness, that the blade cuts both ways. If *we* have a motive for wanting Georg to have done it, or perhaps a motive to do the murder ourselves and make it look like Georg killed the Thelm, then *you* have a motive for proving that Georg did *not* kill the Thelm."

"And that possible motive will evaporate if it turns out Georg ascends even if he didn't commit the murder," Brox said calmly. "However, in that case, *your* motive for the crime becomes even stronger."

"Assuming we knew for sure that Georg would ascend if someone else was the killer," said Hannah. "We didn't. We still don't."

"There are few things as easy to feign as ignorance," said Brox. "And few things as difficult to conceal, if it comes to that."

And suddenly Jamie had it. He saw. It wasn't logic that told him so. It was a gut feeling. But the logic was there. It held together. He was sure of it. But he had to walk through it, lead the others behind, see if it all worked. He was the junior partner here. Brox and Hannah were the seasoned investigators. They had seen it all before. They weren't going to be impressed by some fresh-faced kid spinning one more theory. Facts. He needed to show them *facts*.

"We're going at this the wrong way," he said slowly. "We're trying to say what this or that person *could* have done, and bending the known facts to fit the theory. Turn it around. You'd *have* to know certain things for sure before you killed the Thelm—such as who would ascend to the Thelmship. Or else you might have to *think* you know something—but make a mistake based on incomplete knowledge."

"What do you mean?" Brox asked.

"Well, the weapon, for example. The killer knew some things, but not others," Jamie said. "Wait a sec. I'll be right back." He stood up, went to his room, and came back with the duplicate weapon in its box. "This was waiting on the table when I first got up, while you two were still sleeping. It doesn't have all the fancy stuff on it that the real one had, but it's mechanically identical. I think it tells us a lot."

He held up the rocket-gun pistol. "The weapon itself is almost too simple to explain," he said. "The barrel is a straight tube. It's not even rifled. The breech end has an exterior screw thread. It takes a single round of ammo, which screws into place." He held up the dummy round Darsteel had provided. It was a cruel-looking thing, shaped like an oversized bullet, about four centimeters wide and fifteen centimeters long. "The rocket-projectile round has its base mounted to the screw-on endcap. The electrical connection with the pistol's firing mechanism is made through the screw-on cap. The round loads this way."

He shoved the projectile up into the breech end of the gun barrel and screwed it in place. "That's all there is to it. Pull the trigger and you complete an electric connection and *POW!* the thing fires. The projectile flies out the end of the barrel. The muzzle end of the tube is flared out like a bell or a funnel to keep the rocket exhaust more or less out of the shooter's face. The projectile has snap-out fins that unfold as soon as it is clear of the barrel. The fins are canted to provide spin stabilization of the projectile."

He unscrewed the dummy round, set down the gun, and held up the round. "All you have to do in order to shoot again is unscrew the cap, run a thing like a bottle brush through the barrel, then screw in a fresh round. There are various types available. High-explosive, armor-piercing, even ones that explode just in front of the target to create a really horrible wound. And, if you know who and where to ask—there is the suicide round, also known as a backfire shot. One of Darsteel's colleagues saw a picture of the Thelm's wounds and instantly knew a backfire had done it. Darsteel sent along everything he had on them."

He held up the other dummy round, one that looked much like the first—except the pointed end of the projectile had been sliced off, and the projectile was mounted to the endcap backwards, so that the rocket engine pointed at the muzzle, with two thin electric leads connected to its igniter.

"Suicide round is an ironic name, of course. They aren't meant to be used when you *deliberately* want to kill yourself. They are meant to do what was done in this case—to cause the shooter to kill himself when he tries to shoot someone else. You can see most of the modifications that have been made. The one that's less obvious is that the screw-cap's threads have been very precisely filed down, and that the screw-cap is made of a much thinner piece of a much weaker material. When the rocket fires, the threading will shear clean off, and the screw-cap will be driven into the shooter's body, where it will shatter on impact, with the rocket projectile plowing right through it. We saw what the results look like last night."

"But what does all this tell us that we did not already know?" Brox demanded. "We knew the rocket fired backwards and killed the Thelm."

"Yes, but *how* it was done tells us a great deal we did not know," said Jamie. He held up the suicide round. "This is a premade part, all of a piece. It's not something an amateur could put together on the kitchen table. Either the killer was someone who knew weapons, and this particular weapon, and had the skills to build one of these—or else the killer would have had to go shopping for it—quietly, and very carefully. And that would take time, possibly quite a bit of time. But once the killer had the suicide round in hand, he or she could swap it into the Thelm's gun in seconds." He demonstrated by picking up the gun, unscrewing one round, and screwing the other back in. "That's all it would take," he said. "Now the gun is ready to kill the shooter."

"So you're saying this would take a lot of time to prepare, but very little time to put into operation," said Hannah. "And of course the suicide round could have been put in the gun at any time. Months ago, maybe."

"Yes, but I tend to think it wasn't," Jamie said. "There's a whole line of sporting and target-shooting weapons that use the same type of rocket-cartridge ammunition. According to everything I've read about him, the Thelm went target-shooting pretty regularly—but he has never fought a duel.

"Maybe Plan A was to load a backfire round into his long gun. That way you'd kill him the next time he goes shooting, and you don't have to goad him into reaching for a decorative pistol in his office. Then, for whatever reason, the killer went to Plan B. Of course, it might even be that the killer had the rounds in stock for some other reason, some other intended attack, and simply reached for the tool at hand when he or she decided to kill the Thelm."

"So what does *that* tell us?" Brox demanded.

"That the killer has been on Reqwar long enough to learn about these rocket guns, perhaps long enough to make some contacts with someone willing to come up with a few suicide rounds for sale. Or maybe the killer dreamed them up independently, or found the plans for them on the reference net somewhere and worked from there, and the round *was* homemade. There hasn't been any chance to analyze the remains of the round that buried itself in the Thelm's chest. Once that's done, it might tell us a lot. But it already tells us that the killer has been preparing to kill someone for a while."

"And you two have just arrived," said Brox. "You exonerate yourselves."

Jamie shrugged. "What's the harm in that? It's a start. It eliminates two suspects. I would suggest that it also tends to exonerate Lady Zahida. She has only been on-planet for a month or two, and was keeping well clear of politics until her great-uncle dragged her into them on his behalf."

"Ah, but let us not forget the Reqwar Pavlat fondness for gestures and romance," said Brox. "It was a canceled duel that ruined her family. What more fitting means of revenge than a dueling pistol? It might well be that Bindulan himself gave her precise instructions on what to do, so as to heighten the drama and the justice of it all."

"That might make sense," Hannah conceded. "At least, to a member of the Pavlat nobility. But it's out of character for Zahida, somehow. If she wanted to kill you, she'd just go ahead and do it. She's no fan of all the conspiracies and alliances."

"So she didn't do it because this sort of murder

isn't her style?" Brox snorted with derision. "As for her rejecting the complex web of alliance and loyalty—let me just point out that she risked her life to save the two of you because her great-uncle, from who knows how many light-years away, told her to do so. *And* she returned from off-planet to face a dreary future—when so instructed."

"I'll give you a much stronger argument against her being a suspect," said Jamie. "I think the scratches and bruises on the Thelm's arm also tend to exonerate Zahida—and just about any other possible Pavlat suspect."

"How so?" Brox demanded.

"Because the only possible reason for clawing at his hand after death that way would be to try to get the gun out of it—and any Pavlat would know that was impossible. I think the killer's original plan called for removing the gun, leaving the Thelm dead, with no sign that he had shot himself."

"Except that the fragments of the suicide round's cartridge endcap were embedded in his body," said Brox, "and there were scorch marks from the rocket exhaust on his hand, and—"

"I know, I know, I know," said Jamie. "But I'm suggesting that this was a very last-minute plan, put together in a rush. Maybe not thought through all the way, or maybe the perpetrator knew perfectly well what at least some of the flaws were, but just didn't have any way to fix them, or else was trusting in the fire to destroy the inconvenient evidence."

"All right," said Hannah. "A Pavlat like Zahida

would of course know about the clasp reflex death grip. I agree that does at least strongly tend to exonerate her."

"The death grip issue shows that the killer's actions can tell us what he or she did *and* didn't know," said Jamie. "The crime scene evidence doesn't just tell us what the killer's plan was—it tells went *wrong* with the plan."

"Okay," said Hannah, leaning forward a bit over the table. "I can see that with the death grip. Go on. Tell me more."

"This next is a bit of a stretch—but only a bit," said Jamie. "*Why* would the killer want to get rid of the gun, except to conceal the fact that the Thelm was the one to pull the trigger? Can either of you think of another reason? I can't."

Hannah shook her head. Brox snorted. "That we can't think of any reason does not mean there *was* no reason," he said. "But go on. We'll accept your argument, for the moment, anyway."

"Put the failed attempt to remove the gun together with the shoe print, and I think it's fairly clear that the killer either *was* Georg, or else was trying to frame Georg for the murder. The weird thing in this case, of course, is that it would *benefit* Georg to be guilty of, or framed for, the killing—but the killer would benefit as well, by literally getting away with murder. There were lots of people who might have private reasons for killing the Thelm. So, assuming it *wasn't* Georg, we *can't* assume that making Georg Thelm of all Reqwar was the motive."

"But suppose Georg wasn't the killer, and wouldn't cooperate with the frame-up, because *he* wanted the killer caught?" Hannah asked.

"Then the killer might have a problem," Jamie conceded. "But it might at least seem a risk worth taking. But let's get back to what the crime scene tells us. What happened next?"

"Either Georg the killer left a shoe print behind, in a very awkward spot, or else the killer did it for him—and I think it was obvious to all of us how unlikely that shoe print was—a single, perfect print, all by itself like that." said Hannah.

"I'm no biped, obviously," said Brox, "but I wondered about that myself. Even you humans had to more or less wedge yourselves in between the door and the knocked-over plant to *see* the shoe print—and the print had to be made *after* the plant fell over, because it was in the dirt spilled out from the plant's pot."

"But why just one shoe print?" Hannah asked. "Why not leave a whole trail of both feet all over the place? It would be more plausible, if you did it right."

"Maybe the killer *couldn't* do it right," said Jamie. "A Pavlat would have a lot of trouble putting on human shoes and leaving prints that were convincingly spaced and so on. Or maybe because the killer only had the right shoe.

"Darsteel's people have found the *left* shoe in Marta's apartments. The right shoe, the one that made the prints, is missing. For whatever reason, the killer only had one shoe, and wisely decided not to leave a half dozen right shoe prints and no left shoe prints. Under the circumstances, leaving *one* shoe print was probably the safest course. As for where the print was, the killer didn't have much choice. After all, if not the dirt from the pot, what else was there in the room that would take a clear print?"

"What about the beverages in the bottles that were on the table? The liquid from those bottles pooled up nicely. A shoe could have stepped in that and made a good print."

"I don't think those bottles had been knocked over yet when the killer was placing that shoe print," said Jamie, after considering for a moment. "Or they might have been, but weren't related to it. I think they were part of starting the fire. But I'll come to that."

"It's flimsy stuff, but this business about the shoes and the shoe print and the missing shoe does weaken Georg as the suspect," Brox admitted. "*He* would have been wearing both shoes, and would have been able to leave a real-looking set of prints—because they would *be* real."

"Good," Jamie said, just glad to have Brox offering something more or less positive. "But now we do come to the fire, which I am starting to think wasn't part of the original plan. That there was a shoe print tells us we're supposed to think Georg did it. That there is only one print, and that the shoe that made it is missing, tells us that it probably *wasn't* Georg. But the other big glaring thing that makes it not look like Georg is the killer is a dead Thelm with a booby-trapped gun in his hand. If Georg were killing in order to claim his rights, he would do it as, as *clearly* as he could, so everyone would know he did it."

"Ah, but let us not forget his high and noble Pax Humana oath," said Brox. "If for some reason—such as fear of his daughter's being shipped to Penitence—he suddenly felt the need to kill the Thelm at once—he might still wish to kill secretly, in order to avoid bringing shame on the organization, or himself. Perhaps Pax Humana even suspects something of the sort, and that is why they have avoided getting involved."

Jamie considered it. "I see your point," he conceded. "But he'd have to know the dangers of getting caught would be awfully high. Even if Georg had some other motive beside the Thelmship for the murder—"

"Such as not wanting to be shipped out to Penitence," said Hannah.

"Even if Georg had some other motive, it would still make lots of sense for him to use his legal obligation to commit the killing as a cover story for his real motives. And if he was willing to kill, I think he might be willing to risk looking bad in front of the PH in exchange for making himself safe—and gaining control of the planet."

"Or at least maybe the real killer figured out something along those lines," said Hannah. "He decides to kill the Thelm and pin it on George, knows the gun in the Thelm's hand doesn't fit the picture—but then can't get the gun away from the Thelm. So, the killer sets the fire, in hopes of getting everything to burn enough to hide the fact that the Thelm was holding the gun."

"Things would have to burn pretty completely to hide that fact," Brox objected.

"But the killer could at least hope that the local cops would foul up the crime scene so no one would be able to tell," said Hannah. "Maybe our killer is even someone with the power to *arrange* that sort of foul-up, perhaps ahead of time. But I doubt it, especially if the plan was improvised at the last minute."

"Then why not set fire to the body directly?" Brox demanded.

"Our killer is no hardened professional," Jamie said. "Revulsion. Guilt. Shame. An unwillingness to see the corpse start burning. Maybe just panic. And let's not forget our amateur killer had just been clawing at the dead hand of the planet's ruler, while he lies there with a burned-meat smell rising from the smoking hole in his chest. The fact that someone wouldn't be thinking clearly at such a time shouldn't be all that much of a shock."

"The killer actually *did* try to burn the body directly, or nearly so," said Hannah. "You said yourself there were several scorch marks from a firestarter, and from a burning liquid, on the carpet he was on."

"Or maybe the cold-blooded, carefully worked-out plan was to burn the wooden ceiling and collapse it into the room, literally adding more fuel to the fire, so as to hide the evidence that way," said Brox. "If the fire floaters had gotten there a few minutes later, that's likely what would have happened."

"In any event, our killer tries several ways, and several times, to ignite the room. The killer tries to light the carpet—then tries dumping out the contents of all the beverage bottles onto the carpet, and lighting that."

Brox drummed his fingers on the table. "But what good would that do? The Pavlat don't drink anything with volatiles in it. The bottles on that table would have contained sophisticated Pavlat intoxicants, but those don't have anything in them that burns."

"I guessed that, but I didn't know it for sure until you told me," Jamie said.

"But then the killer *did* find some sort of supply of flammable liquid to serve as an accelerant," Brox observed. "The signs of a fire set that way were absolutely classic."

"And I have a guess as to what that supply was," said Jamie. "But I want to hold off on that until we hear from Darsteel."

Brox was still drumming his fingers distractedly, staring into space. "Your logic is good," he conceded, with a certain reluctance apparent in his voice. "But we must wait and see how closely it resembles events in the real world."

They did not have to wait long. At that exact moment, there was a thud and a rattle on the other side of the door of their apartment. The door swung open, and an exhausted-looking Darsteel in a mussed and rumpled uniform came in.

The two humans stood up, and Brox got up off his haunches. There was something in Darsteel's set, weary, worried expression that told them things had turned upside down.

"It would appear you're free to go," he said without preamble. "There have been developments. A lot of them. Enough that it looks like we won't need you anymore."

Darsteel had had a monster of a night. Locking up his three tame alien lawkeepers was only the start of it—though it did cross his mind that locking them up like that might give him a new murder case or two to solve in the morning. If so, his sympathies were limited. He had not the faintest idea who had killed his Thelm, or why, but it was fairly plain to see that it wouldn't have happened if not for aliens coming in and stirring things up.

But he had more aliens than his three pet lawkeepers to worry about. There were the Stannlar. How to keep the two Consortia isolated from each other, or the comm net, when they were in effect permanently linked to both?

He solved the twin problems, or at least dealt with them both, by throwing personnel and equipment at them. He ordered three whole squads to surround the building, and another to enter it and "observe" the Stannlar. He sent in his best snooper team as well, with orders to intercept and record all the comm they could, but with authority to jam every possible frequency as they judged best. The Stannlar were reputed to use several *im*possible frequencies, but it was the best he could do. He told the snoopers to be as blatant and obvious as they could be setting up their equipment. With any luck, the Stannlar would be sufficiently intimidated by the show of force and the sight of the comm gear not to try anything.

The other aliens still at large—Georg Hertzmann and his family—were physically easier to control—but politically speaking, they were even more dangerous than the Stannlar. Georg Hertzmann might be his Thelm by morning—might, indeed, be his Thelm already, if it turned out to be a case where succession was automatic. And yet, tonight Darsteel had to arrest all three of the Hertzmanns, keep them separate from each other, and keep them from returning to their quarters.

In the event, keeping them away from their quarters was easier to do than he thought. The Keep had been kept sealed after evacuation for "safety" reasons. Of course, the real reason was security. Nearly all of the Keep was intact and undamaged—and Darsteel needed places to keep people under control—such as the three aliens he had locked up in there.

Those displaced by the evacuation were herded into various nearby outbuildings, or sent to find places for themselves in the town. Georg and his family had been placed in reasonably comfortable rooms in a gate-keeper's cottage. Darsteel simply decided to leave them there. Darsteel found one of his most diligent and stubborn-minded subordinates, and told him to split the Hertzmanns up, and keep them split up, no matter how much they—meaning Marta Hertzmann—protested.

They were not to have the chance to compare notes or get their stories straight.

Future Thelm or not, Georg Hertzmann had been in no mood to debate the issue. His wife had been another matter, raising eight different kinds of ruckus and demanding that she and her daughter be allowed to return to their apartments in the Keep. That plainly wasn't going to happen with fire officials and safety inspectors swarming all over the place, and the local police finally getting organized enough to take their turn at the crime scene. And, meantime, the corpse of Thelm Lantrall still lay sprawled on the floor of his Private Audience Chamber. *That* state of affairs could not be tolerated much longer—and it wasn't. An hour after dawn, the corpse was removed by a most respectful team from the coroner's office. Darsteel made it doubly and triply clear that their examination was to be accurate, detailed, and precise—and not so respectful of the dead that there was scarcely any point in holding a postmortem at all.

At the same time, Darsteel had had to find and secure the person of Zahida Halztec. She hadn't been hard to find, and was so distraught that she was far less of a problem to manage than he had feared. She allowed herself to be filed away in another commandeered room in another outbuilding. But she, too, was a person it might well be dangerous to trifle with. Her family's honor had been besmirched a generation or two back—but she had been granted the power of the Thelm's Hand, at least in a limited circumstance. That showed the favor of the old Thelm, and clearly enhanced her status. And it was known that she had met with Georg Hertzmann—who might be the new Thelm. It was not hard to see how she might grow to be powerful, influential. It would be wise to handle her gently, just in case the day dawned when she was in a position to remember how she had been handled—and do something about it.

Which left only the High Thelek. Darsteel reluctantly decided to leave him alone. He would have had to recruit and arm a whole regiment of lawkeepers just to take the Thelek into custody. The odds of the Thelek's cooperating with an effort to detain or secure him were zero—and the odds of any attempt to compel him going horribly wrong were close to a certainty.

That much accomplished, there was nothing more to do than to send lawkeepers to follow up on the young human investigator's odd queries, obtain a binding legal opinion regarding the succession, dispatch investigators to organize interrogations of witnesses, send further lawkeepers out to check on the whereabouts of various opponents of the Thelm, on the off chance that this was a more routine, home-grown, political murder, and order searches, where possible, of the various premises of the persons he had detained. In other words, a lifetime's worth of work that had to be done within a few hours—and that was just the start of it all. A thousand other details, some mundane and trivial, some utterly essential, had to be managed as well.

And then the reports started to come in—the

answers to the questions he had asked, the results of the searches, updates on the prisoners—correction, the persons in protective custody. One of the those protective custody reports brought Darsteel up short.

It seemed that his diligent subordinate had been a little *too* diligent. The Herztmann's little girl, Moira, had been kept separate from both parents and confined in a room by herself. Apparently Moira had been exhibiting a quite remarkable series of hysterical tantrums.

Darsteel felt a sharp pang of guilt as he read the report. He had met Moira several times, even come to know her fairly well. His first instinct was to go to her and personally take her back to her mother at once. But then he thought again. The damage, after all, had already been done. And it might be, *might* be, that great good could be done by keeping her from her parents for just a little longer. Certain threads of logic had been starting to come together in his mind. At the very least, he might be able to test them by talking to Moira.

He thought for a moment about where best to meet with her. Once she calmed down, would she feel safer where she was? Or would she be more cooperative in an official-looking office? His instincts told him to go to her.

He was just about to do so when the next bit of news arrived at his office. It was a large, formal envelope from the Court of High Crime. It had to be the ruling on the succession.

Darsteel had played it all straight, up until that moment. But as soon as he opened that envelope, he would receive official notification of what was, so far, only a theory about who the next Thelm would be—or, in fact, was already.

Darsteel decided it would be best for—nearly—all concerned if it stayed a theory just that little bit longer. It was time to bend the rules a little. He left the still-sealed envelope on his desk and went to have a chat with a frightened little girl.

\* \* \*

Or maybe not so frightened as all that. They had put her in a disused ground-floor room of the gate-keeper's house, and left the door open, and set a guard in the doorway, sitting there on a perching stool, watching her. Every light in the house was blazing, and there was a seemingly constant bumping and thumping as various sorts of officers and lawkeepers headed up and down stairs, trying to look very important indeed.

And there was Moira on a sitting cushion, back to the far well, facing the doorway and framed by it, staring at the guard, solemn-faced and determined-looking, with something of her mother's stubbornness shining through. Streaks of tears shone on her face—but the tears themselves were gone. There was something about the set of her chin, the way her arms were folded across her chest, that told him something more than childish fear was going on here.

She wore an oversized pink flannel nightgown and was clutching a large and rather lumpy object covered in some sort of fabric that had been made to resemble brown fur. It took a moment for Darsteel to realize that it was meant to represent an animal—no doubt an Earth creature of some sort.

Darsteel stepped forward to the doorway and dismissed the guard with a gesture. He stepped into the room and closed the door behind him.

"Hello, Moira," he said.

"Hello," she said, her voice tired, even surly, but with that tone of stubbornness plain to hear. "I want to go to my mother. Now."

Darsteel knew that tone, and what it meant: She had argued a half dozen grown-ups to a standstill already, and was ready and willing to take on another. So he decided not to play the game. "No you don't," he said, pulling over a sitting cushion and seating himself right in front of her. "In fact, that's the very last thing you want."

Moira frowned, cocked her head, and looked at him in puzzlement. "What do you mean?"

"You know perfectly well you can't see your mother now," he said. "But you know that it's what a child you age is *supposed* to want. So you have to play the part in front of the grown-ups. Except I know. I know that your mother told you it was very, very important that you stay away, that you *don't* go to her, until you do something very, very important."

Darsteel had been bluffing, making it up as he went along when he started to speak, but he wasn't anymore. Her reaction told him at once that he was right. "So what you *really* want is to keep up arguing with everyone, demanding what you know you won't get, because that's what a regular little girl would do. Except you're not a regular little girl."

"I am so," she protested.

"No, you're not. A regular little girl would have given it up by now. But the other thing I know is that you haven't gotten a chance to do the job yet, because if you had, you'd stop the pretend tantrums and stop being stubborn. You'd have gone to sleep by now. Because you must be awfully tired."

Moira didn't say a word, and that told Darsteel everything. "And I don't think you've even had a chance to hide it here in this room, or anyplace else," he said, "because people have been watching you every second. So I think it must still be hidden on you somewhere, maybe inside your too-big-for-you night-gown, or maybe—"

"You can't touch me!" she shouted. "No one is allowed to touch me!"

"I know that," Darsteel said. "But you didn't ask me what the job was, or what it was you were supposed to be hiding. That tells me I have it all figured out right." He paused for a moment, then stood up, careful not to get any closer to her. "And I'm *not* going to touch you," he said. "I don't have to. All I have to do is call to the guards, and tell them to get a portable X-ray viewer from the hospital. They can bring it right here, and I can point it at you. It's for looking at bones and stuff inside you—but right next to the view of your bones, it'll show whatever is in your pockets, and whatever is hidden in your gown, and in your—"

"Wait!" Suddenly that stubborn look was gone, to be replaced, for the space of two or three heartbeats with a look of cold and naked calculation—which was replaced in turn by a look of the sweetest, most angelic, and most artificial innocence. "Oh!" she said in patently false surprise. "*That's* what you want. Why didn't any of your guards just ask for it? I would have given it to them," she lied.

Moira set the simulacrum of an animal on the floor, facedown, fumbled with some sort of fastener strip in its back, reached into its interior—and pulled out a human male's semiformal dress shoe for the right foot.

"My teddy bear has a special inside pocket for pajamas and stuff. But Mommy didn't give me the shoe or tell me to get rid of it or any of that stuff," she said. "I just found it, and figured I'd better take it to give to Daddy when I got the chance."

Darsteel stared at Moira, and the shoe. He reflected that even the youngest criminals made the mistake of explaining too much when they were caught. All such explanations were always unconvincing. The idea that she had just happened to find Daddy's shoe and just happened to conceal it in her toy was absurd—but what other story could she tell without betraying anyone? Darsteel made a heartfelt wish that he himself would one day be blessed with a daughter as clever, as poised, as intelligent—and as loyal. But that was all to one side. The main thing now was evidence—finding it, getting it, securing it.

"Thank you," he said. "That was what I wanted."

He resisted the urge to reach out and take the shoe. It showed every sign of having been wiped clean of any finger marks or fire debris or other evidence, but there was always the chance that it still held some clue that might be disturbed if he touched it. And if he just took it, he might spend the next fifty years of his life denying a charge of planting evidence in the case. "I still want it," he said, "but I want to be extra-careful how I take it, so we don't mess it up. And then you can *really* go to your mommy, if that's what you want."

And Moira smiled in genuine relief. "Yes, please. It is. Really."

"Then you'll really get to do it. In a minute." He stood up, opened the door, and called to the guard on duty for a vid recorder and an evidence bag, and witnesses. Then all he'd have to do was have her tell him again that she had "just found it," get the actual transfer recorded, get her to drop the shoe in an evidence bag and get the bag sealed.

\* \* \*

Ten minutes later, all that was accomplished, and Darsteel was headed back to his office.

The letter from the court, the one that would give him a ruling on the succession to the Thelmship, was still there waiting for him.

Until he opened the envelope, Darsteel could at least *pretend* he didn't have a new Thelm. Except he couldn't hide from the news forever—or for long. And whoever the new Thelm was, his first orders were bound to concern themselves with the investigation.

Which meant he had mere hours, perhaps mere minutes, to assemble an honest case, put together legitimate evidence of what had really happened, and secure that evidence against tampering. The task seemed flatly impossible—but at least he could get a start on it. He locked the shoe away in his office safe, along with a full copy of the recordings he had made of its receipt.

Darsteel doubted very much that the shoe itself could tell them anything at this point. But the means by which it had gotten to him told him a lot. It had unquestionably been in the possession of the killer. Hours later, it was in the possession of Moira Hertzmann, who, all but certainly, had received it from one or both of her parents, who obviously felt they had a very strong motive for concealing it if they were willing to involve the daughter they both doted on. All that was suggestive, to say the least.

But with that accomplished, what was there to do next? He sat down at his desk and stared at the pile of reports that was growing even as he watched. Couriers were coming and going, depositing their papers and packages. Nearly all of them were strictly routine, reporting that this site had been searched with no result, twenty-seven eyewitnesses to the fire had been interviewed so far, and so on.

And then another courier came in and dropped another report on his desk, on top of all the others. Darsteel gave up on the heap of papers on his desk and reached for the new one, on the theory that it had the latest news.

It did. He read it and started to get a sinking feeling in the gut of his stomach as he realized that it did indeed. It was, in a sense, the end of the case before it really began. Together with the evidence of the shoe's being concealed by the Hertzmanns, it was all but conclusive.

That should have made him happy, even relieved. But Darsteel had just discovered another little flaw in playing it straight. Sometimes it led to conclusions you didn't really want to reach.

"So that's it," Darsteel said in disgust to Hannah, Jamie, and Brox. "There are multiple witnesses at the fire scene—including all of you—that place Georg Hertzmann here at the Keep once the fire starts, when he's supposedly been staying away in that museum of his all the time. There is the shoe print in the crime scene, and the shoe winding up in his daughter's possession. We found the other shoe of the pair found in Marta Herztmann's apartments in the Keep, which very strongly suggests Georg Hertzmann was there *before* the murder. As you suggested, Lawkeeper Mendez, finding it was central to the case. And then there's this." He dropped the report onto the table in the common room. "It's the information you asked for, Lawkeeper Mendez. Some of it, anyway. Last night, roughly two hours before the murder, Georg logged onto the Keep's reference net node and pulled up all the information he could about the succession. He didn't even try any of the standard dodges for hiding who he was. It's a positive lock ID that he was the one doing the research."

Darsteel looked bitterly at Hannah and Jamie. "He did it," he said at last. "Never mind all that high and proud language about the Pax Humana, and being willing to die but refusing to kill. Some of us on Reqwar admired that notion. We've gotten tired of every political problem being solved with a bang from a gun and a thud as the body hits the floor, tired of no one in the roomful of people seeing who did it. But it turns out Georg Hertzmann killed his adoptive father to become Thelm of all Reqwar. Perfectly legal, and fulfilling all the requirements of the law—but none of that makes it *right*. He might have done what the law told him to do—but the law is wrong."

"But none of this proves anything," Jamie objected. "If Georg committed the murder, he ascends to the Thelmship. That's the most clear-cut case of all. There's no doubt about it. There's no *need* for him to look it up. He knew that. It's only if he *didn't* do it that the question is uncertain."

"And," said Hannah, looking at the report Darsteel had thrown down, "it looks like what he pulled up here were very general texts on succession law—not legal cases or anything like that. Besides, this report doesn't tell you what parts he actually *read*—just the names of the reference files he found and opened up. And he does the lookup just a couple of hours *after* Jamie popped up with his idea about Penitence. And he pulled up a copy of the Pax Humana bylaws too. What could that have to do with anything? Any good Earthside defense lawyer could put together a totally different scenario."

"Such as?" Darsteel asked skeptically.

Hannah shrugged. "His wife contacts him and

reports that the Thelm has been given a very dangerous idea that might threaten the family, please come
over at once. He does. Marta tells him about the Penitence idea. He broods on that, and looks up succession law to see, I don't know, if there is anything
about permanent exile. Or maybe he was trying to figure out what would happen to Moira if he went to
Penitence alone. *Could* Moira be used as a pawn, a
bargaining chip—or a rallying cry? It might be just
about anything. Maybe he hoped there was something
in the Pax Humana regs that would make it harder to
deport the child of a member to Penitence for some
reason. Who knows? Then it's late. He should get
back to his glass house—but he hasn't seen his wife in
a long time. Their child is asleep, but if he spends the
night, he can see her in the morning—perhaps for the
last time."

"And the very sad music starts to play," said Brox,
with heavy sarcasm. "Just the sort of absurd story the
Pavlat would love."

"All right, all right," said Hannah. "But I think I've
made my point."

"Whatever the merits of your story," said Brox,
"it's quite clear that this murder was planned sometime in advance. Why do something as basic as re-
viewing the succession law at the last minute?"

"So you're all saying that you don't think he did it,"
Darsteel said.

"I wouldn't go that far," said Hannah, "but I would
say he seems an unlikely suspect."

"And if he *did* do it, it wouldn't make any sense for

him to keep it hidden this way," said Jamie. "After all, this was the one murder *he* could commit that *wasn't* a crime."

"Unless," suggested Brox, "you consider what our noble friend Darsteel has just demonstrated—that at least some Reqwar Pavlat would like a Thelm who believes that murder is wrong. Legally, he can get away with this murder, yes. But he has the political savvy to realize that a damned alien coming to power by killing the Thelm isn't going to be too popular. He'd have motives beyond strict legality for wanting to keep people from thinking of him as a murderer. And I come back again to his Pax Humana membership as a strong motive for concealing the fact that he had committed murder, even legal murder."

There was a nervous cough from the doorway. Darsteel turned to see one of his more youthful-looking couriers standing there. "Yes, what is it?" he asked.

"Ah, sir, I have a message—"

"Of course you do," he said. "What else would a courier have but messages to bring?"

"Yes, sir," the courier agreed meaninglessly. "But it's a message for *them*. An invitation, really. I think yours is being delivered to your desk by another courier," he went on. "Sorry, sir."

Darsteel looked at the addressing on the big thick envelope. "From 'Thelm Georg Hertzmann' it says here. *He* didn't waste any time." He turned and glared at the messenger. "I seem to remember giving orders to keep Hertzmann in isolation—no contact with outsiders."

"Yes, sir. And they followed those orders—right up until the Court of High Crime ruled that Georg Hertzmann should ascend to the Thelmship."

Darsteel let his ears droop wearily and leaned up against the side of the table. "And someone decided that Thelm Georg ought to be informed. And the new Thelm started giving orders, and people started obeying them."

"Well, ah, yes sir."

"Including you."

A hint of green came to the courier's face as he blushed. "Yes, sir."

"All right," said Darsteel. He pulled a packet out of his blouse. "I might as well open this now," he said. "It's the report from the Court of High Crimes." He pulled out the papers and stared at the top one. " 'The said human Georg Hertzmann-Lantrall, having been duly adopted by the late Thelm, and the late Thelm having duly named him in the line of succession, and all other persons with prior claims to the succession having died, and, conditional to confirmation that the Thelm died properly, the said Georg Hertzmann-Lantrall is provisionally found to have succeeded to all the rights, titles, and powers, of the late Thelm, and shall hereafter be styled Thelm-Designate until such time as the propriety of the death of the late Thelm is confirmed.' "

Brox frowned. "Either I missed something, or that

is a very long-winded way of saying 'we haven't decided yet, but he's probably the Thelm.'"

Darsteel nodded. "You're right. Everything hinges
on the words 'conditional' and 'provisionally.'"

"So he's bending the rules pretty hard right from
the start," said Hannah, taking the message from
the courier. "He's calling himself Thelm instead of
Thelm-Designate."

"And he's sent another message, just by sending us
that one," said Jamie. "He's telling us he knew the
three of us were here, together. Don't you just wonder
how he found that one out, when he was supposed to
be kept in isolation—just like us?"

Darsteel glared again at the courier.

"It—it wasn't me, sir," the courier protested.

"No, it never is. It's always the one who's not here."

Hannah had been reading the invitation. "All that
Thelm-Designate stuff won't matter long anyway,"
she said. "We're summoned to join in witnessing the
'formal declaration of ascension' in which it will be
certified that 'the late Thelm did truly die properly
and thus that his heir-designate is hereby declared his
heir in fact, and named to all his heritable titles,
ranks, powers, rights, and other things.'"

"In other words," Jamie said grimly, "he's going to
wheel out a stack of Bibles and swear that he did it."

"So much for running a proper investigation,"
Darsteel said with savage anger. He turned to the
courier. "You and all your friends who all say 'it
wasn't me' are going to find out the hard way that this
job is not about protecting yourself from your own

actions. It's about protecting others, protecting the innocent from harm."

Hannah was studying the invitation, and only half-listening—until the last words that Darsteel spoke. Yes! That was it. That was the key! She understood. But it was down to two cases, one of two things that could have happened. Did it matter which? It *might* matter, a very great deal. She had to find out, and the answer ought to be in the papers right in front of her. But there was something they left unsaid. She checked the ruling from the Court of High Crime, and saw the same omission. "Neither of these say anything about ruling that Georg killed the Thelm," she said. "They just say the Thelm died 'properly.'"

"Which is a nice, polite way of saying Georg killed him, or whatever," said Darsteel.

"What do you mean, 'or whatever'?"

"Legal nonsense. 'Proper' in this case means 'without besmirching the honor of the Thelm or the heir.' I checked the law over as best I could last night, after locking all of you in. The law covers all the absurd contingencies. The Thelm, while in the act of attempting to commit suicide, is accidentally hit by a car driven by a contract killer hired by the heir. That sort of thing."

"And *would* it be proper for him to die that way?" Brox asked.

"What does it matter?" Darsteel snapped.

"It might matter a very great deal," said Hannah, with some iron in her voice. "Please be so kind as to answer the Inquirist's question."

"It would depend on a lot of things," Darsteel said. "It all stems from ordinary inheritance law, and there's all sorts of precedents for that. If the Thelm was attempting to kill himself by throwing himself in front of a car, that would be proper—so long as the heir had not *compelled* him to suicide, and the Thelm had chosen suicide for honorable reasons—and what is and isn't an honorable reason for suicide is hugely complex. Hiring a third party to do your killing for you is wrong, dishonorable, and illegal. But, if the hired killer was not, at that moment, *attempting* to kill the Thelm, and his death *was* accidental, that would be a proper death. *But* if the contract murderer was in fact on his way to try to kill the Thelm, so that his driving the vehicle at that place and time was due to an intended attempt on the Thelm's life commissioned by the heir, or *if* the heir had bullied or tricked or manipulated the Thelm into suicide, or if the suicide was to avoid shame or scandal—then that would not be proper."

"What if the killer was working for himself, or hired by someone besides the heir?" Hannah asked.

"Well, that wouldn't besmirch the honor of Thelm or heir, would it? It would of course be murder, and a crime—but insofar as touching the honor of the Thelm and heir, it would be an entirely proper death."

"In other words, just looking at the inheritance, and not thinking about criminal acts, it's okay for the heir to kill the Thelm, or for a third party to kill the Thelm—but *not* for the heir to get someone to do his killing for him."

"To do so would smack of cowardice, squeamishness, and venality—very, very, improper."

She flipped through the ruling, puzzling out the Greater Trade Writing, looking for the citations, the precedents. The Reqwar Pavlat loved precedents, the old ways, what had come before. The quickest, most hurried read possible through the strange language seemed to confirm what Darsteel was saying. If the picture she was starting to see was right, this could be bad. It could be very bad indeed. Winning the battle but losing the war would scarcely cover the case.

She turned on the courier. "You!" she said. "Answer my next questions, and answer with the knowledge you have, not with what I want to hear or what will make Darsteel happy with you. Don't answer with what you think will help your new Thelm-Designate. I'm not sure which answer would." *That* was a flat-out lie, but she needed to press the courier hard. She held up the papers the courier had just brought in. "Did Georg Hertzmann help write these? Did he talk things over with the lawyers and judges or whoever it was, or did he just sign what they brought him?"

"It doesn't matter," Darsteel put in. "The papers would have the same force in law in either—"

"Please!" Hannah snapped, cutting him short. "Just let him answer the question."

"I—I didn't see what happened, exactly," the courier said. "But I can tell you they brought those papers in, and took them out again after only eight or sixteen minutes. It might not have even been that long."

"All right then," Hannah said. "Fine. Now you get back to Thelm-Designate Georg—and make sure to address him by that title on our behalf—and tell him we would be honored to attend his ceremony declaring his accession—but first he must—*must* meet with us, an hour before the ceremony, in order to prevent a terrible error—an error that would endanger his ascension and his rule." She thought for a moment—but only for a moment. There wasn't much time. She glanced about the common room of their apartment. It would have to do. No time to look for some more suitable spot. "Tell him to come here," she said. "Yes. We will meet here. Tell him—tell him it concerns *Penitence* for past wrongs." She had been speaking in Lesser Trade, but she shifted to English for that one word.

"It concerns *what* for past wrongs?"

"*Pen-i-tence*," she said, saying the word slowly and carefully. "It's a human word. He'll know it—if you say it carefully. Be sure you get it right. It's *vital* you get it right. Now repeat it all back to me."

"What is—" Darsteel began, but Hannah held up her hand to quiet him.

"Repeat it all back," she said again.

The courier did, three times, before Hannah was satisfied. Once she was, she wasted no time shooing him out the door. When he was gone, she slammed the door shut and bolted it from the inside. "We'll have to clear a lot of the gear out of here, and you'll have to go get some things," she said to Darsteel, "but I want us locked in here just a little bit longer."

"What in the dark devils are you working at?" Brox demanded. "I can't be any part of this game of yours without being told what it is."

"I'm sorry," Hannah said. "You're quite right. But I didn't want to talk until the courier was gone. Let's just say I didn't get the impression that his loyalties were all that clear."

"But what is this about?" Darsteel asked.

"It's about getting what you wanted," Hannah said. "A real investigation that gets down to what really happened. We're nearly there, without even knowing it. And we're going to get there, I promise. But first—" she paused, and looked around the room at the three faces—a human, a Pavlat, and a Kendari—that were staring back at her. That was as it should be. If all of them, working together, brought in the truth, then no one would ever be able to say it was one side or the other, this faction or that, bringing in some of the truth, but not all. "But first," she said, "we've got a trap to set."

Caldon Saffeer, High Thelek of the Realm, stood in the first light of a grim and frightened dawn, and stared out the windows-walls of his Grand Hall. He looked down at the fire-ravaged wreck of the Thelm's Keep in the valley below and lusted for knowledge of what, precisely, had happened.

The whole planet was in a panic, and no one knew anything. He could see the Keep, but the view told him nothing. The authorities on the scene had managed to cut off all outgoing comm as thoroughly as his transparent window-walls cut off all sound from the outside world.

There was the sound of a door opening behind him, and a scuffle, and a thud. The High Thelek turned around to find Nostawniek, full-time steward and part-time informant, standing between two guards and bowing so low that his head was practically burrowing into the carpet.

"Where is he?" the Thelek demanded.

Nostawniek at least had the wit not to feign ignorance, not to ask who the Thelek meant. "I don't know. Brox told me nothing," he said, his head still so low his voice was half-muffled. "He did not tell me he was going. I slept through the first alarm. I didn't even know he was missing before the guards woke me to ask about him."

"Your grand friend, the being you so proudly spy for, said not a word to you?"

"No, Great Thelek. Truly." Nostawniek gestured to the view. "I don't know the first thing about what happened, except what can be seen out the window."

"Take him away," said the Thelek, struggling to control his temper as he turned his back on the prisoner to look down once again on the Keep. "Keep him safe, but unharmed." The infuriating thing was that he, the High Thelek, and perhaps now already the Thelm of all Reqwar, knew almost precisely as much as that miserable little wretch—only what he could see from where he stood.

He dared not act until he knew, clearly and certainly, what the results had been. Who had lived, who had died?

But by the time he knew that for sure, it might already be far too late to act.

* * *

When Georg had been locked up for the night—in the most comfortable room available, he was assured—all that anyone would officially acknowledge were the two facts he knew already: There had been a major fire in a room where the Thelm was known to spend much of his time, and the Thelm himself had not been seen since shortly before the fire.

Georg did not try to get anyone to tell him more than that. Not that they needed to, anyway. You'd have to be a blind fool not to be able to guess, quite accurately, all that you weren't told. There was shouting and crying from downstairs. He did not envy her captors: Marta in a rage was something awesome to behold. He could not hear Moira, but, at a guess, she was somewhere on the ground floor. He worried about her, and the terror she must be feeling. But it would likely be safer for her if he stayed away. He was in great danger, and those near him were likely to be in danger as well.

He was going to have to think his way out of this. He arranged a pile of sitting cushions into a comfortable heap, sat down, and considered the situation. A few minutes' reflection showed there was, in fact, nothing he could do to help himself. *Yet.*

That tiny thought was what sustained him. He knew how the planet Reqwar worked. He knew the turmoil that must be going on outside, the guessing, the rumors that must be sweeping everywhere. And he knew how the Reqwar Pavlat longed for order, for hierarchy, for things set out in a neat and orderly pattern. With the Thelm, the center of the pattern, suddenly gone, the need for order, for continuity, would come to the fore.

They would come to him. His guards, for a start. The lawyers, the judges, the police officials, the nobles. They all *needed* a Thelm at the center for any of the rest of it to work. And if the only possible Thelms available were the dangerously ambitious High Thelek and an alien with a strangely mobile face and half his thumbs missing—then a great number of Reqwar Pavlat would turn to him. And sooner rather than later, for the longer the Thelmship was unclaimed, the more likely the High Thelek was to snatch it for himself.

They would come for him. And soon. Perhaps very soon, in a matter of hours. Which meant he had to *think*, and think hard. He had to figure out what had happened, why it had happened, what it meant. And he had to figure out how to protect his family.

It was a tall order—an impossibly tall one. But Georg was used to thinking big, and thinking fast. If he could not work through every possible variant of likely next events, he could at least work out some sort of rough plan ahead of time.

And he spared a thought for Thelm Lantrall. His Thelm. His adoptive father. Georg allowed guilt, shame, sorrow to wash over him, at least for a time. But he could not afford the luxury of wallowing in such feelings. Not now. Not in the midst of crisis. Later, if he lived through all this, would be time enough to mourn. But it was hard not to think about the grand, garrulous, scheming, generous, cantankerous old character, dead in the midst of those flames.

But he had no official knowledge of the Thelm's death. *Be careful what you say, what assumptions you reveal, what certainty and uncertainty you expose.* It was sensible advice he gave himself. If only he knew how to act on it. It might well be just as dangerous to know too much as too little—and just as deadly to feign knowledge instead of ignorance.

It all came down to some very simple conclusions: There was great danger ahead, for all of them. And it would be safer for all concerned—including one Georg Hertzmann—if he took that danger on himself.

*After all*, he reminded himself, *you're the only one with a license to kill*.

Not exactly a comforting thought, but at least it left him feeling a bit less helpless. And there was another encouraging thought along those lines. If he lived through the next few days, he would be the most powerful person on the planet. And if *that* didn't given him some ability to protect his family, he might as well give up here and now.

But there was one other thought that was entirely comforting. *Now, at least, Marta and I don't have to worry about Moira growing up on Penitence*. Putting *that* nightmare behind them was worth a bad night, and even a bad conscience.

And it was enough to ease his mind, at least far enough to let him sleep.

When he woke, he was profoundly grateful that he had not dreamed.

\* \* \*

It was an hour after dawn when they started to come to him, even sooner than he had expected. A note concealed in the tray at breakfast. Another note, from another source, when the tray was taken away. A whispered conference with a guard, who offered to smuggle in a law-reader who might be helpful. And the law-reader who showed him the findings of the Court of High Crime, and also brought a judge who brought papers to sign.

But he had worked it all out by then. He knew what he had to do to protect the ones he loved and the planet that had fallen, all unwillingly, into his care. He would push past being the mere Thelm-Designate as soon as possible, rush the ascension ceremony, and make a strong and clear declaration that would draw followers to him, before the doubts and rumors could spread, before the investigators could ask too many questions.

He would take the Thelmship, seize it, use it as a shield and a wall—and as a sword and a battering ram, if need be, to do what had to be done. He signed whatever they put before him, boldly, almost blindly. It didn't matter anymore. Not really. Either the Thelmship would be taken from him, in which case the High Thelek would see to it that all the papers were of no use to anyone in protecting him—or else Georg would become Thelm, and the power of the office itself would be a defense against any flaw, any fraud, any double-dealing in the documents he signed so hurriedly.

It was after he had signed the last of them that the change truly began to take place. He could not mark any one precise moment as the one where he ceased to be a prisoner or started to be treated as the Thelm. But the time came when the door to the room in which he had been held locked stood open, and the armed officers were no longer watching over a prisoner but mounting a guard of honor and defense around their sovereign. It was heady. It was exciting. It made it easy to imagine more hopeful days, not too far off, as the couriers and assistants and helpers rushed back and forth, bringing news of the investigation, sending the invitations, and making the plans for his formal declaration of ascension to the Thelmship of all Reqwar.

And it made the crash back to the ground all that more abrupt and jarring, the doubts and fears that much stronger, when one of the couriers brought back a spoken message that contained the single English word "Penitence."

And when a single word from a low-level investigator from a far-off planet could bring all his plans to a shrieking halt and tie his stomach up in fear, then it was plain as could be that he was far, far, far from being Thelm of anything at all.

*  *  *

Hannah never had the least doubt that Georg Hertzmann would come. Not with the vague and implied threat of Penitence hanging over him. Not when she warned of a terrible error that could endanger his rule, and he had just signed a stack of papers without the slightest hope of knowing all that was in them. Getting the rest of the guests to come had not been much of a challenge, either, of course, as most of them were in custody. The exceptions, for two reasons, were the Stannlar. One, they weren't *exactly*

420 ROGER MACBRIDE ALLEN

in custody, and two, it wouldn't be physically possible to fit them into the room where the event was to be held.

The solution was, of course, obvious once thought of, and Hannah chided herself for being surprised when two Pavlat police came in, each carrying a flat, plate-sized disc. The discs were set down on a table, and promptly popped themselves open to reveal two cheerful and animated six-legged starfish, one purple and the other green.

No, the audience had pretty much taken care of itself. The hard part had been in arranging the stage, dressing the set, and, most of all, getting the props ready. But all that was done. She could hear the sounds of a small group in the corridor approaching their apartments. *And now the show begins.*

.* * *

Georg Hertzmann almost knocked on the door himself, but then one of his self-appointed retinue scurried forward and did it for him. He gravely nodded his thanks, and at the same time came to the disconcerting realization that, if he was lucky, he was going to spend a lifetime of expressing insincere thanks for endless acts of such totally useless assistance.

The door swung open, and he saw Hannah Wolfson standing there. He had the strangest sensation, looking at her. For the first time in his life, he found himself regarding a human being as an enemy, someone intent on doing him harm. But no. That was unwise and unfair. She was an obstacle, an opponent, a danger—not an enemy. But even more peculiar was the sensation of looking at a human being and thinking of that human as something *alien*. He glanced behind him, at the Pavlat clustered close. They were his people now. There was already a gulf between Georg Hertzmann and the rest of humankind.

"Welcome, honored sir," said Hannah Wolfson in good if accented Lesser Trade Speech. She bowed to him as she spoke, just deeply enough to signify respect to a Thelm-Designate, but not far enough to do full honors to a Thelm. She had been well briefed. "Please sir, I would ask that you give your followers leave to depart, and come inside." She spoke as if sending them away, and going in alone, were part of some well-known ritual, the normal and expected next step in something that had been done many times.

"I would prefer that they remain with me," he said.

"Honored sir, I think that would be unwise," she said, and switched to English for two quick sentences, spoken in an urgent, whispered tone that had nothing to do with her courtly posture and expression. *"This could get rougher than either of us would like. You might want to limit witnesses."*

It was the false, calm, warm smile as much as the sharp, fast whisper that convinced him the warning was sincere, and no trap. Would he ever understand Reqwar Pavlat expressions, gestures, tones of voice that well?

He glanced at his retinue again and experienced the strange and accurate feeling, not that they were alien—but that *he* was. If he survived, he would forever be between the two worlds, and never fully part of either. "Very well," he said in Lesser Trade. He turned to his followers and spoke. "My friends, it would appear that this is something I should best do alone. I would ask that you all wait for me in the chamber where the ascension ceremony will take place." *If it ever takes place at all*, he thought.

Hannah Wolfson spoke. "It will be our honor to bring the Thelm-Designate to you there," she said.

Georg looked back toward the cluster of couriers, assistants, lawyers, lawkeepers, and law-readers who were the first of all his subjects to proclaim him—and wondered if they would be the last. "Go now," he said. "I shall see you all there shortly."

He nodded once to them as they departed, then entered the room, resolved not to reveal surprise at anything. The moment the door was shut behind him, he could see it would be a hard promise to keep. He saw them all at once. Brox—a creature of the Thelek. Was he there representing Saffeer? Components from his business partners, Allabex and Cinnabex: two hand-sized six-legged starfish, both, bizarrely enough, standing in their open containers—and bowing low to him with deep respect. Darsteel, bowing as well, though not as deeply. The other BSI agent, Mendez, poker-faced, arms folded across his chest, plainly not ready to believe anything or bow to anyone.

The Lady Zahida, performing a precisely correct courtly bow. And his wife, Marta, ashen-faced, motionless, looking as scared as he felt, underneath a mask of calm that was just like the one he was wearing.

There were no chairs, no sitting cushions, no perching stools—only a table on which the Stannlar components' containers had been placed to get them off the floor. The room was empty of furniture except for one small side table that had a cloth over it. There was an odd, ungainly-shaped something or other in the center of the room, likewise concealed under a cloth. Everyone stood, and nobody spoke.

Georg glanced to Marta. She made a quick series of small gestures. She pointed to her closed mouth, then moved her fingers rapidly open and shut to indicate talking, then shook her head and waved her hand very slightly, in a way that indicated everyone in the room. That was clear enough. *I can't talk to you. They have told all of us that we must not speak.* They were spectators, not participants. *Or perhaps they are witnesses*, he told himself. *But for the defense, or for the prosecution?*

Georg turned calmly toward Agent Wolfson and spoke to her in English. "This is your idea of limiting witnesses?"

"Sir, these are the surviving persons present at the meeting held last night, along with the investigators looking into the events of last night. I assure you that it is necessary that all of them attend."

"*Why* is it necessary?" he demanded. "What is the purpose of this—this meeting?"

"To learn the truth," Hannah said. "One or more of this group, which one or ones we cannot say for certain, possess information vital to this investigation—possibly without being aware of possessing it."

"Very well," he said, for plainly there was no other possible answer. He shifted back to Lesser Trade Speech. "Let us get at the truth you seek."

"The signed papers you sent to us proclaimed that the Thelm died 'properly,'" said Brox 231, without preamble. "Did he?"

Georg stiffened. Those sworn to Pax Humana strove to be without hate, without prejudice, but it was hard to forget certain incidents in which the Kendari Inquiries Service had been deeply involved. He did not care for a Kendari speaking that way to him, let alone a Senior Inquirist of the Kendari Inquiries Service. Which was probably exactly why he had been selected to ask such questions. "I do not believe it is proper to question the word of a Thelm," he said, determined to keep his feelings in check.

"Which is precisely why this session had to happen *now*," said Brox. "Because you aren't Thelm yet—and weren't Thelm when you signed that paper. The question stands. Did the Thelm die 'properly'?"

Georg paused a moment before he spoke. It was not hard to sense the danger he was in. "Yes," he said at last.

"What, in your own words, does the word 'properly' mean in the present context?" Brox asked sharply.

Again a pause before Georg was willing and able to answer. "It means I killed him," he said at last, and the words seem to sweep all other sound from the room, leaving it in deathly quiet.

Brox let the silence hang there a moment and looked around the room at all the spectators. "So, to be perfectly clear about this—you, Georg Hertzmann, as required by the laws of this planet, did in fact kill Lantrall, Thelm of all Reqwar?"

"Yes."

"Might I ask what became of your high and noble Pax Humana oath? As I recall, it includes the phrases 'I will die most willingly to stop evil, but I will not kill, even in the name of good.'"

Georg felt a flush of anger he could not suppress. "Your noble Kendari Inquiries Service, and the Kendari military, have made full use of the opportunities provided by that oath to kill us in our hundreds, mow us down like crops in a field, when it suited your purposes."

"That is expressed rather dramatically, essentially true, and completely irrelevant," Brox replied evenly. "Once again, the question stands. What became of your Pax Humana oath?"

"I was forced to make a choice, and I did so," Georg replied coldly.

"A choice between what alternatives?"

That question, at least, was easy, and he could answer without need for care or caution. "On one side the legal and legally required death of the Thelm, who was willing to send not only me, but my wife and daughter, into a hellish exile on Penitence that would mean lives of misery, and, more than likely, early deaths for us all. On the other side, killing the Thelm and thus preventing my daughter from being sent to that place."

"I see," Brox said, turning his back on Georg—a deadly insult to a Thelm—and beginning to pace up and down the room. "So you broke your oath in order to protect your innocent daughter—and presumably your wife as well, though you neglected to mention her."

*And you very carefully did not call her innocent*, Georg noted. But it would do no good to rise to the bait. "That is correct," he said.

"Very good," said Brox. "So the Reqwar Pavlat can celebrate the beginning of your reign, secure in the knowledge that you probably won't go back on your word, or betray them in any way, provided no one threatens your daughter."

It was too much for him, too much for any man who had been through what he had. He was not even aware he had lunged for Brox until he felt Wolfson's arms around him, holding him back. At first he was angry, shocked she would dare touch the person of the Thelm. Then, a moment's fleeting surprise at himself for already thinking that way, wrapping himself in his Thelmhood. And finally, a realization that it was for the good that she had held him back.

Otherwise, he knew, looking deep into Brox's dark and mocking eyes, he would have broken his Pax Humana oath then and there.

The two Stannlar components directed all their senses forward to the drama being played out before them, aiming all their auditory sensors and all four of their available leg-eyes at the struggle between Georg Hertzmann and Senior Special Agent Hannah Wolfson. If they had not needed their other two feet to stand on, they would have used those eyes as well.

It was not merely the fate of Georg Hertzmann that was at stake, not merely the fate of a world. The Stannlar had been caught in the act of preparing to depart Reqwar at once—and for aliens to leave without the permission of the Thelm was, in and of itself, an illegal act. They could be put to death for it. The multiple layers of irony in that fact were not lost on either of them.

Their main bodies might still be in the warehouse, surrounded by armed lawkeepers, but neither of them was more than vaguely aware of the fact. All possible main-body volitional activities were powered down, and their full attention was directed at the data streaming in from their subcomponents. Every available and appropriate sensor, detector, and recorder built into their transport containers was powered up and in use. Neither of them wanted to miss anything. Neither of them fully understood what was happening—but understanding could wait. The moment could not.

"Sir!" Agent Wolfson cried out. "Sir, please!" She looked over her shoulder at the Kendari. "That's enough, Inquirist Brox. That's more than enough." She turned her attention back to Georg, and released her hold on him. "Please forgive us, sir. I didn't intend for it to go quite that far."

Georg Hertzmann glared at her, rage on his face. "I doubt your sincerity," he said, and left it at that.

"You have every right to do so, sir. But the point Brox was making—rather too crudely and baldly—is that the Reqwar Pavlat will have every right to doubt *your* sincerity. The manner of your succeeding to the title endangers the success of your reign. And, to be even more blunt about what is obvious to everyone anyway—you are an alien to your own people. That will be a huge obstacle to overcome. It will breed suspicion and doubt, inspire conspiracy theories, and all the rest of it."

"Perhaps all of what you say is true," Georg replied. "But what does it have to do with us, here, today? What is the terrible mistake you warned against?"

" 'Rumors cannot take root where the facts are planted thick,' " Agent Wolfson quoted from somewhere. "There is little we can do about your being an alien, or about your oath breaking—but there is another area of danger we can at least reduce. You have said you killed the Thelm, as you were required to do by law. Well and good. But no one saw it. There are no witnesses. We do not know how it happened. Unless something is done, and quickly, to plant the facts thick, so they are known to the nobles and the people, rumors will start to grow. Rumors that challenge the legitimacy of your reign."

"What sort of rumors?" Georg demanded.

"The sort that would be—will be—planted by your enemies—such as the High Thelek," said Brox. "You know that I know him quite well, and you know that I would prefer him as Thelm to you. I make no pretense. But—provided your claim that the Thelm died properly is supported—I see no way for the High Thelek to ascend."

Brox made a dismissive gesture and went on. "But I doubt the Thelek views things quite that way. He will want to win—and he *will* plant rumors. Perhaps that it was a palace coup, or that you did not have the courage to do the thing yourself and the job was done by hired killers. Rumors that the Thelm is not in fact dead at all, that the burned body was from the city morgue, because you lacked the courage to kill, and so merely spirited him away, fired the dueling pistol into the corpse's head to make identification more difficult. Or that the Thelm was in league with you, and the two of you conspired together to fake his death, so that you both could live while still denying the Thelmship to the noble and legitimate claimant, the High Thelek. I could go on, but I believe I have made my point."

"But you, of course, would play no part in spreading such stories," Georg said, a sneer in his voice.

"No, I would not," said Brox. "But you are welcome to doubt *my* sincerity, if you wish."

Georg glared at Brox 231 and turned back to Wolfson. "So. You want to know exactly how I killed him."

"Yes, sir," said Agent Wolfson. "We need the specifics."

"I see." Georg paused a moment. "Forgive me, but this is a difficult subject, and it has been a difficult night and day for us all."

"Of course, sir. We might start with how you came to be at the Keep at all. When we left you last night, you were planning to return to—forgive me, I don't know its name. The glass-walled place where you have been staying."

"The Finstar Art Gallery. I did go there, yes."

"Then how did you come to the Keep? Did you go there with the intention of killing the Thelm?"

"No, not at all." He gestured toward Marta, standing off to his left. "Marta called me, very upset, and told me to come over right away, that something very bad was likely to happen, and that we had to talk about it right away."

"Why couldn't you talk over the comm net?" Agent Wolfson asked.

Georg smiled sadly. "It doesn't take long to stop trusting the privacy of the communications system around here. The Stannlar jamming devices couldn't protect against a tap inside the comm net. Besides which, I was staying in as public a place as I could, and I had quite deliberately taken no precautions at all against watchers or listeners—in fact I had made sure to make things easy on them. I didn't even carry the Stannlar device most of the time. For a truly private talk, I had to go to Marta."

"I see," said Agent Wolfson. "So you traveled to the Keep. How?"

"My private aircar. I let the autonav system do the flying. The flight data should all be in the car's log recorder and the city autonav system. You can check it."

"We will," said Wolfson. "So you arrive here. You go to your wife in her apartments—well, your apartments, really, I suppose, though you haven't been there much recently."

"That's right," Georg said. "And she told me all about your associate's brilliant idea to ship me off to Penitence."

Wolfson frowned. Agent Mendez shifted his stance a bit but did not speak, though plainly he wanted to.

"As Agent Mendez said at the time, it wasn't a very good idea. It would seem that events have proven him right."

"They certainly have," Georg growled, making no effort to hide his anger. "My wife also reported that it was the Thelm who thought of sending all three of us there. Not the most lovable thing he ever did."

"What if it had only been you that was to be sent to Penitence?"

Georg shook his head. "I can't say for sure. What I'd like to believe is that I would have accepted it, for the sake of saving the Thelm's life and mine. But who can tell what would have happened?"

"But involving your daughter—and your wife—crossed the line."

"Yes," Georg said, answering Wolfson's question cautiously.

"So what happened then?"

"I told Marta that so long as I was there, and since it was late, and since I had scarcely seen either of them in weeks, I might as well spend the night. I waited until my wife went to sleep, then went up to the Thelm's Private Audience Chamber."

"Did you know he was going to be there?" Brox demanded.

"I wasn't absolutely certain, but I knew that, oh, nine nights out of ten, he was up there working late at night. Thelm Lantrall is—was—something of a night owl, to use a human phrase."

"One moment please," said Darsteel. "There was nothing else concerning the matter at hand that took place with your wife? Just the conversation?"

Georg frowned and shook his head. "I'm sorry. Nothing I can think of."

"Nothing? No calls seeking advice, no checking of references, no trips to the Keep's library?"

"Oh, yes! I forgot about that. I logged onto the reference net and got several general texts about succession law. We were looking for anything concerning exiles, and the families of exiles. We didn't find anything. But looking up the material was just part of the conversation, really. I didn't really think of it as something separate until you asked."

"Very good," said Darsteel. "Thank you."

"If we could return to the point in the story you had reached, sir. You arrived at the Thelm's audience chamber. What happened then?"

Everyone seemed to lean in toward him just a trifle, paying just that little bit more attention.

"He was there," Georg began simply. "Working on some sort of papers. I don't know what. He seemed surprised, but not too surprised, to see me. He told me how good it was to see me again, and how sorry he was about how adopting me had turned into a nightmare instead of being the honor he had intended. But I wasn't there to chat. I asked him point-blank about Penitence, whether he had decided for sure whether or not to send my family there."

Georg hesitated, and looked around the room. Marta gave him a forced half smile. He nodded to her, very slightly. "The Thelm was a politician. He knew how to answer a question—and how to not-answer it—and that's what he did. He went on about how it was only a contingency, a possibility they had to explore. The human lawkeepers were working to prepare the groundwork, so the plan would be ready to go, just in case it was needed. But I knew. It was just a contingency—but there weren't any other options. He wouldn't choose until the last minute—but by the time the last minute came, he would have arranged matters so there would be no choice left but Penitence.

434 • ROGER MACBRIDE ALLEN

"I asked him again, about my family," Georg went on. "Would I go alone, or would he send us all, just on the off chance that Moira would turn into some sort of bargaining chip if she were somewhere accessible, and was my heir of property?

"He answered me with a question. I can't swear to the exact words, but they were something very like 'Do you think it would be right for Moira to grow up without a father?' It was a brilliant, terrible thing to say. It made my going by myself not a sacrifice to protect my family, but some sort of self-centered indulgence on my part. It would be selfish for me to go to hell alone and leave my daughter to grow up without my guidance, and never mind the killers and psychopaths that passed for the general population."

Georg looked around the room at his audience, and turned his hands palms upward in front of him. "That was when I reached my final, irrevocable decision to kill him," he said. "If it was a choice between the old man who was, ultimately, ready to betray me, and the little girl he was willing to betray as well—well, I made my choice."

He shrugged again, looked helpless, appealed to the spectators. "The rest of it—the rest of it is still kind of a blur for me. It all went by so fast—and it was so terrible, so unpleasant, that I don't think that I'm remembering it all quite right. Maybe later I will, and I'll have nightmares. Maybe it will never come back to me."

"Tell us what you remember," said Wolfson, her voice a study in neutrality.

"Well, you seem to know about the dueling pistol and the head shot," he said.

"There's some guesswork," Wolfson said. "The, ah, corpse was in very bad shape after the fire. We still haven't located the weapon in the debris. But the wound pattern was clear enough to Darsteel and the locals. They'd seen it before. In fact, the corpse was burned and crushed enough that it was easier for them to identify the wound as what a dueling pistol would do than it was to say where, exactly, on his body the round had struck him."

"The head," Georg told her. "Very definitely the head. He turned his back on me. That was his mistake. I went to the table where the guns were on display. He sat back down at his desk to work at his papers again. And I stood a few feet away and fired." He paused. "Fire. Smoke. Dust. It wasn't pretty. I was in shock for a moment or two. When I came back to myself a few seconds later, sparks from the gunshot had already started the fires going. I decided to help them along a little. I fed papers to them, then more papers, then some of the furniture."

"Why?" Brox demanded. "A fire after a murder is almost always used to conceal and destroy the evidence. It was in your best interests to admit to the killing, once you had committed it. It would ensure your ascension to the throne."

"Panic," said Georg. "Shock. Shame. A gut feeling that I had to hide what I had done. I wasn't entirely rational—not by a long shot. Maybe it was just that I wanted to hide what I had done from my Pax

Humana oath. I can't really say." He shrugged. "The fire started to get pretty big. It was time to go."

"What about the business with the shoes?" Darsteel asked.

Georg looked at him and frowned. "What shoes?"

"Not important," said Darsteel. "Please go on."

"There is not much more to tell," said Georg. "I came back to our apartments just in time. I sat up and waited for the alarm to be sounded, then I gathered up Marta and Moira and took them downstairs."

"You set a fire in the upper floor of a building, then went downstairs, to where your wife and child were sleeping, in apartments directly below the fire, and sat and waited for the fire alarm to sound?" asked Brox. "Why? Why didn't you rouse them at once and get them out of there, out of danger?"

"All I can say was that I was not entirely rational," Georg said again. He looked straight ahead, at no one, at nothing.

"And so the good Pavlats of Reqwar can look forward to life under a Thelm who becomes irrational in moments of danger and crisis?" Brox asked.

But before Georg could protest, a new and completely unexpected attack came from another side. "Thank you, sir," said Agent Wolfson. "That was an excellent summing-up. I think it will suit our needs admirably. But there is one other item." She gestured to the other agent, Mendez. He stepped forward. "Agent Mendez is our resident expert on weaponry," Wolfson said.

Georg's eyes flitted to the table off to one side with

the cloth concealing whatever was on it "Weaponry?" he echoed.

Mendez crossed to the table and stripped off the cloth to reveal a scorched and damaged, but still largely intact, dueling-pistol display case. One of the pistols was gone. The other was blackened by smoke, its ornate decoration masked by soot and ash, but otherwise quite undamaged. Mendez moved to the center of the room and removed the cloth from the large and ungainly shape it concealed. Underneath it was a tailor's dummy with bendable arms and legs, borrowed from somewhere in the Keep. It was balanced, rather unsteadily, on a perching stool, with its back to Georg.

"This is our best guess as to how the Thelm was sitting when he was shot," said Agent Mendez. "It sounds like it more or less matches up with what you just described." He nodded toward the display case and the remaining gun. "Both case and weapon are just as they were when we found them in the audience chamber," he said. "You can use the duplicate gun."

"What—what are you asking of me?" Georg demanded.

"The devil is in the details," said Mendez. "You have given a quick and sketchy account of what you did, and how, and why. That's all very well for things like what books you consulted, or how you left the scene. But the shooting itself is the center of it all." Mendez gestured at Wolfson and himself. "We two humans are mainly interested in confirming the mechanics of the shot. The angle, the distance, the direction, that sort of thing. The Reqwar Pavlat authorities have another emphasis."

Darsteel spoke. "The people and nobles of Reqwar want their Thelm to be strong, resolute, ready to act. They will want to know what your actions say about your character. And there is no recording, no imagery, of how the Thelm died. We Pavlat need to see that you could have done it, that you *did* do it. That you can handle the weapon, aim it, operate it, understand it. That you can aim it and fire it at another living being."

Georg pointed at the tailor's dummy. "That is no living being."

"No, sir. Of course not. But it would be a very rare being indeed who could aim the same kind of gun he used a few hours ago and point it at something representing the victim, and *not* have a very strong emotional reaction. We will see it. We will believe. And then it will be all over."

Georg stood there, staring at the gun, then at the dummy, for a long time. "The gun," he said. "It has live ammunition in it?"

"We haven't done anything to change it in any way, sir," Mendez replied. "It is just as it was when we recovered it from the wreckage, less than an hour ago."

"And 'one must be ready to resolve a question of honor at once.' The Thelm kept the damned things loaded. But what if the gun was damaged in some way by the fire?"

"I have examined it carefully sir. There was some ash that was blown into the barrel. I cleared that out.

Other than that, it does not appear to be damaged in any way. And it is an extremely simple mechanism. Either it will work perfectly, or it won't work at all. Please, sir. Take up the gun. Position yourself by the dummy as you did by the Thelm. Aim. Fire. And we will be done. It will satisfy us, and buttress your claim to the Thelmship."

Georg hesitated one last time, then walked toward the table that held the ruined display case.

"Georg!" It was Marta, calling out to him. He did not answer, did not look behind him. He stretched out his hand and picked up the pistol. A little loose ash and dust fell off it as he did so, and sprinkles of soot hung in the air for a moment. The grip, designed for the Pavlat hand with two thumbs and four fingers, was awkward for a human hand, but he did not have any great difficulty.

"Georg! Please! Please don't!"

He did not respond. He turned and walked the few steps back to stand facing the back of the dummy's head. He moved as if he were underwater, in slow motion, through some medium that offered firm resistance but gave way under steady pressure. He raised the weapon—then lowered it again and released the safety mechanism's twist-and-slide switch. He lifted the gun and aimed it straight at the back of the dummy's head. The sweat was streaming down his face, his back, his arms.

He hesitated and eased off his aim. He seemed to come back to himself after a few seconds. He took a deep breath and resettled himself. He sighted along the aiming guides set into the top of the barrel.

"Georg!" Marta said again.

"I'm doing this for us, Marta," he said without looking behind. "For all of us. To make us safe at last." He leveled the gun. He sighted in on his target again, from a range of less than two meters. He put his finger around the trigger. He pulled it back—

And Marta leapt forward, her arm slamming into the top of the gun barrel, shoving it down, hard, just as the trigger engaged and the rocket projectile fired. With a roar and whoosh, the projectile blasted not through the head of the dummy, but through its mid-section, slicing it clean in two, dropping the two halves to the floor, already ablaze.

The projectile crashed into the floor and stuck there, engine spent, spewing smoke, for a count of one, two, three—then it went off with a flash and a pop that threw the projectile up hard enough to bounce against the ceiling before dropping back to the floor.

Smoke and dusk and the smell of burned propellant and spent explosive and burned wood, shouts and cries and yelling, filled the room. The dust and sound and flash of light seemed to have stunned everyone.

Or almost everyone. Agent Hannah Wolfson made a flying tackle to bring Marta down just a step or two shy of the door. Wolfson coolly and professionally restrained Marta, held her down, and produced a pair of restraint cords from somewhere, wrapping one cord around Marta's wrists and another around her ankles.

Marta spat and cursed and hissed at her captor, struggling long after struggle was pointless. "You! You switched the ammo after all, you nasty little—"

But Wolfson taped Marta's mouth shut, before Marta could say any more. "No," said Wolfson, with an expression of intense and feral satisfaction. "I didn't do that. I told your husband—Agent Mendez is our weapons expert." She grinned, and a bright spark of blood dribbled down from her lower lip, split open at some point in the scuffle. "But I'll take all the credit I can get for that takedown," she said. "You definitely weren't that easy to catch."

Georg dropped the gun, and it hit the floor with an empty and meaningless clatter.

A few hours in an improvised cell served to calm Marta Hertzmann down a bit before questioning, but did nothing to improve her disposition.

"Where did the suicide rounds come from?" Jamie asked for the dozenth time.

"You've got all the proof you need," Marta Hertzmann snapped—which was actually more of an answer than she had given up to that point. "Why in the devil do we need to go through with this?"

"For more or less the same reasons we gave to your husband," Darsteel said, lounging back on his perching stool. The more tense and angry Marta got, the calmer and more relaxed Darsteel became. "To make sure that rumors cannot grow, to see to it that the facts are planted close together and make each other strong. You know you're going to tell us what we want, sooner or later—and I think we both know the process will be a lot gentler with your fellow humans present. Let's get it over with before I tell them to leave. Answer the questions."

Judging by her expression, the not-very-well-veiled threat made an impression.

"The suicide rounds," Jamie said once again.

"Where did you get them? Where did you buy them?"

Marta snorted disdainfully—but this time, she actually answered. "Buy them? I *made* them. I'm an engineer, when I don't have to waste my time playing adoring wife to my brave and noble husband. Twenty minutes' work for each of them—and that was only because I was working carefully. Get a standard round, cut here, glue there, reroute some wires. Simple."

"When did you make them?" Hannah asked. "And why? And when did you load them into the Thelm's dueling pistols?"

"Or to put it a trifle less delicately, whom were you planning to annihilate?" Brox asked.

"Just after Georg was recaptured and handed back, things got very, very ugly between our own great and noble Thelm and that fiend incarnate, the High Thelek," said Marta, sarcasm dripping from her voice. "For a few days there, it looked like they actually might fight a duel and try to kill each other. That seemed like a good idea to me. The Thelek would be no loss. Most people would tell you that, though they thought the Thelm was some kind of saint. But he was ready to sell Georg out the first moment that the price was right. *You* helped prove that, when you told him about Penitence.

"I decided to make the duel as lethal as possible. But once I had swapped the rounds, I wanted to get as far away from Thelm's Keep as I could. If there *were* a duel, and the suicide rounds were found, there would be an investigation—and I didn't want to be in the neighborhood for that. I decided it would be a good idea to stay safely on the other side of the planet for a while. Once I heard you were coming, I figured I had to be close to the scene."

"I do not understand the point of booby-trapping the pistols before the duel," Darsteel said. "Why would it matter? One or the other would die, and that was what you wanted."

"Not quite. She wanted them *both* dead," said Hannah. "If both guns shoot backwards, straight at the shooter, the odds are much better that someone is going to die—probably two someones. If you don't want *either* side to win, why not get rid of both? Furthermore, if either duelist *did* survive, he'd be the obvious suspect for rigging the guns. His reputation would be destroyed because he had acted dishonorably. If it was the Thelm, he'd be removed from office—if the Thelek, removed from the line of succession. If both the Thelm and the Thelek were out of the way—who did that leave to inherit the power? Georg."

"That's all about right," Marta said.

"But it would also mean that Georg's adoring wife Marta would have inherited the Thelm's wealth, his property, his land—and the income that property produced," said Brox.

Marta's eyes gleamed with enthusiasm. "The income flow generated from the Thelm's wife's share is amazing. Even getting a small percentage of the gross planetary product for a poor, backward planet means a truly astounding amount of cash," she said wistfully. "I could have done some grand things for Reqwar with that money." She glared at Darsteel and the BSI agents. "Now, thanks to you, none of that can happen."

Hannah snorted. "Right. It's our fault."

Darsteel stared at Marta. "You humans look enough like us, and act enough like us, that, sometimes, I can forget how alien you are. How could *you* blame *us*?"

Marta tossed her head back, glared at him through half-closed eyes, but did not answer.

"I might be able to give a hint on that point," said Jamie. "Your husband is a true believer. He believes that his oath *requires* him to do what's *right*. You're an absolutist, and your oath merely confirms what you already know—that *you* can do no *wrong*. He feels obliged to do certain things—and you feel entitled to certain rewards."

"Very cute phrasing," Marta said. "But meaningless."

"Is it?" Jamie asked. He gestured to Hannah. "It puts me in mind of a talk we had about the ends justifying the means. Rob a bank to feed the poor, and if the bank guards get killed trying to stop you, it's their own fault for interfering with your act of benevolence. Your cause is good, and therefore you can do no wrong." Jamie looked at Marta. "You were going to spend the money you got from killing the Thelm and Thelek—or at least most of it—on doing nice things for the planet, and so it was all right to kill them, and besides they weren't nice men anyway. And you worked so hard to do good that you deserved to be rich anyway. Is that about it?"

Marta shifted her poisonous stare to Jamie. "Go to the devil."

Jamie chuckled. "Let the record show that wasn't a denial."

"But what about that Pax Humana oath of yours?" Darsteel insisted.

" 'I will die most willingly to stop evil, but I will not kill, even in the name of good.' " said Jamie. "Simple. Marta didn't kill anyone. Did you, Marta?"

"No, I didn't, as a matter of fact."

"Of course not. How could she, when she is sworn to Pax Humana? Instead she found a way to get her victim to kill *himself*. When the Thelm died, it was because he was willing to kill Marta, and it was his own finger on the trigger that killed him. What would you call a plea based on that theory, Marta? Premeditated self-defense?"

Marta said nothing. Hannah decided to do some talking. "Stop me if I go wrong, Marta. I want to see if I have this put together right. Weeks ago, when you thought the Thelm and Thelek might have a duel together, you bought or borrowed a couple of standard dueling rounds from somewhere, modified them into suicide rounds, then took advantage of your position as a trusted member of the household to sneak into his audience chamber and swap the standard rounds for the suicide rounds. If they had had a duel, and had used the Thelm's weapons, then both of them would die, or at the very least one would die and the other be badly discredited."

"It would have been the Thelm's weapons," said Darsteel. "The Thelm may not issue a challenge, but only accept one. And the challenger is always required to accept the challenged party's weapons."

"Except the duel never came off—and you either never saw a reason to swap the rounds back, or else you never got the chance. Maybe you just liked having a weapon like that handy, right where it might do some good. Maybe you even amused yourself, a little harmless fantasizing, working out ways you might use it.

"Then, suddenly, last night, you had to act at once, before the machinery for deporting you to Penitence could be started up and put in motion. Maybe the Thelm would have decided today to take no chances and lock you and Georg and Moira up someplace safe to prevent your causing trouble."

"He should have done it last night," said Darsteel, unhappily.

"True enough," said Brox.

Hannah went on. "You got Georg to come to the Keep, on a perfectly legitimate errand that would also give him the same motives for killing the Thelm that you had. You convinced him to spend the night, so he could take the blame, or credit. And of course, you needed his shoe, in order to do some evidence planting. You figured—rightly, as it turned out—that he would figure out you were guilty, without being told, and that he would act to shield you—or at least shield your child."

Hannah had received the distinct impression that Marta did not hold her husband in the highest possible regard, though she didn't really have a good sense of the depth of feeling that Georg had for Marta. Did he love her—or had he merely accepted that he was stuck with her, and that his daughter needed a mother? She hoped for his sake that it was the latter.

But best not to be sidetracked too far. "The rest was pretty straightforward. You simply had to go the Thelm's chamber—easily done, for you, a trusted member of the household—and goad him into firing at you. But he would only die if *he* tried to kill *you*. Attempted murder would be punished, instantly, by a death sentence. You were setting yourself up as judge and jury, but making the Thelm his own executioner. How, exactly, you got him to fire I don't know. At a guess, you tried—or pretended to try—to blackmail him, threatening him in a way that so enraged his sense of honor that he would have no choice but to kill you."

"No," said Marta. "You're wrong there."

*And you'll start talking if someone tells you how clever you were, and then you get a chance to prove it by correcting them*, Hannah thought. "All right," she said. "How did you make it happen?"

"By playing on what the Thelm knew about the succession, and knowing that he obsessed on it, saw everything first by how it affected it, or was affected by it. I set up a plan I knew wouldn't work, knowing it would inspire him to try a plan of his own. I waited until Georg was asleep in our bed. Then I went up to the Thelm's audience chamber, carrying a gun—a small-caliber slug thrower—which I made very sure had exactly one round in it. I went into his audience chamber and started an argument. Easy enough to do, believe me. He didn't like me any better than I liked him. I told him that he was not going to send us to Penitence, that there was a better and more honorable solution that he had never even considered. I told him he should abdicate, at once, in favor of Georg."

Hannah frowned. "I must admit I never thought of abdication. Can a Thelm do that?" she asked Darsteel.

"If so, none of them have done it for a long time," he said. "It wouldn't be very healthy, for one thing. One faction or another wouldn't like something the new Thelm was doing, and would gear up a plot to put the 'rightful' Thelm back in the job. Which would leave the new Thelm with very few options. Thelms die in office, because they'd die pretty fast if they left the job any other way."

"Abdication is perfectly possible, and legal, and there are precedents," said Marta. "I researched that point long, long ago."

"Abdications are legally *possible*, yes," said Darsteel, "but an abdicating Thelm might as well sign his own death warrant."

"That," said Marta, "would have suited me fine. In any event, I pulled out a letter of abdication that I had drawn up myself, and slapped it down on the table—and I 'accidentally' chose the table that had the dueling pistols on display.

"I pulled out my pistol and threatened the Thelm with it, demanding that he sign the letter. I fired the one round in my gun past his head, a deliberate miss. The slug lodged in the wall behind his head."

"We didn't find any spent rounds lodged in the wall," Darsteel objected.

"We had no reason to look for one," said Brox. "But we have a reason now." He gestured to Marta.

"It's there," Marta said. "And I'm sure the Thelm thought it was a gift from the gods. It was beautiful, perfect evidence that *I* had tried to kill *him*. He could shoot me, and say quite truthfully it was self-defense—and all his troubles would be over. I could see it in his eyes. He worked it all out in the blink of an eye. So far as he could tell, I had just handed him a golden opportunity."

"Wait a second," Jamie said. "Why? How?"

"Because the eldest son is only required to kill his father the Thelm if the Thelm is over a certain age, if the son is over a certain age—*and if the son is married*. The Thelm's children are not permitted to divorce during the Thelm's life and for four years after his death, for various purposes of protecting inheritance—but also to prevent them from using divorce as a loophole in a situation like this one. But the succession law doesn't deal with the case of a father ending the son's marriage by killing the daughter-in-law in self-defense."

Hannah stared at her prisoner, and her guts ran cold. What sort of mind could set up a trap within a trap within a trap like that—and have the nerve, the will, to set it in motion against the ruler of an entire planet? Marta Hertzmann was one tough piece of work.

"I lowered my gun, just a trifle, and demanded again that he sign. Instead he snatched up one of the dueling pistols and pointed it at me. He ordered me to put my hands up, to drop the gun. I did. And he raised his gun, and fired."

The room was silent for a moment, but then Marta went on. "I had used low-power, low-yield dueling rounds to make my suicide rounds. A bit more powerful than a training round, or whatever it was, that you tricked Georg into firing. But even so—the damage it did was remarkable. I was stunned, shocked. But I didn't have the luxury of staying that way. I got out the shoe I had brought with me, knocked over a plant, and placed one shoe print. If there hadn't been two human investigators on-planet, I would have risked putting both shoes on and walking through the dirt, and then around the room or something—but I assumed you two would spot that the shoe prints were too shallow for a man Georg's size, or that I'd get the length of stride wrong, or whatever. One print was risky enough.

"Then I went to get the gun out of the Thelm's hand—and I couldn't. It wouldn't look much like Georg had done it if there was a gun in the Thelm's hand, and there was obvious evidence that it had literally backfired. I tried like blazes to open his hand, but I had to give it up. I didn't have much time before some servant came in or the like. I decided to hide my evidence with fire. I had brought a firestarter with me to get rid of the abdication letter, and I tried using it to light the carpet he was on. Nothing. I tried pouring out the liquors in the drinks cabinet, and setting fire to things with that, and found out the hard way that Pavlat liquor isn't flammable. I knocked over the drinks cabinet, to make it look like the bottles had fallen out during a fight or something—just to confuse the issue.

"But then I remembered. Georg liked a vodka martini of an evening, now and then, so naturally the Thelm had gotten some vodka in. But he hadn't just ordered a case or two brought in from Earth. He had ordered two-hundred-liter tanks of the stuff—and they were kept in the pantry, behind the service door I had just blocked by knocking over the tree and making the footprint. It wasn't easy getting through that door without disturbing the plant or the footprint, but I did it. I filled whatever burnable or meltable containers I could and brought them back in the room. I splashed the vodka where I could, then started the fires."

"Ah!" Darsteel cried out, and turned to Jamie. "That is why you asked for a report on Earth-style food and drink stored in the pantry. Now I understand."

Marta glared at Darsteel, annoyed that someone would interrupt her story, and apparently forgetting that it was also her confession. "Anyway, I poured vodka on the carpet and tried lighting it again. The liquor lit up immediately, but the carpet fabric itself just wouldn't burn. But the rest of the fire was going very nicely, burning so hot I had to retreat. Some big chunk of burning debris dropped down on the display table, so I couldn't get to the other dueling pistol and swap out the second suicide round. Besides, I didn't want to get too close, for fear the heat would touch off the rocket propellant in the round. I got out, got back down to our apartments, and waited for the fire alarm to sound. I woke Georg and Moira, and we left the building together."

The room was quiet again, and Marta looked around at all of them, a defiant look coming back to her face. "So that's how I did it," she said. "That's how I saved my daughter from your brilliant idea to have her exiled to a place full of killers and psychopaths. That's how I saved my husband's life. That's how I kept a pompous idiot like the High Thelek from ascending to the Thelmship and wrecking the planet. And that's how I *nearly* made myself the richest woman in the universe. Do you really want to tell me I was wrong?"

Hannah Wolfson thought of how close the planet had come to civil war, how close to the Thelek's coming in and wrecking the genetic decrypting project, treating it like a building project where the low bidder was your brother-in-law and maybe he'd skimp on the concrete mix, but everyone would get a cut.

She thought of an old man, guilty of scheming and plotting and worse, manipulated into defending himself, and getting himself killed in the process. She looked at Marta and thought again of the mind capable of setting up such a circumstance. What would Reqwar have looked like, five, ten, twenty years after the person capable of *that* plot got her hands on the planetary finances—then started deciding she deserved a reward or two for doing the world so much good? What sort of reputation would *that* have earned humans among the Elder Races?

She thought of the simple, clumsy, naive, heartfelt, lovely Pax Humana oath, and the ocean of good intentions it represented. Did the Reqwar Pavlat, or humanity's reputation, or Pax Humana need a woman capable of turning those words inside out in charge of *anything*? Hannah looked Marta Hertzmann in the eye, and spoke. "Yes," she said. "I do want to tell you that you were wrong. With all my heart, and all my soul, I do."

She stood up, and so did Jamie. Hannah looked at Darsteel, and gestured to Marta. "Take her away," she said. "She's all yours. Maybe, once you decide how you want to handle her, you'll want us to come and collect her to serve her time on Earth, or Center—or Penitence. Just give us a call, and we'll come get her."

\* \* \*

The ascension ceremony went off without a hitch, albeit a few minutes late, and in spite of the fact that the Thelm-Designate, and several of his guests, complained of a loud ringing noise in their ears, and looked slightly disheveled, and had the slightest smell of gunpowder in their clothes. The inevitable recep-

tion—a most subdued affair, under the circumstances—followed immediately afterward. The
Thelm-Designate, that was, the newly minted Thelm,
stayed in the main room long enough to greet everyone, thank everyone, and accept everyone's condo-
lences. Then he vanished, leaving the party to go on
without him.

Hannah was not surprised when one of Darsteel's
people relayed a whispered summons to her a few
minutes later. She was even less surprised to be led to
a comfortably appointed side room, stocked with
human-style chairs as well as sitting cushions and
perching stools—and least surprised of all to see
Brox, Darsteel, and Jamie coming in right after her, or
the new-made Thelm relaxing in the biggest and most
comfortable chair, drinking what looked very much
like a double vodka martini.

Thelm Georg greeted them all, had someone take
their orders for food and drink, and sat them all
down. Once the pleasantries were done, he did not
speak at first, but instead merely took a sip or two of
his drink and stared off into space. At last it seemed
he had found the words he needed, and he spoke.

"This is the strangest, saddest, happiest day I have
ever had," he said. "I am guest of honor at a party the
day after my adoptive father's death. My daughter is
safe from Penitence, but she has lost her mother. My
wife has killed my father—but now the way is clear
for us to save this planet's terrestrial ecology. It is too
much, and it is too sudden—and there is far too much
that must be done at once, too many duties I must see

to immediately. I don't have *time* to feel all the things I should feel.

"But I knew I *must* take time to speak with all of you to say thank you. Thank you for more services done for me and my people than I can even express. One of the judges of the Court of High Crime explained to me what, exactly, dying 'properly' means. It's a lot more complicated than I thought. If I had been allowed to go on the way I was going, it would have been just about impossible to convince anyone that I wasn't in a conspiracy with my wife—she does the crime, I take the blame and credit. I shudder to think where we would have been a few months from now if I hadn't flunked your little test."

"You *passed* the test, with flying colors," said Hannah. "Except for the questions where we knew you knew the answer, you got every single answer wrong. You told a good story, a convincing one—except you included all the misleading details we had given you."

"But why, exactly, *did* you give them to me?"

"By that time, we knew, or just about knew, either you or Marta had done it. As a matter of physical possibility, you *might* have done it. And you had a good strong motive for it, too. But as a matter of logic, if *you* were going to commit the act, it made no sense at all for you to do it in the way it was done— but it *did* make a sort of strange, warped sense for Marta to do it that way. For her, it was rough justice. The Thelm would only be punished if he tried to attack her. When you declared that *you* had done it, we assumed you were acting to shield her."

"I was acting to shield *Moira*," Thelm Georg said sharply. "The moment the Thelm was dead, I at least knew all of us, most importantly Moira, were safe from Penitence, and that was the main thing. But it didn't take me long to figure out it was very likely Marta who had done it, and all the information that came to me during the night confirmed it. I realized that I was very likely to become Thelm very soon."

He sipped his drink again. "Pax Humana likes Paxers to marry among themselves, and the Senior Members like to do matchmaking. There was a lot of pressure put on me, and on Marta, to marry each other—but they didn't worry so much about compatibility. The Senior Members look for pairings of talent, and trust for love to blossom between the couples once they are together. Sometimes it works. Not with us, even though we tried. Things between Marta and me had been rocky for some time. And let's just say that her killing my adoptive father wasn't going to improve our relationship." His face hardened. "But I did not want Moira to lose her mother. If I took the blame for the crime, I could keep Marta from facing charges."

*Did it occur to you that Marta more than likely had figured all that out, and probably* expected *you to take the blame for Moira's sake, counted on it, manipulated you into it?* Hannah wondered. But that was not the sort of question you asked the Thelm. "That was basically what we worked out," she said.

"But then you had to decide what to do about it," said Thelm Georg. "I must admit I am very curious. How did you come up with your plan?"

"Well, sir, we needed to prove you *hadn't* done it— and also that Marta had. We decided to give you all the hints we dared that the fire damage to the room, and to the Thelm's corpse, were worse than they really were. We fed you a version of the crime that *Marta* knew was wrong—but we needed her to believe that *we* had gotten everything wrong. We wanted her to think we had very scanty evidence, and that we were misinterpreting what we had.

"She knew it was a chest shot, not a head shot. The Thelm was shot from the front, not the back. He was standing, not sitting on a perching stool. He was killed by a shot from less than a meter away, not one from more than two meters away. But she didn't dare warn you, in case we *were* getting it all wrong for real."

"But what was the point of it all?" asked Thelm Georg.

Hannah answered. "The Thelm would not have died 'properly' if you had conspired with Marta and had her do the killing. What we needed to know, beyond a doubt, and needed to prove, was that you had *not* conspired with her, that she had done it all herself. If you were prepared to buy into all our false clues— and fire a gun that the killer had to know might still have a suicide round in it—then that would be the proof we needed."

"I'm not quite sure I should be cold-blooded

enough to ask this question," said Thelm Georg, "but, leaving all morals and ethics out of it, why would it have really mattered if I *had* conspired with her?"

"Because, sooner or later, conspiracies fall apart," said Hannah, "even small ones. If you had been involved, sooner or later it would have been discovered. Some forgotten clue, some slip of the tongue, something told in confidence to someone who turned out to be less than reliable. Maybe, even, somehow, down the road, your wife simply spilling the beans. And then your whole reign would be called into question. The High Thelek would have made a career out of looking for holes in the story and circulating them. He wouldn't need to prove anything. Brox was right about the Thelek's rumor mill."

"But now," said Jamie, "with the recordings we have, and the witnesses, you have cast-iron proof that you *weren't* involved, that you believed your wife had done it, and that you were bravely trying to shield her by allowing false dishonor—the breaking of your Pax Humana oath—to fall on your own head. Just the sort of grand romantic noble gesture the Reqwar Pavlat love."

"And I have sent the Thelek a copy of that recording," said Brox, "so that he knows that *you* have it. He won't ever dare try to put it about that you were in on the killing, for fear that some loyal flunky of yours will accidentally-on-purpose get that recording to the public, and make the Thelek look very bad, and have the whole planet fall in love with you."

Thelm Georg shook his head. "I'm going to need some practice getting used to how they—we, I suppose—play at politics on this planet. But one other question. Was it really necessary to expose, well, everyone in that room to the danger of using a live round? Wouldn't you have achieved pretty much the same effect with a dummy round, a dud? I pull the trigger, Marta leaps to knock the gun out of my hand, and nothing happens at all?"

"The round in the gun was a training round with a minimal propellant load and a small delayed-burst flash charge that wouldn't go off until people had a few seconds to take cover," said Hannah. "With that kind of round in the gun, yes, there was some slight risk of someone getting hurt, but mostly it was just flash and noise. Besides, we figured that it was unlikely that it would get as far as your actually pulling the trigger. The most likely scenario was that she would snap before then, make some slip, break into the reenactment to keep you from incriminating yourself, take the crime back on herself." *And we won't talk about how she didn't do any of that.* "When she jumped for the gun, she was in a panic, or near to it. She had seen you digging either your grave or hers, getting detail after detail totally wrong, watching us lead you down the garden path."

*Or maybe,* Hannah said to herself, *she realized that if the suicide round was still in there, when you died it would just about prove, by process of elimination, if nothing else, that it had to be she who had killed the Thelm. You would be dead, the High Thelek would*

*become Thelm—and she would be in very, very, very
big trouble. She didn't dive for the gun to save you—
but to save herself.*

But Hannah didn't offer up those theories out
loud. Georg Hertzmann would have enough shock
and sorrow and hurt to deal with, even if such ideas
never crossed his mind. "But she *did* let it get as far as
the gunshot," Hannah went on. "Then she dove for
the gun and it went off with a lot of noise and smoke.
What she did in the midst of the shock and the smoke
and the noise was dive further into panic, run without
thinking toward the door, and that was as good as a
written confession to us.

"We were worried that if we used a dummy round
and she jumped for the gun, then there was just the
anticlimactic click of a trigger, she might have been
able to pull herself together, maybe claim she had
done it because she couldn't bear to watch even simu-
lated violence. After all, she was Pax Humana."

"That's the real irony," said Thelm Georg. "I'm
not, not anymore. Last night, I didn't just check the
reference net information about the succession. I also
looked up a few things in the Pax Humana regula-
tions. The moment I became Thelm, I was automatically expelled from Pax Humana and released from
my oath."

"Sir?" Jamie asked. "What—what do you mean?"

Georg spread his arms wide, taking in the whole
planet. "I wouldn't last five minutes running this place
if I was sworn to renounce all violence at all times.
That would just bring on a civil war and get everyone

killed. But the Pax Humana bylaws recognize that there can be circumstances when renouncing violence would simply invite chaos. If a Pax Humana member was on the Podunk town council and the mayor and police chief were convicted of fraud and forced to resign, all of a sudden you'd have a sworn pacifist as acting police chief. In such cases, it is mandatory that the PH member be automatically released from his oath in order to be able to enforce the law and keep the peace. That rule applies here—just on a slightly larger scale."

\* \* \*

It took a few days to sort things out. It always did. And a few nights of uninterrupted sleep on more or less human-style beds, and days of eating human-style food that came from the same kitchen that was feeding the ruler of the planet, were just what the doctor ordered. And so was a walk about the grounds of the Keep. The Keep itself was already undergoing repairs, and the purposeful bustle of the work crews seemed to add energy and enthusiasm to everyone around them.

Jamie and Hannah were strolling with Zahida. Moira was up ahead, taking the Stannlar Consortia out for a little run. At least, that was how *Moira* saw it. The sight of the two huge, immortal, translucent slug shapes cavorting with a human child was not one seen every day, and Jamie was very glad they were there to see it.

On the night of the killing, the two Stannlar had been nearly ready to summon their spacecraft from orbit and use it to flee Reqwar. The destruction of

their antijamming coins, which, they assured everyone, acted as tracking devices, but *not* as listening devices, had been enough to make the Stannlar think
they were already under attack—for the coins were
integrated subcomponents of the Stannlar. Given all
the other events of the night, the Stannlar had, perhaps understandably, regarded the wrecking of the
coins as something very close to a preliminary assault
on themselves.

Thelm Georg was strolling as well, in between the
two groups, keeping just a bit to himself—except for
the discreet presence of his security detail.

"I don't know if you've heard the latest," Zahida
was saying. "That wise-guy suggestion you made
about a plea of premeditated self-defense? It's just
possible the Court of High Crime is going to buy it."

"What?" Hannah cried out. "Marta Hertzmann
murders the head of state, and my sarcastic comment
gets her off on a technicality? It's not safe making suggestions around you people."

Zahida laughed. "No, no, no," she said. "You people still don't understand how this places works."
Zahida held up the fingers of one hand and starting
ticking off offenses. "Tampering with a Dueling
Weapon with Malicious Intent. Unlicensed Modifi-
cation of Certified Ammunitions. Arson. Unlawful
Discharge of a Firearm. Contemplating the Death of
a Sovereign. Unauthorized Manufacture of False Evidence."

"*Un*authorized manufacture? You mean you can
get a *permit* for producing false evidence?"

"Yes, but the paperwork is a monster to get through," Zahida said, in a perfectly serious tone of voice.

Jamie couldn't tell if she was kidding or not, and decided it didn't matter. "So she's being charged with all that?"

"Oh, no. She's already been declared *guilty* of all that—and probably a few other crimes, in a courtroom that doesn't go out of its way to attract publicity. Enough to disqualify her from the inheritance, which was the main thing, and also to put her away pretty much wherever and for however long the government wants. They can do all that a lot more quietly than executing the Thelm's wife for high treason. So they let her off on the main charge on a technicality to avoid a death penalty, and throw the book at her otherwise. Don't forget, she *is* the Thelm's wife. Georg can't divorce her for four years after the death of the old Thelm. Besides, it's considered bad policy to announce that the sovereign has been murdered. It gives malcontents ideas. Lantrall, Thelm of all Reqwar, died in a tragic and accidental fire."

Jamie had to wonder if that was good justice, or wise policy—and then decided he was glad it wasn't his problem. "So what will happen to her?"

"Weirdly enough, it was Allabex who came up with the idea—from ancient Earthside history. Some group called the Romans, ruled by people called Caesars. Ever heard of them?"

Jamie smiled. "A little something." It was a startling glimpse behind that California-accented English, that easy assumption that she "knew" Earth. Zahida obviously had never heard of the Romans. And he had known even less of her culture when he had been mad enough to make suggestions about how the Thelm should conduct his affairs and run his family. He hoped fervently that he had learned his lesson. "The Romans are named after the city of Rome," he said. "It's still around."

Zahida nodded eagerly. "Oh! Right! I didn't make that connection. Anyway, when one of the Caesars had a daughter or a wife or whatever who caused too much trouble, but was too prominent to execute—or maybe the Caesar just could not bring himself to sign the death warrant—they picked out an island far enough from everywhere else that you couldn't swim back from it, and put the offending family member on it, and dropped off supplies once in a while. They're going to update the plan a little bit—arranging for Moira to visit, for example—but they're shopping for an island now." Zahida nodded at Thelm Georg and his daughter, up ahead. "It's the two of them I worry about," she said. "Aside from Marta, the only two humans on-planet, wrapped in a security service blanket at all times. They're going to be two very lonely people."

"No they won't," said Jamie. "The decrypting operation is about to kick into high gear. They'll need contractors, technicians, specialists. And you can bet UniGov will want to plant an embassy full of advisors here. There was a deal to allow human settlers on at least one continent under the old Thelm, and I'd be very surprised if that wasn't expanded. There will be lots of techs coming in with their families. Lots of children for Moira to play with, sooner than you might think."

"What about someone for Thelm Georg to play with?" Zahida said, and the expression on her face made it clear how she meant that.

It was Hannah's turn to laugh. "Your people still don't understand how *our* people work. '*Young, handsome, likable male, separated from spouse and awaiting divorce decree, runs own planet, in search of female companionship. Respondent must be willing to become incredibly wealthy.*' A lot of those technicians and specialists are going to be female, you know. *He* won't be lonely one day longer than he wants to be. I'd be willing to lay odds Georg marries his new consort four years and one day after the death of Thelm Lantrall."

"Good," said Zahida. "He and Moira both deserve to be much happier than they are."

"I agree, all around," said Hannah. "But my information is that there's another deal brewing—one that concerns you. But for some reason no one will tell me anything."

"Well, yes," Zahida said. "It's all in the early stages, but we're putting something together to, ah, regularize the succession. I know, I know, a week into Georg's reign, and we're sweating the succession. But we all just got a lesson in why it's important to keep these things tidy."

"So what's the plan?" Jamie asked. There was a certain hesitancy in the way Zahida was talking about it that gave him the sense that she needed a little push to say more.

"Georg will decree that a Pavlat must succeed him, and that henceforth all Thelms must be born Reqwar Pavlat. It was always assumed they *would* be—but the law says nothing, and we've seen what happens to assumptions. Georg will go further and specifically disbar his own children and their descendants from the succession. *He* doesn't want Moira turned into somebody's chess piece or hostage thirty years from now. He will pick out one or two of the High Thelek's illegal activities and discover to his regret and surprise that they disbar the Thelek from the succession. He will therefore declare the High Thelek ineligible for the Thelmship, *but* he will designate the Thelek's male descendants as heirs to the Thelmship."

"Except the Thelek doesn't have any descendants," Jamie objected. "His wife and daughter died years ago, and all his sons have gotten themselves killed one damn fool way or another."

"That's, ah, where I come in," Zahida said primly, but blushing bright green. "The Thelmship will descend through the Thelek's male line—on condition that the Thelek will, well—provided that he marries *me*, thus closing out a blood feud that has caused so much trouble for so many years. The High Thelek will not take the Thelmship—but he could live to see his son do so, and possibly serve as his own son's regent. And, ah, of course, with the line of property inheritance broken by Marta's criminal convictions, *she* can't inherit. Georg would therefore make me his heir of property—provided I marry the Thelek."

The two humans said nothing, but walked along, staring at Zahida in stunned silence. Jamie could think of a thousand things he *could* say—but none of them would be very diplomatic.

Zahida walked along, staring straight ahead. "Don't go all horrified on me," she said. "One, don't forget, we Reqwar Pavlat do things differently from humans. Two, this was my own idea. I sold it to Thelm Georg as the plan with the best odds of getting the Thelek to stop plotting ways to get the Thelmship, by giving him a stake in the present arrangement. It might even work. Three, don't forget, my family ordered me home for the express purpose of being bargained about in the marriage market, and I obeyed the summons, even if I wasn't that enthusiastic about it. I've just come up with a far more profitable arrangement than anyone expected—and one that ought to lift the exile off Bindulan, and the unfair stain of dishonor from the clan. Four—there are plenty of human women who might trade life with a wearisome husband in exchange for stewardship over the wealth of a whole world."

Jamie kept his mouth shut, and let Hannah be the one to answer. "Good points all," she said. "I wish you well," and left it at that.

"Thank you," she said. "And don't waste time feeling sorry for me. I am going to do very, very, very well out of this bargain."

Jamie had to smile at that. He glanced over at

Zahida, and wondered if the Thelek knew exactly what he was getting himself into.

"The one *I* really feel sorry for is Brox," said Zahida, obviously trying to change the subject. "He behaved with perfect honor in all this. He had the good sense to watch out for the Kendari's long-term interests, instead of the quick win that would turn into a permanent headache. I just hope his government has the sense to see it that way, once he goes home empty-handed."

"Who says he's going home empty-handed?" Hannah growled. "Thelm Georg is already thinking like a Reqwar Pavlat instead of a human. He figures the planet is going to need all the help it can get, all the contacts, all the investment. And maybe a little healthy competition will keep the prices down. Brox has hired some off-planet Pavlat named Nostawniek as his local rep, and he's going home with a stack of contracts taller than he is."

"Good," said Zahida. "Good for us—and I'll bet it's good for you Younger Race types too, in the long run. Both of you. Get you working together—or at least, working next to each other, without trying to kill each other."

"I suppose," Hannah said. "I'd have to admit I'd vouch for Brox a lot sooner than I'd vouch for a lot of humans I could think of."

There wasn't much else to say after that, and they walked in silence through the weary, worn-out grounds of the Keep. But if the Keep could be repaired, then, with a little luck, so too could the landscape, the whole ecology, be renewed, reborn, reset. *And we're the ones who gave it the chance for that to happen,* Hannah told herself. That was worth taking pride in.

Night was coming on. The stars were coming out. In the morning, a Pavlat ship would take Jamie and Hannah back to the *Hastings*, and they would begin the journey back to Center, and home. "Well," said Hannah, "mission accomplished. Assuming the *Hastings* doesn't blow up when we light the engines—but that's not going to happen."

"What do you mean, 'mission accomplished'?" Jamie asked.

"Commandant Kelly gave me strict orders to get you home alive," she said. "I came pretty close to disobeying that one."

"Yeah, but you didn't," said Jamie. He looked up at the stars, bright and clear, shining points of hope and promise in the nighttime. It was a sky, a galaxy, a universe full of possibilities.

"I wonder," Jamie said, "where they're going to send us next."

# ABOUT THE AUTHOR

Roger MacBride Allen was born September 26, 1957, in Bridgeport, Connecticut. He is the author of twenty science fiction novels, a modest number of short stories, and two nonfiction books.

His wife, Eleanore Fox, is a member of the United States Foreign Service. After a long-distance courtship, they married in 1994, when Eleanore returned from London, England. They were posted to Brasilia, Brazil, from 1995 to 1997, and to Washington, D.C., from 1997 to 2002. Their first son, Matthew Thomas Allen, was born November 12, 1998. In September 2002 they began a three-year posting to Leipzig, Germany, where their second son, James Maury Allen, was born on April 27, 2004. They returned to the Washington area in the summer of 2005, and live in Takoma Park, Maryland.

Learn more about the author at www.rmallen.net, or visit www.bsi-starside.com for the latest on the BSI Starside series.

Don't miss the next exciting
mission!

# **BSI**STARSIDE

Coming in 2007